BRONZE
DRUM

BRONZE DRUM

PHONG NGUYEN

GRAND CENTRAL
PUBLISHING

NEW YORK   BOSTON

Grand Central Publishing
Hachette Book Group
1290 Avenue of the Americas, New York, NY 10104
grandcentralpublishing.com
twitter.com/grandcentralpub

First edition: August 2022

Grand Central Publishing is a division of Hachette Book Group, Inc. The Grand Central Publishing name and logo is a trademark of Hachette Book Group, Inc.

The publisher is not responsible for websites (or their content) that are not owned by the publisher.

The Hachette Speakers Bureau provides a wide range of authors for speaking events. To find out more, go to www.hachettespeakersbureau.com or call (866) 376-6591.

Library of Congress Cataloging-in-Publication Data

Names: Nguyen, Phong, 1978– author.
Title: Bronze drum / Phong Nguyen.
Description: First edition. | New York : Grand Central Publishing, 2022.
Identifiers: LCCN 2022004314 | ISBN 9781538753705
(trade paperback) | ISBN 9781538753699 (ebook)
Subjects: LCGFT: Novels.
Classification: LCC PS3614.G95 B76 2022 | DDC 813/.6—dc23
/eng/20220204
LC record available at https://lccn.loc.gov/2022004314

ISBNs: 9781538753705 (trade paperback), 9781538753699 (ebook)

Printed in the United States of America

LSC-C

Printing 1, 2022

For Vũ Thị Hoà (1919–1947):
grandmother I never met,
shot by a colonial French pilot;
she died holding her one-year-old son.

Nothing ever dies.
> *—Toni Morrison*

Nothing ever dies.
> *—Viet Thanh Nguyen*

Nothing ever ends.
> *—Alan Moore*

Nothing ever ends.
> *—Peter S. Beagle*

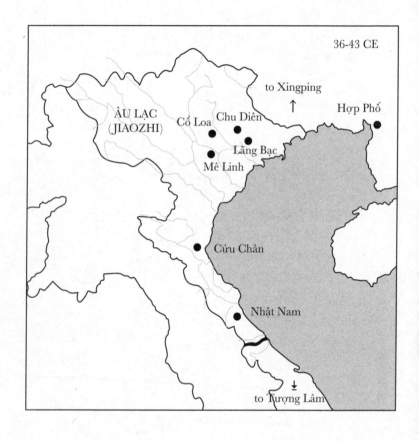

The story of Vietnamese independence begins, not with the victory over the French at Điện Biên Phủ, not with the rise of Hồ Chí Minh, nor even with the Fall of Saigon and the withdrawal of US troops from Việt Nam, but two thousand years earlier, with two sisters from a village overlooking the Red River.

In 40 CE, in what is known today as northern Việt Nam, a regional lord by the name of Trưng stood up to the oppressive laws of a brutal Hán governor, which included conscripting young Việt men to fight in distant wars, banning the worship of Việt gods, and forcing Việt aristocrats to marry and form traditional family units, the better to pay taxes to the Hán. Eventually, his daughters took up arms, raising an army of women and leading them to victory against the Hán Chinese. They briefly ruled a free and independent nation, creating the precedent for Việt Nam that would come into being a thousand years later.

The Trưng Sisters are a historical reality, but one veiled in myth. The traditional Vietnamese account canonizes the Trưng Sisters as saints and attributes their success to divine favor. It is full of legends of daring, seemingly impossible feats, and a thirst for independence that pervades Vietnamese literature throughout the ages.

At the center of the story of the Trưng Sisters is the symbol of the bronze drum. With carvings representing sea birds in flight, splayed frogs, and other figures, these drums are tools of narrative as much as instruments of rhythm. The story they tell is of the indomitable spirit of the Việt people.

After the fierce General Ma Yuan reconquered ancient Việt Nam for the Hán, he decreed that all the bronze drums across the land be seized, smelted into base metal, then reconstituted into two giant bronze columns as a symbol of Hán power. "As long as these columns stand," he said, "the Hán will rule in this land." But many Việt women did not willingly submit their bronze drums; they hid them, or buried them, and two thousand years later, archaeologists still find these artifacts in excavation sites scattered throughout the north, as a reminder of the enduring legacy of the Trưng Sisters.

Gather around, children of Chu Diên, and be brave. For even to listen to the story of the Trưng Sisters is, in these troubled times, a dangerous act. The Hán gods are jealous of Việt heroes, and while the Hán have ruled Lạc Việt for a hundred years, our legends threaten to reduce the empire to ashes.

Behold the lacquered puppets dancing on a clear pool of water under the moonlight, and think back farther than you ever have before, to your ancestor-memory, and witness:

Here are the Trưng Sisters! Trưng Nhị is wild and venturesome, while Trưng Trắc is disciplined and proud. They ride into war on the backs of elephants, wearing golden armor, brandishing swords that flash in the sun, leading an army of women. And in the distance, the thrashing of the bronze drum, announcing the battle at hand.

Look! The wicked Hán governor enters the stage. He takes Việt honor and blood as if they were shimmering coins in his hands. He will settle for nothing but total subjugation.

Soon the armies will clash on the field. The Việt women love freedom and will not bow. The Hán men fight to conquer what was never theirs to rule: the soul of this country, its unobtainable heart.

Now watch as I, Kha the guardsman, ride between the two, and carry the heroic secret of how to vanquish the Hán to the Trưng Sisters, She-Kings of the Việts. I will not presume to claim responsibility for their victory—suffice it to say the outcome would have been uncertain without my help.

Let us clear the stage before we go too far. Let us focus instead on this sublime moment: the cusp of the Trưng Sisters' triumph. There is nothing more beautiful than the intake and outflow of breath from the bodies of free men and women.

Today, on the sands of Tượng Lâm, there loom two vast bronze columns. General Ma Yuan, who erected them, said that the Hán will rule in this land as long as they stand. Yet the shift in the fortunes of women and men is as swift as the darting of the black-winged kite, soaring in one direction, then jinking suddenly in another. The work of nature upon us is more patient and, like the crawl of the snail, seems to leave only a faint trail behind it. Yet the shell endures, emptied of its life, to be worked on by the elements until it is indistinguishable from a rock, until it, too, joins with the grains on the beach.

Children, I say to you *this*: the bronze columns on the sands of Tượng Lâm one day will sink, to be swallowed by the tide and, over time, taken by the ocean as easily as a body.

PART ONE

THE TALE OF TWO SISTERS

Lạc Việt Year 2734–2735
(36–37 CE)

CHAPTER 1

The Courtyard of Cung Điện Mê Linh

Lady Man Thiện stirred restlessly beneath the furs. Her neck twinged in the recess of the stone pillow. Soon, the lord lying beside her would begin to dream, and within these troubled dreams, another night of frantic fear would ensue. But rather than wander the grounds at night, as was her habit, Lady Man Thiện shook her husband awake and asked him to tell her a story.

"What kind of story?" the lord asked.

"Something other than a nightmare," said Lady Man Thiện. "I've heard enough of your nightmares."

"Right now? You know how much trouble the night brings."

"I want to hear something pleasant for once. Tell me how our daughters come to prosper."

"Okay," said the lord, blinking the sleep out of his eyes. He leveled a placating stare at his wife and spoke in his most assuaging tone. Hers was not an idle worry. Their daughters would one day rule in Mê Linh, though neither showed the right disposition for it. The lord shared his wife's fears for the future, that Trưng Trắc might never possess the forcefulness of a leader and Trưng Nhị may never yield to tradition. Yet Lady Man Thiện needed his assurances. "Years from now, Trưng Trắc will be the most desired woman in Lạc Việt, and though she will receive the attention of the strongest and handsomest men in the region, she will choose to marry none of them. Instead, she will give birth and raise children here in Cung Điện Mê Linh."

"What about Trưng Nhị?" Lady Man Thiện asked.

"Well, Nhị is skilled at horse riding, so she will join the army, and rather than starting out as an officer, she will train cavalrymen until she learns enough discipline and responsibility to become a leader. Then she will marry a lord—"

"Why should she marry?" Lady Man Thiện asked.

"Nhị is too wild. She needs the taming influence of a husband," the lord said.

"Oh? And have you tamed me?"

"That would be impossible," said the lord, but his playful smile gave way to worry lines upon his brow. "Yet the Hán have tamed us all."

Silence prevailed in the complete darkness of the lord's chamber.

"I thought you were going to tell me a happy story?" Lady Man Thiện said.

"The only happy story you want to hear begins with a revolution."

Trưng Trắc, the elder sister, was imperious, solemn, and filial; Trưng Nhị, the younger, was ardent and restless to become a woman. Trưng Trắc had recently reached her age of maturity, and Trưng Nhị was not far behind. Trưng Trắc could often be found indoors, studying the history of the Việts and the Hán, while Trưng Nhị was usually out in the garden, idling among the marbled cats and painted turtles and peacocks, if she could be found at all. The one space they shared with comfort and equanimity was the courtyard of Cung Điện Mê Linh. Here the sisters recited poetry and sparred with lacquered wooden staffs on a dirt-floored, sun-speckled patch of earth, in the shadow of a great stone sculpture of an elephant. The ointment of music soothed the sisters' restless spirits and focused the mind so that even the most contentious wills could sync as one. Outside the courtyard, they never spoke about how each sister inspired the other, but in the songs they sung, one could imagine a unity that was impossible to break. When they sang together, their harmony reached the far corners of the palace and seemed, from a distance, like the keening of unhappy ghosts.

It was easy to glean each sister's temperament by watching her spar. Trưng Trắc's movements were patient and controlled, her every strike flawlessly executed but performed dispassionately, as she threaded the air with her staff like a needle in the hands of a seamstress. Trưng Nhị struck wildly, guided by the same instinct by which an ox charges a rival. Trưng Trắc's formal style, honed through innumerable hours of practice, bested Trưng Nhị's powerful but undisciplined stance. At the end of a spar, Trưng Trắc would help the fallen Trưng Nhị to her feet and apply a balm of camphor and paraffin to the bruises that covered her sister's arms, her torso, her back.

Mornings, the golden light upon the dun clay walls of Cung Điện Mê Linh ascended over the ceramic tiles and through the slats in the wooden windows, like a purifying fire. For the night was full of the sounds of their father's howling and crying.

Lord Trưng's visions were occasionally so powerful that he believed he could see the future. The voices threatened to strangle him in his sleep. Many nights he would stir his family awake and beg them to leave their home, clothed in rags, and become a family of peasants. Lady Man Thiện would soothe him by stroking his hair like a child's, though he was an old man whose gray beard had grown down to his navel.

Trưng Nhị often listened to her mother's calm entreaties from the hall, as she lay down on the cold stone at the threshold of her father's chamber like a guard dog. The sound of her father's whimper excited the deepest protective instinct of her nature. Her memories of childhood were still sharp, and she recalled the times when, after being lulled to sleep by his sweet singing, she refused for days afterward to leave his lap. Back then, Trưng Nhị wished never to leave his embrace.

Every night, she swore to protect him; and every morning, after another night of listening to his howling in the dark, she swore that she would become nothing like him—that she would never be controlled by her fears.

The foundation for the lord's latest dream was the

introduction of a new governor, Tô Định, who was rumored to be ruthless, and who forbade the men and women of Lạc Việt from honoring the Guardian Spirit, forcing them to worship Hán gods. The governor, the lord dreamed in one of his nightmares, had learned of a plot among the Việt people to rise up.

For three generations, the Hán had occupied Lạc Việt and imposed their laws and customs on the Việt people. The Việts—tribal, communal, and matriarchal—were now separated into familial units governed by men, according to the Confucian tradition. Yet the legacy of their ancestors was preserved in stories passed from mother to daughter and sung in the corridors of every home, and the next generation of Việt aristocrats were emboldened to challenge the Confucian order.

But a new Hán governor in Lạc Việt asserted his will among the populous. He demanded the conscription of young Việt men to fight in distant wars, strict adherence to Hán law and religious practice among the peasantry, and marriages for Việt aristocrats so that the Hán could keep track of households and therefore debts.

The Trưng Sisters watched their father maintain an uneasy peace with the Hán, their historical enemy and their current regents—a powder keg that threatened to explode with the slightest spark.

In his dreams, the Hán swarmed the palace, the mud of their boots scuffing the stone floor, overwhelming the meager guard of Cung Điện Mê Linh, and leaving headless bodies everywhere they went. "If they mutilate our men, what will the Hán barbarians do to our daughters?" Lord Trưng begged his wife to understand.

"Our daughters are safe from the Hán," said Lady Man Thiện. "If the time comes, they will know to take their lives rather than to have it taken from them by an enemy. If you are born to die by your own hand, then you have nothing to fear from war."

From her perch outside the lord and lady's chambers, these words rang and echoed in Trưng Nhị's ears. She felt detached from this vision of her nobly taking her own life, landing with all the force of prophecy as though it were the fate of a stranger. Why did Man Thiện insist that war would shape their lives' contours? Trưng Nhị did not believe she was born to die by her own hand, and imagined the day that she could run her own palace and entertain visitors freely—the kind of guests who would laugh at the solemnity of duty and the sacredness of war. She defied her mother's notion of what it means to be a leader; but she was utterly alone in this defiance. She longed for friendships twined in pleasure, not forged in battle.

Framed by the window, the turtle named Kim Quy canted its leg and crooked its neck, as though to bring itself into perfect synchrony with the bending branch of willow buds behind it. A cicada from the field chirped its shrill ascending clicks, and the stalks of wheat waved slightly as though in response.

Seated ceremonially on the floor beside Trưng Trắc, Trưng Nhị was brought back from her reverie of this never-

to-be-repeated moment in nature by a swift strike on the neck
from their mother. Trưng Nhị's attention immediately fixed
itself on the assortment of stones, shells, and coins in front
of her, representing the three constituencies of war: enemies,
allies, and innocents. If she could trace a path to the stones
through the sand without touching any of the coins, she would
win. These war games were Trưng Trắc's favorite challenge of
her martial education, but the lure of battle—simplified and
abstracted into shapes representing the field of combat—was
lost on Trưng Nhị.

"What is your move?" Lady Man Thiện repeated now that
Trưng Nhị was finally focused.

Trưng Nhị pinched her brows together in concentration.
Her eyes always seemed to glint with mischief, and her high
forehead formed an arch, unlike the widow's peak upon her
mother's and sister's browlines. Taking her stick in hand, she
traced a line in the white sand between a shell and a stone that
passed through a coin in the middle.

Lady Man Thiện let out a restrained laugh. "You cannot
just trample over the innocents," she said. "You must find
another way to reach your enemy."

Trưng Nhị resented being corrected in front of her older
sister, who always seemed to find favor with their mother. She
retraced the line, making a harder mark in the sand than the
first time. "There are no innocents in war," she said. "I must
make them my ally, or they will *become* my enemy."

Lady Man Thiện walked over to the table, took up a
brush, and returned to the floor near the window where her
daughters sat. She carefully erased the line Trưng Nhị had

drawn with her stick. "That's what the Hán say," said Lady Man Thiện. "But if there are no innocents, then the Hán have already won. It is their purpose to divide Việt from Việt."

Trưng Nhị felt the thumb of her mother's disapproval pressing down upon her, but she refused to be cowed. "The Hán *have* won," she said. "Otherwise we wouldn't live by their laws."

Lady Man Thiện turned to look at Trưng Trắc hopefully. "What would *you* do, elder daughter?"

Trưng Trắc lifted the sleeve of her robe with one hand; then, with contained eagerness, deftly flanked the rear position with two shells. Her movements appeared to flow in and out like a breath, and matched her pacific expression. The arcs in the white sand, one short and one long, looked like the trajectories of two arrows.

"Why?" Lady Man Thiện said. "You have trapped yourself in the snake's nest."

"To cut off the snake's head," said Trưng Trắc.

Trưng Nhị scoffed. Her sister's move was bold, but it angered her to think of a cadre of generals sitting atop a hill and plotting while the war raged in the valley. "The generals are cowards, and always place themselves at the rear, where they are spectators to war."

"A leader should never be a coward," said Lady Man Thiện. "Especially not a Việt."

Trưng Nhị said nothing, though she knew she would never be a leader and suspected herself to be, deep down, a coward.

Cung Điện Mê Linh was more than a palace. Overlooking the Red River, where the city of Mê Linh resided, Cung Điện Mê Linh was like a town unto itself, populated by workers and surrounded by a low stone wall. The servants and their families lived in separate longhouses on the grounds, and the Trưng family, the guardsmen, and their guests lived in the main palace, which, though its corrugated roofs were no higher than the back of an elephant, boasted a terrace overlooking the gardens.

Trưng Nhị strolled in the flower garden with the gardener's son, Phan Minh, who was one year younger than Trưng Nhị. His father was responsible for keeping the animals. Trưng Nhị called Phan Minh "Keeper of the Names," and presently she tested his knowledge of them. "One day it will be your duty to care for our animals, and you must treat them like your equals," she said.

"My equals?" Phan Minh said. "They are my superiors. A gardener's son has no status and no name but that which you bestow upon him."

The fountain burbled as the water spilled from the mouth of a stone fish into a pool of real ones, multicolored and moving in every direction, popping their mouths above the surface of the water as if waiting for flakes of feed to fall from the heavens. The palace stood squat and wide and gray in the background, a horizon over which the late morning sun shone. Trưng Nhị thought that, with a little bit of luck, every day could be like this.

"All right," replied Trưng Nhị with a wicked smile. "I now bestow upon you the name of Animal Acquirer. Furthermore, it shall be your job to bring more animals into our parks and gardens."

"I am already struggling to remember the names of the fifty-five animals," said Phan Minh.

"You aren't counting the fish! The fish have names, too," Trưng Nhị said, gesturing at the fountain. The idleness of a sun-warmed day and Phan Minh's banter, alternately earnest and playful, blended into an ointment that spread along the surface of her skin. His friendship demanded nothing but her presence and her attentiveness, which he returned with equal fervor. She basked in it. She did not have to strive to earn his respect, as she would with her sister and mother, because it was easily given. "So, Animal Acquirer, when will we get a dog in Cung Điện Mê Linh?" Her voice was sincere but her eyes betrayed her mischief.

"A dog," said Phan Minh, "would harass the marbled cats, scare away the painted turtles, and snap its jaws at the peacocks." He made a snapping motion with his hands to show her how the peacocks would feel about such an arrangement.

"If we cannot get a dog," said Trưng Nhị, "then I declare *you* to be the dog of Cung Điện Mê Linh. I hereby bestow upon you a new name: Minh the Dog."

Playfully, Phan Minh immediately dropped to his hands and knees, barking and bounding around the garden like a new puppy. His boisterous play was infectious. Trưng Nhị laughed, taking a stick and hurling it over Phan Minh's head, which he chased and brought back in his teeth, dropping it at her feet. He panted like a dog, and Trưng Nhị patted his head fondly. But when Phan Minh licked her hand, Trưng Nhị slapped him for his impertinence. It was an innocent reflex, though she was immediately flooded with both a yearning and pride, at once embarrassed by his audacity yet desperate for the kind of familiarity that it implied. He looked at her with wavering, watering eyes.

"Fine," Trưng Nhị said, offering her hand condescendingly. "You may lick."

Trưng Trắc sat on a stone recess in the wall, while Trưng Nhị leaned against a pillar. The great hall was the innermost room of the palace, allowing the sisters to look out upon the courtyard, the great elephant statue, and the moss-covered stone. This vision of the elephant was so familiar that it was like a silent, watchful parent. "Do you want to wander in the garden?" asked Trưng Nhị. She could still feel her muscles aching from their morning bout and she wanted her sister's tenderness now that she had been beaten and mended. Trưng Trắc's quiet studiousness simultaneously frustrated and impressed her. She could not help but seek her sister's approval.

"I'm too old to wander in the garden," said Trưng Trắc, her face impassive. Her expressions were slighter than Trưng Nhị's, yet to those who knew her, the slightest curl of the lip or bend of the eyebrow could communicate more than any sutra.

"What do you do all day indoors?" asked Trưng Nhị. She felt sorry that her sister was content to be confined to pacing within the clay walls of the palace, while her own domain was all the world outside it.

"I write." Trưng Trắc gestured with her arms to indicate the scroll upon her lap, feeling vulnerable at the prospect of sharing her private musings with her callous sister.

"Military strategy," Trưng Nhị said dismissively. Trưng Trắc's filiality almost sickened her in such moments. She might as well have been talking to Lady Man Thiện. How could she have a real relationship with her sister when Trưng Trắc spent her whole life emulating her parents, living accordingly to their will and whim?

"No," said Trưng Trắc defensively. "I write letters, notes, lists...jokes and riddles."

Trưng Nhị laughed almost witchily, but with an undertone of warmth. Trưng Nhị's crooked, comely smile always risked a look of impishness.

Trưng Trắc looked at Trưng Nhị. "You're laughing," she said. "But I haven't even told you a joke yet."

"It's just that you never mentioned this before," she said. Trưng Nhị pictured her sister diligently and dutifully and humorlessly crafting a joke. "I never imagined you trying to be funny. Please tell me one?"

"Okay. Let me think of one you'd like." Suddenly Trưng Trắc sprang to her feet and performed the joke like a puppet, shaking her head from side to side and saying in a shrill voice, "Our Hán cat never sleeps. He keeps us up at night, making bad smells. Why does he never sleep?"

"Why?" asked Trưng Nhị.

"Because he's dead!"

Trưng Nhị's expectant face turned indignant. "Dead cats are not funny. You are not funny. Go back to studying."

"Maybe you didn't get it," said Trưng Trắc. "He never sleeps, but smells bad because he's dead, right?"

Feeling cheated by the promise of a moment to smile and laugh together, Trưng Nhị's eyes lingered for a moment on her sister's face. She wished to find her own wildness, the inner animal that stirred and roared, reflected back at her in Trưng Trắc's expression, but saw only the tight line of her mouth with the slightest bend to suggest that she had been amused by her own joke. Trưng Nhị stood up and walked away, her egg blue silk robe gently undulating in the wind from the courtyard.

"Wait, I have others," Trưng Trắc said.

"I don't want to hear them," said Trưng Nhị to the air. She had tried to connect with Trưng Trắc and felt pitiable now for abasing herself in the name of familial harmony—a virtue she detested.

Trưng Trắc stared at the space vacated by her sister, before turning her attention to her pages of military strategy. "Each opponent is different, but their universal quality is fallibility," it read. "Every enemy is vulnerable in its own way, whether an excess of pride, or a habit of indulgence, or a surfeit of will. To discover where the ship is weakest, you must use an awl to prod the wood, cubit by cubit."

A month later and the monsoon season was almost upon them. For the feast of the Golden Turtle, Lord Trưng and

Lady Man Thiện hosted the Lords and Ladies of Chu Diên, Cửu Chân, Nhật Nam, and Hợp Phố at the palace. The dining hall was lit by beeswax candles, and all the lords and ladies sat on the floor, holding their bowls to their lips to taste of the ox broth. Only when the last bowl was emptied, and the wine poured, did the talk begin.

"Your daughters are grown now and beautiful beyond any parent's fondest hope," the Lady of Nhật Nam said.

"Yes, grown," said the Lord of Nhật Nam. "So when will they marry?"

"My daughters are not made to marry," said Lady Man Thiện. "Marriage is an economic arrangement for the benefit of the Hán."

"What will they do?"

"They will do as our mothers did and take whatever lover will bring them joy, and make them the best children, to raise in their own homes."

"To raise children alone?" asked the Lord of Nhật Nam.

"Maybe," said Lady Man Thiện. "What does a husband do but let himself be taken care of?"

The Lord of Nhật Nam scoffed. "But who will protect them?"

Lady Man Thiện raised an eyebrow. "You speak like a Confucian."

The Lord of Nhật Nam, his legs crossed and his hands planted on his thighs, raised his chin as though he had just awoken. "Maybe I am a Confucian, then. I am just thinking about what is best for your daughters. It is my intuition that, even though our society has allowed women to choose mates at their own will, what women secretly want is a husband and head of household."

"Maybe so, maybe not," said Lady Man Thiện. "There's only one way to know. Let's ask."

The Lord of Nhật Nam looked amused by the challenge. "If we are going to ask your daughters such a question, it is not enough that they give an answer. They must be persuasive."

"You and I have already shown our bias," said Lady Man Thiện, then gestured across the table to a thin, elderly woman, whose bowl of wine shook in her arthritic hands. "Why don't we enlist the Lady of Cửu Chân as an impartial judge?"

The Lord of Nhật Nam's lips pinched into a straight line, failing to conceal his amusement. "If we have a lady judge, we must also enlist a lord. The Lord of Hợp Phố will serve as a judge."

So Trưng Nhị and Trưng Trắc were called in. Trưng Trắc stood with her arms rigid at her sides, like a soldier, as Trưng Nhị crossed her arms and scanned the room with a sour expression. Both women wore *áo dài*, the flowing silk gowns embroidered with floral patterns, Trưng Nhị draped in the orange of sunrise, and Trưng Trắc in the dark blue of twilight. When the sisters learned of the terms of the contest, they looked at each other for some invisible cue as to who should make the first attempt, and it was Trưng Trắc who finally spoke.

"A woman wants the same things a man wants," she said, as though repeating instructions from a manual. "Glory in battle, comfort in bed, and the freedom to choose one's own fate."

"What of marriage?" asked the Lord of Nhật Nam.

"Marriage is an institution forced upon us by the Hán. It is the legacy of Confucianism, and should be abolished," she said. But she felt the cold draft of disapproval wafting from the judges, and added, "Though marriage is fine for your generation, which has had to accept the yoke of Confucianism, and your own marriages are, I'm sure, sacred things." As she spoke, everyone in the room could see her confidence waver.

Trưng Nhị, seeing her sister beginning to flail, interceded. Despite her feelings of rivalry with Trưng Trắc—despite her hope to surpass her in their morning sparring sessions and her dream to one day reign in her own palace far from Mê Linh and the Hán occupation—she hated to see her elder sister wriggle like a carp in a net. She stepped forward and gestured wide with her arms, a posture that suggested a story was forthcoming.

"Here in Mê Linh there was once a beautiful and proud girl named Hoàng Tâm, whose silken hair grew so long that it brushed the floor. She wanted nothing more than to mate with Trần Thuận, a handsome boy who lived in the same quarter. Trần Thuận was simple and happy, always quick to smile. His mother had never known marriage, and she was happy to see her son grow into a lover of women. But Hoàng Tâm's parents were united in the system of marriage, and they would not agree to a coupling without the promise of eternal loyalty. Hoàng Tâm loved Trần Thuận but could not say whether she would love him forever.

"So Hoàng Tâm secretly visited Trần Thuận at night and enjoyed his favors, her hair becoming a dark blanket around their bodies, and she soon became pregnant with his child. In most houses, this would be a blessing, but in Hoàng Tâm's home, this was cause for shame. Her parents chased their daughter out of their home, and Hoàng Tâm had to live among the peasants, where she gave birth in a stable, and had to beg in order to eat. The baby contracted a disease and died shortly after its birth. One day an unscrupulous trader saw the beautiful girl with long hair begging in the street, and lured her into his carriage with the promise of riches.

"Instead of caring for her, he traded her to a Hán, who used Hoàng Tâm as his concubine. Having vowed never to marry, she was now the property of a Hán devil. Rather than submit to a man, she shaved her head, wove her beautiful long hair into a rope, and used it to hang herself."

Trưng Nhị drew her arms into her chest and stepped backward, to indicate the story's end. This game of unsettling the thoughts of so many distinguished lords and ladies thrilled her. The room hummed with murmurs from the emissaries gathered there.

"What should we take from this, Trưng Nhị?" asked the Lady of Nhật Nam.

"What *do* you take from it?" asked Trưng Nhị.

"Her stubbornness is to blame," said the Lord of Hợp Phố. "If she had just married the boy she loved, then this terrible fate would not have befallen her."

"But," said the Lady of Cửu Chân, "if Hoàng Tâm's mother had simply accepted the Việt way, and allowed her daughter to mate with Trần Thuận without making vows and promises for the future, then all would be happy."

"We should have anticipated this situation," said Lady Man Thiện. "We have a tie."

"Unless you can find an impartial judge who is neither male nor female," said the Lord of Nhật Nam, "then the matter can never be resolved, and will remain a mystery."

"I have an idea," said Trưng Nhị impishly. Lady Man Thiện caught her daughter's eye and issued a silent rebuke, which she ignored. "Ngốc, the snail, is both male and female. It can impregnate other snails, and can be impregnated itself. Therefore, it is the most impartial creature on this question. I will bring Ngốc to the table, and if it slithers towards the Lady of Cửu Chân, then I am telling the truth when I say I do not wish to marry. If it crawls towards the Lord of Hợp Phố, then I secretly wish to be married like a Hán."

All of the men and women arrayed there agreed this was a fair plan—an entertaining resolution to the game being played out that evening. And when Trưng Nhị returned with Ngốc the snail, she placed him on the long table, where the Lady of Cửu Chân and the Lord of Hợp Phố sat on opposite sides, then said, "Listen to me, Ngốc. If you go east, to the Lady of Cửu Chân, then you accept that the tragedy of Hoàng Tâm and Trần Thuận is the fault of the institution of marriage; if you go west, to the Lord of Hợp Phố, then you agree that the tragedy of Hoàng Tâm and Trần Thuận is the fault of the girl Hoàng Tâm for refusing to marry." Then she let go of his shell.

Everyone was silent while Ngốc crawled the table lengthwise, neither east nor west but north, toward the end of the table. When it did not stray in either direction, but continued its journey away from both the Lady of Cửu Chân and the Lord of Hợp Phố, the silence gave way to howls and gasps of surprise. Seated at the end of the table was the Lord of Chu Diên, named Đặng Vũ, who had maintained his silence throughout the game. When Ngốc reached the Lord of Chu Diên, it affixed itself to the end of the table as though making a home there.

"The final verdict is yours, Đặng Vũ," said Lady Man Thiện. "Who is to blame for the misfortune of Hoàng Tâm? Is it Hoàng Tâm, who wished to live independently in spite of her parents' commands, or is it Hoàng Tâm's mother, who wished to impose marriage on her daughter?"

Đặng Vũ reached over and clapped his hand on the shoulder of Lord Trưng, and smiled. "I am not a scholar, and am innocent of higher forms of interpretation practiced by the monks, but my ear must be tuned to a different pitch than that of my friends from Hợp Phố and Cửu Chân. I cannot lay the blame upon either Hoàng Tâm or her parents." Đặng Vũ's smile folded down like a wilting rose. With his free hand, he slammed a fist down on the table, shaking the bowls of wine and causing Ngốc to crawl to the underside of the table, where it affixed itself. "I blame the Hán!" he said. "The men and women of our generation married, yes, but we never accepted the Confucian ways. Hoàng Tâm's story only proves their folly, for it is a Hán scoundrel who forces a girl into concubinism. Our people are not property, and the story should provoke only one response: outrage at the injustice of living under such a people."

The Lord of Nhật Nam was stern. Lord Trưng stood and

said, "Surely we can agree that the Hán are to blame, and that my daughters are in earnest when they declare they will not be married."

The prevailing silence meant many things: that no answer was possible; that the Hán were surely to blame; that Mê Linh, Cửu Chân, and all the lands of Lạc Việt were beyond saving by men.

CHAPTER 2

The Dog of Cung Điện Mê Linh

Phan Minh listed the names of the animals for the fourteenth time: "Drunk-fish, Beetleback, Pok-pok, Soup-bones…" The catfish were the most difficult to keep track of, as they flicked the surface of the water one by one with their fins, their mouths jutting out and throbbing open and closed like the valves of a beating heart. Each had a differently colored pattern on its scales, so they could be distinguished from one another by a discriminating eye, but the way they weaved and tumbled in an orchestrated chaos defied the bureaucratic imperative of the Keeper of the Names.

"Why do you count the catfish?" Phan Minh's father the gardener asked, picking the dead blooms off a sapa orchid. It frustrated him that his absentminded son needed constant watching, constant instruction. For a gardener in training, he lived too much in his head. "That's the one animal that doesn't need your ministration."

Although they carried no real responsibilities, Phan Minh wished to keep his titles as Animal Acquirer and Keeper of the Names secret, as he knew his father the gardener felt protective of the fauna of his garden and treated her ladyship's interest in this realm as unwelcome meddling by a spoiled aristocrat. "There are fewer today than yesterday," he said idly.

"Huh? A fisherman has been sneaking into our gardens at night? I bet it is that beggar Duy, who must be shooed away from the gates of Cung Điện Mê Linh every morning."

"I must be mistaken," said Phan Minh, concerned that having Trưng Nhị in his thoughts all day may have inadvertently stirred up trouble by distracting him. "They are too difficult to count."

"There are exactly sixty-seven," the gardener said, crouching over the edge of the pond to count the catfish. Behind him, the low stone wall that defined the border of the palace grounds ran jagged into the distance.

"What are the chances that we could bring a dog into Cung Điện Mê Linh?" Phan Minh asked, eager to change the subject.

"Never. A dog would harass the marbled cats, scare away the painted turtles, and snap its jaws at the peacocks. Why would you want to take care of a filthy beast who tears up our garden?"

"They are faithful guardians," said Phan Minh, "and can protect the gardens from intruders like Duy the beggar."

The gardener stopped counting fish. "So it *was* Duy who stole our catfish? Why did you lie?"

"I saw nothing. I don't know if it was Duy," Phan Minh said. "Maybe it was the tiger?"

The gardener frowned. He would have whipped Phan Minh for the slightest provocation, but an insult this deep he somehow abided. "Răng the Tiger," he said, "has only one appetite."

Phan Minh was just old enough to remember his mother, who had died six years earlier. Võ Tuyến had been stalked and mauled to death by a tiger—a tiger that still terrorized the village, a sleek and silent killer whom they called Răng and was believed to be of supernatural origin. The villagers said that Răng was inhabited by the spirit of a jealous man who wished to own a woman whose favors he had once enjoyed, but the woman wished to be free and had become pregnant with another man's child. The man died of grief, but when he came back as Răng the Tiger, his spirit was full of vengeance, and he was afflicted by an insatiable hunger for women who were full with child, as Phan Minh's mother had been when Răng devoured her.

Phan Minh had been nine years old then, old enough to remember his father before his mother's death—when he was just a charming visitor in their home, sharing the bed with his mother every few days. Ever since her passing, the gardener had been Phan Minh's resentful caretaker, who cared more for his garden than his child, and seemed to be forever looking for culprits to punish for perceived wrongdoings. For this purpose, Phan Minh was usually nearest at hand.

Vines spread their leafy fingers in the grooves of the palace's clay walls, and upon each tendril, a thousand more curled tendrils clung to the earthen surface. Rather than clear them away, the gardener had tamed them into a shape that defined the borders of the walls. The wooden structure of the ceiling offered open slats to allow the light and weather to enter in. Trưng Trắc stared up at a ray of angled light through the slats and pondered how by simply leaving a thing unsaid, it could be perceived as an act of deception. A quiet girl like Trưng Trắc risked the reputation of a liar, when even the fact that she spent her days composing riddles surprised her own sister. So much of her inner life was unvoiced, but it was not in her nature to withhold; she simply lacked a counterpart with whom to share her thoughts. Trưng Nhị certainly would not have appreciated her insights; her sister's impatience with anything that resembled philosophy repelled Trưng Trắc. It was unthinkable to her that one could live their life without questioning their own thoughts and impressions, rather than seeking answers from the great thinkers of the past. And as far as her mother went, Lady Man Thiện possessed an aloofness that did not invite confidences. Perhaps *secret* was merely another name for loneliness?

However, even if it didn't mean true companionship, Trung Trac's parents' insistence that she learn the art of war provided her a clear path to acceptance and approval. In her loyalty to Lord Trưng and Lady Man Thiện, whose ancestors had fiercely yet unsuccessfully defended their homeland from invasion, understanding military strategy—and specifically the history of war between the Việts and the Hán—had become her life's pursuit. Trưng Trắc's latest revelation came not from the library, but from the kitchen. She had been idly listening to the chatter of the cook, Phùng Thị Chính, when she overheard this mother of four say that, though she was but one mother, she had to become a different mother to each son. When she gave praise to her shyest son for the meagerest bold act, and her rowdiest entered the room, she would find something to scold him for. Sometimes she had to pivot from child to child, from tone to tone, within an instant, and she said that the siege of their needs upon her motherly soul was like an army at the gates of a citadel. To Trưng Trắc, this had become more than idle banter, and was hardening into a philosophy of war. She wondered, "What is military strategy but *speed of thought*?" Yet there was no one with whom to share this new knowledge.

Trưng Nhị stepped out into the garden. She was never far from the animals, especially the painted turtles, her favorite of which was Kim Quy, who was so old that her mother had grown up with it. She suspected Kim Quy was older than Cung Điện Mê Linh itself. Watching Phan Minh tending to the fish, Trưng Nhị's rising heartbeat startled her. Maybe it was merely the body's response to the fun they had together. She had been aware, up until now, of how their closeness emboldened the gardener's son, but not how her own mind and body responded to it. She felt an addiction to the quick smile that brightened his eyes and revealed his dimpled cheeks. But perhaps the roots of this new interest went deeper than the honeysuckle. She crept up to Phan Minh from behind, though he showed no surprise when she spoke. "I saw how you tried to obtain a dog for Cung Điện Mê Linh, and I will reward you one day when I have my own palace," she said wispily, as though she were already halfway into such a glorious future.

"I need no reward," Phan Minh said, lowering his chin with due humility but raising his eyes to meet hers, "other than your approval."

"But surely you aspire to a title of some sort, a military rank?"

"But I am rich with titles and ranks. I am the Keeper of the Names; I am the Animal Acquirer…and I am Minh the Dog." With this last utterance, Phan Minh turned around and boldly took Trưng Nhị's hand and stroked it with his thumb. Trưng Nhị's hand radiated with heat as the blood in her veins rushed to the spot where Phan Minh touched her. She recalled the sensation of his rough tongue on her fingers as he, doglike, cleaned the flavor from her hand with absolute devotion to the task. The memory awakened an awareness within Trưng Nhị, alerting her to her own desire. She felt it run through her legs. Trưng Nhị pulled it away when she noticed that her hand was sweating from the heat.

She looked up at Phan Minh and noticed, as though for the first time, the flowering of his irises, blooming out from the pupil into the brown vase of his eye. She studied him as carefully as she studied the natural world and noticed how Phan Minh's eyes both withheld and revealed his longing, how they trembled from the effort of containing what he could never put into words.

Behind Phan Minh, a kingfisher alighted from the branch of an evergreen and made a languorous arc toward the stream that ran through Cung Điện Mê Linh. The shift, from moment to moment, of lightness and weight, from play to solemnity, felt like rolling too fast down a hill and landing in a bed of moss. The animal joy that Trưng Nhị took in sharing such a simple thing with Phan Minh unsettled her. "Quick, what is the kingfisher's name?" she asked, assuming again an aristocratic air.

"His name is Mở," Phan Minh said, turning away from Trưng Nhị's gaze and glancing at the kingfisher stepping in the stream. In profile, his chin descended to a point, and his hair strayed ahead of his brow, giving a sharp, half-moon quality to his visage, silhouetted by the morning sky. Whatever happened, she could not show this gardener's son how much more *herself* she felt in his presence—how he made the days fuller and easier and far, far shorter than they should have been.

"What a dull name. I thought he was called Lồng," Trưng Nhị said.

"Lồng is her ladyship's parakeet."

"But *Cage* is such a sad name for a parakeet," Trưng Nhị said. Then Trưng Nhị spoke with greater conviction. "Lồng will henceforward be the kingfisher's name, and the parakeet will be called Mở."

"But *I* am the Keeper of Names," said Phan Minh. "Is it

not my duty to keep the names of the animals of Cung Điện Mê Linh?"

"You are the Keeper of Names, not the Decider of Names," said Trưng Nhị. "Besides, you have more important duties now."

"What is my newest title?" Phan Minh asked, with a confidence unbefitting a gardener's son.

"Well," said Trưng Nhị, offering her hand, this time to pull herself up. "Do you ride?"

Trưng Nhị and Phan Minh sat atop their horses at the crest of a ridge overlooking an endless valley of rice paddies. The evergreen forest that surrounded Mê Linh was far behind them, and each one knew the trouble that awaited them upon their return, but neither one spoke of it. For Phan Minh to wander off the grounds of the palace with the Lady Trưng Nhị was to invite the attention of his father and the lord, neither of whom would see their ride in the wilderness as innocent.

"There is already a stable master," said Phan Minh, "and there is already a riding tutor."

Trưng Nhị turned toward Phan Minh and saw, as though for the first time, more than a peasant boy riding on a horse. Away from the palace, he seemed as proud as a noble yet as fierce as the animals he cared for, and which she loved.

"Minh-ơi," said Trưng Nhị, using the affectionate, familial form of address. That *ơi* was more passionate than a kiss would have been. "I am running out of names."

"Why don't you call me Gardener's Son, like you once did?"

"Why don't you give *me* a title? I don't want to be called her ladyship any longer."

"I cannot give you a title," Phan Minh said, and the boldness he had shown in holding Trưng Nhị's hands and holding the horse's reins dissipated like a dream in the daylight. "I must call you her ladyship, and you must always know what I truly mean when I say it."

"Say my name," she said, straining to remember a time when she had heard those simple syllables on his lips. "Just once." Nothing but the words themselves mattered to her at that moment, as long as she could thrill to the sound of her name vibrating in his delicate throat.

The horses stared straight ahead at the rice paddies. Trưng Nhị and Phan Minh looked at each other, then followed the horses' stare into the valley as if by the same instinct. They knew that a return to the pretense that she was merely a lady and he was merely a gardener's son awaited them beyond the evergreen forest, far behind yet never forgotten.

Spotting something that shined in the foothills, Phan Minh dismounted from his horse and walked up to it. He knelt down next to an amethyst, which he pried from the earth and discovered had cracked into two with a jagged edge. The pair admired the purple and green crystal patterns, which appeared otherworldly in the light. He handed half to Trưng Nhị, which she stretched to receive.

"Say my name," said Trưng Nhị, accepting his gift.

"Nhị-ơi," Phan Minh said.

The slight wind on Trưng Nhị's cheeks felt as powerful as a monsoon, and the dimpled flesh of her arm anticipated a touch that never came.

"Say it again." Trưng Nhị reached out to touch Phan Minh's face, but she sat high up on her mare, and he was out of reach. That Trưng Nhị would one day rule these lands, these animals, and determine his own fate, battered him like a squall. How could he begin to imagine a life by her side? Whenever he dared dream it, she was always Lady Trưng and he was always Phan Minh the Dog, Phan Minh the gardener's son, Phan Minh the Animal Acquirer and the Keeper of Names.

"I do not deserve this," Phan Minh said, and pulled on the reins of his horse, named Mực, and reversed course.

Left in his wake, Trưng Nhị felt cut by the reminder of their roles and titles, by the truth that they could never be equals. "*Deserve* this?" called Trưng Nhị after Phan Minh. "Am I a prize to be won?"

When Trưng Trắc planted herself in a secret spot by the doorway in the dining hall, listening to the kitchen conversation, the servants' talk was somber. Võ Danh, the oldest son of Phùng Thị Chính, was nearly at an age when he would be conscripted by the Hán to fight in a war for a cause he would never understand. His mother was determined to prevent such a fate. She talked about disguising her son as a girl, or hiding him away in the mountains. "Death would be better than serving in the armies of the Hán," said Phùng Thị Chính. All the mothers agreed.

How could the Hán break up our families and send our young men off to die? Trưng Trắc thought. *How could the lord allow it?* Troubled by this question, Trưng Trắc wandered dazed through the corridors of the palace until her feet had taken her to the quarters of Bác Huy Vũ, the astrologer. A confidant of Lord Trưng and Lady Man Thiện, the astrologer was both a wise man and as close to a member of her family as a commoner could be. Bác Huy Vũ had cultivated a particular fondness for the Trưng sisters, having watched them grow since their birth.

"I was just setting out for a walk in the gardens," said Bác Huy Vũ. Trưng Trắc followed the astrologer on his ramble, though she strode with her chin pointed toward the path, indifferent to the lure of the outdoors.

She failed to notice the fickle wind that blew one way, then another, making overlapping ripples in the surface of the pond and changing the flight patterns of a flock of birds.

"Watch how the leaves dance and even sing!" said Bác Huy Vũ, spreading his arms as though to embrace the whole of nature.

"How can I think of dancing leaves when the husbands and fathers and sons of Mê Linh are being sent off to fight and die for the enemy?" said Trưng Trắc.

"You must seize joy, for without joy you will become indifferent to others, shirking your duties because nothing will seem to matter," said Bác Huy Vũ, pausing mid-step to pivot in her direction. "You must remain ready, for one day Cung Điện Mê Linh will need you."

Trưng Trắc's expression betrayed her uncertainty that she could ever live up to that duty, but only for a moment, and it was quickly washed over by a smile. She possessed the kind of will that overcame anything, even her own frailty. "When have I ever shirked my duties, Bác Huy Vũ?" she asked with a confidence that was almost brash, if Trưng Trắc could ever be brash.

"One of your duties stands above all others," said Bác Huy Vũ.

"I know," said Trưng Trắc. "I will never forget my duty to my mother and father."

"No," said Bác Huy Vũ. "Your highest duty in this life is to be an example and a protector to your sister."

At night, the gates of Cung Điện Mê Linh were locked by a thick wooden brace. Phan Minh found himself outside them, looking for the low place where the stone wall was sunken to eye level, a spot over which he was accustomed to hurdling. In his arms he carried a brown-coated *bạc hà* puppy, a breed of dog known for its discretion—the quietest dog in the land—but he hadn't formulated a plan for scaling the wall with a dog in his arms.

He walked back to the gate, even debated knocking upon it, unsure whether the guardsman on duty would be his friend Kha or another guardsman unfriendly to his schemes. He paced the length of the wall until a figure stumbled into view—it was Duy the beggar.

"Hey, Duy," Phan Minh called out in a loud whisper. "Come here."

Duy eagerly complied, bowing as he approached and repeating, "I am hungry, my children are hungry, and my mother is hungry. Please. A handful of rice."

"Okay," said Phan Minh. "I'm just the gardener's son, but I will bring you a sack full of rice tomorrow. Only help boost me over the wall."

Duy was surprised to be offered the promise of rice, rather than rice itself. "Won't you give me something so that we might eat tonight? That animal?"

"This dog belongs to Her Ladyship Trưng Nhị. It is not for anyone to eat."

Duy the beggar shook his head. "Only the rich," he said.

"Listen," said Phan Minh. "Just bow down, the way you just did a moment ago, and I will stand on your back to get over the wall. Then you must pass the dog to me on the other side."

Duy agreed. But when Phan Minh was over the wall and reached over it, there was nothing.

"I must have your promise," Duy said. "Your *word*."

"You have it."

"Swear on your father's garden and on all of Cung Điện Mê Linh, that if you break your promise to me of a sack of rice tomorrow, then doom and misfortune will rain down upon your home and the home of your precious ladyship."

Phan Minh hardly gave the beggar's words a thought. "I swear it. Now give me the dog."

The dog silently passed from Duy's hands to Phan Minh's over the wall. "Thank you," said Phan Minh, rushing off to her ladyship's chamber.

"Does he have a name?" Duy called out.

"Ngoan," said Phan Minh, deciding that the dog deserved the name "Obedient."

Trưng Nhị startled awake in the middle of the night at the sound of her chamber door being opened. Instantly, her training took over, and she rolled to the wall, grabbed a spear, and ran with a light tread at the intruder in the doorway. In the moonlight she caught a glimpse of Phan Minh's dimpled cheek and managed to stop the thrust of her spear in time.

"It's me!" Phan Minh said, and his own instinct was to wrap his arms protectively around Ngoan the dog. Then, when Trưng Nhị lowered her spear, Phan Minh revealed the contraband animal, presenting it to her ladyship by placing it at her feet. Ngoan proceeded to rub itself affectionately against the leg of its new master. "His name is Ngoan," he said.

"Ngoan, sit!" Trưng Nhị said. The dog continued its cat-like prowl around Trưng Nhị's legs.

"He's just a puppy," explained Phan Minh.

"Ngoan! Sit!" This time Ngoan looked up at Trưng Nhị, but stood its ground. She couldn't help but notice that she and Phan Minh were alone. She could hear her own shallow breath in the near-dark and she rushed to fill the void with banter. "I think we should call him Xấu," said Trưng Nhị. It proceeded to earn its name by peeing on the floor of her ladyship's chamber. "Disobedient" seemed the more fitting name after all.

Phan Minh laughed. "Okay, but Xấu must be kept a secret. Do you have a place for him to go where my father won't see him?"

"A secret dog?"

"Xấu is a *bạc hà* puppy," said Phan Minh. "They hardly make a noise. Would you please help me keep him hidden?"

Trưng Nhị hesitated. The gardener was old, and even though Trưng Nhị was an aristocrat, she had known him since she was a baby and was still somewhat frightened of him and his harsh demeanor. "I will hide him in the armory, and let him out into the gardens only when the gardener is gone. But if this is your way of becoming worthy of me, then you have much work to do."

"Nhị-ơi," Phan Minh said, and the yearning in his voice was impossible to miss. He looked at her wildly and warily, as though she were a spirit that had descended from the clouds. Yet his gaze held the warmth of an embrace.

Trưng Nhị looked down at her hands and noticed that she still held the spear. She noticed, too, that she was dressed only in her night robe. "It will be our secret," she said.

Back in the courtyard, as always, at the behest of their parents, Trưng Nhị and Trưng Trắc faced each other in the light of dawn, shaded partially by the statue of the elephant. Their family history was also the military history of the Việts, and so, for aristocrats, martial training was an inevitability. It was the lord's first and perhaps only decree upon the subject of their education. It was as routine as a meal, a fixed star in the constellation of the morning. But the lord's insistence upon daily trials of war was more than that of his neighbors, more than that of anyone in their sphere. Two generations without war, the lord often said, did not mean the Hán had given up on their designs to wrest control completely from the regional lords. As his night terrors taught him, war waited around every corner.

At their sparring session, Trưng Nhị's ferocity nearly overwhelmed her sister's rhythmic, almost musical strategy: block, block, block, counterstrike. Trưng Nhị could usually be counted on to wear herself out on the offensive and lose the strength of her stance as she advanced prematurely into Trưng Trắc's range of attack. But Trưng Nhị's energy seemed to flow unabated and undiminished that morning, and it was Trưng Trắc who shook wearily under the repeated blows from her sister's staff. Trưng Trắc retreated to the wall and started to counterstrike from both ends, hoping in this way to surprise her opponent with a two-sided attack. Instead, Trưng Trắc found she had to yield her grip to avoid having her knuckles crushed by Trưng Nhị's onslaught, each blow encroaching further on the center of balance on Trưng Trắc's staff, until finally she had to let go. Trưng Nhị may not have had the aptitude or the appetite for war her sister had, but as long as she was forced to train relentlessly, she refused to be beaten. She needed to show that she was not the second in everything— in intelligence, in obedience, in military prowess. But just as Trưng Nhị was about to come down upon Trưng Trắc with a finishing blow, Trưng Trắc noticed how her sister planted her front foot too heavily in order to gain more power. Trưng Trắc ducked and pivoted in one swift motion, extending her leg and spiraling around to sweep under Trưng Nhị's and send her careening to the floor, where Trưng Trắc pounced upon her and delivered seven swift punches to her chest, her neck, and her cheek. The match was over, Trưng Nhị called "enough," and Trưng Trắc helped her sister to the infirmary, since Trưng Nhị had briefly fallen unconscious. The words of Bác Huy Vũ echoed in the back of Trưng Trắc's mind, that her first duty was to her sister. She resented being told that Trưng Nhị was her responsibility, and she had taken it out on her sister that morning. It was expected that Trưng Nhị would get carried away, as it was in her nature to do so, but Trưng Trắc had always been able to handle her sister's overzealous style without resorting to such violence. Yet it was not the first or the last time that Trưng Nhị would wake up with her sister's sympathetic face hovering over her.

At the infirmary, the physician looked in Trưng Nhị's eyes and nose and ears and mouth, and said that she needed ginseng root to stimulate her yang energy and needed to extend her arms outward and move them in circles throughout the day to improve the flow of blood back to the brain. For Trưng Trắc, the balm of camphor and paraffin on her knuckles would be enough. Trưng Trắc kissed her sister on the forehead and said that she had some studying to do that morning.

"Before you go, tell me another joke," said Trưng Nhị, attempting, once again, to find a connection with her sister that was more than the thrash of a weapon.

"No," said Trưng Trắc. "You don't like my jokes. But I will tell you a riddle."

Trưng Nhị nodded.

"What creature whistles and blows, but never swallows? It knocks you down and licks you with its tongue, but has no teeth to chew. It spits and it pees but never feeds; it buffets its wings but never takes flight."

Trưng Nhị thought about being knocked down by her sister, of her hand being licked by Phan Minh, of the dog Xấu peeing in her chambers. But none of these creatures fit the description in its entirety. Lost in thought, Trưng Nhị walked into the hall, leaving Trưng Trắc to the contemplation of her narrow victory.

The mating call of the peacock sounds like the wail of a woman in distress. When the peacock is stalked by a predator, its cawing becomes bark-like, warbling and shrill. Such a sound, erupting over the gardens of Cung Điện Mê Linh, drew a crowd of laborers and servants, who were the first to discover the dog Xấu guiltily pawing at the carcass of the elaborately plumed bird.

The gardener, when he arrived, lost all the color in his face. The cost of the peacock alone would beggar him if he were found guilty of its death. The chance that the lord would dismiss him was an even greater horror to contemplate.

"Where are the guardsmen?" the cook, Phùng Thị Chính, wondered aloud. She was accompanied by her four children, all gawking boys.

"It's just a puppy," said a servant.

The gardener took the shaft of a bamboo pole and struck the dog, who fled the scene, but finding itself walled into the garden, began to let out its own desperate yelps.

Phan Minh broke free from the crowd that had gathered and put himself between the gardener and the dog, who had once again proven himself worthy of the name.

"You?" said the gardener. "Is this your doing, Phan Minh? Did you want a dog so badly that you sneaked one into our garden, against my wishes?"

"No," said Phan Minh automatically.

"Then who did this?"

Phan Minh scanned the faces in the crowd and found no one to blame. "Duy the beggar."

And the words were hardly out before the guardsmen had seized Duy from his route around the wall's perimeter and dragged him into the garden. By then, the lord had been alerted and found himself reluctantly set up to arbitrate this minor dispute. His mind was on the increasing efforts of the Hán officers to interfere with affairs within his jurisdiction, and it was pure distraction that caused him to sentence the beggar to be flogged in the public square of Mê Linh.

Phan Minh decided in that moment that he would attend the flogging, silently declaring this to be his own punishment— to witness the shame of his deception.

"Just because a beggar sent a dog into Cung Điện Mê Linh to poach our fowl," said Trưng Nhị to her mother, "that doesn't mean the dog should be punished. Let Xấu stay, and I will keep him in the courtyard, away from the outer gardens." She worried only about how to keep her secret family—she, Phan Minh, and the dog Xấu—intact and gave just a passing thought to the beggar Duy, who wandered the perimeter of the palace at sunset.

"Let's keep this simple. I will make you a bargain," Lady Man Thiện said. "I will let you keep the dog if you promise to stop spending your days with the gardener's son."

Trưng Nhị's mouth went dry, and for the first time in her mother's memory, her daughter was struck speechless. Trưng Nhị and Phan Minh had been so careful, so clandestine. Had her mother known all along? She knew that the palace was a nest of spies, but hadn't suspected that the spies had been watching over her.

"You are at an age when you need to think about what kind of man will bear you the best child," Lady Man Thiện said.

"But I don't want a child," said Trưng Nhị. "How do you know about Phan Minh? Have your spies been watching me?"

"How can I help but notice that you spend all your time in the garden, and that your fascination with animals is growing into a fascination with boys? But this is precisely when you need your mother to introduce you to the best stock of young men in the land. Phan Minh is simply the first boy you are acquainted with. He is surely not the best."

"I won't," said Trưng Nhị. When it came to her mother, Trưng Nhị always imagined she could outplay her. Lady Man

Thiện was so much like Trưng Trắc and neither of them possessed Trưng Nhị's subtlety or wile.

"Either the dog or the gardener's son."

Trưng Nhị looked down at Xấu, whose facial expression was fixed in an eternal plea for mercy. She was determined to find a way to keep Phan Minh and Xấu both. Trưng Nhị would not have to choose. Fearing the dog would be put down if she named Phan Minh, she said, "I choose Xấu."

Her ladyship's appearance at the gardener's longhouse that night was unprecedented, and the gardener scowled when he found Trưng Nhị upon the threshold, her hair and clothes wet with a coat of rain. Trưng Nhị, however, was driven by a purpose that did not wane with intimidation. She shoved the gardener aside and called out for Phan Minh, who, when he saw her shivering, brought Trưng Nhị a fresh bowl of broth and a fur.

Helpless to command the young aristocrat to leave his home, the gardener left to report this breach of law to Lady Man Thiện, and the two young lovers were alone. Phan Minh wrapped the fur around Trưng Nhị, whose clothes still shed water on the floor. She shrugged it off instinctively, unwilling to let herself be cared for. Phan Minh smiled indulgently and Trưng Nhị returned it tentatively. They looked down at the fallen fur on the ground between them. Now that their secret had been discovered, Trưng Nhị felt no hesitation, only a hunger for his presence, closer and ever closer. She wondered how long she would have to plead with her eyes before he touched her. Phan Minh's hand found her cheek, and then he slowly lowered his hand to her chest, feeling the thump of her heart. The lovers shed their clothing and buried themselves in the fur, kissing and nuzzling each other's bodies. The wind howled outside the longhouse, and the sound of pounding rain was like the stamping of horses on the roof. Phan Minh kissed her ladyship's inner arms, neck, and breasts with the same faithful devotion to the task that he exhibited in his care of the animals of Cung Điện Mê Linh. Each kiss carried the weight of his full attention, and lingered on Trưng Nhị's skin as though he were spreading balm down her chest, to the soft pad of her belly, to her thighs, where she began to quiver with new sensation. Trưng Nhị surrendered her body to his lips. She felt no need to return his kisses and simply let the servant serve.

After, as she lay among the furs in the glow of an overwhelming feeling, Trưng Nhị's mind moved in unfamiliar ways—as though she was barely aware of her thoughts swimming in front of her eyes. She didn't feel altered so much as she felt a greater belonging to herself. She felt close to Phan Minh, connected as two separate trees may be interlaced at the roots. She listened to the wind-driven rain knock at the wooden windows of the longhouse.

"A monsoon!" Trưng Nhị called out, sitting up. She laughed, grudgingly impressed with her sister's riddle. "Of course!"

Phan Minh looked crookedly at her and rubbed her back with his hand languorously.

"'What creature whistles and blows, but never swallows? It knocks you down and licks you with its tongue, but has no teeth to chew. It spits and it pees but never feeds; it buffets its wings, but never takes flight,'" Trưng Nhị recited. "A monsoon!"

CHAPTER 3

The Flogging

In the region of Lạc Việt there were three subregions, and a river flowed through each of them. The largest, the Red River, broke into prongs before flowing into the East Sea. North of the delta, where the effluence of rivers is strongest, there resided the city of Mê Linh. The regular flooding of the valley made this region ideal for growing rice, and the migration of loach and catfish made it perfect for fishing.

But today all the rice farmers and fishermen of Mê Linh broke from their work to see the commotion in the public square. Among the gathered crowd was Phan Minh, who burned with guilt but did nothing to interfere with the proceedings of the day. Duy was tied by his hands to a pole, bare back exposed to the sunlight, skin shiny with sweat but otherwise undisturbed. The man designated to enact this punishment was Kha the guardsman, the longest-serving and most faithful of the lord's guard.

"What crime did such a pitiful beggar commit?" said a woman carrying a basket of jackfruit.

"Why don't you flog the tax collector?" said another, guiding an ox hauling a cart of goods.

Kha just continued to count the strokes, knowing that with each blow the beggar's punishment was closer to its completion.

Then a Hán officer approached and stood at the outskirts of the small crowd. He wore a leather jerkin over kapok cotton and carried a poleax. He had a mole on the middle of his forehead like a third eye. "What is this man's crime?" he asked several of the citizens gathered there, but no one could answer him.

Kha finished the twentieth stroke and reached to unbind the broken, sobbing beggar from the wooden pole. The officer stopped him, saying, "For what crime is this creature being punished?"

"For the crime of poaching on Lord Trưng's lands," answered Kha. "And he has faced the penalty today."

"Nonsense," said the officer. "The Hán penalty for thievery is amputation of the hands, and the penalty for stealing from an authority is death."

"Death?" said Phan Minh, stepping out of the crowd to declare his presence before the guardsman, the officer, and the beggar. The torment of watching his proxy abused and debased was too much to abide. It ruptured and rent him. Phan Minh could not sit by watching an innocent man punished. The spectacle stung, every lash like a rebuke to his honor. "Hasn't he suffered enough?"

"And who is this?" said the officer.

"Just a noisy bird," said Kha, casting a warning glance toward Phan Minh, "who has wandered too far from his nest."

The officer sneered at Phan Minh, as his eyes took the measure of the scene. "You Việts are a strange people," he said finally, with a laugh. "You are far too lenient with the criminal element, and it fosters rebellious attitudes and encourages a lack of respect for authority."

Kha laughed as though he were in on the joke. "We cannot help it. We are an indulgent people," he said, grabbing his substantial belly as proof.

"Well," said the officer. "We must draw the line somewhere." For a moment it seemed to Kha as though the officer would leave it there, but then he announced, "You must execute the poacher, as is consistent with Hán law."

"Please—" Phan Minh pleaded, stepping forward as though to take the ax stroke himself, but Kha shushed him by raising a fat finger.

"Wouldn't it behoove you to learn the facts of the case first? Would you overturn the ruling of our Lạc lord for something so small?" Kha asked.

"The decrees of your lord cannot countervail the law of the land," the officer said.

If the flogging itself drew dozens of bewildered citizens trying to reconcile the scene, the argument between the guardsman and the Hán officer drew twice as many spectators.

Kha stood as if his body had been sculpted from the earth beneath him. "If this is Hán law, then why don't *you* execute him? It won't be on my conscience." Duy cried helplessly and bowed his head, too resigned for a plea.

The officer pointed his polearm, topped with a bronze

pediform ax, at Kha the guardsman. "If you do not obey the law, then you are an insurrectionist, and it would be my duty to execute you and your family."

"Then I suppose I should count myself thankful that I have no family," said Kha, his eyes briefly glancing from the bamboo bundle in his hands to the bronze ax pointed at his belly.

A tense silence prevailed. The crowd whispered among themselves.

Then through the haze of his fear and pain, Duy spotted Phan Minh in the crowd and shouted, "*He* is the one! The real poacher is Phan Minh the gardener's son! Execute him!"

Kha flogged Duy again with his bamboo bundle wrapped in straw, until he fell silent.

"All right," said Kha. He had no time to grieve or doubt or agonize over this fate, but as Kha lifted the bundle, ready to strike again, he saw the beggar's desperate gaze, and it stayed his hand. If a man would die that day, at least he would no longer suffer. "I will execute the beggar, but I cannot kill a man by flogging him to death, no matter what his crime. May I use your ax?"

"May the Guardian Spirit protect me!" called out Duy. He clenched his eyes shut and tensed all the muscles of his body involuntarily.

The officer warily handed over his poleax to Kha, who as soon as he took hold of the instrument, felt the weight of this moment—the different destinies that might come to pass should he choose to wield the ax against Duy, or against the officer who had pronounced his sentence. He held his breath, begging the Guardian Spirit for forgiveness, then he let the ax fall swiftly upon the beggar's neck.

Compromise by compromise, Trưng Nhị had regained her mother's trust. By taking other men to her bed—a diplomat, a soldier's son—she had proven herself immune to the boyish love of a gardener's son. Thus, Trưng Nhị was given the freedom to explore the town outside the walls and grounds of Cung Điện Mê Linh. What she found there, in the marketplace, at the banks of the Red River, and in the public square, bored her. She began to spend her mornings riding as far from the town as her horse—whose name she couldn't recall—would take her, and spent her evenings in game dens, consorting with gamblers and prostitutes, who always spoke in street proverbs that sounded world-weary and pennywise. When these commoners spoke, it was without the burden of guile, unlike the reserved and careful speech of her own family. They did not act as though the world would fall apart without them; each man and woman knew their place in the life of the village, which was small. Among them, Trưng Nhị could have been a cat stretching out in the sun for all they cared of her "duty." She thought that they would be intimidated by such an important personage as she; instead, they regarded her as an ornamented bird, decorated with frills but occupying the same air. They could conceive of nothing more important than their own pleasures, and this was sweet relief to the taut string on the bow of an aristocrat. She was always seeking for that which was hidden, and to open every locked door just to discover what waited on the other side.

It was in the Cá Sấu Street game den that Trưng Nhị met Ngô Cầm, the tattooed one, a man from the mountains and a notorious tale-teller. He claimed that each of his tattoos was a Lạc Việt legend, and the more of his body that became exposed, the more the viewer would come to understand the culture and history of the Việts. He revealed that his chest held the likeness of a princess who divorced her husband and took half of their one hundred children to the mountains. Lower down, there was the turtle-claw crossbow of An Dương Vương, which rendered his armies invincible in war. Even lower still, there were references to deep myths that weren't known to any but those who had been honored and blessed to have seen them with their own eyes, or so he said.

In telling these stories, the tattooed man tried to get Trưng Nhị to pull down his trousers for him. The other men, seeing the crude seduction at work, tried clumsily to ride in his wake. "Pull my trousers down, too!" said one. "Yes, I have a tattoo you won't want to miss," said another.

Trưng Nhị, uncowed by their crudity, thought that the tattooed man possessed a rough charm, though his audacity demanded a swift rebuke. Trưng Nhị looked for a moment as though she would ignore their effrontery, but she stared them down as one might do with a feral dog.

"Leave her alone," said Mai the prostitute halfheartedly.

What happened next would be retold by those in the room for days afterward. Trưng Nhị stood up with her head held high, then struck Ngô Cầm in the chest with a solid fist that sent him curling to the floor in pain, kicked another man so that he collapsed on a table, then took a third by the arm and bent it behind his back, throwing him down to the floor.

"What did you do that for?" asked a fourth man.

"Words are fleeting, but actions are lasting. I want you to remember this lesson." Trưng Nhị wondered how these unruly men would fare in a real contest of discipline. They fought like children fight, with eyes closed and hands outstretched.

Ngô Cầm stood up and, walking gingerly, offered a drink to the beautiful young stranger. She took the drink and gulped it down, then asked him kindly where he kept his ointments, for there was blood on her knuckles.

CHAPTER 4

The Summons

It was during the height of summer that the lord was summoned by the new Hán governor, Tô Định. The servant of the royal messenger tolled the bell at the gate, and Kha the guardsman was wearing a mere wrap, seeking a reprieve from the oppressive heat, but his lack of clothing showed a failure to observe ceremony, inciting a disrespect that the messenger could scarcely conceal.

"Why does the lord's guardsman present himself without clothes?" the messenger asked, making no motion to pass over the threshold.

Seeing that the messenger and his servants had no intention of being welcomed inside Cung Điện Mê Linh, Kha took the opportunity to catch his breath and plant his hands on his knees, which had the unfortunate effect of exposing his behind to the open air. "You tolled the bell so insistently," Kha said, breathing heavily. "It would have been rude to make you wait." Kha wore his hair in a chignon, and his chin rested atop another chin that reached all the way around to the back of his neck. "His lordship expects for etiquette to be maintained," he said.

"Either clothe yourself in the appropriate garb, or fetch another guardsman." The emissary put his feet together and stood stiffly with his arms folded.

Kha sighed, his hands still planted on his knees. "You are in Lạc Việt," he said, "so whether you are the emissary or the governor himself, *you* must learn to respect *our* ways." He handed the emissary and his servants each a pair of sandals. "Wear these. At least your feet will be comfortable."

It was early in the day and the lord, seated on the mat when the emissary arrived, projected confidence and authority.

"Greetings on behalf of Governor Tô Định, overseer of all of Jiaozhi," said the emissary, emphasizing the Hán term "Jiaozhi" for Lạc Việt, the Việt territory.

"You are most welcome in Cung Điện Mê Linh," said the lord. "Please enjoy our grounds and gardens while you are here. Allow us to prepare a feast in your honor."

From his seated position, the emissary bowed his head slightly.

The lord sensed hesitation from the emissary. "Please, speak your mind," the lord said.

"You will think me rude if I speak of business right away, but my message is urgent."

"Oh?" the lord said. "I had assumed that you were speaking to all the Lạc lords."

"Just you." The emissary looked up.

The lord ran his hands through his beard, looking over at

Kha seated in the corner, and back at the emissary. "To what do I owe this distinction?"

"A summons to the palace."

"The governor wishes to see *me*?" said the lord as he tried to tabulate his earnings and calculate the taxes owed and paid. "Whatever for?"

The emissary nodded respectfully. "I am merely sent to prepare you for the journey."

"Does the governor ask that I should leave immediately?" said the lord.

"I am to be your escort," the emissary said.

How unlike a summons, thought the lord, *and how like an arrest!*

The lord dismissed Kha the guardsman. Then he turned to the emissary and spoke in a hoarse whisper. "I must give my people notice, or at least a reason why I am to leave Cung Điện Mê Linh so abruptly. Can't we devise some explanation for my sudden absence?"

"The governor wishes it," said the emissary. "That should suffice."

A peacock barked its two-tone call from the gardens.

"I will bring Trưng Trắc," the lord muttered to himself. "And we will say we are headed to Cổ Loa to find her a husband to marry."

After the lord had left the palace, taking Trưng Trắc with him, Trưng Nhị sang mournfully in the gardens while Xau followed her wherever she went, and took on the same somber mood as his master. Surely the lord brought Trưng Trắc to Cổ Loa because she was the elder sister; but this did little to soften Trưng Nhị's bitterness at being left behind. She and Phan Minh would never be trusted alone again, so Phan Minh had been exiled from the palace, leaving behind him an absence of names. Unknown birds alighted from the trees, and strange catfish puckered their mouths from the ponds.

It seemed unjust that Phan Minh could be banished without having committed any crime other than loving Trưng Nhị and following their own bodies' wills. Her pride told her that Phan Minh was no one, a mere gardener's son, but this was no salve for a wound that originated with a mother's decree; this reasoning simply muted her loss, leaving her numb to joy.

At the governor's residence, the lord and his elder daughter were separated, each prepared for the court in their own way: the lord arrayed with the regalia of his station, the lord's daughter perfumed and clad in layer after layer of silk. This tiresome ritual was a relief to the lord, who supposed that the governor's intentions upon his guests must therefore not be terminal. To Trưng Trắc, to be buried in silk seemed a gentle way to be ignored, shoved away, and ornamented. Although she knew of her father's night terrors, she always trusted in his strength; at that moment, as her form was drowned in fabric, she felt too heavy, and wondered if the kind of strength they needed to face the governor was even possible.

In the governor's court, the lord and his elder daughter were made to wait, crouching with their backs straight and eyes facing forward, to formally greet the governor. But an hour passed in silence, and the heat combined with the heavy clothing caused their bodies to sweat and itch. The lord's legs cramped, and his shoulders quaked from the effort of maintaining his posture.

Trưng Trắc felt oddly soothed during their wait, as she rarely found herself alone with Lord Trưng; her father was the type of man whom one needed to seek out, as Trưng Nhị would, to catch his attention. To Trưng Trắc, the lord always seemed preoccupied, if not in business then wrapped up in his own worries; she feared disturbing the delicate balance of his mind. His life was made up of consequential things and Trưng Trắc's own concerns appeared small by comparison. He was also the type of man who hid his vulnerability throughout the day, until night, at which time he could no longer hide his weakness. She wished somehow to entertain him, to impress him, but the only words that occurred to her to speak were, "Father, why am I here?"

It was at this moment that the Governor Tô Định, his bodyguard, and his advisor Li Hong, all dressed in the Hán red and gold, poured into the room. The faint smell of liquor tinged the air, and their smiles faded.

"I'd welcome you to our court and our city," said the governor, "but neither of you look pleased to be here. Have the accommodations not been to your liking?"

The lord placed one fist inside his other hand and bowed. "I am most grateful to be invited to the governor's court, and we have brought a ceremonial drum as a gift, which signifies the pride of our people, which we now share with the Hán."

The governor looked down at the gift he was presented, yet did not touch it. "A bronze drum," he said. "Is that not the same drum that the Việts would strike on the battlefield when at war with the Hán?"

"The governor knows his military history," said the lord. "The bronze drum is used for rites and ceremonies as well as for war. It is important to our people in times both of war and of peace."

"It is also a musical instrument," added Trưng Trắc. She thought of the drum's place in the history of her people, and she watched the scornful sneer on the governor's face. She wanted to demand that he respect the instrument, to respect *her father*. An object forged with such care, one that took on a thousand meanings depending on where it was struck and how light the touch was, should not be a gift to dismiss lightly. "Watch." She played a flam on the surface, the grace note resonating throughout the high-ceilinged court.

The governor frowned. "Forgive me, Lord Trưng," he said, without acknowledging Trưng Trắc. "But to the Hán, an impertinent daughter is like a curse upon one's family. If we might continue without her interruptions?"

The lord's impulse, which he wisely withheld, was to laugh at the suggestion of Trưng Trắc's disrespect. He wondered what the governor would think of his younger daughter's manners. "Of course," he replied. "My daughter is still young and unschooled in the ways of Hán society."

"Then it is your own failure to educate. For Việt society is Hán society now, and you must aspire to teach all in our region how to behave properly, starting with your own household."

The lord bowed again. "If it pleases the governor, may I ask for what purpose I have been summoned to Cổ Loa?"

"Sons," said the governor.

"I'm sorry?"

"All the other lords have borne sons to inherit their domains and serve as representatives of their cities to Cổ Loa. What am I supposed to do when you pass away? Host your daughters at the palace? Politics is not a tea ceremony."

It was as though Trưng Trắc were rendered invisible, and she looked down at her hands to remind herself of her own solidity. She inwardly rebelled against the governor's assumptions about her capabilities; in fact, the governor's manner struck her as skittish and undisciplined in comparison to her own. She opened her mouth to speak, but the lord anticipated this and immediately put his arm out in front of her to halt her speech. "My lawful wife, Lady Man Thiện, is at an age when giving me new heirs has become impossible. My daughter, impertinent though she may be, is trained to be the next Lord of Mê Linh."

"That won't be possible," said the governor. "Take a concubine if you must, but produce a male heir if you wish to keep the city under your family's domain and duties." The governor made as though to stand, and as he did so, his bodyguard and the advisor Li Hong stood with him.

Trưng Trắc felt her father's urgency and despair, and she was moved to soothe him, but to do so would further prove his weakness before the audience of the governor. She thought of what this proclamation might mean for her family, for her life. She had always been told, growing up, that she would govern Mê Linh one day as a lord in her own right.

"A husband!" gasped the lord, more loudly than he had intended.

"Pardon?" said the governor.

"If my daughter marries, will her husband be recognized as the Lord of Mê Linh?"

"*If* your daughter marries?" the governor said. "Do you mean that she might go forever unmarried, like an immoral woman? Is all of this—the bronze drum and the impertinent daughter—a demonstration of defiance? Do you mean to slight me and challenge my authority?"

"Never," said the lord, "would I presume to challenge the governor's authority. I vow that my daughter will be married within the year, and I beseech the governor to acknowledge my future son-in-law as the lawful heir to the Mê Linh region."

A cascade of conflicting emotion flooded Trưng Trắc at that moment: she thrilled at the opportunity to do her filial duty and be her father's salvation; yet this was tempered by the sword point of the governor's wrath, which corrupted this duty and made it a prison; and all of this churned up by the monsoon of being promised to a husband in marriage, a condition that her whole life up until that moment she had been told was like a Hán curse.

CHAPTER 5

The Lord's Nightmare

It was the lord's last night in Cổ Loa. He had avoided sleep entirely the first few days, certain that the Hán spies were watching him, and loath to reveal his night terrors to the Governor of Lạc Việt. But those nights of sleeplessness left him more vulnerable than ever. His already deep-set eyes looked sunken and gray, and his tired posture accentuated his thinness. By the time he left Cổ Loa, the lord appeared changed, colorless and aged, with less of the vital force that animates the living body.

When they arrived back at Cung Điện Mê Linh, it was late. The lord's attendants hoisted his platform and led him, already sleeping, into his chambers. Trưng Trắc saw a lamplight flickering in Trưng Nhị's room, and announced herself at the entrance. "Come in," Trưng Nhị replied flatly. "Welcome home."

Trưng Trắc could sense a distance between them greater than the length of a sparring staff. She supposed that her sister must have resented that Trưng Trắc had been the one chosen to accompany the lord on his journey to Cổ Loa. Trưng Trắc felt most comfortable in the role of the favored daughter, but anticipating her sister's anger, she lingered at the door for a moment before flowing into the room, crouching next to the dog, and petting him distractedly.

"Did you come to boast of your travels?" Trưng Nhị said.

The elder sister showed no sign that the younger's question cut at her. "I missed our morning spars," Trưng Trắc answered simply and sincerely.

"I rather enjoyed the reprieve, to be honest," said Trưng Nhị. She knew that the gamblers and prostitutes she kept company with in the game dens would never join her in the palace, yet they held a place in her life that, she imagined, would one day be filled by nobler rascals. To give herself over to their carefree ways was her first step down the path of leisure that she had always envisioned. Her sister simply followed their parents' commands and felt no yearnings other than to meet their approval—what an uninteresting life it must be, thought Trưng Nhị. The frustration of always losing at sparring was another thing her sister would never know. Of course Trưng Trắc missed the spars in which she was the constant victor. Now she expected that Trưng Nhị would long for the sting of losing? Her sister, always the favored one, must be clueless. "What did you and father see at the citadel?"

"I saw his age," said Trưng Trắc, "maybe for the first time."

"The lord is more formidable than you or I or the ancestral lords from whose loins he came."

There followed a silence that uttered only truths. That

Trưng Trắc and Trưng Nhị may look out upon the same vista, yet never perceive the same reality.

"Can we sing together?" said Trưng Trắc, seating herself by her sister's furs, where the impression and warmth of a recent body still lingered. She hoped that, over time, her bond with Trưng Nhị would transcend the morning combat and return to its childhood roots, when they played unselfconsciously and didn't define themselves against the other. "As we used to?" In their youth, one game had been to hum the first three notes of a song, then pass the melody to the other, who would have to guess the tune based on the scant evidence of those three untethered notes that came before. Once the other sister picked up the melody she assumed to be correct, the one who started the game would resume the original song, until they sang in rounds, two clashing melodies that somehow found the same key.

Trưng Nhị hummed a familiar melody from the reservoir of songs from which they had drawn all their lives. Trưng Trắc took the low harmony, and this once, the joining of their voices was a quilt that gave her shelter and comfort, as though order had been restored. To Trưng Nhị, it represented a momentary reprieve from the daily indignity she suffered at her sister's hands.

They sang about a young woman named Vũ Thơm, who fell in love with a soldier and became pregnant with his child. It was the first time, since experiencing love herself, that Trưng Nhị had sung this song. It carried a new resonance now that made her swell with unwanted tenderness.

In the song, the soldier went off to war and every day the child would ask about his father, and Vũ Thơm would point at her shadow and say, "There is your father." When he returned, the boy claimed that the soldier wasn't his real father, and the soldier became so jealous that he chased the woman away, who went into the mountains and ate *lá ngón*, the heartbreak grass, which closed her throat and ended her life, to prove her faithfulness. The next day, the boy pointed at the father's shadow and said, "My father has returned!" The soldier then built a temple in her honor, and grieved for his callous misunderstanding.

Trưng Nhị wondered why suffering was rendered even more tragic when it was the result of a great misunderstanding. Such songs sharpened the mind and made one alert to the role that whim played in deciding our fates. But after the song was over, Trưng Nhị thought simply of the stupidity of a woman who would let a man chase her out of her own home, then flee to the mountains and eat heartbreak grass.

The next day, Lady Man Thiện and Lord Trưng held hands in the anteroom. Lady Man Thiện was outraged by the demands of the governor, but maintained her composure throughout the briefing. They summoned the astrologer, Bác Huy Vũ.

"According to the position of the stars, there will soon be a burgeoning of the mind—a fertility of knowledge and imagination," said Bác Huy Vũ.

"So we hire a scholar to introduce our daughters to the life of the mind?" said Lord Trưng.

"This burgeoning will take place with or without formal instruction, but if you mean to guide Trưng Trắc and Trưng Nhị towards leadership and away from idleness, then they would do well to study under a master," said Bác Huy Vũ.

"Then I will search all of Lạc Việt for a master-scholar worthy of my daughters."

Trưng Nhị and Ngô Cầm strolled the village that night, where they could roam anonymously petting each other under cover of darkness. Trưng Nhị challenged Ngô Cầm to a competition of brazenness. To tug on an old man's beard and sprint away from him, leaving him cursing and growling in her wake, left Trưng Nhị craving more childish mischief. To crouch on a roof's edge and spit on a passerby made her feel as though war—and the martial discipline it demanded—was the farthest thing from the life of the village. In this realm, the lady could shed her propriety and become anonymous and free.

They vied in the scale of their public improprieties, until, after several escalations, Ngô Cầm victoriously strode down the street wearing nothing but the tattoos on his skin. Merchants and fishermen and farmers shook their heads and proceeded on their way, and Ngô Cầm nodded or saluted them as they passed.

Trưng Nhị, never to be outdone, prepared herself to do the same, but Ngô Cầm surprised her. "It's too much. The villagers expect a scoundrel like me to dwell in filth, but a noblewoman..." All men, even the scoundrels, thought Trưng Nhị, talked like a dull aristocrat.

"So do you win simply because you are a peasant from the mountains?" said Trưng Nhị. It was deep in her nature to compete and she was still fixated on the victory.

"No. You win, because my sense of propriety won't allow you to bring yourself shame."

Trưng Nhị's cheeks reddened. "Why is *my* shame *your* responsibility?" she said.

They walked in silence, a small void between them. She was reminded of Phan Minh's striving to "earn" her love. Trưng Nhị recalled riding in the fields overlooking the rice paddies with him, the cracked amethyst he offered to her—his gentle speech, his gentle touch. It felt like many years since that moment, though it was two short seasons past. The memory startled her with its clarity and she found her eyes clouded with tears that she would not let flow. Trưng Nhị and Ngô Cầm passed through the square, nearly empty at this hour. The lights in the windows cast an array of shadows into the street.

"When do you think we might introduce a child into this world?" said Ngô Cầm.

Trưng Nhị laughed, but saw that he was serious.

"Are all men this way?" said Trưng Nhị. "Are you determined to make me your concubine?"

"A concubine?" said Ngô Cầm. "But how can you say that? These three weeks have been a gift. Haven't you been enjoying this?"

"Then let us continue to enjoy this," said Trưng Nhị. "Without the distraction of making plans. Another drink?"

She took out her wineskin and took a dram. Ngô Cầm consented to a sip.

Later, in the oceanic depth of night, the drunken lovers stumbled to the edge of Mê Linh, where Trưng Nhị's mare was tied. The horse stamped her feet restlessly, gnashed her teeth, and yanked the rope that held her fast against the post. Trưng Nhị tried to calm her, but she circled around the post to the opposite side. "C'mon, girl," Trưng Nhị said, but she stood rooted in this defensive stance. In the wan moonlight, they could barely make out the white spot on the mare's forehead, and the fearful eyes that stared out from beneath them. But into the darkness, the roar of a tiger resounded as clear as a beam of unwelcome light upon the eyes of a sleeper.

Ngô Cầm took cover behind the mare, at the risk of being kicked by the troubled beast. But Trưng Nhị's head swam with so much liquor that she made it only two steps before she collapsed on the dirt road that led to Cung Điện Mê Linh, reaching helplessly around her for a stick or other weapon, her hand finding only a root so firmly buried that it was like a shackle, keeping her fixed in that vulnerable spot.

Răng the Tiger—white fur gone gray and brown like a wolf's, the majestic yellow eyes peering out from his orchideous face—prowled in a zigzag pattern as though to show he understood how helplessly his prey clung to the root as though the very earth could save her. Baring his teeth, Răng stepped down from his higher perch and, as he approached, seemed to achieve an impossible height. The mare squealed and strained against the rope; Ngô Cầm's body heaved with fear. Trưng

Nhị wanted to clench her eyes shut, but resolved instead to stare her killer down until the moment he sank his teeth—the shape and size of knives—into her. But instead their eyes met and fixed upon each other, Răng and Trưng Nhị, until her whole field of vision was filled by the fan of his willowy mane. She smelled death on his rough tongue, blackened gums, and teeth stained with the blood of her folk. Then Răng lowered his noble nose onto Trưng Nhị's torso and sniffed, down where Trưng Nhị bled, not from injury, but from womanhood. Then, suddenly indifferent to her helpless heap of sodden flesh, Răng turned his head aside, and made his slow way up a low cliff into the jungle.

It was nearly morning, and although all the other drunkards in the game den were asleep, Trưng Nhị and Ngô Cầm were wide awake and full of the kind of energy that comes from an encounter with one's mortality. Trưng Nhị sat on the floor and Ngô Cầm crouched nearby, a bowl of alcohol and a bottle of ink at his side. He wielded a needle, and was in the process of etching the likeness of a tiger on Trưng Nhị's upper arm. Trưng Nhị stared ahead and replayed the encounter in her mind, Răng's enveloping size, his breath like a cloud of death, the tiger eyes tracking his prey's motion.

Ngô Cầm's tiger, drawn in black ink on Trưng Nhị's upper arm, was unlike the tiger that had just stalked them. The real Răng had been terribly bright, despite the gray of his fur and the dirt hanging from his underbelly; and the only lines that

Trưng Nhị remembered were the blades of his fangs, and the only circles that lingered were his fierce, indifferent eyes.

The lord and lady paid a visit to the courtyard where Trưng Nhị and Trưng Trắc were sparring again, after weeks of reprieve.

"To what do we owe your visit this morning?" said Trưng Trắc.

Lord Trưng and Lady Man Thiện looked at each other, then beheld their daughters.

"Nhị-ơi," said Lord Trưng. "We hear that you have been making trouble in Mê Linh—fighting in public, groping around with strange men, gambling, acting indecent."

When accused, Trưng Nhị's usual habit was to smile in the face of those who sought to shame her. But under her father's gaze, she lost the spirit to rebel. "Not gambling," she said.

"What?" said the lord.

"I haven't been gambling," said Trưng Nhị. Trưng Trắc flinched as though struck. She knew her sister to be immodest, but never thought of her as the subject of a scandal.

"So the rest of it is *true*?" The lord's voice took on a tremor that mixed pain and anger, a tone that he used only with his daughters. "I thought my spies were mistaken. Do you mean to bring shame on all of us? To bring down the Trưng clan?"

Trưng Nhị lifted up her sleeve to show the tiger tattoo. "I was attacked by Răng the Tiger. I only escaped because I was not full with child. If you wish to confine me to the palace, then I will heed it. But something must be done about that beast."

"You are using your silver tongue to distract us," said Lady Man Thiện. "The issue we are discussing right now is your ill-used freedom."

Trưng Nhị took a harsher tone with her mother than she dared to with the lord. "Which is it that you want? That I should settle down in a domestic peace with a man I care for? Or that I should reject a Confucian marriage and become a free woman?"

"There are *better* men," said Lady Man Thiện, "than these peasants and scoundrels."

"It's our fault," said Lord Trưng, "for not having suitors from other regions."

"Your actions have convinced us that we have been too permissive. We must give you more direction for you to learn the burdens and privileges of your station," said Lady Man Thiện.

"Am I to become a nun?" said Trưng Nhị. She looked from mother to father to mother again, sensing the conflict within them, wishing one of them would give voice to the complicated truth of living under the yoke of the Hán, wishing they would stop pretending that it was in their power to make decisions for their own future. That was what this was really about: if Trưng Nhị stepped too far out of line, the Hán would rebuke her. That despite their titles, the four of them were ultimately powerless.

"No," said Lady Man Thiện. "But you must only leave Cung Điện Mê Linh under the supervision of a guardsman. This is for your protection."

Lady Man Thiện and Lord Trưng left the courtyard, leaving a complicated knot of emotion behind in the room. The sisters felt their parents' conflict, and took on their help-lessness. Their sense of defeat was more profound for being borrowed. How could they alleviate a sorrow that originated outside of them, in the hearts of their mother and father? It was a door that could not be opened; a rock that could not be moved. Trưng Trắc reached out and held Trưng Nhị's shoul-ders, her head bowed, soothing her sister while her mind con-jured the memory of Lord Trưng promising that she would be married in a year. Trưng Nhị's expression showed no pity or remorse. And that morning, as though to prove she needed no protection, Trưng Nhị bested Trưng Trắc for the first time in their sparring match, and afterward applied the balm of camphor to her sister's aching back as Trưng Trắc had always done for her.

CHAPTER 6

The Tutor

The tutor arrived during sunset, to little fanfare. The golden light upon his white robes gave him a holy, healthful glow. Kha the guardsman received him at the gate, and remarked how fortuitous was the hour of his arrival.

"Are you an astrologer?" asked the tutor, unaccustomed to such a garrulous guardsman.

Kha handed the tutor a pair of sandals. "I know nothing about the positions of the stars," he said. "But I can track the sun, and it was lucky you arrived before dark. There's a tiger in these woods who has been known to feed on unsuspecting travelers."

"Thanks for the warning," said the tutor absently. He surmised that this guardsman had a habit of speaking his mind, even to the disturbance of the lord's guests. "The tiger must keep his teeth sharp somehow." This last utterance was a proverb, spoken reflexively, and Kha rolled his eyes when he heard it.

The guardsman and the tutor heard the plaintive strains of

song through the palace halls, on the way to the guest chambers, as the last rays of sunlight blinked out over the garden wall.

"What is that haunting, lovely music?" the tutor asked.

"That," said Kha, "is your new pupil."

"But I have two students," said the tutor.

"Only one will be susceptible to education. The other you will find immune to learning."

"That may be so," said the tutor. "But the petal can scarcely shed before it blossoms."

Kha stopped, and the tutor stopped next to him. They looked at each other expectantly.

"What is it?" said the tutor.

"Oh," said Kha. "I was waiting for you to spout another aphorism."

"Ah, and I was waiting for you to show me to my chambers," said the tutor.

"Here we are," said Kha, gesturing to the door beside him. "His lordship will give audience in the morning. He is occupied with other business at night."

The click of staffs resounded in the courtyard that morning. This was a mere warm-up exercise, and had none of the ferocity of a sparring match.

"I saw our tutor last night," said Trưng Nhị.

"I hope you left him alone," said Trưng Trắc.

"I kept my distance, but I couldn't help but hear his conversation from the garden. He speaks in aphorisms, and wants to tame me," said Trưng Nhị.

"You were spying on him?" said Trưng Trắc. Inexplicably, she worried that her sister would get the chance to meet the tutor before she herself did. "You shouldn't be so nosy. Our tutor will be introduced to us formally, after his meeting with Father."

"He's handsome, in a severe way. Maybe I will *let him* tame me," Trưng Nhị teased.

Trưng Trắc laughed stiffly. "Our tutor is a master-scholar, and a man of learning. I don't think he will make for your usual prey."

"Is that a challenge?" Trưng Nhị said with a sly smile.

Trưng Trắc broke formation, and lowered the staff. Despite the lightness of their talk, she balked at Trưng Nhị's casual attitude toward everything those days, especially the introduction of an honored guest. "Must everything be a game to you?"

"Only men," said Trưng Nhị with her characteristic smile, both coy and mischievous. "If we aren't sport for each other, then what are we?"

"Equals?" said Trưng Trắc.

"Nonsense. I've never met a man who is my equal." And Trưng Nhị advanced on Trưng Trắc with the confidence of one who knows she is the victor before the battle has even begun.

The scholar, Thi Sách, sat in the reception room, and rose when his host entered. The two men exchanged a friendly bow and sat across from each other, maintaining steady eye contact. Each man's assessment of the other was filtered through his conception of the ideal, and therefore sank into an inevitable sense of disappointment. Lord Trưng, with his beard that went on and on, and his thin frame, appeared less august than the Lạc lords of Thi Sách's imagination. Meanwhile Thi Sách, the famous scholar, had a youthful smile and bespoke an innocence at odds with his purpose at Cung Điện Mê Linh. Thi Sách wished that his host's presence demonstrated more of the storied strength of one of the descendants of the Dragon Lord, and Lord Trưng wished that his guest's face showed the maturity and austerity of what he imagined a wise man to be.

"Welcome to Cung Điện Mê Linh, our humble home overlooking the Red River," said Lord Trưng. "I trust your accommodations are satisfactory?"

Thi Sách bowed. "Living in the palace of a Lạc lord is more than this lowly scholar ever imagined or deserves."

"As the son of my former physician Thi Vũ, you deserve high esteem," said Lord Trưng. "He was a learned man as well, and a loyal friend."

"He taught me much about medicine, but my real facility was with literature," said Thi Sách.

Lord Trưng looked pained by this news. Were his daughters to study literature? "Walk with me through Cung Điện Mê Linh, and I will show you the glories of the palace, such as they are."

Thi Sách stood and followed Lord Trưng into the Great Hall, to the rock garden, to the horticultural garden, and the patios and terraces that overlooked them. The entire structure seemed built for the purpose of bringing the outdoors indoors, and the indoors out. There was a harmonious relationship between the clay and stone that shaped the contours of the buildings, and the shoots and vines that climbed up the buildings and shot up between the cracks. If nature had not been so obviously invited in, the trees interwoven with the stone would have resembled a ruin, but with the canopy of leaves over the bronze latticework, it suggested instead a place where men and women coexisted with the vegetal.

"So what is your plan for my daughters' education?" asked Lord Trưng.

"I'm unsure what you mean," said Thi Sách. "Isn't education an end in itself, a divine state of being, one that is sought after by paupers and emperors alike?"

"Do you intend to teach them poetry? If so, you will learn that my first daughter is already instructed in verse. Do you intend to teach them the art of persuasion? If so, my second daughter will not need your persuading." Lord Trưng guided Thi Sách to the inner, lamplit halls of the palace, past the bedchambers and past Thi Sách's own guest room.

"The life of the mind is a vast and complex terrain," said Thi Sách. "I cannot chart its geography because the landscape is ever-changing."

The two men reached the courtyard, where the sour-sweet smell of a recent sparring match combined with the odiferous lichen and moss that covered the great elephant statue. "Bác Huy Vũ the astrologer warned us of the girls' restless minds. Yet it is my greatest wish that you might channel their energies into *military* training."

"From what I have observed in your library, it appears as though your daughters have had a good deal of military training." Thi Sách looked directly at his new employer. "But I will honor your wishes, as long as you allow that the military arts are subtle, and leadership is more than knowing the Lạc lords and their history of war with the Hán. A strong leader must understand the human soul."

Which is why, thought Lord Trưng, *I wish that you were more experienced in the world.* For all his own shortcomings, Lord Trưng at least had known the tribulations of war. What, after all, did this mere boy have to teach his daughters?

Trưng Trắc and Trưng Nhị met their tutor, Thi Sách, on the terrace overlooking the stone garden. A bad idea, Trưng Trắc thought, for Trưng Nhị would be distracted by the lure of the natural world. Yet Thi Sách had a presence that drew one's attention like a flame. He had a wide face, high cheekbones, and eyes that looked both tired and alert in the way that a mind, close to sleep, can be rife with thought. When he raised his serious eyes and parted his lips, the listener leaned in. And when he spoke, the tone was gentle, loud without boast, full of thoughtful pauses and earnest interrogatives.

"Together we will explore not only that which is known, but that which is unknown, because it is the unknown that fires the imagination," said Thi Sách.

"Do you mean that we will no longer have to study history?" said Trưng Nhị with undisguised pleasure.

"No," said Thi Sách. "You will still be responsible for

knowing the history of the Lạc Việts and the Hán. Yet there is much about that history that is unknown. And we will explore it together."

"By *unknown*, you mean that *you* do not know it," said Trưng Nhị, toying with him as a cat with a turtle tucked in its shell. "Did you ever think maybe it *is* known, and that you are just a lazy scholar?"

"It's true, there are many things I do not know," said Thi Sách.

"You are not much older than we," said Trưng Nhị.

"I am as close in age to your mother as I am to you," said Thi Sách. "But if you expect wisdom to come with age, without the rigor of study, then you will find yourself one day merely old and boastful. If you seek true knowledge, then you must first accept your own unknowing."

"*To know that you know nothing, that is the meaning of true knowledge*," said Trưng Nhị, walking a slow circle around her tutor like a tiger stalking its victim. "Do you get all your wisdom from Confucius? Are you a Confucian?"

"In fact," said Thi Sách. "This, right now, is an opportunity to learn the appropriate stance of humility and subtlety that is conducive to learning. We know, of course, why you are angry towards the Hán. But why should a scholar like Confucius make you angry? Did his teachings not save Hán government from overwhelming corruption and perpetual internal struggle?"

"His teachings," said Trưng Nhị, "deny women their natural right to live as they please. It forces them to obey their fathers and brothers and husbands."

"Not so," said Thi Sách. "Hán society had already con-
signed women to such a status, and Confucius merely gave
name and structure to what already existed in society. What
he *added* to the social sphere, however, is immeasurably valuable. Confucianism is about virtue in leadership, about being
a responsible steward of power. As the daughter of a lord, you
would do well to study him."

"Ha!" said Trưng Nhị.

"May I speak?" said Trưng Trắc, who had been standing shyly against the wall, while her sister and her tutor
paced and gestured. She found the dance of their argument
exhausting.

"Of course," said Thi Sách. "You always have permission
to speak in your own home."

"It seems to me," said Trưng Trắc, "that your positions are
reconcilable. It is possible for a person to contribute greatly to
the progress of society and still fall victim to the limitations of
the society in which he lives. Just because Confucius suffered
from blindness toward the role of women, it does not mean he
is incapable of teaching us about virtue in leadership. And just
because he is a great teacher, that does not mean he is without
his failings."

Trưng Trắc's face showed that she was untouched by the
heat of the argument, and would have gladly proceeded in
this manner for the rest of the afternoon. Thi Sách possessed
the same weary but alert expression that gave no hint of how
much energy he kept in reserve.

"Your impulse to make peace is admirable," said Thi Sách,
"but argument may lead to growth, and learning is about

allowing yourself to be wrong. What are your thoughts on Confucius?"

Trưng Trắc looked straight ahead and poked her chin forward. She could not hide her pleasure at being asked a question for which she had a ready answer: "Confucius introduced the virtues of *jen*, *li*, and *yi*—benevolence, propriety, and righteousness—that each individual must aspire to, because these give dignity to human life. Benevolence is the greatest virtue, because it is the acknowledgment that each human has a self that is as valuable to them as yours is to you. It can be achieved through the rule *Do unto others as you would have them do unto you*."

Thi Sách was silent for a long moment, which Trưng Trắc chose to interpret as having been impressed with her learning. Then he spoke. "I did not ask you, 'What does Confucius teach?'" he said. "I asked you, 'What are *your* thoughts on Confucius?'"

Trưng Trắc looked down, embarrassed. She had only recently been challenged physically, by her sister, and she was unprepared to be challenged intellectually now, and in the realm of philosophy, which she had always thought of as *her sphere*. Wasn't it enough to know the answers? "I..." she began, but, her face flushed, she retreated into the hallway with a bow and a muttered apology.

Trưng Trắc searched Cung Điện Mê Linh for her sister, checking the courtyard, where the statue of the great elephant overlooked the slow growth of tropical plant life. Then she inspected the bedchamber, where Xấu lay curled up on the furs, but Trưng Nhị was nowhere to be found. Strangely, she envied the dog's connection to her sister. Trưng Trắc herself had never felt truly at peace with Trưng Nhị's presence, or not since they were young children, and even then her sister always seemed to grasp at more than was her share: whether it was sweet buns from the kitchen, or affection from their father.

The last place she thought to look was in the library, where she doubted Trưng Nhị would even set foot, but she vainly hoped that her sister had been persuaded by the tutor. Instead, in her rush, Trưng Trắc nearly crashed into the tutor himself, who was standing near the entranceway, a scroll lifted to catch the sunlight through the open door.

"Oh, I'm so sorry," said Trưng Trắc, bowing and backing away from the entrance. Then she fully took in the curious scene in front of her. "What are you doing standing in the dark?"

"I was reading Mencius," said Thi Sách. "I didn't want to remove the scroll from the library."

"Why not light a lamp?" Trưng Trắc pointed out the oil lamps, one on the desk and one mounted on the wall.

"I wasn't going to be long," said Thi Sách, "and I don't work well by firelight."

Trưng Trắc covered her mouth to disguise her laughter, but her eyes betrayed her amusement. "What scholar doesn't like firelight?"

Thi Sách smiled indulgently, and Trưng Trắc thought that the expression suited him. When his smile faded away, Trưng Trắc was moved by the impulse to make him smile again.

"I once worked for a scriptorium in Chu Diên," said Thi Sách. "And I worked by lamplight. All of the scribes practiced their careful calligraphy on scrolls much like the ones that fill this library. We worked throughout the night, and we knew that the slightest error would affect our livelihood. My training in calligraphy was such that I would never make a single error in the stroke or the line. Yet physical and mental exhaustion performed their weary work upon me, and in a moment—just a moment—of waking sleep, I dipped my brush not in the ink bowl, but in the lamp oil, and as I drew it out, the brush caught flame."

Trưng Trắc could tell the story was a confession of great shame for the teller, yet the image that arose in her head of the scholar's surprise at his flaming brush stirred her to laughter.

To her relief, Thi Sách smiled again. "My dreaming mind was so completely under its spell that I brought the fiery brush down upon the scroll, and the whole text was consumed in flame." He was laughing now as he recounted this story. "We were far from the well or the river, so I had no means of quenching the fire other than to use the spout I was born with."

Immediately sensing that, in his amusement, he had gone too far and become too familiar with his charge, Thi Sách apologized and excused himself. "Thank you," was all Trưng Trắc could think to say to his hastily retreating form. But all she knew was that she wished for their conversation to continue, were it about his history as a scribe, or about philosophy, or about nothing at all in particular. His presence both calmed her and roused her. She could not explain it, but she yearned to try. It presented such a contrast with the lord's alternating sternness and fearfulness, Lady Man Thiện's aloof watchfulness, or the brash intensity of Trưng Nhị. It was like a canopy on a hot day—a reprieve from the incendiary world.

Kha followed a comfortable pace behind Trưng Nhị as she navigated the woods. "This is a shortcut," she told Kha. The thickness of this jungle meant climbing over tangled brush and ducking under low branches. Despite his own thickness, Kha soldiered through this obstacle course and always stayed within shouting range of his charge. Trưng Nhị looked back, saw that Kha was still behind her, and sighed. Kha sighed, too, at the same pitch.

"Your duty is to protect me, not to mock me," said Trưng Nhị.

"I am capable of both. I have always been known to go above and beyond the call of duty," said Kha, with a bow so exaggerated that a clumsier man of similar size would have tumbled over.

"You are lucky that your antics amuse me," said Trưng Nhị, hopping with ease over a nest of brambles. "Otherwise I would tell Mother that you tried to kiss me and you would be banished."

Kha lifted his leather-bound feet and stomped down on the brambles, trying to pack them low enough to step over, leaving his ankles covered in small red lines. "Ah yes," said Kha, "the corruption of the innocent. I'm sure she would believe your story. I'm quite lascivious, you know."

"How *do* you manage to live without a woman in your life?" said Trưng Nhị, teasing the burly guardsman who used to tease her as a child. She now understood him to be a harmless, avuncular chaperone. "I haven't even seen you so much as visit a brothel. Are you a monk?"

Kha stopped, and put his hand against a tree trunk to balance himself and take a breath. "I have achieved a state of enlightenment that has no name, beyond nirvana, beyond moksha."

"So you are completely without desire?" said Trưng Nhị.

"No," said Kha. "Being without desire would be dull, like being asleep. I have achieved instead a state of being that is blissful in a perpetual state of wanting. I am happy with my own unfulfilled yearnings. These pangs tell me I'm still alive."

"I understand," said Trưng Nhị as though she were privy to a secret.

"How can you understand?" said Kha. "I just told you that it is a state of being far greater than anything another human being has achieved throughout many lifetimes of discipline."

"I understand that you must touch yourself," said Trưng Nhị, "and think about ladies who would never touch you in real life."

"Self-love," said Kha, "is the summit of enlightenment."

"If only everyone could be content with so little. Ambition is the food of the wicked."

"So what do you think of your new teacher?" said Kha.

"He is interesting," said Trưng Nhị, changing tone and taking the question earnestly. "He looks severe, but he, in fact, lacks the severity that I always imagined of a master-scholar."

"Would you like to know what I think?" said Kha.

"No," said Trưng Nhị. "I wouldn't."

"Thi Sách is repeating things he has read and it makes him sound smart, but in fact, that's all he knows. I don't believe he's ever been tested," said Kha. "He lacks the heart of a true education."

"Ha," she said. "I see that you are jealous of the esteem in which my mother holds him."

Kha waved his hand in front of his face as though fanning away an unpleasant odor.

They arrived now at a tiny shed on the outskirts of Mê Linh—a shed where Phan Minh, the gardener's son, lived out his exile from Cung Điện Mê Linh.

CHAPTER 7

The Shed

The sky grew dark, and the fading sunlight was obscured by the swarming insects in the air. Phan Minh lit a fire, and Trưng Nhị and Kha joined him around it, seated on the bare earth. The only sounds that rose over the flame's crackle came from the crows heralding the nightfall.

Trưng Nhị closed her eyes and bit her lip. She came to Phan Minh expecting the rekindling of their joy. Instead the gardener's son seemed changed, disturbed. He wanted to talk to Kha about Cung Điện Mê Linh. He asked after the cats, the birds, the fish, the turtles, as though in his absence these animals might suddenly disappear. He asked after the kitchen staff, the laborers, the other guardsmen. He asked about his father, who refused to speak to him. Trưng Nhị would have shut the door on her guilt, and she resented Phan Minh's clinging to so many irrelevancies of the past.

"I didn't know that Duy the beggar would be killed," he said. "I thought he would be flogged, and I would have years to repay him with rice and wine. I did not know he would be killed."

"It was I who killed Duy," said Kha. "It was that Hán official who ordered it. Not you."

"But it was our dog. Trưng Nhị's and mine. *Our* wicked lies that he suffered for. We are cursed," said Phan Minh. The fire caught a log that Kha had placed atop it, and burned green where the bark was ringed with fungus. "It is a moral universe." The fire fizzled as though in answer.

"What is moral?" said Trưng Nhị. She lifted her chin in the air defiantly. It was easy for commoners to talk about morality. A commoner—if only she could consign Phan Minh to this. Yet his torment would become her torment, his mental anguish like a pain in her liver. "If we give our kingdom to the peasants, are we then moral? If we burn Cung Điện Mê Linh to the ground, then we would all be equals." Trưng Nhị folded her arms and stuck out her chin. "But there would be no one left to govern but the Hán."

Knowing that her sister had been told to remain in Cung Điện Mê Linh, and was disobeying the lord's command, Trưng Trắc had followed her in the night to the shed—a rare departure from the palace. She listened closely to the three voices, watching from behind a felled tree, and wrapped her robe more tightly around her shoulders, not for warmth, but for momentary comfort from the troubled thoughts within her. Strangely, Trưng Trắc found that she envied how their lives were interconnected. Though it was shame and guilt that brought them together, Duy's death had forged in them an incorruptible bond—they could be exiled or imprisoned or separated forever, yet they would still be tinged with the same dye. Trưng Trắc herself felt no sense of identity, no such sense of belonging, not even to her family, and it was only at the altar of her ancestors that she felt that connection, and that was to the dead.

"But Phan Minh," Trưng Trắc overheard Kha saying, "if Duy's ghost is restless for justice, as you say, then how do we pacify his spirit?"

"We must make him offerings," said Phan Minh, "of salt and fish."

"I've never met a restless ghost," said Trưng Nhị, "but if it was me, I would want vengeance instead of fish."

"I'll take fish," said Kha. "Besides, on whom would you take vengeance? Upon his executioner?"

"Against the man who *ordered* his execution," said Trưng Nhị, pointing in the direction of the officers' barracks. Now that she knew the suffering to which Phan Minh was privy, she felt that the only course of action was to exorcise that guilt through vengeance. "Against the official who forced you. He must be dealt with. No one wants a Hán official deciding whether a Việt lives or dies, beggar or no beggar."

It occurred to Trưng Trắc that she was overhearing a dangerous scheme that, if followed through, could spell the downfall of Cung Điện Mê Linh. For a moment she was tempted to reveal herself and scold her sister for her impertinence, but then . . . to learn that these three were responsible for the killing of Duy and were now discussing the killing of another man to avenge the first—a Hán official! To speak so plainly and bluntly about murder and insurrection! What was happening to Trưng Nhị, that she could set out for a shed in the woods to plot with fellow conspirators to take a man's life?

"Absolutely not," said Kha to Trưng Nhị, raising a chubby finger. "You are not to even think of vengeance against the Hán official. It would mean the end of Cung Điện Mê Linh."

Though she held her tongue, Trưng Nhị's stolid eyes concealed a fire within that Trưng Trắc alone could see. She prayed to the Guardian Spirit that the fire would never catch.

Thi Sách undertook an education in military strategy by default, for going in to teach his lessons each day was like going to war. Trưng Nhị was always prepared with a new deflection tactic or argument as to why the topic of the day was unworthy of study, and he needed the armor of facts and authorities to steer his reluctant student. He spent so much time persuading Trưng Nhị of the benefits of learning that there was little time for learning itself. He noted, regrettably, the loss to Trưng Trắc's education when, after each day of verbal sparring, she would request more work.

It was only a month until Thi Sách sought advice from the guardsman Kha, who had been the first to warn him about the challenge of teaching the unteachable Trưng Nhị. He found Kha scratching himself by the north gate and Thi Sách almost reconsidered, but after hesitating under the archway to the outdoors, Kha spotted him. Thi Sach sheepishly approached him with his request.

"You must be strict, like Lady Man Thiện, and assert your status as master-scholar," said Kha. "When she misbehaves, order her to write 'I will practice obedience' in perfect calligraphy a thousand times. She understands boundaries."

"But you misunderstand," said Thi Sách. "I mean to inspire them to learn. Education has nothing to do with rote and repetitive tasks. You cannot punish a student into wisdom."

"Then, by all means, keep doing what you are doing," said Kha. "It's no matter to me if you are sent away from Cung Điện Mê Linh for failing to fulfill your duties. That way, Trưng Nhị wins."

"But education is not a game with winners and losers," Thi Sách meant to say with great conviction and authority, but it came out instead as a whine. His problem with the younger sister, he was coming to understand, was the frustration of dealing for the first time, not with ought-to-be, but what-is.

"It is the way Trưng Nhị is playing it," said Kha. "But if you can harness her competitive instincts, then you might lead her into this new understanding of yours."

Thi Sách bowed slightly in Kha's direction. "Thank you for your counsel," he said. "The bird may learn to fly by watching the leaves fall."

"Spare me the aphorisms," said Kha, scratching an itch on his belly with both hands.

"I know that you aren't my most ardent admirer. So I appreciate your advice."

"I'm getting used to hearing you talk," said Kha. "But in small doses. So—"

"I see!" said Thi Sách, excusing himself and walking the gardens, pondering the quandary of how to harness Trưng Nhị's competitive nature to benefit her education.

Trưng Trắc and Trưng Nhị sat across from Thi Sách on the terrace. The sun was at its zenith, and the fountain below shone pale. Even the rocks seemed to shimmer with reflected light.

"From now on," said Thi Sách, "each of you will earn points for accomplishing learning goals, and the more advanced the goal, the greater the number of points rewarded. This system starts today, so—"

"What do we win?" said Trưng Nhị. Her attention, for once, was focused on the content of her tutor's speech, rather than her next skillful evasion.

"Excuse me?" said Thi Sách.

"If we are earning points for learning, then what do we win at the end?" Trưng Nhị said. "Surely there is nothing you have that I want."

"You *win* knowledge and perspective," said Thi Sách. "These are the highest rewards that one can ask—"

"You can keep your reward," said Trưng Nhị, not bothering to mask her disappointment that this game turned out to be a ploy. "I have as much perspective as I care to possess."

Thi Sách tried to frown, and the resulting scowl always

looked theatrical, as though performed for the benefit of his students. "Suit yourself," he said. "But there are titles that go along with meeting these goals and acquiring these points. Right now you are *không ai*, a nobody. But once you acquire one hundred points, you will be an apprentice scholar."

A title was something that Trưng Nhị could understand. She turned again to regard the tutor. "And how do we acquire these points?" said Trưng Nhị.

"By meeting learning goals," said Thi Sách. "For example, the first one of you to explain the role of religion in military life according to the ancient philosophers will gain twenty points."

"I can tell you all about the role of religion in military life without their help," said Trưng Nhị. "You see, An Dương Vương had a crossbow with a trigger fashioned from a turtle claw, which made his armies invincible in warfare—"

"I want you to tell me what the authorities say on this matter," said Thi Sách. "*Then* you may offer your own opinions."

"Fine," said Trưng Nhị, standing up, and proceeding to the library.

Trưng Trắc gleamed, both for Trưng Nhị to learn this lesson of obedience, and for the excitement of engaging in a contest with her sister in which she was guaranteed to win.

CHAPTER 8

The Suitors

Lord Trưng decreed that Cung Điện Mê Linh was to host suitors from throughout all of Lạc Việt. These suitors were to arrive during the Spring Festival, the only time of year that the villagers of Mê Linh were welcomed into the palace. Ordinarily, playing host to lords and ladies meant that ceremony and etiquette must be maintained; but during the Spring Festival, propriety fell away, such that men and women of every station were treated as equals, and everyone was just a Việt.

Trưng Nhị had fond memories of the Spring Festival because as a child she was always called upon to perform—to sing, and dance, and tell stories—and there was no audience quite like the villagers of Mê Linh, starved as they were of entertainment other than drinking and gaming, and who expressed their honest appreciation in howling and whistling.

It was the elder sister, however, who was expected to greet all the guests and manage the servants and act in all other ways as though she, not Lady Man Thiện, were the hostess of this affair. For Trưng Trắc, she would almost rather face Răng the Tiger than to face the burdens of nobility.

It was during the Spring Festival that many of the women of Mê Linh had met their first lovers, and the fathers of their children. The sights and sensations of love were so thick in the air that its lure was said to be irresistible. But the romantic mood of the palace was no accident; it was painstakingly wrought by the servants of Cung Điện Mê Linh, under the supervision of Trưng Trắc. Now that she herself was expected to find a suitor, she felt as though she were trying to sculpt her own destiny. It was she who oversaw the hanging of the garlands from the bronze latticework in the gardens. It was she who ensured the puppeteers trained and prepared for the day in question. It was she who employed the musicians and dancers. There was no room in this for her own anticipation, for her own joy.

The noblemen of Lạc Việt are beautiful and proud, Trưng Trắc observed, worthy descendants of the Dragon Lord and the Princess Âu Cơ, strong of build, and keen of eye. But none seemed to possess the sort of intellect that would make conversation into a journey, who could venture with her deep into the wilderness of the mind.

There was the dutiful Võ Quan from Nhật Nam, whose perfect posture bespoke a martial discipline, his face round and unblemished, as though sculpted from wet clay. When he spoke, it was of his solemn duties to the people of Nhật

Nam. Trưng Trắc found him exemplary, commendable, but dull, like a good cabbage.

Then there was the dissipated Trinh Sang from Hợp Phố, good-natured and amenable to all company, charming but undiscriminating. Trưng Trắc got the distinct feeling that she could be anyone and he would still regard her as a worthy object of his attention. A baritone voice and a manly beard gave him a classical air, but the causes to which he leant his attractive speech were all vanities.

The pensive Đặng Thảo, son of the Lord of Chu Diên, was the most similar to Trưng Trắc—thoughtful and serious, well studied—but it was through listening to his conversation at the Spring Festival that Trưng Trắc realized that she was looking for more than a man who could mirror her own restless intellect. She desired a mind that was practiced in the art of exploration; she desired a guide through the wilderness of the mind—a guide like the master-scholar Thi Sách.

She could never before have admitted to this burgeoning within, but at the Spring Festival, feelings that were concealed, even from oneself, would become manifest. When she looked around her now, Trưng Trắc saw more than a palace garlanded with flowers; every object, every plant, seemed to glow with newness. Carefully avoiding staring at Thi Sách over the crowd of revelers, she looked instead at the incipient orchid buds and found them astonishingly alive. She longed for nothing now more so than to be alone with Thi Sách, son of Thi Vũ, and to hear his disquisitions on history, philosophy, and myth.

Surrounding Trưng Trắc now were sights and sounds of the Spring Festival: the flickering lights of the fire dancers, the bright shapes of water puppets crossing and recrossing the stage, the thrum and rattle of the bronze drum. The darkness just beyond the grounds of Cung Điện Mê Linh made everything within it appear tentative and brief but undiminished in its brevity. Glimpsing her own reflection in the firelight revealed truths to Trưng Trắc that were hidden in the daylight. Trưng Trắc knew not what she was thinking, only that her whole self inclined toward the tutor. What she had seen all along as a breeze of intellectual affinity she now had to admit was a monsoon that upswept her, body, mind, and soul.

It was forbidden, she knew from her sister's example, to love a man beneath her station. Lord Trưng and Lady Man Thiện had, after all, gathered these noblemen from throughout Lạc Việt specifically for the purpose of courting her. If there was no declaration of marriage to another Lạc lord, they would consider this endeavor a failure. It was dangerous, and this yearning for what was forbidden was new to Trưng Trắc, whose mission in life until that moment was to bring pride to her parents.

Of course, thought Trưng Trắc, it is the dissipated Trinh Sang from Hợp Phố—the deep-voiced and broad-shouldered stranger, the garrulous and glib raconteur—who captured Trưng Nhị's attention. He was equally enamored with her energy and wit. They spoke with a quickness with which few could keep pace, and as a result they formed their own co-orbit, the two alone in the stone garden, basking in the light of an open fire.

Trưng Nhị seized upon every opportunity to stroke his dark, curly beard. To Trưng Trắc, the beard was off-putting, reminding her too much of their father.

Yet, as the kindling that starts the fire is the first to burn to ash, the courtship between Trịnh Sang and Trưng Nhị was brief, and lasted only until they found themselves alone, and then love's momentum—no longer fueled by the exhilaration of performing for the crowd—slowed to stillness. During their first wordless hour, it became clear that their bodies were not as willing to be charmed.

The dutiful Võ Quan had Trưng Trắc all to his own, but the lady's attention was on the servants bustling in and out of the kitchen; on the assorted musicians, dancers, and entertainers preparing their amusements for the villagers of Mê Linh; and on the ambling tutor who took no wine but stood upon the bridge and let the flow of the river intoxicate him. The young man Võ Quan, however, was accustomed to being ignored. He treated her distraction as natural and normal, and continued speaking to her about the way the farmers of Nhật Nam yoked metal ploughs to their water buffalo, rather than pulling them with draft horses, which were better served for riding.

"I apologize," said Trưng Trắc, "for being so divided. I must play hostess to the people and somehow also partake of the merriment of the Spring Festival."

"My mother is hosting the Spring Festival in Nhật Nam right now. She has no daughters, so she worries that her sons will move away and leave Nhật Nam with no Lạc lord. But I plan to bring my wife back to Nhật Nam someday and together we will support my mother and father."

The company of Võ Quan pitted Trưng Trắc's two most dominant traits against each other: her courtesy toward others and her yearning toward the intellectual sublime. The first kept her yoked to this gentlemanly suitor like a water buffalo to a plough; the second cried within her to flee this boor who thought of nothing but his filial duties.

She nodded as he spoke, but looked over his shoulder at Thi Sách and Đặng Thảo as they conferred quietly and purposefully on what she imagined was a vast conversation, full of mysterious depths and sudden clarities like sunlight on water. But then she felt in the periphery of her vision what was unmistakably the sensation of Thi Sách's gaze upon her. Sunlight on water. With the slightest shift of her eyes, she found him looking directly at her, and the two most curious minds in Cung Điện Mê Linh were now locked in a single, shared thought: *If only we could be alone.*

CHAPTER 9

Duy's Vengeance

The morning after the Spring Festival, Trưng Trắc visited the shrine of her ancestors, and praying with bruised hands and scarred forehead pressed against the stone floor, she gave her thoughts over to the tutor Thi Sách and the dream that they would one day be together. Then, out of a sense of propriety, she made a plea to Duy's spirit. If it were true, as Phan Minh said out in the woods, that his spirit cried out for appeasement, she wished that it could be at peace.

At their afternoon lessons, Trưng Nhị was absent. Trưng Trắc and Thi Sách sat opposite one another in silence for a time, as they awaited the younger sister who never arrived. Then, as abruptly as the tolling of a bell, Thi Sách began his lesson on the philosophy of restraint. Trưng Trắc felt conflicted, for this was an arrangement for which she had long hoped—to be Thi Sách's sole student, and to occupy the whole of his attention—yet she feared that Trưng Nhị was truant for an evil purpose.

"Em Trắc?" Thi Sách said, calling her *Em*, for she was

younger than he. He had just finished a statement, the content of which Trưng Trắc could not recall.

"I'm sorry," said Trưng Trắc. "I was distracted. What did you say?"

"I was saying," said Thi Sách, "that for restraint in leadership to be possible, there must first be a reservoir of will, according to Đặng Quốc. That reservoir of will cannot come from education alone, but it must derive from experience, the kind of learning that cannot be undone."

"So I must take action?" said Trưng Trắc, standing and looking out toward the garden wall, a rising panic for her sister's safety, and for the fate of Cung Điện Mê Linh, creeping up her spine.

Thi Sách looked up at Trưng Trắc from his seated position with eyes wide and confused.

"And I must acquire experience of the world, and not just accept what I read in the scrolls?"

"Well, yes," he said, and at that, Trưng Trắc left the terrace and headed toward Mê Linh.

As she entered town, Trưng Trắc realized she had no idea where to find this Hán official, nor did she know anything about Trưng Nhị's plan. She knew that her sister frequented the game dens, but even these could hardly be differentiated, as there were scarcely any signs posted over the doors. You had to simply follow the noise at night to find them.

She stood in the public square, at the site of Duy's execution, and her eyes darted around the afternoon crowd. The sun could not have shone higher and brighter in the sky, and all the villagers wore *nón lá* except for Trưng Trắc, who used her hand to shield her face from the light, which shone over the valley of conical hats.

She visited the fish market, which was bustling with activity, but whenever she thought she had spotted Trưng Nhị, it turned out to be a long-haired stranger. "Trưng Nhị!" she called out, surmising that the cries of one woman could be ignored by the crowd. The longer she searched, the more agitated and desperate she became. She had always feared that her sister's rashness would lead them all into disaster, yet she hated to be right. "Trưng Nhị!"

"Is your sister missing?" said the head cook, Phùng Thị Chính, who was returning from the fish market with four children of her own, the eldest of whom was a boy with a long, skinny neck that made him slightly taller than his mother. "Can I help?"

"Yes. Please help us find Trưng Nhị."

"Your sister is a bully and a braggart," said Phùng Thị Chính. "I have no wish to help her."

Trưng Trắc nodded in agreement. She knew that Phùng Thị Chính was fearless, even in the presence of an aristocrat, yet Trưng Trắc had no quarrel with the cook. "That's what I'm worried about," said Trưng Trắc, "that she is up to no good. Help me find her?"

Phùng Thị Chính sighed. "If it will keep the peace in Mê Linh, I will help. Your sister seems to have a talent for making trouble," said Phùng Thị Chính. "Let's follow the crowds." Then, to her son, she said, "Danh-ơi, go and bring your brothers home. I'll be there shortly."

As the day went dark, the activity moved from the fish market back to the square, where the din of bartering and the chatter of gossip were like the chittering of insects in the night. The *nón lá* fell away, tied around the necks of the men and women of Mê Linh, but no longer hiding their faces.

Eventually Trưng Trắc spotted a figure with a familiar height and girth—Kha the guardsman, whose wide eyes recognized her simultaneously.

"Where is Trưng Nhị?" said Trưng Trắc. Finding her sister's guardian without Trưng Nhị anywhere in sight was dispiriting.

"I followed her here," said Kha.

"So she's not with you?" Trưng Trắc said, who could not do otherwise but state the obvious.

"She left Cung Điện Mê Linh dressed all in black like a thief," said Kha.

"She's after her death," said Trưng Trắc.

"She's after all our deaths," said Kha.

"Where do you suppose she went?" said Phùng Thị Chính.

"The Hán officials live in a barracks north of town—" said Kha.

"Like soldiers," said Trưng Trắc.

"Like an invading army," said Kha with a growl, "with a tower overlooking the Red River."

Trưng Nhị had been sneaking out at night to watch the tower for weeks. She knew the shift changes, and she knew the room assignments. She had identified the Hán official with the mole in the middle of his forehead like a third eye. She knew the hour, after he was relieved of his shift, shortly after sunset, when he walked to the bank of the river alone and watched the fishermen retrieve their nets. He would set down his poleax and wait until every soul was gone from the river, then shed his leather jerkin and kapok cotton and bathe in the light of the moon.

Now she followed him, robed in black silk, wearing a *nón lá* like a villager, blending into the night, as he underwent this ritual cleansing. There was a shallow ingress with still-warm rocks upon which he laid his body. On the bank, Trưng Nhị reached out and seized his clothes and hid them away in a thorny bush, then she took up his poleax and stepped toward him in the shallow water. Soon, she imagined, Hán blood would be washed away by the current of the river.

There was something about his vulnerability that gave her pause. Her training, and her instinct, told her that it was wrong to attack an unarmed opponent. She had to force herself to remember that he was a Hán, responsible for Duy's death and an oppressor to the Lạc Việt people. But her hesitation was enough to alert him to her presence; as dark as her figure was as she moved through the night, her slight shadow under the moonlight revealed her.

The Hán official stood and spoke. "Please," he said, seeing the familiar shine of his own blade in the hands of a stranger. "My name is Wan Fu. I am from Szechuan province. I am here in Jiaozhi on orders from the governor."

"Give me one reason not to kill you," said Trưng Nhị, surprised by her own mercy.

"I am just doing my job," he pleaded as he turned to run. Trưng Nhị chased him through the ingress of the river until it became knee deep. Then when his pace slowed so that he was within striking range, he stumbled and fell, his body drifting a few feet away in the shoal.

Just then she heard splashing from behind her, and she turned to see three figures approaching, silhouetted by the half-moon. One of the figures was plump and scarcely clothed, and even without discerning their features, she knew this was Kha.

"Sister," said Trưng Trắc, "you are not a killer. Leave the man alone, and let the Guardian Spirit see to his punishment."

Trưng Nhị laughed. "*Sister*," she said in a mocking voice, "would you have me spare this villain because of *the Guardian Spirit*? Even your betrayals are self-righteous." At that moment, there could have been nothing worse, to Trưng Nhị, than a lecture. Sick of idle words, the warrior within her awakened. Seeing Trưng Trắc, full of holy purpose, standing across from her and opposing her, made Trưng Nhị grip her weapon even tighter.

Wan Fu was standing again, and trying to maneuver himself around Trưng Nhị so he could reach the bank, but she stepped in his path.

"I'll stop you," said Trưng Trắc, holding her staff in an offensive position. She held one blunt end toward her sister, but her stance felt weak. Would Trưng Nhị see her folly and retreat, or would she truly advance upon and strike out at her elder sister? She let a silent cry for peace remain unvoiced, for she could not at that moment risk weakening her position even further.

"Be careful," said Trưng Nhị, holding her poleax upright. For a brief moment, her will faltered. Trưng Nhị had supreme confidence in her skill, yet she remembered all too well succumbing to her sister's attacks in their youth. "I'm holding a weapon of war, and you are wielding a sparring staff. Would you risk your death to save a Hán dog?"

"Don't threaten me," said Trưng Trắc. She did not even consider that Trưng Nhị could have meant to attack her with a bladed weapon. Despite the many battles between them, she never once imagined her sister might kill her. "I am your elder. Show some respect."

"Spoken like a true Confucian!" Trưng Nhị shouted.

"Em Nhị," Trưng Trắc replied. "Do not mistake me for your enemy."

"You are outnumbered," said Phùng Thị Chính, pulling out a short gutting knife.

"Please," said Kha. "If you fight, it will be *me* who faces punishment. Put down your staffs."

Wan Fu splashed through the shoal, hoping to cover the short distance between him and Trưng Nhị, and to wrestle away his poleax, but he underestimated the indolent pace of a body's movement through knee-deep water, as well as the skill of his aggressor. Trưng Nhị lifted the blunt end of the poleax and jammed it into the notch below his knee, sending Wan Fu down to the wet rocks. She raised the sharp end, and just as she was about to lower it upon his torso, Trưng Trắc struck her savagely on the shoulder, and one hand's grip was released, so that the blade merely nicked Wan Fu's arm as he raised it to shield his body.

Then the melee began. Trưng Trắc had no time to acknowledge the fear that shook her legs and unsteadied her grip. The elder sister prayed for this moment to come to a peaceful end, deflecting and attempting to disarm, while the younger thought only of vanquishing the opponent in front of her, possessed as though by a tiger spirit. As Trưng Trắc advanced upon Trưng Nhị, Kha took Wan Fu over his shoulders and carried his body toward the bank, where they hid behind a rocky outcropping.

From a distance, the river roared louder than the sisters, whose fierce exhalations were like bass notes to the terrible treble of wood against wood.

"We need to warn the others," said Wan Fu.

"I saved your life," shouted Kha in a deep authoritative bass, for he knew how the Hán would react if they ever found out about the attack on Wan Fu. "You must do me a favor! Say nothing about what happened here tonight. If you go around telling the Hán officers that you were attacked by the lord's daughters, they will talk of insurrection, and bring disaster to our doorstep. This is just the act of one overzealous girl, and you must swear to me that I will be the one to determine her punishment, and that you will not seek vengeance upon her."

"But there are laws," said Wan Fu.

"I don't care about Hán laws! I will decide her punishment, or I won't protect you now."

Wan Fu looked grimly at Kha. Then he looked through

the dimness and between the trunks of trees to see the form of his attacker, robed in black, swinging the ax at her own sister.

Phùng Thị Chính crouched so low that her nose barely hovered over the surface of the water. She circled Trưng Nhị at a distance, holding the gutting knife so close to the river bottom that it occasionally clicked against a stone. If she could get close enough to her target undetected, she could slice her at her heel, and the fight would be over. But Trưng Nhị seemed to have the upper hand. Trưng Trắc was frightened by the blade that kept sweeping closer and closer to her fingers as it cut across the staff. Once, the blade stuck in the wood of Trưng Trắc's staff, and the two women struck out at each other with kicks, and the splashing made it difficult for Phùng Thị Chính to see.

Trưng Trắc swept at Trưng Nhị's leg but Trưng Nhị launched herself into the air and her poleax became unstuck from the staff, which splintered and broke in two. Trưng Nhị stood now over her prone enemy, wielding a newly sharpened blade at the end of a staff of sturdy oak, and pointing it at Trưng Trắc.

"Get out of my way," said Trưng Nhị, "and give up the Hán enemy."

"Sister, what are you going to do? Kill me?" Trưng Trắc said. She wished she could be confident of the answer. The ferocity in Trưng Nhị's eyes was animalistic, instinctive. Her whole visage made Trưng Trắc feel as though she were staring down a wild dog, not her sister at all. She realized, then, that she could actually die by her sister's hand.

Trưng Nhị hadn't thought through her next step; she

hadn't thought at all. She hesitated, and her pause gave Trưng Trắc time enough to get to her feet. She saw the protrusion of Phùng Thị Chính's forehead coasting toward Trưng Nhị from behind, like the belly of a koi poking out of the water, and knew that she must distract her sister for just a moment longer.

"I'm in love with the tutor," Trưng Trắc said, and though she meant to startle her sister with this revelation, voicing it aloud was like hitting the perfect high note in a song; and it had the effect of disrupting her sister's rage. Trưng Nhị cocked her head to the side, her *nón lá* slipping a bit, and said *Huh?* just as Phùng Thị Chính sliced her heel with the gutting knife, and she collapsed under the water. Trưng Trắc seized the poleax and hurled it like a javelin into the current of the Red River, which lived up to its name as Trưng Nhị's blood rose to the surface.

The Great Hall boasted murals on every wall that depicted the history of the clan's war with the Hán. Every victory—and every tragic loss—was recorded in stark black and white. The figures, and the landscape, and the blood that was shed upon the landscape, were all rendered in the darkest ink. Underneath the dripping lines of the mural, Kha explained how he had taken responsibility for Trưng Nhị's punishment—how, in the act of saving Wan Fu's life, he had won this concession— that the Hán official would save them from shame by keeping silent on the attack at the Red River, and instead Trưng

Nhị would be punished severely in a way determined by Kha himself.

"In what way shall she be punished?" asked Lord Trưng, who could not hide his discomfort at the lack of control he had over his daughter and her punishment.

She would spend one year alone in a prison away from Cung Điện Mê Linh, where food and water would be provided to keep her alive, but no one was to speak to her for the duration of that year.

"She could die," said Lady Man Thiện.

"She will surely die if we leave it up to the Hán," said Kha.

"I accept it," said Lord Trưng, "though it pains me to know she will suffer, and to be kept away from my daughter for a year. If this is the way to spare her life..."

"Your majesty is wise," said Kha with a bow. As he backed away as if to excuse himself, Lord Trưng held up his hand, palm forward, to indicate the guardsman was not yet dismissed.

"But how will *you* be punished?" said Lord Trưng.

Kha remained in a bowed position, in uneasy silence.

"Keeping track of Trưng Nhị and keeping her out of trouble and danger was your charge," said Lord Trưng. "So your failure must surely warrant punishment as well."

"I will be her warden," said Kha. "To bring her food and water every day and night."

"No," said Lord Trưng. "You are needed as a sentinel for the south gate. But here is your punishment: as long as Trưng Nhị is captive, you are not to eat any fish, fowl, or cattle, but must only eat the fruits and vegetables that grow in the gardens of Cung Điện Mê Linh."

Kha's head poked up from its downturned position, and he opened one eye, which peeked all around him. "Are you sure you know what you're doing?" he said to Lord Trưng.

"Why?" said the lord. "Do you find these conditions unacceptable?"

"It's just that...do you really want a grumpy guardsman? I can go without fowl and cattle, but *fish*..." But Kha saw that the lord was in no mood for compromise, and his wrath threatened to erupt like a volcano long thought to be extinct, made all the worse for the length of its dormancy.

There was a holding cell in Cung Điện Mê Linh that had only been used twice in Kha's memory, and both times as a habitat for thieves. Now it held the lord's younger daughter, who was unable to stand due to the injury on her heel, and whose hair fell in front of her face in thick bunches, salted by the river water. There was a window on the door with bars of bronze, and other than the slats of light that fell through the bars, no relief from the utter monotony of darkness. Then all at once the slats of light disappeared, obscured by a shadow passing in front of the door.

"You won't be here long," Kha promised, speaking through the bars.

"If you let me out," said Trưng Nhị, "you will be rewarded. I have little to offer you now, but one day I will be Lady Trưng, a possessor of land, and I will repay you tenfold."

"I didn't come here for you to use your silver tongue and talk your way out of punishment."

"I am not deceiving you. If promises for the future are too insubstantial, then there are beautiful women in Mê Linh, in the game dens, who would give themselves to you."

"Trưng Nhị!" Kha shouted in a tiger's voice. "I am here to pronounce your punishment. For one year you will be held a prisoner in the old Temple of Âu Cơ, where you will be provided food and water but never spoken to until the day of your freedom."

"Bastard!" said Trưng Nhị, banging against the door that held her captive. "I have admirers who will come to my rescue. You will see! Phan Minh will save me, and then you will regret not freeing me when you had the chance!"

"Phan Minh won't set foot in Cung Điện Mê Linh. Did you forget that he was punished?"

"Ngô Cầm will save me! Or Trinh Sang!" said Trưng Nhị. "I will be freed somehow, and I will have vengeance!" She felt the circle of conspiracy widening. It was not just the cook, the guardian, and her elder sister. It encompassed anyone who failed to work toward her freedom. She could not be caged; she could not be confined, even for a moment.

"I suggest you reflect on your crimes, and commit yourself to redemption," said Kha.

Trưng Nhị spat through the bars and laughed when the glob struck Kha in the eye, where he rubbed it away with his fat thumb, then walked off, leaving her in a checkered rectangle of light.

Trưng Trắc went to the courtyard the next morning out of habit. There she met only the statue of the great elephant, and reflected how that statue had overseen her whole childhood, every morning bout, all her struggles with Trưng Nhị, and now that it bore witness to her solitude with its blank gray eyes, she wondered if the great elephant judged her harshly for her vindictiveness. How much did her rescue of the Hán official come from a wish to be alone with the tutor? How could she have stood against her sister, and how could she have watched as her heel split open and she clutched her wound? She hardly recognized herself over the course of the past few days. The change frightened and repelled her.

"Now that Trưng Nhị is gone," she said, "I will honor the ancestors each morning. I shall be more devout than I have ever been." She bowed to the sun and repeated her mantras.

By the end of the dawn devotions, Trưng Trắc had resolved to be the obedient daughter and do as Lord Trưng and Lady Man Thiện wished, even if it meant sacrificing her own happiness. If her parents desired that she should marry a lord, then she would not do as Trưng Nhị had done and countervail their wishes. If the Trưng line would be strongest in a union with Đặng Thảo of Chu Diên, she would tolerate the lord-to-be's awkwardness and youth. His manners were repellent, but his mind was alive and his face was comely.

As though to challenge her resolve, the form of Thi Sách appeared in the archway that led into the courtyard. He was wearing the same white robe that he wore when she first laid eyes upon him. The brightness on his robe seemed to defy the mantra, that the sun was the source of all light.

"I just heard about Trưng Nhị," he said, taking Trưng Trắc's hands. "I'm so sorry."

Trưng Trắc let herself be comforted, and rested her head against the master-scholar's chest, though she could not cry. She felt the residue of anger at Trưng Nhị, but no sorrow.

"She lost control. All of us feel anger toward the Hán, but Trưng Nhị had no restraint."

She could hear Thi Sách's heartbeat accelerate underneath the layers of cloth. "She wasn't wrong to attack the Hán official," said Thi Sách. "The fist of the Hán is tightening in Mê Linh. A fisherman returned Wan Fu's missing garb, and he was repaid by having his hands cut off."

Trưng Trắc looked up at Thi Sách's face, which was empty of irony.

"Nhị acted too soon, without coordination, and without support," said Thi Sách. "But make no mistake: the Hán laws are meant to subdue and colonize us, and eventually destroy us. One day, we will have to fight just to preserve our right to live as we choose."

"But you..." said Trưng Trắc, unsure of what to say next. "You speak the Hán's language, and you read their scrolls, and you study their history."

"The gardener nurtures every seed, though some grow thorns and some grow poison."

"Poison?" Trưng Trắc pulled herself away from the man she loved. "You speak like an insurrectionist, all coded and masked, but your meaning is plain as can be."

"There is no one here," said Thi Sách, "but the statue of the elephant, and he is our ally."

"I cannot believe," said Trưng Trắc, "that revolution is the answer. The blood of the people is too high a price to pay for freedom from taxation."

"But the Hán have forced us to live unnaturally, in clannish solitude according to the Confucian order," he said. "They aim to change our way of life."

Trưng Trắc's eyes were like minnows turning upward, like extensions of her lashes. Thi Sách thought her impossibly lovely, like a visitation in a dream. "I am not an enemy to the idea of marriage," she said, and though it was *all* she said, Thi Sách read a lengthy discourse in her eyes.

CHAPTER 10

The Condemned

Thi Sách was summoned by Lord Trưng, and the summons was odd for its formality.

The tutor worried that the lord would find some fault with his teaching—as though Nhị's madness was his responsibility—for he had known scholars often suffered blame at the hands of those who misunderstood their trade.

"For what purpose has his lordship called me?" said Thi Sách, seated opposite the lord in the Great Hall.

"So quick to get to the point!" said Lord Trưng. "Such impatience is unbecoming in a master-scholar, I think."

"Please pardon this poor country bumpkin," said Thi Sách, bowing. "I am merely restless for knowledge."

"I will indulge your restlessness," said Lord Trưng, "because the nature of our meeting is a request."

Thi Sách's eyes could not help but wander around the room, as though looking for clues. He would have preferred a punishment to a request.

"You were tasked with the education of both my daughters, and that is the term of your payment," said Lord Trưng.

"That's correct," said Thi Sách.

"And now you are only responsible for one daughter's education, so this will entail half of the work for which you were employed," said the lord.

"I'm not sure I understand your lordship's request," said Thi Sách.

"All of our servants are occupied with their duties day and night, but you spend four hours tutoring one student, then spend the rest of your day reading and wandering the grounds of Cung Điện," said Lord Trưng.

Thi Sách merely awaited the lord's request.

"I therefore request that *you* be assigned the duty of bringing Nhị food and water at the old Temple of Âu Cơ, each morning and each night. There will be a door of stone built to contain her, and in the stone a window, too small for Nhị to crawl through, but large enough to pass portions of leaf-wrapped rice and salted fish. You must not speak to her, no matter what. She will try to instill sympathy, to compel you, to seduce you, to get you to utter even a single word, but you must resist, or her term of confinement will be extended another year. I ask you because you are our only choice, but it is our good fortune that you are a master-scholar, and have the fortitude of will to resist Nhị's pleas."

"I admit," said Thi Sách after a moment, "that this is a most unusual request, and not the purpose for which I have trained and studied all these years. Yet if it is his lordship's belief that this treatment is toward the education of his younger daughter, then I must accept that it is my burden."

"I thought you would see things as I see them," said Lord Trưng. "But I did not expect you to accept this charge so quickly..."

On the night before Trưng Nhị was to be sent to her prison in the Temple of Âu Cơ, Phan Minh appeared outside the dungeon gate, carrying a bronze drum at his side. Trưng Nhị's black silk had worn thin, and her face took on the pallor of the moon. Other than the bright circle of her face, it was as though she had no more vitality in her, but when Phan Minh appeared, she came alive.

"Ha!" Trưng Nhị shouted. "I am saved!" It was as though the presence of Phan Minh restored, not just her freedom, but the innocence that had been stolen by such a punishment. As though the bars would melt away at his touch.

"No," said Phan Minh. "I cannot release you. I am risking my life even coming here."

"Then why are you here? Have you come to mock me?" Trưng Nhị said.

"Kha told me that you would be confined for one year at the old Temple of Âu Cơ. Since the old temple is near to the shed where I live, though I cannot visit you, I will play for you the bronze drum every night," said Phan Minh. Trưng Nhị anticipated the sweet succor of this nightly ritual, almost wished for it, as proof of something still pure. Her own heartbeat thrashed like a drum. "Whenever you hear this rhythm, you will know that there is still someone in the world who loves you—" And Phan Minh struck the bronze drum alternately with the two drumsticks, first at the edge then at the middle of the drum, letting out a hollow ring at the end. Ka-*shock*, ka-*shock*, ka-*shock*-a-*shock*-a-*shuick*. Ka-*shock*, ka-*shock*, ka-*shock*-a-*shock*-a-*shuick*.

PART TWO

THE GOVERNOR AND THE TIGER

Lạc Việt Year 2736–2737
(38–39 CE)

CHAPTER 11

The Betrothal

While all of Trưng Nhị's romances took place out-of-doors—riding horses in distant fields with Phan Minh, parading around the town of Mê Linh with her tattooed man from the mountains—Trưng Trắc's courtship took place under a roof, across the study table. The feelings that flowered between Trưng Trắc and Thi Sách may have been hidden from the outside world, but became the most tactile reality for the two. Their moments together felt inevitable, more solid than packed earth, as though they stood at the holy center of things, and all-that-was-not-them dwelt in a fog of unreality.

But to Lord Trưng and Lady Man Thiện, it appeared Trưng Trắc was as devoted to her studies as ever. Their burgeoning love manifested in coy glances, restrained laughter, and the rare touch when a scroll or a quill was passed from hand to trembling hand, so that that love expanded to fill the halls of Cung Điện Mê Linh, bringing the palace to life. A touch that never seemed to dissipate, even when the warmth of his hand upon her hand had faded, was utterly new to Trưng Trắc.

"It is time," said Lord Trưng one day in autumn with resignation, "for you to find a husband." He stood in the doorway, lit from behind by the morning sun, a robed and bearded shadow.

Trưng Trắc sat in her white silk robe on the floor of the meditation room, her feet bare. Although she could do nothing to abrogate her sister's sentence of one year of isolation, at least she could share in a portion of it. Trưng Trắc's role in Trưng Nhị's downfall left her with complicated feelings of duty and guilt and solidarity with the fallen. But the force that drove her to the meditation room was also that which prevented her from achieving perfect focus. She flinched distractedly as she replayed the events of the past months in her head. In particular, she thought of her own silence as Trưng Nhị was delivered to the Temple of Âu Cơ.

Trưng Trắc, buoyed by love's levitation, could not fathom at that moment any impediment to her joy. She nodded compliantly to her father, but deep within her she dwelled in the certainty that the stars would align in her favor. Deeper still, she knew that a union with the tutor was forbidden, but the problem seemed abstract and theoretical when compared to the overwhelming reality of their love.

A thrill shot through Trưng Trắc when she imagined a world in which the Lord Trưng and Lady Man Thiện would bless her union with Thi Sách and she would no longer need to hide the most profound feeling her soul had ever known. It was soon overtaken by a wave of guilt, as she imagined feeling the greatest pleasure of her life while her sister was trapped in an old, dark temple without a single voice to comfort her. She longed to relieve Trưng Nhị of loneliness by running to the Temple of Âu Cơ and confessing her joy, but the breach of law would only prolong her captivity and their last murderous encounter had stained their sisterhood, perhaps forever.

Trưng Trắc and Thi Sách were often distracted by their separate burdens: that Trưng Trắc carried the weight of having been the one to send Trưng Nhị into a year of isolation, and now Thi Sách was tasked with bringing food to Trưng Nhị in the mornings and evenings.

Why did it have to be you? wondered Trưng Trắc, when she thought of Thi Sách's new duties. Must she still compete with Trưng Nhị when her sister was so far away, trapped in an old temple and shut away from all human contact? She scarcely believed Trưng Nhị would seduce Thi Sách from inside her prison; yet now she felt the tutor's heart inclining in two directions.

Thi Sách's attention was divided. He had been a tutor and a scholar for most of his life, but he had never before been a warden, and he treated this new duty with the utmost solemnity. He never jested about this change in his role, and Trưng Trắc thought that, if he had been able to view his plight as though it were playing out on a stage, with a comic distance, then Thi Sách's disposition would not be so altered, and he could once again focus upon her education.

Each night, Thi Sách listened to the cries and pleas and

promises of his charge, a desperate young woman whose great crime was her brash patriotism, through the small slot in the door of the temple. Then each day he was expected to pivot to idle acts of instruction—the fond familiarity of philosophy, language, and literature. He lamented all the lessons that Trưng Nhị would miss. Yet the days' consolation was every hour he spent with Trưng Trắc on the terrace—the lithe and lovely Trưng Trắc, for whom the tutor was cultivating an affection that was almost frightening to him. At thirty-three years of age, he had had many occasions in the past to believe himself to be in love; but this was love of a different order, a whole-body love that would risk all for a fond glance. By all logic, he should not feel what he felt. A love for the young aristocrat risked his livelihood, his reputation as a scholar. Yet what good was logic in the company of chemistry? Her humility and deference only heightened the boldness she concealed. The power she held was much greater than she exhibited; now that he truly knew her mind, he felt an awe and reverence for her more befitting a student than a tutor. He understood, even then, her potential for greatness, and felt immense privilege at becoming her partner in affection.

The temple, like Cung Điện Mê Linh, was rendered all in stone, but unlike the palace, its orientation was vertical, where each side of the temple was both roof and wall, a pyramid covered in a loose scree that, from a distance, formed a corrugated pattern that jutted farther out the higher up it went, until it recessed again. Though he had never been inside the temple, Thi Sách knew from other temples that this second building atop the first was not accessible by stair or ladder, but rather it formed a nave inside where lozenges of light intruded upon the stony darkness within.

The door was built of stone too, and contained one window small enough for Thi Sách to pass his hands through, but no larger. One day when Thi Sách was in the act of passing a package of leaf-wrapped rice through the gap, the captive seized his hands, and he was helplessly bound by the young warrior. She could have snapped his wrists easily, or broken his fingers one by one. She could have enacted promises through torture, but after a moment it became clear that the lord's daughter had no plan or scheme, and seized his hands just to feel, once again, a human touch. Trưng Nhị's heart thrashed in her chest. She caressed his palms, and let them go. For a moment, she felt like herself again, and this man's hand was like her father's hand guiding her safely over stepping-stones on the creek. It was as though she could hear the rush of water. Thi Sách, meanwhile, thought of how easily she could have snapped his fingers or wrist, or trapped his arm. Ever since then, Thi Sách did not take the risk of reaching through the window, but left Trưng Nhị her food and walked away before he could regret anything.

On the road back to Cung Điện Mê Linh each night, he heard the rhythm of a bronze drum in the distance. He wondered who would welcome the sunset with this nightly lone performance.

The mind assigns personality to everything, Trưng Nhị told herself, *even the void*. Yet she could not deny the presence of ghosts surrounding her in the darkness, and the darkness itself took on a human cast. As she moved through the thickness of the air, an oppressive heat seemed to be an entirely separate and sentient entity. What she did not feel was confined. If anything, the space within the temple felt vast and borderless. She would see a specter rise before her in the faint light, then she would rush toward it to attack, only to find herself in the middle of an inconceivable darkness. She would crouch to the ground and touch the clay to remind herself of the solidity of the earth.

A lifetime of preparing for war had not equipped Trưng Nhị for the trials of solitude. For months, she raged against invisible enemies until they manifested out of nothingness, the Temple of Âu Cơ becoming crowded with Hán officials, soldiers, generals, the guardsman, her own parents, the lovers who had betrayed her, and her wicked sister. Trưng Trắc haunted her in the darkness most of all. She thought of her girlhood, and the thousands of sparring sessions when she was beaten by her sister. She remembered the aloof disregard with which Trưng Trắc had treated her when she begged her sister to play in the gardens—how she had always been treated as an obstacle in her sister's path. She cried helplessly and struck out at the conjured ghost of Trưng Trắc. Her knuckles grew calloused from attacking the walls. Just at that point in the fight when she might have given up, and allowed Trưng Trắc to apply the balm to her bruises and to bandage her cuts, she heard the thumping and ringing of the bronze drum from afar. Ka-*shock*, ka-*shock*, ka-*shock*-a, *shock*-a, *shuick*! The drum roused Trưng Nhị, like the tool of war it was, replenishing her strength even after her energy had abated. She stood up again, and returned to the task of assaulting the ghosts with renewed fervor.

When both her will and her stamina were depleted, Trưng Nhị resorted to her second-greatest gift: her voice. She gathered the spirits around her in a circle and tried to pacify them. In her mind, she was using her silver tongue to persuade them to retreat, to surrender, to admit defeat; but to Thi Sách, who came by each day to silently deliver food and remove her waste, it sounded like the mumbling and rambling of a madwoman. And when she sang to her enemies, it was high and shrill and unburdened by melody.

Trưng Trắc stood in the sunlight of the courtyard, protected by her nón lá, practicing her form, without a sparring partner. As her stance shifted, she sensed a slight displacement of air behind her. Thi Sách was watching from the opened gate. When Trưng Trắc became aware of being studied by the tutor, her cheeks blushed.

"Do you wish to join me?" said Trưng Trắc.

Thi Sách laughed. "I am not a fighter," he said.

"There are a thousand ways to be joined," Trưng Trắc teased as she wiped the sweat off of her brow with a cotton sleeve. "Fighting is but one of them."

"What are you suggesting? That I join you in song?" Thi Sách jested. "I fear I'd fare even worse in that arena."

"Yet you love poetry," said Trưng Trắc.

"It is true," said Thi Sách, "that poetry and song share an

origin. Yet they have diverged into distinct bodies like man and woman."

"So which is which?" said Trưng Trắc, resting her staff against the elephant statue, and taking up a silk cloth to cover her sweaty chemise.

Thi Sách smiled indulgently, playing along with Trưng Trắc's game. "Poetry is the male, and song is the female," he answered, "because poetry is thought and song is feeling."

"I would have had it the other way around, I admit," said Trưng Trắc. She looked up at the tutor with uncharacteristic boldness. She mimicked her sister's blithe ease.

"How so?" said Thi Sách.

Trưng Trắc circled the tutor, appraising him and educating him all at once. "Because poetry speaks quietly and bids the listener to lean in, while song cries out in a booming voice and exposes its whole self at the first introduction."

"How do you know that I have exposed all of myself? Perhaps there are still depths to be explored?"

Trưng Trắc stopped in her pacing to stand in front of Thi Sách. She looked down intently at his feet. The things she wished to say could not be said directly into his eyes. "Is it possible that I might explore those depths?" She reached out her hands and felt his fingers like lightning upon hers.

At that moment Trưng Trắc noticed another presence, and turned to behold the Lord Trưng striding forth. She stepped away from Thi Sách, in despair at the thought that she could be deprived of this feeling, a sense of wholeness that she only felt in the tutor's presence. The lord took the measure of the scene, and grimly stared at the floor. When he looked up, his eyes were glazed. "I have found you a suitable husband."

Sitting in the Great Hall like a guest, Trưng Trắc sat opposite her father in formal attire. The flat, decorative walls stood in contrast to the modest clay of the rest of the palace's rooms. "I will not marry a Hán," said Trưng Trắc, and looked up at her father with a fire that evoked her sister.

"You will marry whomever your father wishes you to marry!" said Lord Trưng. Then he added, "We cannot reject the suit of Commander Ho without drawing the ire of the governor."

So it was the Hán authority who had designs upon her. To Commander Ho she must have been a means to an end, a convenient gamepiece in a strategy that would place him in the seat of local power, doubling his influence in the region. Trưng Trắc could not hide the strain in her mind as she struggled to reconcile her habit of obedience with news of an intolerable reality. She tried to channel her sister's revolutionary spirit, to reject the Hán, through violence if necessary, but the filial pattern was too intricately woven into the cloth of her being. She clutched her knees until her knuckles whitened.

"If only you had chosen a suitor at the Spring Festival…" he began. "If only you had kept better watch over your sister, none of this…" But Lord Trưng could not finish the thought, as hopes for the past were idle.

"Where is Mother?" she asked desperately. "Does Lady Man Thiện approve?"

"It matters not what she thinks," said Lord Trưng. "What matters is that Cung Điện Mê Linh, and stewardship of our land, remain in our hands; too many Việts depend upon us. We cannot give the Hán cause to take away what is ours."

"Then let us not hand Cung Điện Mê Linh to them through accepting a Hán devil as its next lord," Trưng Trắc beseeched. "There is another way. I will marry Đặng Thảo. But do not compel me to marry a Hán!" In her stomach, there was more than turmoil, more than ache. It was like a rot that threatened to burrow through and spill upon the floor beneath her.

"It has already been arranged," said Lord Trưng.

In the prevailing silence, Trưng Trắc looked and looked again at the Great Hall, which became foreign in its ornate design and its pretension to excess, like a Hán box. Even when she stepped out into the gardens, all of Cung Điện Mê Linh seemed strange, as though the scenes in which she had lived out her whole life had been an illusion that, once removed, revealed an arid landscape full of dry husks.

Trưng Nhị sat cross-legged with her back aligned with the curved wall. In the dawn light shooting down like arrows from the height of the temple, her long dusty hair clumped and dangled over her chest like icicles. The hum in her throat harmonized with the drone of insects outside the prison. For months, she had nothing to mark the time other than the arc of light from the high windows, and the two meals left in the slot in the door, and she had nothing to look forward to other than the thunder of the drums at sunset. Now, as she transitioned from rage to confusion to acceptance, the drumming unsettled the peace she had achieved within the rhythms and cycles of the natural world. It tormented her with the reminder of the outside world, whereas she had now learned to dwell harmoniously in the world within.

It was just as the sun declined, its last orange beams softly illuminating the bas reliefs of the temple, that the bronze drum would awaken Trưng Nhị into her plight, dragging her back into the human world of betrayal. All day, Trưng Nhị sat by the wall, a stone among stones, and listened to the chorus of warbling frogs and birdsong, felt the trembling crepuscular organisms of life in her blood, as though she were a part of the earth upon which the temple stood.

At that hour, inevitably, Trưng Nhị leapt to her feet and cried out to Phan Minh to stop the incessant drum song, but he was never so near that he could hear her screaming. She was no longer crying to be saved; she was calling out to him to let her go, to allow her to sink into the soil and be forgotten. In order to let go of her rage, she needed to let go of everything.

After hearing of the lord's intention to marry her away to an unfit suitor, Trưng Trắc spent many days without leaving her bed, in a numb defeat that looked like acceptance. Then one morning Trưng Trắc rose with the dawn bell and visited the library, the meditation room, and the courtyard for training before arriving early at the terrace, where she awaited Thi

Sách. She could only temper her despair and fury with an unfeeling torpor, and this she could not sustain for long.

"I am ready to return to my studies," said Trưng Trắc flatly when her tutor entered.

"And what did you do on your break from learning?" Thi Sách feigned disinterest, but he ached to know what she had felt and thought and done in his absence.

Her intention had been to separate herself emotionally from imminent realities, as she had succeeded in doing these last few days. But the presence of the beloved tutor thawed her cold determination. "I am being punished for my obedience," she said, "for being the good daughter."

"Whatever you are suffering, it cannot be worse than that visited upon your sister."

"You think I do not know how much Trưng Nhị hurts?" said Trưng Trắc with a fire that she had suppressed and contained for so many days and nights. These listless days she spent, not only grieving her own loss, but with pangs of guilt like a cramp in her side at the thought of her sister's plight. No matter which direction she faced, she saw only unscalable walls; her helplessness was absolute. "Don't speak to me of my sister's pain. To force me to marry is bad enough, that I should have to take as my betrothed a Hán devil, and that it should be Commander Ho, of all the souls in this world."

Thi Sách lifted his hand to his cheek as though to feel the sting after it had been struck by an open palm. He lost his breath momentarily. He crouched to avoid falling. "What can be done?" he said.

"I dream of running away. How can my father ask me to

share a home, a bed, with a stranger and a Hán?" she said, her eyes wide and vacant with renewed incredulity. "It is unthinkable, that I should become a Confucian wife, preparing his food, cleaning his clothes, bearing his sons, who should, in turn, have dominion over me." Even as she spoke these words, she found herself disbelieving their reality.

"Yet this is how the Hán want all of Lạc Việt to be. As though our whole people are made to serve."

"The problems of the Lạc Việt and the world are too large. What can one woman do?"

"*Two* women," Thi Sách said, as a reminder that she would never truly be alone as long as she had a sister.

"You really care for her," said Trưng Trắc, looking into Thi Sách's eyes carefully to read their movement and to measure his response.

"I respect her," said Thi Sách, his gaze unwavering, "but I care for you."

"I care for you, Sách-ơi," said Trưng Trắc, and it amazed her that this was the first time she had said so aloud.

"Trắc-ơi," said Thi Sách, simply to feel her name on his breath.

CHAPTER 12

The Runaway

When Kha reached the Temple of Âu Cơ, it was full dark save for the lantern in his hand. And the jungle was silent except for the clangor of insects and the sound of a distant drum. The tutor had taken ill, and Kha had brought food for the prisoner in his stead. The smell of ox shank was almost irresistible to him as he delivered it. Kha's stomach rumbled loudly, for he had had no dinner, and it had been almost a year since he'd eaten anything other than vegetables and broth.

He brought the lantern up to the hand-sized hole in the door, and peered in, seeing nothing and hearing nothing within. Just when he was prepared to sprint back to Cung Điện Mê Linh to sound the alarm that she was missing, Trưng Nhị's face appeared in the lamplight. Startled, Kha stumbled backward, almost tripping on the weave of roots that surrounded the temple.

"Thi Sách?" she said. "Have you brought me a new scroll?" Reading and writing by the wan light through the high apertures of the temple had become a matter of survival. Each day

she awaited their arrival eagerly and each night she resented
the darkness for taking her sight so that the words of sages no
longer sounded in her head.

"It is not Thi Sách," answered Kha automatically, forget-
ting for a brief moment the moratorium on speaking to the
prisoner. Kha was about to turn around and return home
when he realized what the prisoner had just said. "Wait a
moment! Has the tutor been smuggling you *scrolls*?"

There came no reply. In fact, this was the first real human
voice other than the tutor's that Trưng Nhị had heard in eleven
months, and the sound was so beautiful, it caused tears to flow
from her face. She had not eaten that day, yet the sound of
Kha's vacillations and accusations were greater delicacies than
the sweetest longan would have been.

"Give them to me," said Kha, and though Trưng Nhị
understood that her compliance meant a severe punishment
for the tutor, she reluctantly and dutifully passed to Kha a
sheaf of scrolls upon which she had been writing, by the light
of day, her thoughts.

"Go in peace," said Trưng Nhị. "You needn't fear me. I am
just another stone piled upon the temple's cairn."

Kha stood stricken with doubt. For her voice seemed calm
and wise, not wild and frantic, as he had anticipated. "You
scare me more," he finally said, "when you tell me not to fear
you."

Trưng Nhị laughed and the sound was so free of scorn that
it struck Kha anew. "Then fear me. But I seek no revenge."

A great struggle raged within Kha between his newfound
affection for the tutor and his duty to his lord. Yet when he

looked at the evidence in his hands of the tutor's disobedience, he knew that he would not hide this act of indiscretion.

The light of the lantern retreated and faded until Trưng Nhị was left in the full dark.

Rather than meeting in the Great Hall, where the Lord Trưng always pronounced his official decrees, he insisted on speaking to Thi Sách in the garden as soon as the dawn bell tolled. Yet it was still dark, and the lord and Lady Man Thiện were wide awake. "I will not receive him in the Great Hall like a man of dignity," said Lord Trưng angrily to Lady Man Thiện. "I should never have listened to Thi Vũ, that physician."

"Do not blame Thi Vũ," said Lady Man Thiện, shifting her body to feel his warmth against her own and placing a hand on his chest. "At least Nhị is safe."

"I have to hide Nhị from the Hán and keep her a secret, and all this while we are expected to receive the suit of Commander Ho, who reports to the governor," Lord Trưng sighed with exasperation. "It will be a miracle if we survive the month. I told you that we should have just abandoned Cung Điện Mê Linh and become a family of peasants."

Lady Man Thiện laughed. "A descendant of the Dragon Lord abandoning his people and allowing his children to beg in the streets? You are the one who is too proud to have a daughter in love with a scholar."

"Should we defy the Hán and go on pretending that we can live as our ancestors did, that we are not vassals?" said the lord.

"We *must* live as we wish to live; otherwise we are not Việts," said Lady Man Thiện. "If the Hán truly want to make Confucians out of us, at least they will have to fight for it."

"Is it war then?" said Lord Trưng incredulously. There was nothing more unfathomable, it seemed, than the plain truth and the inevitability of war.

"If only it were war," sighed Lady Man Thiện, "then I would know how to win."

As the first rays of the sun shone upon the ceiling through the window, the dawn bell rang, and Lord Trưng stood, donning the golden robe he saved for the most solemn decrees.

"I feel as though I should bow," said Thi Sách, still in his night robes while the lord sat arrayed in his most regal apparel that morning in the garden. "But I will not."

"You are no longer employed at Cung Điện Mê Linh," said Lord Trưng, barely masking his enmity. "So you can forgo your false gestures of respect."

"I am not false," said Thi Sách, "neither is my respect. Just because I am a man of learning, do not assume that my words are subterfuge and my actions are schemes. I speak in earnest, and I have always prided myself on this, ever since I was merely a doctor's son."

"I did not invite you here in order to listen to your speeches. I called you here so that you could listen to my decree: for disobeying your lord and giving comfort to the prisoner, you are dismissed from your position as tutor."

Thi Sách nodded and the skin of his brow tightened, as

though he had just been presented with a difficult theorem that it would be a challenge to refute. "I accept the terms of my punishment," said Thi Sách. "But now that I am no longer Trắc's tutor, I would like to become her husband."

Lord Trưng laughed. "And whatever convinced you that my elder daughter would take you as a husband?"

"Her eyes, her words, and her touch all convince me," said Thi Sách. "They teach me. They are all that I live for."

"Who do you suppose made those eyes, and taught her those words?" said Lord Trưng, no longer laughing. "She has no idea what she wants, or what is best for her."

"She may surprise you," said Thi Sách.

"I reject your proposal to marry my daughter," said Lord Trưng. He would have been amused if he had not been so angry. The audacity of this tutor knew no bounds. Lord Trưng felt as though he were being pulled down below the earth by his unruly children, and now here was a lowly tutor dragging him lower. What new depths of despair would he discover next?

"Then I am thankful that a Việt woman does not have to ask leave of her father before choosing a mate."

"That may be how things still work for the sons of doctors," said Lord Trưng. "But it is different for the daughters of lords. Furthermore, I decree that you are to be exiled from Cung Điện Mê Linh. Be grateful you have a family to return to. Go back to your father and tell him that you have brought shame to his legacy by your conduct here."

"I will make you a bargain," said Thi Sách. He understood that he was powerless to change the law, or turn the heart of the lord. Yet he believed in the force of Trưng Trắc's will more than he believed in anything else in this world. "I will leave Cung Điện Mê Linh as you have decreed, and return to the home of my father, Thi Vũ. But you must tell your elder daughter where I am, and if she follows me to Chu Diên, then you should lift my banishment."

"I will do as my conscience wills," said Lord Trưng. "No more, and no less."

Thi Sách waited outside the east gate in his traveling clothes, all his worldly goods stuffed into his pack. Beside him stood a statue of the Dragon Lord, mighty and fierce, onto which he leaned for support. He could not believe that he and Trưng Trắc's love story could possibly end this way—without so much as a farewell. Thi Sách had known this was a possibility all along, that he could be cast out on the whim of the lord, yet now that that day was upon him, his heart rebelled.

Kha delivered his final bundle and said, "When I first met you, I thought you were a fool in fancy clothes, but your commitment to your charges has won you my respect."

Thi Sách nodded, looking over Kha's shoulder for any sign of his beloved.

"Please," said Kha, "do not shatter the respect I hold for you by lingering here outside the walls of Cung Điện Mê Linh. Faithfulness is commendable, but pigheadedness is folly. Salvage your pride and go home to Chu Diên."

"If you felt as I feel," said Thi Sách, "you would not speak to me of pride."

"You are not the first to wait desperately outside the walls of Cung Điện Mê Linh because of heartache," said Kha.

Thi Sách shook his head. "Although we are two Việts, engaged in conversation like men, and looking upon one another like men, we do not truly see one another. Imagine you are not a guardsman, and I am not a tutor."

"But I am a guardsman," said Kha. Between them, the statue of the Dragon Lord stared straight ahead with nostrils flared and eyes inflamed and spear upraised. "And you are an outcast."

"Then, please, just give this to Trưng Trắc," said Thi Sách, handing Kha a bound sheaf of vellum. "It is a book of aphorisms that she may use to guide her through this troubled world. I recorded them all on these papers when I was still a scribe."

Kha sighed. "So we lose the tutor," he said, accepting the book, "but he leaves his tired sayings behind."

"You will tend to your legacy," said Thi Sách, "and I will tend to mine."

"I will be taking over as tutor until we find a replacement for the last one," said Lord Trưng. Trưng Trắc knelt on the stone terrace; behind her, the glory of early spring was framed by an arch.

"Where is Thi Sách?" said Trưng Trắc, looking down with her hands folded. She tried to make the question sound idle.

"He has returned to his father's home," said Lord Trưng.

"The tutor and I agreed that he could not continue to teach you after he disobeyed the laws of the palace."

"But he was unwell," said Trưng Trắc. She thought of his recent bout of illness, which left him bedridden for days, from which he had only begun to recover. She thought of him in the ornate white robes on the day he arrived—his whole body lit by the sun—when she had pretended not to have seen him; when she acted as though he were just another inhabitant of the palace. "Has he left already?"

"The guardsman saw him off at the east gate this morning."

She could not hide her sinking, drowning expression. Her head bowed low suddenly as if she were a puppet's head whose strings were cut. In her gloom, she pictured the sickly tutor forced out of the palace at spearpoint, shambling down the road with his meager belongings, the most ignominious end to the most beautiful courtship. Her heart felt detached, as though, while her body sat in the palace speaking emptily to the lord, it ambled down the road a pace or two behind the banished tutor.

"Did he leave a letter, or...?" Trưng Trắc began. That he would have left for good without a good-bye, without even a respectful farewell note, was unthinkable.

Lord Trưng held his daughter's hand and looked pleadingly in her eyes. "You must try to forget your former tutor, though I know he charmed you. He and I agreed it would be best for all involved if he simply...walked away."

Trưng Trắc could not help but think about her walks with Thi Sách, their long conversations upon the bridges and under the arches, where feelings were layered upon meanings, and meanings were layered upon texts, so that they appeared to be talking about the philosopher Mozi and the virtue of *ai*, or universal love, but they both understood that the real subject was their own imagined intimacies. Now that she knew these feelings, what good was a life without them? She could not take comfort in any of the activities that formerly brought her joy. Mere study, without the amplification of love, was impossible to her now.

"The Spring Festival is nearly upon us," said Lord Trưng, letting go of Trưng Trắc's hand and reaching for an empty scroll to be written upon. "Commander Ho will be our guest of honor. You can practice calligraphy by writing invitations to be sent to young noblemen throughout the province."

Trưng Trắc foundered in grasping after words. She imagined returning to the basics, as though her mind had not been awakened. She imagined trying to live in the banal as she used to. "I can't...just...practice calligraphy."

"And why not?" asked Lord Trưng.

"This is a task for a child. We have been reading the works of the great philosophers, and debating their precepts. Even when Lady Man Thiện taught us, and we focused on military technique, it was more advanced than penning invitations to a festival."

The lord tried to mask his surprise at Trưng Trắc's countervailing. Rebellion was a foreign posture for his older daughter. "So you think calligraphy is easy, do you? The great calligraphers would disagree."

"Do you want your daughters to be great calligraphers, or

great leaders?" said Trưng Trắc, her chin jutting forward as a challenge.

"Either one is preferable to turning you into philosophers' wives!" Lord Trưng crushed the scroll and threw it on the floor.

Thinking that all she could do at that moment was placate the lord, Trưng Trắc picked up the empty scroll and lifted the brush, obediently writing out the invitation in her elegant hand, marred only by the creases in the hide made by the lord's fist.

Though Kha had given her the tutor's book, Trưng Trắc had merely glanced at the artifact, then tucked it away among her things. For the first time, she found reading to be no comfort or consolation. She could not bear to consign him to ink yet, as though Thi Sách were another myth, another subject for literature. She would not read his book. Yet she would always keep it near.

Trưng Trắc no longer dwelled in the library or the meditation room. When she wasn't on the terrace looking out into the gardens, she was out in the gardens themselves, among the flora of the palace. Whereas Trưng Nhị would have perched by the edge of the pond, or stroked the shell of Kim Quy, the ancient turtle, or lay in the grass staring up at the birds that flitted past, Trưng Trắc simply gazed upon the palace walls, as though aware for the first time what they kept in, and what they kept out.

As the days passed, Trưng Trắc thought more and more

about Hoàng Tâm, from the story Trưng Nhị once told, who had hanged herself with a rope made from her own hair rather than serve as a concubine to a Hán. The story used to seem tragic somehow; though, as she considered it now, it felt heroic. Hoàng Tâm refused to be helpless and took her fate into her own hands.

As for Trưng Trắc, there seemed to be no other choice. She could not obey her father *and* obey her heart. A beautiful death, like Hoàng Tâm's, was the best result she could hope for. Yet Trưng Trắc's hair did not spill to the floor so that one could make a rope of it. In fact, every death she could think of felt ugly. To stab herself in the heart, or to hang from a tree, or to throw herself on the rocks. But the longer she contemplated the act, the more practical and inevitable it seemed. It was then that Trưng Trắc had a realization: if she went into the mountains, she could find the *lá ngón*, the heartbreak grass, and eat its leaves, and her throat would close, and at least she would die far from anyone who might discover her corpse.

Trưng Trắc's utter resignation appeared no different from her usual attitude of modesty and reserve to the residents of Cung Điện Mê Linh. But it was Lady Man Thiện who noticed the change, that this was more than a sour mood or a shy retreat from society.

Lady Man Thiện was combing her hair one morning when she was struck suddenly with a dark fear. She held at arm's length the jade comb that Trưng Trắc had gifted to her, and thought about how jealously Trưng Trắc used to guard this comb from Trưng Nhị's covetousness. Lady Man Thiện leapt up and searched the grounds for her daughter. She went to

Trưng Trắc's chambers, where, instead of her daughter, she found a scroll written in fine calligraphy that read: "Gone to find my roots. If you should ever seek me again, look to the earth."

This behavior was so unlike her elder daughter that Lady Man Thiện's fear for her rose like a note in a song that rings in one's head after the melody is over. It left a throbbing in her ear. She could not fathom losing Trưng Trắc. *Another riddle*, Lady Man Thiện thought with increasing fear and frustration. *If only the tutor were here to answer it. What are Trưng Trắc's roots, if not Cung Điện Mê Linh, where she was born and raised?*

CHAPTER 13

The Rescue

Trưng Trắc wondered what her education was worth if she could not identify a simple plant. All she knew about heartbreak grass was what she learned from the song: that it was found in the mountains, and that it ended one's life quickly by closing one's throat. But now that she stood on the mountain path, all the grass looked the same. Things she knew instead: the core philosophical precepts of Confucius, Laozi, Mencius, and Mozi; the literature and songs of the Red River Valley, and all the accompanying myths; the military history of the Lạc Việt and the Hán, and the strategies of war put forward by Sun Tzu and Sun Bin; how to subdue a charging opponent; how to disarm a swordsman; how to execute a reversal from a prone position; how to sweep, swoop, strike, and end an enemy's life. But for the task of ending her own life, she was miserably underequipped.

The path narrowed until it disappeared; tall grasses encroached on the space where she walked, and the trees grew thicker and more abundant, the landscape steeper and rockier, until she found herself climbing to reach the next plateau. As she lifted herself onto the high precipice, she thought about letting go. Would she survive the fall? If so, how long would she writhe in pain before death overcame her, or she was discovered? This chain of thought was interrupted by the sight she encountered as she pulled herself up to the next elevation and rose to her feet. In front of Trưng Trắc stood a group of tattooed women clothed in hides. Degar. Mountain folk. They carried bows and arrows, but from their casual postures and expressions, she guessed it was not a war party.

"How goes the hunt?" Trưng Trắc said. She knew enough of the Degar to treat them respectfully, rather than act the aristocrat. The assembly of women intrigued her.

"You are standing on the eagle's landing. This is a sacred rite of passage for our daughter, Ly Anh, who will prove her worth in the tribe by downing the black-winged kite," the apparent leader of the women began. Her tattoos covered her body from head to foot. "You are disturbing our ancient traditions, prairie dweller. Go back down to the valley, or you will be thrown down."

Trưng Trắc was unaccustomed to being addressed so frankly and familiarly by strangers. Her first thought, which she suppressed, was to reprimand them for speaking so to an aristocratic Lady. "Your threats are unconvincing," said Trưng Trắc, "since I've come here to die anyway. But if you can assist me in finding the heartbreak grass, then I will be on my way."

A young girl pushed her way to the front of the group. She

announced herself as Ly Anh. "Mothers," she said, "it is the will of Âu Cơ that we should meet this prairie dweller on the day of my trials."

"It must be," said Trưng Trắc. She felt no sense of duty toward these women to which she might rise, only the anchor of her own suffering, sinking within. She thought of nothing else. "So will you help me?"

"To end your life like the lovesick girl from 'The Lament of Vũ Thơm'?" the leader said. "If Âu Cơ sent you here, surely it was not so that we could feed you poison."

"Perhaps she was sent here to join our tribe?" said Ly Anh.

The leader laughed. "Among the People, even our children are stronger than this stranger, as you are here today to prove."

"I can hunt," said Trưng Trắc. She needed them to reach the heartbreak grass, but she also yearned to know more about these strangers. Although she had scarce experience with actual hunting, she was skilled at the crossbow. At least when it came to stationary targets.

An eagle shrieked as though to dare her.

The leader handed Trưng Trắc two arrows, and a bow. "This is it. If you can down the black-winged kite in two shots, then you may become one of the People."

Trưng Trắc pondered the fate before her. If she had already inured herself to death, then being absorbed into a tribe of strangers was no great leap of the imagination. She tried to quiet the voice within her that said that this one act would determine the arc of her future; she would either become a Degar, or die a jilted aristocrat. Perhaps starting over among a new people was just as good as dying. Perhaps the hardy mountain people possessed a wisdom that would allow her to live with the near-fatal wound she suffered. She took the bow and arrow, drew it back to her eye, and aimed expertly at the circling birds of prey. She waited for a landing, but the eagles seemed to have no intention of obeying her will. Finally, Trưng Trắc let fly the first arrow, which soared true and would have hit its mark if the kite hadn't been in motion, but as it was, the missile flew past its target and into the valley below.

With the second arrow, Trưng Trắc was more patient. She felt certain that there would be a landing, and then she could hit a stationary target. If only she could know the future. Nothing seemed certain any longer. But she channeled all her confidence into her hands. She would prove herself to them; perhaps she would belong somewhere again, if only she could focus. The women gathered there upon the mountainside listened to the changing of the wind; it lasted so long that several of the women sat, but none spoke. Finally, one of the kites perched on the opposing bluff, close enough for a sure shot, and Trưng Trắc let fly her arrow. Yet she could not have accounted for the wind upon the mountain, which pulled the arrow to the right, where it shattered on the face of the rock. She let out an exasperated breath, thinking her fate as a dead woman had now been sealed.

"You are not one of us," the leader said. She took the bow from Trưng Trắc. "But Âu Cơ has brought you to us for a reason. Before you return to the prairie, you will witness the prowess of the People. Behold our daughter Ly Anh, who will prove herself a true member of the tribe."

The young girl was given two arrows, and she nocked one. Then, as quick as instinct, she let it fly and it pierced the black-winged kite in mid-flight, sending it tumbling into the trees.

"If you mean to discourage me from my aim to die here in the mountains," said Trưng Trắc, "then having a young girl humiliate me does not serve your ends." For all her bluster and confidence, Trưng Trắc felt unfit to join the mountain folk, unworthy even of equal status to a Degar child. She absorbed this new understanding alongside the rising inevitability of her life—that it would end as soon as she found the heartbreak grass.

"Your life is your own to take as you wish," said the leader. "But if you are suffering from heartbreak, as Vũ Thơm did, then death will not bring you peace. Your ghost will live in these mountains forever."

"We cannot allow even your ghost to live among the People," said another woman.

Trưng Trắc set her stance so that she felt rooted to the earth beneath her. Moments before, the Degar had briefly given her a reason to live, and she felt now as though they somehow possessed the answer to the despair that plagued her. She had never seen so many women working together with such power and trust in one another. "I cannot simply go back to my father's home and agree to wed a stranger."

The women huddled together and conferred among themselves, whispering of their duty to the sisterhood of Việts, the will of their common ancestor, the Princess Âu Cơ, until the leader broke away from the group and announced, "My name is Ly Chau and this mountain is my home. You may stay with us for three days and three nights, and learn our ways. When you leave here, you may end your life, or not; either way, you are not to return here in any form, and you are not to speak of our ways to the prairie folk." Thus Trưng Trắc, her curiosity about this tribe of women as acute as when she first saw them, decided to live for three more days.

Lord Trưng had gathered together Lady Man Thiện, Bác Huy Vũ the astrologer, and Huỳnh Quyền the master of spies. Kha the guardsman stood by awaiting command.

"How could this happen, that no one knew of my daughter's disappearance from Cung Điện Mê Linh?" demanded Lord Trưng.

Huỳnh Quyền, who rarely appeared in public, felt the lord's gaze land upon him like a lash. "I have ears in every market in Mê Linh, and eyes upon every corridor in the palace, but I have not yet learned to box the minds of your daughters so that their thoughts could be taken out and read at my convenience," he said. He paused, then added, "One might say that the will of your daughters is particularly difficult to discern."

"Then why was no one posted at the west gate?" the lord said, turning his gaze upon Kha.

"We are still short one guardsman since Bình was dismissed," Kha said apologetically. Bình's loyalties had been divided, it seemed, as he insisted on obedience to the laws of the Hán.

"And who was responsible for advising our daughter?"

Lord Trưng turned to Lady Man Thiện, who flashed a fierce look back at him.

"I would say," she said, composing herself, "that Trưng Trắc has never demonstrated any impulsivity in the past, and we had no reason to suspect that this latest compromise would leave her in such a state of mental fragility."

"You said to me this morning that Trưng Trắc had been feeling helpless and hopeless. What if she has run away forever, to seek comfort in the arms of that snake, Thi Sách?"

"Then I would say," said Lady Man Thiện, "that our daughters are not destined to be controlled."

"Once again, I must fall upon the wisdom of our astrologer," said the lord. "Bác Huy Vũ?"

The old man rose and shook his robe, then strode to the center of the room to address the lord and his retinue. "What question would you ask of the stars?"

"Where is my elder daughter?" said Lord Trưng.

"All the heavenly animals descend from the sky at once, but for two: the phoenix and the tiger," he said. "Lady Trắc seeks her own death somewhere far from home. Lady Nhị must be set free to follow her and find her." Bác Huy Vũ allowed a moment for his words to sink in.

"And what, in the end, will become of my elder daughter?" said Lord Trưng, his voice quivering with fear of the answer.

The astrologer was silent.

"What happens to Trắc?" said the lord, steadying himself.

"Do you really wish to know?" said Bác Huy Vũ.

"Yes!"

Bác Huy Vũ took a deep breath, gave a meaningful look

toward Lady Man Thiện, then spoke directly to the lord. "Lady Trắc lives, and will be forgiven. What's more, you will find the mercy and compassion in your heart to permit her to marry Thi Sách, and will invite him back to Cung Điện Mê Linh as an honored guest."

Silence prevailed in the room, the unnatural quiet of a storm-eye.

The lord laughed, thrown at first by the astrologer's audaciousness, then driven by temper when he thought of the trap he had sprung. Soon, mercy prevailed in him. To act otherwise would be to pit Việt against Việt and would only serve the wicked designs of the Hán. "You could learn something from Bác Huy Vũ," he finally said to Huỳnh Quyền, the master of spies. "Here is a man who has not only boxed my thoughts and read them, but who knows all our past, present, and future as well."

"All I know is what the stars tell me," said Bác Huy Vũ humbly.

"Then go and release Trưng Nhị, who will help us to track down her wayward sister," said the lord, dismissing the guardsman, the master of spies, and the astrologer with his command. Lady Man Thiện stayed by his side, reaching for his hand. If he had any fury within him, it collapsed with this gesture, and he leaned his head upon the shoulder of his wife and sobbed. If no power on earth could turn his heart, then the stars would do this difficult work.

Lady Man Thiện, Phùng Thị Chính, Kha, and Mai gathered at the Temple of Âu Co. They stood with regal postures and wide stances. Lady Man Thiện called out in a strained voice, "Trưng Nhị! We are here to set you free! Your torment is at an end!" She was so moved by the sight of her daughter's prison that she could have torn away the stone door all on her own. Lady Man Thiện had been so afraid of her own tenderness that she had not visited the Temple of Âu Cơ since Trưng Nhị was imprisoned there; not even to observe from a distance. Seeing it now filled her with the desire to look upon her younger daughter's face once again. The four Việts planted their feet firmly on the clay beneath, and pushing with such force that the loose scree of the temple tumbled to the ground under them and their sandals tore from the exertion, they shifted the portal until an arc of light poured in and shone upon the thin and ropy form of Trưng Nhị, her skin red with dust and her hair long and tapered and turgid like the temple itself. Underneath the layers of grime, there were welts from insect bites. Her knuckles and elbows were scarred, calloused. Though her body looked ruined and weak, she bowed before her rescuers and said, "I am here." As soon as she uttered the words, she felt the force of their truth, which had seemed impossible moments before. "I am here."

Lady Man Thiện embraced Trưng Nhị and whispered a thousand sorrows and pleas. "Forgive me!" she cried, holding her close, afraid to look her own daughter in the eyes. "I have driven you to such a fate. You must despise me!"

"No," said Trưng Nhị. In her gratitude of being freed, Trưng Nhị thought no longer of vengeance. She registered a profound change, not just within herself, but within her captors, too. The threads that wove them into a family seemed more visible than ever, sturdier in spite of the fraying. Somehow Trưng Nhị had never before understood how much her beloved family mattered to her, how her mother had once created her and was here again at her second birth. "I should thank you. While I had seen my reflection before, I had never truly met myself until this moment, the hour of my freedom."

"I promise you will never be caged again," said Lady Man Thiện.

As Trưng Nhị bathed, Lady Man Thiện brought clay jars of hot water and ladled it in until steam rose into the night sky. She had dismissed the servants, and performed the servants' duties with solemnity. Lady Man Thiện had imagined that her daughter, after a year of solitude, would have been driven to madness, or else her wrath would keep her sane, but here was a tamed Trưng Nhị quietly soaking in the baths.

"You are rather quiet," said Lady Man Thiện. "I thought you would be full of questions."

"I prefer to listen," said Trưng Nhị, clearing the clods of dirt from her hair and untangling the individual strands. Indeed, the sonorousness of each human voice, especially her mother's, carried a sweet and nourishing particularity. Nothing else on the earth was like it.

Trưng Nhị closed her eyes, listening to the night noises and breathing the open air. Lady Man Thiện combed her daughter's tangled hair gently. Though it was a struggle, Trưng Nhị did not wince or complain.

"You are not the same woman you were," said Lady Man Thiện, noticing her daughter's calm.

"I'm sorry," said Trưng Nhị, opening her eyes, registering her mother's pained expression. "Why was I set free?"

"Your sister is missing, and you are the one who knows her heart best, and can find her," said Lady Man Thiện.

"Why did she run away?" said Trưng Nhị with disbelief. It was so unlike Trưng Trắc even to leave the palace, much less to flee beyond the reach of the guardsmen. She sank deeper into the bath, fearing the answer.

"Thi Sách has been banished from Cung Điện Mê Linh," said Lady Man Thiện.

"She loves the tutor," said Trưng Nhị, as though speaking it aloud would manifest their happiness. She only wanted her sister back and living a happy life as she deserved.

"She regrets what happened between the two of you," said Lady Man Thiện.

"Trưng Trắc did the right thing. I would not have stopped at Wan Fu, and would have kept on killing until the tiger inside of me had had his fill," said Trưng Nhị. This was, finally, Trưng Nhị's revelation: not that she had done wrong in confronting the Hán, but that she had put her family in danger while doing so. The tiger within her now was patient.

CHAPTER 14

The People

In the recess of a shallow cave, surrounded by Degar women absorbed in the task of shaping and stringing their bows, Trưng Trắc carved the bon-bon branch until it was precisely the width of her two thumbs pressed together. Though it was sturdy and thick, the wood could just barely be bent. "Just right," said Ly Chau when she examined the bow. Notches were needed for the bowstring, made of animal sinew, to become taut. But when it came time to string the bow, Trưng Trắc found it impossible to bend the bow and tie the string at the same time.

She witnessed the other women bending and stringing their bows without trouble, and thought what a hardy race these mountain folk were. Over and over again, these women bent their wood and strung them, yet here was Trưng Trắc helplessly pulling on the sturdy bon-bon branch that she had been given. "I cannot do this alone," said Trưng Trắc. "How can I learn to string a bow like you and your kinswomen?" She had never before been given a task without a solution—not by

Thi Sách, not by Lady Man Thiện nor by Lord Trưng. "Your tribe must possess a strength beyond my understanding, for I simply cannot do it. If there is a secret technique, then teach me."

"There is no secret technique," said Ly Chau, pointing at the unbent bow in Trưng Trắc's hands. "It is simple. Our bows are all made of white pine, and yours is made from a bon-bon tree. Bon-bon wood is not made to bend."

"So there isn't any way to finish it," Trưng Trắc said, frowning at the wood in her hands.

"There is always a way," said Ly Chau. She removed the bowstring from one end, took a longer string of sinew, and tied it to each notch without bending the bow. "This is called a straight bow. It is for short arrows at short range. It gives great power and accuracy for enemies within your sight."

"There is always a way," Trưng Trắc repeated to herself. Then Ly Chau handed Trưng Trắc furs to lay out and sleep on. While the women gathered around the fire and told stories of the hunt, Trưng Trắc took out Thi Sách's book of aphorisms to read by firelight. The aphorisms in Thi Sách's book had none of the spirit of his lectures and lessons—there was an aloofness to them; the words did not speak with the same gentle tones as his voice. The words did not smile. Yet reading them stirred, somewhere beneath her awareness, the desire to live and endure. Thi Sách exuded faith in the future, in his writing and in his speech. It was his gift to the world, Trưng Trắc now understood. She let her heart stumble at the terrible thought that she could never be with him again.

On her second day among the People, Trưng Trắc was told that the tribe's home was near the peak of the mountain, and that she would not receive any help climbing it.

"Is this an impossible task that will teach me some kind of lesson, like bending the unbendable wood?" she said.

"No tricks, no lessons," said Ly Chau. "Just the one way home."

Trưng Trắc waited for some kind of equipment, or any sort of advice, but none was forthcoming. Ly Chau led the tribeswomen on a winding upward path, and Trưng Trắc followed.

It wasn't long before the path tapered off into nothing, and each woman had to find her own way by feel. The People found handholds and footholds where Trưng Trắc saw only sheer rock, and if she allowed herself to gawk in admiration, she would quickly fall far behind. She decided that she would follow them, at the risk of falling, because she was beyond the fear of death. Several of the women had found a vertical fault in the mountain that made climbing easy, and though it was a strain to reach that fault in the first place, she succeeded in leaping and gripping a jutting rock and using that momentum to swing into it. But as she climbed, Trưng Trắc endured two rather imminent realizations: one, that she would have to abandon her sandals if she wanted to survive the ascent; and two, that she wanted indeed to survive the ascent.

The second realization, once it dawned upon her, rendered her paralyzed. She felt her arms strain to their limit; one of her feet barely gripping the rock by the toes, and panic started to set in. When she had no fear of death, climbing was effortless; but as she contemplated now the senses shutting down and losing all awareness, even of pain, she could not proceed any farther up the mountain. But neither could she descend.

"Enough!" she cried out. "I need help!"

To her surprise, Ly Chau was there at her side, scaling down to her level with ease. "I told you: no help, and no lessons."

"You have to help me," begged Trưng Trắc. She thought of falling to her death, never to be seen by her family again—what a mystery her disappearance would become.

"Do you want to live?" said Ly Chau.

"Yes!" said Trưng Trắc. "Save me, and I will renew my commitment to life."

Ly Chau smiled. "Now take a step to your left, reach down, and lower yourself back into the crack's opening. From there, I will show you an easy path."

Following Ly Chau's instructions carefully, Trưng Trắc landed on a narrow but solid outcropping. From there, Ly Chau led her up a chimney to another plateau, and to safety. Her mind now caught up with her body's desperate struggle for preservation. She forswore the fool she had been.

"I thought you said *no help, no lessons*," said Trưng Trắc, giddy with relief.

"Would you rather live?" said Ly Chau. "Or would you rather I keep my word?"

"Who am I to question your methods?" Trưng Trắc was

moved to embrace her mountain guardian, but the tattooed woman was not the kind to comfort a stranger.

Chu Diên was not far by horseback, and Trưng Nhị did not tarry or round up servants to accompany her on the journey. She simply pushed Mực at a gallop, whispering to the mare as she rode, "Keep going! Keep it up! Good girl!" Mực's hoofs would be travelworn and even fractured by the exertion, but Trưng Nhị resolved to hold off her concern for the animal for later. A more imminent fear seized her—that her sister, despite being the elder, was innocent in the ways of the world and, now that she had run off, would fall into some predicament beyond salvation. Her sister, Trưng Nhị now understood, had actually saved her that night by the Red River. It was unfathomable that Trưng Trắc might die believing herself unloved by her family.

At the home of Thi Vũ, the first thing Trưng Nhị saw was Thi Sách, finishing the task of chopping wood. His brow slick with sweat, he dropped the ax and took up a small pile of wood to bring to the house.

It distressed her to see her revered tutor dressed in working clothes, his arms full of wood. The circumstances of his dismissal prevented him from employment elsewhere, and now he simply helped his elderly father with daily chores. When Thi Sách saw Trưng Nhị, he dropped the wood at his feet. She dismounted, approached the tutor, and grabbed his hand, just as she had once held it through the opening in the stone door at the Temple of Âu Cơ. "What is wrong?" Thi Sách asked. "Does your father know that you are here?"

Just then Thi Vũ, the elderly physician, stepped out of the door and walked up to his son and the strange woman who held him familiarly. "Is this Lady Trắc? I have not seen you since you were a little girl."

"No," said Thi Sách, gently detaching himself from Trưng Nhị. "This is Lady Nhị, her younger sister."

"The baby?" said Thi Vũ, making a cradling gesture. "I delivered both of you, you know."

"The lord is grateful to you," said Trưng Nhị. "In fact, I am sent here to lift your son's banishment and to offer the lord's apology for his mistreatment."

"That's how a father's love is," said Thi Vũ, nodding philosophically. "No man is good enough for his daughter."

Trưng Nhị smiled indulgently. "Lord Trưng would like to welcome back Thi Sách as an honored guest, not as a tutor, but as a suitor to Trưng Trắc."

Thi Vũ bowed low and made such a show of gratitude that Trưng Nhị flushed. Though obliged to honor the solemnity of the moment, she felt her impatience for finding Trưng Trắc tug upon her.

"Please," she said. "I would like us to depart right away for Mê Linh." She could not let the old physician, or anyone outside Cung Điện Mê Linh, know that Trưng Trắc had fled home, perhaps to seek her death. It would sow distrust in the lord's authority in Lạc Việt.

"But it is now sundown," said Thi Vũ. "Surely you can rest the night here first."

"At least let me pack my things and dress properly," said Thi Sách with a laugh.

"Of course," said Trưng Nhị, with forced patience. She paced the room as packing and dressing were extravagant luxuries of time.

And when he was ready, and they traveled the road home upon horseback at an amble, Trưng Nhị said in as flat a tone as she could muster, "Trắc is missing. She may have taken her own life."

Thi Sách looked at her with a look of confusion, which turned to horror.

"But if we find her," said Trưng Nhị, "and she is alive, then she is yours to marry. We have the lord's promise."

From atop the mountain, Trưng Trắc observed the proximity of the sky. The clouds appeared earthly, touchable. They lumbered like water buffalo across the firmament. Soon, the wind gusted, and they began to stampede while the sky darkened and crackled with lightning. It was the morning of her third and final day with the People. The moon still lingered in the sky despite the hour, and Trưng Trắc bled early this cycle. She had synced with the tribe, all of whom had been away from their menfolk, she learned, because they had been bleeding, too.

The storm reached the peak, and the day darkened; the moon and the sun disappeared. A heavy rain began, leaving rivers in the grooves of the mountain, cascading below. The tribeswomen found a shallow cave, where the ground was wet, and the wind blew the rain in, yet it was sheltered from the downpour. "You must make a fire," Ly Chau said to Trưng Trắc. "Otherwise you will take ill from the weather. We are accustomed to surviving the elements, but you are of the prairie folk."

"Make a fire?" said Trưng Trắc. "Even if I had the wood, and kindling, and chert, everything is wet. I thought we were close to your village. Can't we go there?"

"We return to the village tomorrow. And you will return to the valley," said Ly Chau.

"But up here there's nothing but barren rock," said Trưng Trắc.

"You must know where to look," said Ly Chau. "Now go."

So Trưng Trắc left the relative comfort of the cave to gather the materials for a fire. "This is crazy," she muttered. Luckily the rain let up enough for her to see at a distance, though what she saw did not reassure her. There was some wet grass and moss, but no trees, nor roots, not at this altitude. Would she really have to go back down to the last plateau? It seemed likely to harm her more than a little rain. Perhaps she could find the village on her own?

Left with nothing to go on but her roaming thoughts, Trưng Trắc reviewed her trials among the People. She had failed to hunt the black-winged kite, failed to bend the bon-bon wood, and failed to climb the mountainside on her own. This was likely to result in failure, too, so why not just return to the tribe and beg them to skip the trial and go straight to the lesson? Her thoughts suddenly focused as thunder clapped nearby like a drum. *The bow!* she thought. It may not bend, but it will surely burn. Getting rid of what *seemed* indispensable appeared to be the rule of the tribe. In her first task, after all, the bowstring was meant to be thrown away and a new one made of animal sinew. In her second task, she had to abandon her fear to scale the mountainside. *What else can I give up?* It was not long before Trưng Trắc took inventory and realized the only other thing she had brought with her was Thi Sách's book. Its vellum pages would have to serve as kindling.

Trưng Trắc rushed back to the shallow cave where the People crouched and huddled in the momentarily dry space. She shone with pride at her cleverness, but the women of the tribe did not return her smile. Trưng Trắc had done nothing yet, and carried nothing with her when she returned.

"I know where to look," said Trưng Trắc. "Right here." She proceeded to take the straight bow and prop it against a rock, then stomped on it so that it split into shards. She snapped several arrows in two and laid them among the shards. She took all the pieces and arranged them in a small pyramid, surrounding the wood with rocks to contain it. Then she took out Thi Sách's book of aphorisms, and offering a silent apology, she began to tear out the pages, placing each crumpled sheet underneath the apex where the wood met.

Trưng Trắc cut a groove with an arrowhead into a segment of the bow, then rubbed the shaft of one arrow into the groove. The storm had picked up again, and spat its rain into the cave so that the wood remained damp and resisted the friction. Yet Trưng Trắc kept constant pressure until finally, a thin trail of smoke arose, and in moments, a small fire caught.

She lit the paper underneath the wood pyramid, and watched as the orange glow played upon the walls.

"Now give me my lesson," said Trưng Trắc, weary in body but invigorated in mind. With a fire lit, now this damp cave felt like a home.

"Is the warmth of a fire not enough?" said Ly Chau. "To survive the day?"

"I've succeeded at your trial this time," said Trưng Trắc. "Is there really no lesson?" She realized, then, that she herself did not know what she was expecting. Surely a lesson was forthcoming, as that seemed to be the way of the Degar.

"What do you think?" said Ly Chau.

She could only think of Thi Sách, and how she was now sacrificing the only thing that remained of him. She imagined him as one of the heavy clouds passing over them. "I think that the fire is a woman's passion, and the rain is a man's passion," said Trưng Trắc, taking strength from this tribe of women, understanding that her love for Thi Sách was not the only thing that she lived for. When they were together, they might pass joy back and forth, one to another, but she was as worthy of life without him as she would be in a happy union with him. "And though they struggle against one another, one must not quench the other."

"You are wise beyond your years," said Ly Chau. "But observe how the passion of the rain and the passion of the fire do not *need* each other. They are opposites. Do not forget this."

But Trưng Trắc was distracted by another matter entirely. As she looked into the fire that she had created with such pain and effort, she saw the pages of her beloved tutor's book

catch the flames and spread, but she could still read one particular sentence before it was consumed: "If Heaven made it,
there must be some use for it." Something about the use of "it"
struck her as odd—the character had a doubleness to it that
made it look like an accidental pair. Yet Thi Sách was a scribe,
and he would have made no such error. And as soon as she
thought it, the revelation came in a flood that the book was
not a list of aphorisms after all, but a love letter to her, coded
into the language of philosophy so as to defy scrutiny by any
eyes other than hers. Every reference to "it" in the book meant
the love between them.

Trưng Trắc reached into the fire and drew out as many
pages as she could rescue.

"What are you doing?" asked Ly Chau, confused.

"This book!" cried Trưng Trắc, unfolding a single page
that she had rescued without any damage. She suddenly saw
how every reference to "the wise man" actually meant Trưng
Trắc, as the character for "man" had a stray blot of ink that
looked like a staff, and "the foolish man" meant Thi Sách
himself, for the characters looked surprisingly like his name.
She saw how the word "virtue" meant "desire" and the word
"kingdom" meant "marriage" and the word "love" remained
"love" but no longer signified the abstract love of one's fellow
man, but the immeasurable spiritual and bodily love between
two souls as inflamed with passion as theirs.

"The passion of the fire and the passion of the rain may not
need each other." Trưng Trắc's eyes filled with joyous tears.
"But what beauty when the smoke rises and mixes with the
clouds."

CHAPTER 15

The Conquest

S o what does it mean?" said Trưng Nhị. She had handed Thi Sách the scroll with Trưng Trắc's riddle on it, and they had been riding quietly ever since. To spare Mực's hooves, Trưng Nhị rode at a trot. She spoke again, to fill the silence: "'Roots' could mean a plant. It does not refer to the ancestors, as I had originally assumed. I already checked the temple of the Dragon Lord."

"Hm," said Thi Sách. He handed back the scroll. The road narrowed so that they had to ride single file, and Thi Sách trotted ahead.

"What?" said Trưng Nhị.

"It's just... You are descended from the Dragon Lord, of course, but you seem to forget that you are also descended from the Princess Âu Cơ," Thi Sách said.

"They checked the Temple of Âu Cơ," said Trưng Nhị. She had avoided going there herself, but other searchers had gone to investigate the possibility that her sister was hiding in her former prison. One day, perhaps, the Temple might become a fond and familiar structure, even a marker of the growth and change within her. But now it felt more like the maw of a tiger that threatened to swallow her and keep her churning in the darkness.

"The Temple is just a place to honor her," said Thi Sách. "The real Princess Âu Cơ lived—"

"In the mountains!" said Trưng Nhị. She tried to pick up the pace, but Thi Sách's mount stood in the way. "Out of my way!" she said.

"If I know your sister," said Thi Sách, "then there is more than one meaning to 'roots.' What plant grows upon the mountains?"

But Trưng Nhị, animated by the fear of losing her only sister to the earth, was already passing Thi Sách on the horse Mực, off toward the mountain path, the melody for "The Lament of Vũ Thơm" ringing in her head, thinking of the deadly *lá ngón*, the heartbreak grass.

Ly Anh, the newest tribeswoman of the People, was the one to lead Trưng Trắc back to the mountain path. The day was sublime, with a post-storm coolness and distant golden clouds on the horizon and the smell of pine upon the mountain. When Trưng Trắc returned to the plateau where she had first encountered the People, she felt a twinge of regret that she did not down the black-winged kite and become one of the tribe. A life consists of so many moments of chance. But she would return to Cung Điện Mê Linh, declare herself insubordinate to the lord's decree, and seek out Thi Sách to live out the rest of her days as a tutor's wife, where they would live a life of learning. Perhaps she would become a great philosopher.

Ly Anh bade her farewell and good luck, and suddenly Trưng Trắc was back on a familiar trail, taking the route home. Halfway down the mountain path, she saw two searchers approaching on horseback. When they came out of the shadow of the trees and into the dazzling sunlight, she recognized her sister, freed from her bondage, and her beloved tutor, in peasant's clothing. Her throat opened as though to cry out with joy, as though she were a thirsty traveler passing through a waterfall, and these two familiar faces were the cascade's source. For that moment, it felt as though all three of them would be forever safe, forever free.

The riders slowed to a trot within shouting distance of the lost sister. To Trưng Nhị, who was experienced at sizing up an enemy, Trưng Trắc appeared curiously stronger in herself than when she had seen her last. To Trưng Trắc, her sister appeared older and wiser.

"What took you so long?" Trưng Trắc said, and their laughter was like a revelation. To tease her sister, whom she feared would hate her forever, and the tutor, whom she believed to be exiled, was like a tired body falling into the furs of her own bed. They were finally together and would not be parted so easily again.

"Your riddle," said Thi Sách, "gave everyone a fright."

"Not you, though," said Trưng Trắc.

"Not me," Thi Sách agreed. "I knew. Even the emerald dove loves its grief song."

"What does that mean?" said Trưng Nhị, who felt as

though she were back at the palace, on the terrace, learning another lesson. Then she gave herself over to the exuberant relief of seeing Trưng Trắc again, of being granted another opportunity to prove that their love for one another was not so brittle as to be shattered by the Hán.

"That those who love," said Trưng Trắc, never feeling more fully herself than when she instantaneously solved the subtle speech of her tutor, "would rather suffer from love than to be numb to feeling."

Trưng Nhị and Thi Sách dismounted, and Trưng Trắc embraced them both. Noticing Mực's agitation and pained whinnies, Trưng Trắc said, "You rode her nearly to death. I'm sorry you had to search for me. But I am so happy to see that you are free, sister."

"You can repay her by returning with us now to Cung Điện Mê Linh," said Thi Sách. In his eyes there was an openness and intensity that had never been so overt, so direct. He beckoned to Trưng Trắc, for he never wanted to be parted from her again. The despair of almost losing her was too great for them both.

Trưng Trắc pulled back from their embrace and said, clear-eyed and full of resolve, "No. We must run away. The farther the better, so that the lord will never find us and the Hán will never interfere with us again."

"But there is no need," said Thi Sách. "The lord has consented for us to be married."

Trưng Trắc's smile was so full and genuine that a kiss from Thi Sách was the only natural response. Warmth spread from the sensation, so long denied her, of Thi Sách's lips upon her lips. Such a secret moment, announced in the presence of a witness such as her sister, knowing that the lord's heart had changed, made Trưng Trắc swell with hope. The future couldn't truly be so beautiful as this, could it?

"What about the Hán?" Trưng Trắc said.

"It is up to Kha now," said Trưng Nhị, "to convince the governor."

Trưng Trắc looked back the way she had come, from the mountain, then looked north, over the range of trees toward Hán territory. "Oh no," she said. "The fate of Cung Điện Mê Linh is in the clumsy hands of our guardsman?"

"We must put our faith in him," said Trưng Nhị. "He plays the bumbling fool, but he possesses an astrologer's wisdom."

Kha vented his frustrations upon the herald, Pham Vien, as they rode. They had been sent north to Cổ Loa, to act as the lord's emissary to the governor, and had been tasked with announcing that Lord Trưng had found a husband for Trưng Trắc, and that she would be married to Thi Sách. "Clothes were too confining," Kha said, causing itches that were difficult to scratch. He was forced to dress in clothes from head to foot. It was a part of his duty as a herald. His kapok cotton tunic and leathers trapped the heat, so that sweat collected in uncomfortable places and the fabric chafed the skin. That's why Kha never owned any clothes, he said, and had to use the clothing left behind by a dismissed guardsman. Having abstained from meat for more than a year, he could now fit into Bình's old apparel.

Kha and Pham Vien soon arrived in Cổ Loa, the citadel shaped like a snail's shell, and were greeted unceremoniously. They were unexpected, uninvited guests, and the guardsmen at the palace were reluctant to admit them at all. While they waited, Kha picked his nose vigorously and, after wiping the gunk on his tunic, stared at it a moment before exclaiming, "So *that's* why the aristocrats insist on wearing clothes!"

"Why are they making us wait outside?" said Pham Vien. "We could easily wait inside, couldn't we?"

"These guardsmen," said Kha. "I have to give them credit. They've got our number. By the time they let us inside, we'll be so relieved that we won't have the energy to ask them for anything."

"But we just have to deliver a message," said Pham Vien.

"Delivering a message is more than just saying the words," said Kha. "It's about interpreting the will of the writer and making the listener understand the thrust of its meaning. It's a subtle art."

"You just told me that the herald's job was too easy!" said Pham Vien.

"Experience is the greatest teacher," said Kha. "And now that I have been a herald these two days, I appreciate the difficulty of our charge."

"Pah! What experience? We haven't even delivered our message yet."

At last, the gates opened. They entered into the great citadel, bustling with activity and commerce, a settlement unto itself. The roofs were corrugated with thousands of ceramic tiles, and lights shone from dozens of red lanterns suspended from the eaves. Kha and Pham Vien looked up and around them at the vastness of Cổ Loa, while the guardsman stared straight forward, leading them on a walkway to a courtyard, where a thin man stood in elaborate yellow robes and a headdress.

"Greetings to the governor, from the Lord of Mê Linh," said Kha, putting a closed hand inside his other hand and bowing. He turned slightly to Pham Vien and winked, proud of his display of proper Hán etiquette.

"Please," said the man, "there is no need for honorifics. I am Li Hong, the governor's advisor. I will decide whether to relay your message to the governor."

"I'm confused," whispered Kha to Pham Vien. "Do I deliver the message now? Or do I convince him to allow me to deliver the message to the governor?"

Pham Vien shook his head and looked down at the floor.

Li Hong reached out to receive the scroll that Kha now clutched in his arms. But instead of handing it over, Kha began to recite its contents. "The Lord Trưng sends good tidings. The taxes collected by our treasury exceeded our projections by twelve percent, and the surplus has been added to the amount owed, which we now deliver unto your care."

Pham Vien stood up to retrieve the chest of copper coins that they had hauled on their packhorse. Kha motioned for him to sit, for he did not want to hand the money over to anyone but the governor himself.

"Furthermore, the lord's elder daughter, the Lady Trưng Trắc, is engaged to be married, in the traditional Hán arrangement, to the esteemed Thi Sách of Chu Diên, who will assume the title of Lord of Mê Linh upon the day that it is relinquished by Lord Trưng. The union shall be sealed at Cung Điện Mê Linh, in the presence of all the lords and ladies of Jiaozhi."

"It seems congratulations are in order?" said Li Hong. "But I have a question for you, messenger. How can the Lady Trắc be engaged to be married, when I have already received news that she has been promised to another suitor?"

"Hmmm," said Kha, looking around the room, and to Pham Vien, as though for a cue. But no answer was forthcoming. "Frankly, we had hoped to get ahead of that news, and to report to the governor about her imminent marriage to Thi Sách before you heard anything from Commander Ho. So if you could let us talk to the governor..."

"I'm afraid that won't be possible," said Li Hong. He spoke in the Hán language to his guardsmen, who proceeded to bring in the chest of copper coins from the packhorse, and he reached for the scroll, plucking it from Kha's reluctant grip.

"Please," said Kha. "If I could just look the governor in the eyes and deliver this news... Trưng Trắc and Thi Sách will marry, no matter the circumstance, and the governor must know that this is not an act of defiance."

"If I allow you to look into the governor's eyes," said Li Hong, "he may decide he doesn't like the way you are looking at him, and have your eyes removed."

"That is a risk I am willing to take," said Kha.

Li Hong raised an eyebrow. "What a noble-minded herald," he said.

Kha looked again at Pham Vien, but this time when

he winked—for the advisor had just acknowledge him as a herald—he could not help but imagine a life without eyes.

The lord and Thi Sách sat in ceremony in the Great Hall, as they had upon first meeting, two years before, when each man struggled with his own unmet expectations for the other. Back then, Thi Sách was not the wise elder that Lord Trưng had hoped for; neither was Lord Trưng the great leader and descendant of the Dragon Lord that Thi Sách had imagined. Now they knew how formidable the other could be, and were bound together by their mutual love for the lord's elder daughter.

"The Spring Festival is only days away," said the lord. "You must be eager to profess your love to Lady Trưng Trắc before Lạc Việt and the world. Despite our differences, I know what it means to be young and in love."

"In fact," said Thi Sách with quiet reserve, "Lady Trắc and I were hoping to wed *during* the Spring Festival."

Lord Trưng stifled a gasp. If he had harbored any hope that he could prolong the time before this news reached the ears of the vengeful Commander Ho, they were now dashed.

Lord Trưng let out a heavy sigh. "This may all come back to haunt us, but you have my blessing to wed on the day of the Spring Festival. You have impressed me with your courage in confronting me and by proceeding indifferently to the will of the Hán. Just remember that, as the future Lord of Mê Linh, you will be the one to reap the consequences."

Pham Vien waited outside the receiving room. Inside, Kha had been waiting all evening, and it was now past the hour when he would have slept under ordinary circumstances. It was his charge, after all, to toll the dawn bell every morning. He yawned, then shook his head from side to side to stay awake, smacking his cheeks now and then. To pass the time, he hummed to himself a drinking song. His stomach rumbled when he thought about drink, which led to visions of a hearty four-course meal.

Finally the governor—and there could be no doubt that this was the Governor Tô Định—walked with an unhurried pace into the room, followed by a burly guardsman carrying the chest with the copper coins. Kha put one fist into the other hand and bowed, as he was instructed. But the governor merely stood there. Meanwhile, the guardsman placed the chest on the floor, and opened it. He proceeded to count the copper coins.

"You have until the coins are counted," said the governor, "to explain why I should allow this audience."

"There is nothing controversial about the message that I am duty-bound to deliver," said Kha. "We have exceeded our tax projections by twelve percent, and the Lady Trắc is due to be married in the Confucian fashion to Thi Sách of Chu Diên, and he will inherit the role and responsibility of Lord of Mê Linh after such time as Lord Trưng abdicates."

The governor took his time responding, but while he

waited, he looked straight into the eyes of Kha. "When the Hán conquered Jiaozhi a hundred years ago," said the governor, "we bestowed titles upon a few leaders, to maintain order. Your lord is a lord only because the Hán say so."

"Nevertheless," said Kha, "the lord has followed your decrees faithfully and honorably."

"Then why are you here? Why send a guardsman rather than a herald?" said the governor. "Why worry, if Lord Trưng is doing as he has been instructed?"

Kha felt a tingle on his neck, and he apprehended that his answers to these questions would be consequential. The governor's spies had revealed him as a guardsman—what else did he know? He made the calculation that the governor knew nothing else, and was simply fishing for trouble, to satisfy a mere suspicion that something was awry with the guardsman's sudden visit. Yet now that he had met the governor, Kha understood that here was a man with grand designs who would not stop at levying taxes and conscripting soldiers. He needed to keep this enemy close, if the Trưng clan were to live and if Cung Điện Mê Linh were to endure.

"I volunteered for this task, in order to offer you my services," said Kha, with no hesitation nor hint of reservation. "I have served Cung Điện Mê Linh faithfully since I was a child, and though I am loyal, I am ambitious to work in the court of the governor."

The governor did not respond directly, but asked Kha to recount the coins as his first act of loyalty to his new employer.

When he was done tallying, he announced the total proudly.

"The yield from Mê Linh is troubling," said the governor.

"Troubling?" said Kha. "It is twelve percent greater than projected!"

"That is what troubles me," said the governor. "It means our expectations are too low. In the future, projections and yield should match perfectly. If you come in too low, then you might be skimming; if you come in too high, then that implies that we could have asked for more. The solution is simple: we will just raise taxes by twelve percent."

Thi Sách's chamber was empty, save for the furs pushed into the northeast corner. A high window shone in barely enough light from the full moon to read by. Thi Sách sat on the floor, his eyes scanning a scroll by Mencius, when there came a knock upon his door. "It's me," said Trưng Trắc in a whisper from the other side.

Standing, he strode to the door and listened for a moment through the wood, wondering if she came alone, and if she came as former student or future wife.

Upon opening the door, he had to step back from the vision of his betrothed in a silver sere gown, as though the moon had granted him the power to see through her clothes as some poor illusion. Thi Sách could not find his voice.

"I'm here," she finally said. He wordlessly stepped aside and welcomed her into the room. Trưng Trắc pulled Thi

Sách's body close to hers. They stood with nothing but straining cloth between them, and she gazed up at him pleadingly.

Trưng Trắc recalled the thousands of times they had brushed hands when exchanging a scroll, or how he had whispered some riddle so that she could feel his breath tickle her ear, or the time she lay her head against his chest once in the courtyard. These memories arrayed themselves like an audience to this moment.

Thi Sách placed his lips on Trưng Trắc's forehead and moved them, in a slow path of kisses, down to her neck. "What do you want?" he whispered, his lips pinching the lobe of her ear and his nose brushing aside a lock of hair. His face was half in shadow, and half in moonlight.

"I want," she said, covering his neck with her hands, and returning his hungry kisses. "I want, I want, I want." Trưng Trắc loosened his belt and pulled off his robes so that he stood before her unclothed, his long body pale in the moonlight. For two souls who often dwelled in the plane of the abstract, who delighted at confronting intellectual problems, the realness of bodies in contact and in motion struck each of them with a transcendent clarity.

"Let me light a lamp," said Trưng Trắc, her voice hoarse with yearning. "I need to look upon you, and I need you to look upon me," she said.

"There is a full moon tonight," he said.

Trưng Trắc pushed him backward toward the light of the window.

There was a trail of hair on his belly, pointing down toward a thicker crop of dark hair above his penis. He had a mole on his hip, and a few other glad imperfections that gave her the confidence to approach what was the first human body she had ever deemed beautiful.

"Sách-ơi," she said, closing her eyes from a transport of joy, and reopening them to gaze upon her beloved.

CHAPTER 16

The Vow

When the servant Pham Vien returned to Cung Điện Mê Linh, the palace was as festive as he was mournful. He alone bore the burden of this awful knowledge: Kha had sworn himself into service for the Hán, and that the taxation on the rice, salt, iron, and other goods of Mê Linh would be raised an onerous twelve percent. He ambled through the north gate tethered to a second horse with no rider. Passing in front of him, a young man and woman played chase, with a giggling that echoed through the passageway.

He wended his way to the Great Hall, only the second time that he would ever have the honor—the first being when he was a boy and his mother first found work as a servant in the palace. A servant ran to notify the lord of his return. Pham Vien bowed all the way to the floor and awaited the lord's arrival with trepidation. He knew that he was not to blame and would not be punished, but who knew what could happen if he somehow became associated with this terrible turn of events—whether it would trouble his life in small ways, such as being given the most unpleasant duties, like gutting fish, or scrubbing tubs, or heaven forbid, collecting taxes for the Hán.

When the lord marched into the Great Hall, he wore the red silk ceremonial garb with golden stitching—such as is worn at a Hán wedding—and a Việt headdress, and in that moment Pham Vien realized that he had interrupted the wedding day of Lady Trưng Trắc and Thi Sách. "My daughter will be married in moments," the lord said. "I hope this is important."

"Felicitations on your daughter's wedding day," said Pham Vien. "All of Lạc Việt and beyond smiles upon this union and we pray for generations of joy and a fruitful family."

"Let's get to the quick," said the lord distractedly.

"I am sorry to bring you such terrible news on your day of celebration, but it is my duty to report that the governor has demanded that every tax yield in the future match the estimate—no more, no less—and that the rate of taxation for the city of Mê Linh and its environs will henceforward be raised by twelve percent." Pham Vien's voice strained as he reported this news. The job of a herald was indeed harder than he had ever thought.

"We cannot..." said the lord, then trailed off, for there was no one to hear him.

"My lord, I am sorry!" said Pham Vien. "There was nothing to be done. The governor had made up his mind from the beginning, and there was no way to appeal his decree!"

"I should have gone myself," said the lord, remaining as stoic as possible in the face of this news, which caused him great grief and worry. "Wait...where is Kha?"

At the Spring Festival that year, there were a few young men, but it was otherwise a gathering of noble daughters and village women from Mê Linh. The poor young men had all been conscripted by the Hán to fight in distant wars, and the sons of lords and ladies had already gotten reports from their informants that Trưng Trắc was no longer seeking suitors. So the few men who had come were happily surrounded and swimming in a sea of women.

The Spring Festival was an event for coupling, and courtship, and comradeship. Yet the imminent wedding only increased the heat of the Việts' passions. By the time that Thi Sách started his procession around the palace walls to arrive at the south gate and invited Lady Trưng Trắc to join him on this fateful walk, the crowds swayed with intoxication. At the end of the day, the spirit of pleasure prevailed at the Spring Festival in Cung Điện Mê Linh, and any grudges were drowned. Then the procession completed its second circuit of the palace and arrived at the arch under the terrace, between the gardens and the Hall. Lady Trưng Trắc and Thi Sách exited the covered wagon, which protected the couple from inauspicious sights, such as a wilted flower, or a widow, and stood in their grand headdresses and long silk gowns, signifying the height and depth of their mutual love.

Bác Huy Vũ, the officiant in ceremonial garb, stood under the arch, but according to the Lạc Việt tradition, it was the bride and groom themselves who made speeches, rather than standing passively and repeating the vows of the authority, as was done in a traditional Hán wedding.

Thi Sách, more colorful than he had ever been and face painted in the style of the Dragon Lord mask, stepped forward to orate, and his experience in addressing an audience was evidenced by the confidence of his gestures and the sonority of his voice.

"The day of the Spring Festival is here, and on this auspicious hour, I am here to say that all love is true love. Now imagine that you come into a discovery of something even truer. It is as though you've reached the summit of your climb, and there is a higher mountain beyond it.

"It is only natural, upon making this discovery, that you would want to devote yourself to this feeling forever, and that is why I am here before you today, to surrender myself, not to the Hán institution of marriage, but to a woman who renders moot the most profound philosophy.

"I will risk prophecy and say what the future brings: a life of joy and conversation and study, a communion of souls that knows no interruption or end.

"So, Trắc-ơi, I promise you this: to always uplift you, to be steadfast and faithful, and to make your happiness my life's work." And this was precisely what love was to Thi Sách, a craft that could only be perfected over the span of a lifetime. In these words, simple as they were, he invested his loving soul.

The howls of appreciation were drowned out by the thrashing of the bronze drums, the typanum of which showed circles expanding around a radiating sun, and at the center of the sun, stylized frogs.

Now it came Trưng Trắc's turn to speak, and though she was not as comfortable with an audience as her husband-to-be, she projected louder than her usual faint treble. Her *áo dài* was embroidered with a colorful pattern of elephants, and her headdress shook with her movements.

"I am not an eloquent orator, nor am I a loquacious bride. But I come to refute the vows of the great master-scholar," said Trưng Trắc with an uncharacteristic mischief in her smile. She was indifferent to the attention of the village folk. It could have been she and Thi Sách alone for all it mattered. Their pattern would be, forever after, interwoven. "We are here to make promises, yes, but also to fulfill them. The promise I am fulfilling is this: that I will not bow nor bend to the will of the Hán, the lord, or anyone. Our marriage is not a surrender, for our love was never a struggle. And we are not trees grown from the same seedpod, but we are two branches on the same bough, forever together yet separate.

"Sách-ơi, I promise to protect you in times of adversity, to comfort you in times of grief, and to continue the quest for meaning along with you." For Trưng Trắc, the promise of their life together was like looking out on the foothills of an exciting journey, a climb in which every precipice offered a new vista. By his very presence, Thi Sách becalmed her on this journey and she wished only to return that same peace in kind.

The bronze drums roared to life again, and the pair clutched hands while stepping under the arch. Bác Huy Vũ declared them married, but the crowd had already risen and moved on to their rowdy celebrations. In their midst, Trưng Trắc and Thi Sách embraced, her cheek pressed against his chest, and though the joy pervaded and overwhelmed her, there were no tears, because Trưng Trắc's was the passion of fire.

The final stage of the ceremony, in Việt tradition, was a journey to the *dinah*, the communal temple in Mê Linh. Here sacrifices of meat and rice and fruit were made to the Guardian Spirit. It was the family of the betrothed that made this journey at night, while those at the festival subsided into sleep.

When the party reached the communal temple, the servants who had carried the offerings handed them to the bride and groom, who placed them on an altar and recited prayers in thanks and beseeched the Guardian Spirit for good fortune. Next, the family of the bride stepped up to the altar and made their offerings.

"Have you forgotten something? Or someone?" This came from a new voice at the entryway of the *dinah*. It was Commander Ho, accompanied by six Hán officials, armored and at attention. "I heard word of a disturbance, but I did not suspect I would stumble upon the wedding of my intended to another man, and the one who, I'm told, ought to be imprisoned in the Temple of Âu Cơ, as free as though she had never been captive at all." Here he turned toward Trưng Nhị with a leering eye. "Besides, you are only permitted to worship the gods of the Hán."

"You must be joking," said Thi Sách acidly. "You cannot compel the heart of a Việt to love your ridiculous bureaucracy of gods."

Commander Ho tightened his grip upon his poleax. "This low-born, insolent scholar is the snake that steals from my nest? *And* he offends the gods of my people? How do you intend to leave this temple alive?"

"Wait," said Lord Trưng, standing between Thi Sách and the commander. "You must give us time to accommodate ourselves to Hán laws. It takes more than a generation to change a people. How can we prove that we are still loyal to the Hán?"

Commander Ho nudged Lord Trưng out of his way, then lifted his poleax to Thi Sách's head. Thi Vũ gasped and clasped his hands together in prayer. Trưng Trắc threw herself to his side. She foresaw trouble, but she would not allow violence on her wedding day. As though possessed of the same thought, Lord Trưng bowed low and pled with the Hán interloper. But the commander simply gestured with his weapon at Thi Sách's hair. "You Việt men keep your hair too short. You must start to grow it out. You are all Hán, too, after all." Then he moved his weapon over to Trưng Trắc's *áo dài*, ruffling the bottom of the long ceremonial skirt. "And no more of these gowns. A Hán lady must wear breeches, and proper footwear. None of this barefoot nonsense, nor sandals of straw."

"Breeches and footwear and functionary gods," said Trưng Nhị. "*That* is nonsense."

"And what," said Commander Ho, turning his weapon

upon Trưng Nhị, "are we to do with this one, who was never properly punished for her insurrection?"

"I will die before I submit to punishment by a Hán," she said proudly.

"Don't be so sure I won't oblige you," said Commander Ho. Then he lowered his poleax. "Though all can be forgiven. If this wild one here submits herself to be my bride, then I can promise leniency. Otherwise, I can offer you neither protection nor mercy."

Trưng Trắc drew her sister close, whispered, "We are outnumbered, with no weapons, and among family and friends who cannot defend themselves. Let us not provoke this animal."

Trưng Nhị's instinct warred with her intellect, but this once, at the bidding of her sister whom she had learned to trust, ever since she was freed and the two were reunited, the mind won. "Believe me," she said, "when I say that you don't want me for a wife."

The commander sneered. "I promise you," he said, "that one day I will take Cung Điện Mê Linh as my own. One way or another."

A crowd had begun to gather outside the temple, and from this crowd a woman stepped forward. Over the commander's shoulder, Trưng Trắc could see that it was Mai the prostitute and spy. She boldly placed a hand on the commander's back, petting him through a layer of iron and leather. "Come with me tonight," she said familiarly. Evidently, the two were acquainted. "There will be many other occasions for proposals of marriage. But there is only one tonight. I will be your Việt bride this evening, and you can fashion my hair, my clothing, and my footwear in any way you please." Mai giggled enticingly, and the commander laughed in spite of himself. He had shown his strength, and made his demands. He would marry one of the Trưng sisters one day. He could do with some comfort in the meantime.

CHAPTER 17

The Letter

Now that Trưng Trắc and Thi Sách had tasted each other's bliss, they sequestered themselves in the dark womb of their chambers, acquainting themselves with the scents, tastes, and touches of the other. Trưng Trắc thought at first she might miss the coded language, the furtive touch, the riddles where their clandestine love had once resided, but she did not. She took great pleasure in the explosive joy of the unfettered body and mind. Thi Sách had begun to allow lamplight into the room, and the lovers would read aloud from scrolls relating ancient myth, philosophy, and tales of war, which were comfortingly remote. Other times, they would crouch across from each other naked, admiring and anticipating, or falling into laughter over nothing.

When they left the chamber, it looked like a two-headed creature emerging from a cave. They clung to each other, and covered their eyes from the too-bright sunlight of the daytime. They would stumble into the dining hall, eat from the same bowl, and retreat into their den. Trưng Trắc began to wonder how she had spent her girlhood playing war games and trying to thrash her sister with a stick. It seemed a great mystery and absurdity, all of a sudden, her life until that moment.

In the comfort of utter acceptance from her beloved, she could try on a thousand ways of being in the world without condemnation, without expectation that she would have to hew to a foolish consistency.

One childhood joy, song, returned to her. On the rare occasion when she was on her own, in the baths or in the meditation room, she found herself slipping into a cheerful melody. Even sad songs had a buoyancy now that she had never noticed. Once wistful, now jaunty, these beautiful tragedies seemed somehow necessary in order to offer to the world their sublimity.

Thi Sách met the lord in the Great Hall, and the lord was crouched over his scroll like a cat lapping at a puddle of water. The lord had been awake all night struggling to revise a letter, composed by Lady Man Thiện, that laid out in no uncertain terms that the Việts could no longer live under the oppressive rule of the Hán. The commander's challenge at the Communal Temple, the lady said, had forced their hand.

"Your lordship," said Thi Sách, and Lord Trưng turned to acknowledge him.

"Ah, Thi Sách," he said, breathing in loudly through his teeth. "I cannot figure out how to say what I want to say without provoking the ire of the governor. These pronouncements feel too forward, too much like demands."

"Let me see." Thi Sách crouched next to the lord, perusing the document. "I think I know what the problem is. These *feel like* demands because they *are* demands. The author must decide whether the purpose of the letter is to show our strength and resolve by facing head-on the oppressive policies of this regime, or whether its purpose is to show subservience and obedience to those policies."

"What do you think?" said the lord.

"The emperor's laws bow before the village customs." Thi Sách invoked an old Việt saying.

The lord and the lord-to-be looked upon the other's visage. What Lord Trưng saw upon Thi Sách's face was naive courage, born not out of self-knowledge, but out of ignorance in the ways of the world. What Thi Sách saw in the elder's face was naked fear. Neither man took comfort in the countenance he beheld.

"You shall write us a new letter," said the lord, "*humbly requesting* the end of the conscription of young Việt men in Hán wars; *modestly asking* for a moratorium on new taxes for rice, salt, iron, and other goods; and *begging* for the end of forced marriage for those aristocrats who do not elect it."

"Are you certain, Lord?" said Thi Sách. Such was the price, he thought, of a reputation for tact. Yet the deep implications of the letter troubled him and he wondered whether, in this case, tact was enough.

"I trust in your ability as a scholar and a scribe, to state our case perfectly," said Lord Trưng, relieved to be rid of this duty and throwing his faith in with the mysterious mental work of the scholar.

"Perhaps *you* would be more suited to write such a letter," said Thi Sách.

The lord squinched his brow but his eyes did not conceal the temperature of his mind, nor did his voice betray his roiling mood. "Let this be your first lesson in statecraft," said the lord.

So Thi Sách retreated to his chamber with a bronze stylus, a bowl of ink, and a blank vellum scroll. As he walked into the room, Trưng Trắc moved to embrace him, and he let himself be embraced. "What is the matter?" said Trưng Trắc.

"I have been given an impossible task: to defy the Hán without declaring an insurrection."

"Yet the Hán will take every act of defiance as a mortal threat," said Trưng Trắc. "Maybe Nhị could help, with her gift of eloquence?"

"Tact is not her greatest asset," said Thi Sách. "It's the irony of human nature that the most rarefied in thought and expression are also the fiercest in opposing rules and conventions. She and I both have the power to speak with subterfuge, but no inclination to do so."

"Well, you must try," said Trưng Trắc, placing her hand on her husband's shoulder reassuringly. She believed him capable of carrying any burden. "Here. I will light a lamp and bring you a drink." At that, Trưng Trắc left her husband to his solitary work.

By next morning, there were two letters: the original, full of demands, which proclaimed the lord and his people in defiance of Hán law; and a new draft, full of apologies, which announced their loyalty to the Hán above all else, and begged dispensations for the people of Lạc Việt. The letters represented two disparate destinies, and Thi Sách became conscious of wielding the future in his very hands. In his left hand, a revolution. In his right hand, a long but subservient life under an oppressive Hán government. Despite every concession he made to the lord, it was not in Thi Sách's nature to bend. A scholar had never before been given such an opportunity to test his beliefs and virtues. He was irresistibly drawn to freedom in the abstract. He wished to know how true freedom felt.

The sleepless son-in-law sought out the lord; read aloud the contents of the second letter, to the relief of its hearer; then passed along the first letter to the herald to be delivered to the governor.

It was Li Hong who first read the letter, and a wide rictus crept upon him when he reflected that the opportunity to have a firmer hand in the affairs of Jiaozhi had finally presented itself. He had counseled the governor that leaving regional lords in power over three generations had emboldened and strengthened the Việts. Now was their chance to impose their will upon the Lord of Mê Linh, to show the rest of Jiaozhi the consequences of noncompliance to Hán law.

"It is the beginning of an insurrection," Li Hong said to the governor, handing him the letter.

Tô Định received the letter reluctantly. Unfolding the

scroll, he observed the crisp lines and delicate curves of the calligraphy, the high diction, the use of poetic repetition. If he wasn't holding in his own hands what amounted to a declaration of war, the governor might have been impressed by the lord's eloquence. The governor was not as gleeful as his advisor about this act of rebellion. He preferred obedience, a Confucian order, clean and undisturbed. The Lord of Mê Linh had always struck Tô Định as controllable and yielding; it was regrettable, yet the governor would have no hesitation executing his punishment.

The governor reread the letter, shaking his head and letting his eyes take on a darker cast:

A just law must do more than compel obedience. A just law is not made just by the exercise of power, but through the eternal measure of its congruence with our humanity.

Because Hán law compels the Việt people to worship Hán gods, it is unjust. Because Hán law conscripts Việt men to fight in wars not of our choosing, it is unjust. Because Hán law forces marriage upon the aristocratic class of the Việts, it is unjust. Because Hán law imposes taxes upon our yields that cannot be sustained while supporting the survival of Việt workers, it is unjust.

In the name of the Dragon Lord, Lạc Long Quân, and his descendant Lord Trưng of Mê Linh, the people of Lạc Việt will no longer sacrifice our sons and fathers, our beliefs and traditions, and our goods to the

Hán. We do not seek war, but a peace on equal terms, where the laws that govern the Việt people are not only just but relevant. To achieve peace under the law, we declare a withdrawal of our people from the jurisdiction of the Hán.

The governor looked around the room. There stood Kha and Li Hong the advisor and a dozen courtiers. Outside in the hall, the herald Pham Vien awaited a message to return to Lord Trưng. The governor leaned over and whispered to Li Hong. Then he addressed the men of the court.

"Virtue in government," the governor said, "begins with unity. We are as a family. If there is discord in a marriage, it is the duty of the wife to yield to her husband. If she does not, then it is the duty of the husband to turn her heart. Gently if possible. If not, then with the utmost severity."

Li Hong closed his eyes to relish the adrenaline coursing through his body. Then, when he opened them again, he forced himself to look somber and grim. "I think, Governor, that you and I should continue this discussion in the map room."

The governor headed for the door, and Kha started to follow, but Li Hong stopped him. "I have a task for you," Li Hong said. "Do you wish to prove your loyalty to the Governor Tô Định?"

Kha bowed and said, "Anything at all, I will do to prove my worth to the governor."

"Something must be done with this herald. We must send him back with a clear message."

CHAPTER 18

The Siege

It was now Tran Ngai the guardsman's charge to toll the dawn bell. He was the only one in Cung Điện Mê Linh to awaken before the sun. Tran Ngai had been a hunter in his youth, and retained the habit of trusting his animal impulses, which at that moment spoke to him of an unseen danger. He feigned obliviousness, continuing his route to the belfry, picking out from the corners of his eye human figures in the shadows on the periphery. When the figures advanced upon him, he broke into a run, intent on sounding the alarm. He had time for a single shout before his lung was pierced by an arrow.

Meanwhile, Trưng Nhị slept through the first beam of light through her window.

Meanwhile, Trưng Trắc and Thi Sách dreamed dreams of their future life of blissful marriage, their future children and grandchildren.

Meanwhile, the lord dwelt in the most untroubled sleep he had ever known, and Lady Man Thiện was undisturbed by the sounds of keening and moaning that usually awakened her.

Meanwhile, the sky bled dawn.

It was Phùng Thị Chính, the cook, who heard the guards-man's shout, and shot awake, scrambling to the window of her longhouse to peer out into the thinly illuminated field. That morning, the trees had been infested with tent spiders that spread along the bower, leaving sacs of sere gray webbing on the boughs.

"What is it?" said her son, Võ Danh.

"Stay here," Phùng Thị Chính said, dressing herself. In her life she had never conceived of a danger greater than the reck-lessness of her sons. But her instinct reported a threat unlike any she'd felt before. Her first thought was that Răng the Tiger had somehow found his way onto the palace grounds.

"I'm coming with you," said Võ Danh, tying his trou-sers and pushing his hand through his unruly hair. "What's going on?"

Phùng Thị Chính gestured at her son to be quiet, and she returned to her perch by the window. This time she saw the Hán soldiers gliding close to the fogged earth, wielding swords, spears, and axes. She turned back to Võ Danh and whispered, "I must alert the lord and lady. You stay here and protect your brothers and sisters."

"No," said Võ Danh. "I will go. You must stay. What if the baby wakes? I cannot comfort him as you can."

Phùng Thị Chính winced at the thought of her son in the midst of this swarm of Hán soldiers, but she nodded and ges-tured for him to hurry.

So it was that the stealthy Võ Danh crossed the field in the red light of dawn after he believed the wave of Hán had safely passed in front of him, and just before he reached the palace, was struck in the neck by an arrow from a hidden soldier, falling to the edge of the stone floor and letting his dark arterial blood spill upon the recently swept hall. For the mother, it was as though the arrow had pierced her own eyes. This thought gave birth to the wish that she could have taken the arrow for him, that she could have died a moment before this—anything but being a helpless witness to the horror her life had suddenly become. Watching from her window her skinny son twisting in agony, Phùng Thị Chính let out an unrestrained scream.

The Hán burst into the longhouse and silently went to work subduing, tying up, and gagging Phùng Thị Chính and her children. She offered up a prayer to the Guardian Spirit that the youngest, who had known nothing of life but mother's milk and its own wails of need, would be spared. But the baby awoke and would not be consoled, and was stifled into an eternal silence.

The lord and his family had been bound, dragged into the Great Hall, and lined up in a row, still in their nightclothes, a grotesque parody of a reception for an honored guest.

Commander Ho, Wan Fu, and a coterie of Hán officials paraded into the room, congratulating each other on the perfect execution of their plan. Tromping back and forth in front of the Trưngs like a predator gloating over its kill, Commander Ho heaved with pride and laughed a joyless laugh.

"I told you," said Commander Ho to Wan Fu, "that the Việts are a naturally docile and subservient people. They have loud voices, but skinny throats."

Lord Trưng tucked his chin into his chest, instinctively protecting his neck while he beheld the patterned floor. He had never been the man of action that his family deserved. That was his violation and this was his chastening. But spare my daughters, he thought. Spare *them*.

"I have been tasked by the governor to 'turn your hearts' toward the right path," said the commander, strutting like the peacock who at that very hour crowed the coming of morning. Behind him, a dozen Hán officers including Wan Fu leaned against the walls, contemptuous and undisciplined. He moved uncomfortably close to the lord so that he could smell the porridge on the commander's breath. "Would you like to see what I've got for you?"

He placed three boxes in front of the lord, and revealed, one by one, the heads of Pham Vien the herald, Huỳnh Quyền the master of spies, and Tran Ngai the guardsman.

Trưng Trắc could not help but turn away, unwilling to confront her own helplessness in the face of these common thugs, while Trưng Nhị confronted the scene with trembling wide eyes, intent on fixing this moment into her memory, that she should never forget their faces. The lord began to weep. Lady Man Thiện said nothing and the expression of her face never changed. She lived her life anticipating the worst but never in fear, always in preparation. She only lamented that her hands were not free to slit the commander's throat.

"I ought to thank you," said commander Ho to the lord.

"That letter you wrote. Without it, I would never have received the order from the governor to lay siege to Cung Điện Mê Linh. Now, as promised, it is all mine: your palace, your lands, your daughters. Thanks to your pitiable pride."

"The letter? We have done all that you've asked and more. What possible insult can you have taken from my letter, begging the indulgence of your Governor?" said the lord, then his tone shifted to pleading. "It is all my doing. You have no need to involve my daughters. They are dutiful and obedient, and have nothing to do with the letter. If you need to execute someone, execute me."

"Don't be impatient," said Commander Ho. "You will be executed soon enough. But you are an insurrectionist. Maybe execution is insufficient. Should I let you live long enough to watch your daughters suffer?"

"Please!" said Lord Trưng. "I beg you as a man to a man, take my life, but leave my daughters alone." Still staring at the floor, he wept tears into his beard, his nose running mucus down to his mustache, unable to move or gesture or struggle beyond his plea of "Mercy! Mercy!"

Commander Ho moved over to face Trưng Trắc, who stared straight ahead without crying or pleading. He took her chin in his hand and moved her head to the side, as though judging the worth of a horse. She said nothing.

"Should I thrash this whore within an inch of her life," said Commander Ho, "who was promised to me once, then betrayed her family's word in order to wed a common peasant?"

He then reached over and gripped Trưng Nhị roughly by

the neck. "Or should I whip this wild horse until it bleeds, so that it learns how to behave in the presence of a Hán officer?"

Trưng Nhị spat in the commander's face. "If you are cowardly enough to keep me tied up like a hen, then you had better stay away from my beak, because any part of you that comes close is going to be bitten off."

Commander Ho wiped his face with a cloth. He maintained his composure but moved instinctively away from Trưng Nhị's range. "Which one shall it be?" he said.

The lord ceased his whimpering and let out an animal groan, straining uselessly against the ropes by which he was bound, falling facedown on the floor.

The commander turned to Lord Trưng. "Because I am merciful," he said, "I will kill you first, but know with your dying thought that everything you once owned is now mine."

"It was I," said Thi Sách defiantly, "who sent the letter. There is no need to kill the Lord of Mê Linh. Take my life instead."

"How interesting," said Commander Ho. "I was going to kill you anyway, but now you've made up my mind: first you will watch as your wife is beaten."

The commander gestured to Wan Fu, who stood above the lord, prone and heaving with unceasing sorrow, before letting down his ax upon his exposed neck, twice and thrice until the head came loose from its spine, a segment of bone now jutting out from the torso, spasming uselessly for a minute before subsiding into stillness. It was Trưng Nhị whose scream gave voice to their agony. Her howling did not end when she fell, breathless, to the cold floor. She thought of the lord holding her hand as she stepped from rock to rock across a narrow creek; she thought of sitting in his lap as he told her the stories of their ancestors.

Wan Fu kicked the lord's body over to its side, while Commander Ho placed the lord's head in a box as a prize for the governor. "Is he looking at me?" said the commander, and the soldiers laughed. "Let's shut his ugly eyes. A dying man weeping like a child. This is the descendant of your great Dragon Lord?" He held up the head for a moment, before dropping it into the box.

With blood still on his hands, he grabbed Trưng Trắc roughly. "What? No scorn or threats like your sister?" the commander said.

"I do not make threats," said Trưng Trắc in a voice so quiet that Commander Ho had to lean in to hear it. She had never known such bone-deep fear, and though she maintained her composure, inwardly she bucked and struggled and screamed out for blood. "I make promises. I promise you, if you take my husband from me, then there will be nowhere in Lạc Việt that you can hide from my vengeance."

Commander Ho smirked and turned to his lieutenant Wan Fu. "As soon as I'm done teaching her," he said, "take off the arrogant head of that peasant tutor."

"You win!" said Thi Sách in utter desperation and defeat. "We understand now how far the Hán will go to keep the Việts under their yoke. I will let my hair grow long. I will worship your gods. I will fight in your wars. But please, have mercy, have humanity, and let Lady Trắc go."

Commander Ho took up a whip and struck the bound

Trưng Trắc like a stray dog, repeatedly, unmercifully, until her skin flayed.

Strange noises, like those of an ox whose horns had been caught in a yoke, issued from Trưng Trắc's dry and cracked lips. She retched, green and bilious strands of filth flowing onto her tunic. Yet the commander continued his assault.

Trưng Trắc was beyond sense. She could no longer even smell her dead father. She felt nothing from this attack but the sober awareness that, once it was over, she would lose everything—her home, and her husband, who meant all to her. Nothing she could do or say would prolong his life one minute. She had never known this depth of helplessness—not when her sister ran away to take vengeance on Wan Fu—and how she wished now that Trưng Nhị had succeeded!—not when her father decreed that she must marry a Hán—if he had only known the sort of man to whom he had promised her!—not even when she had thought that Thi Sách had given up on her and left her for good. It was unlike even the most powerful memento mori, when the certainty of death comes upon us like a cloud obscuring the sun. Life became weighted with numinous meaning, and that meaning, to last the rest of her days, was revenge. As soon as that revelation occurred, she opened her eyes, ceased the howling and grinding of her teeth, and resolved to look upon the naked truth. Commander Ho finished, leaving her skin marked with many fresh and open wounds. An owl hooted mournfully in the distance. Thi Sách laughed maniacally and shouted, "Do you hear that? Do you, Commander Ho? Listen to the owl! It calls in the daytime. He announces your death!" Just then Wan Fu's ax came down upon his shoulder, sending his body toppling to the ground. Then the ax came down and landed true, leaving his head to roll upon the patterned floor.

"Skinny throats," said Commander Ho with a laugh. Then he gestured to his soldiers to follow him. He ordered Wan Fu to "Take these whores and cast them out of Cung Điện Mê Linh. Let them fend for themselves for once, rather than living fat on the land."

"We aren't going to kill the women?" Wan Fu said, whose memory of Trưng Nhị's assault was fresh in his mind.

"One hundred women are not worth a single testicle," Commander Ho said, invoking the Hán proverb, then strode out of the room with his head high as though he possessed a modicum of honor.

Passing by Bác Huy Vũ's fly-bitten corpse on the bridge, the four women walked solemnly, Trưng Trắc held in their arms and carried between them, ruined into silence by woe upon woe. Trưng Trắc, Trưng Nhị, Lady Man Thiện, and Phùng Thị Chính shuffled with feet bound by rope.

"It ends here," said Wan Fu, prodding them forth with his spear. They reached the east gate and, beyond it, wilderness. "If you try and return to Cung Điện Mê Linh, we will not be so merciful."

Trưng Trắc looked back at Wan Fu. Too injured to protest or argue, she simply stared at him and memorized his face, with the mole on his forehead like a third eye, knowing with grim certainty that she would one day look upon this face again.

"What are you looking at?" Wan Fu raised his spear threateningly at Trưng Trắc.

"The future," Trưng Trắc said cryptically as the women continued on, arms and feet still bound, toward Mê Linh. Clinging to the shoulders of her sister and mother, Trưng Trắc grasped wildly for something to anchor her heart. Every handhold slipped away. The space under her feet crumbled to dust. The only edifice she found was in the unknown. The past was irredeemable; but the future in its obscurity provided the promise of vengeance.

Once arrived in Mê Linh, the fallen aristocrats were greeted by no one. The Hán had conducted their siege of the palace surreptitiously, and the normalcy of town life as it carried on all around them that morning had a surreality that left them numb; with her feet feeling as heavy as lead, Lady Man Thiện beckoned for her daughters to follow, and they all veered onto a residential street, where they found themselves at the door of a modest thatch-roofed home.

It was Mai the prostitute who took them in, untied the ropes that bound them, and fed them rice porridge. Although there were no baths in her home, she fetched water from the well, heated the water on an oil stove, and sponged down her guests, all of whom still wore the evidence of the attack and the journey, with splatters of mud and blood and salty streaks of mucus and tears. Trưng Trắc flinched at Mai's touch, then simply stared into the empty space in front of her while she cleansed away anything that could be washed away. Mai was poor in many things, but rich in apparel, and she clothed these noblewomen with *áo dài* from her extensive wardrobe.

Lady Man Thiện said to Phùng Thị Chính: "Your sons and daughters..." But she could not finish the thought. Her grief was too great. If she tried to speak, she would only choke on syllables that fell apart and became nonsense. The fresh memory of the lord, reduced to nothing by the Hán barbarians, bore into her foreskull from moment to horrible moment, emerging unbidden as she struggled to speak.

"The only one to blame," said Phùng Thị Chính stiffly, "is the Hán."

"The Hán invaders will pay with their lives," said Trưng Nhị with iron resolution.

"But when?" said Phùng Thị Chính.

Trưng Trắc stood up and walked to Mai's wardrobe. She took out a ceremonial white headdress. "I am a widow," she said, "and I will wear this mourning turban for one day. Then, tomorrow, I am no longer a widow. I am an instrument of revenge. Thi Sách may be but a ghost and a memory, but I am now his tooth and claw in this world." She placed the headdress on her brow, and turned to face these Việt women who suffered as she suffered, for their husbands and brothers and sons. If she had been another woman, she would have rocked back and forth, keening and wailing. But Trưng Trắc's grief was a lump of wet sand, numb and heavy and as plain as earth, and it buried her; meanwhile her mind circled around the problem of the Hán like a riddle she had proven too simpleminded to solve.

Phùng Thị Chính collapsed suddenly. She thrashed against the floor, risking injury to her own fragile body. She was then held down like an anchor by the arms of Trưng Nhị.

"I am sorry," said Mai, witness to a suffering beyond her understanding. "If only I had achieved greater intimacy with the enemy, I might have known his evil plan and averted it."

"No one has failed," said Trưng Trắc, fighting injury and weakness to stand heavy on her own. "All that has befallen us is exactly how it had to be. To think otherwise is to live helplessly in the past. But the future, no matter how long it takes, will be ours."

Lady Man Thiện stood, then Trưng Nhị, then Mai. Lady Man Thiện's resolve had always been the family's spinal column. They needed her now, and so she stood up in the name of the future, her daughters. Trưng Nhị, with all of the youth and abandon that animated her spirit, was now released from all pretense of courtesy toward the Hán. She stood for the sake of her father. For Mai's whole life, she had had to live with the abuse of the Hán officers, who now abused even the Việt aristocrats. She stood for her people. Phùng Thị Chính, with the ghosts of her children surrounding her, stood with them.

CHAPTER 19

Day of Mourning

Trưng Trắc had grown accustomed to solitude whenever she sought it, which, with her contemplative nature, was often. Now when she needed solitude the most, it was elusive. She foresaw that the Việts needed leadership, and that the leader must project strength, and could not be seen to suffer as she suffered. Vowing never to be seen in public wearing the mourning headdress, she was confined to Mai's home, but the house was so small, it barely accommodated the living members of the Trưng clan. So she found a spot near a wall to sit and contemplate the fresh horror that the Hán had made of her life.

In light of the facts, such as they were, she felt that grief was a wasteful indulgence, so Trưng Trắc's busy intellect forced her instead into a cycle of forecasting, testing out manifold paths of action, and landing every time upon an inevitable future devoid of the one she loved. These calculations obeyed the logic of time, but did not cohere in sense. Physical realities such as these could be repeated forever in speech and unravel into abstraction, to arise in the heart as an object less real than the myths or the stars.

Whenever Trưng Trắc opened her eyes and beheld the immediate world, she would be thrust back into the awareness that the women around her had lost as much, or more, in the past twenty-four hours. Trưng Nhị, too, had lost a father; Lady Man Thiện had lost her husband of twenty-nine years; and Phùng Thị Chính had lost five children—a fact so unbearable that to quantify that loss would be an evil in itself. All Trưng Trắc knew was that degrees of sorrow existed and that, though she herself had never known a reef of pain as high as that upon which she now sat, there were even higher precipices. *My suffering will never be as great as some*, she told herself, *and I have no business suffering when justice is yet to be done.*

Grief was strange and tentacled, winding itself around the room and gripping it, tightening around and strangling any other feeling that entered. Other feelings entered anyway— hope, levity, anger, consolation—but each was strangled in its turn, leaving merely the room, defined by the utter absence of their beloveds.

If I were stronger, thought Trưng Trắc, *I would simply shed my tears, and purge this feeling as it arises. But it is my weakness that I cannot appear weak, even in the presence of my mother and my sister. No one but I can bear witness to the depth of this pain.*

Trưng Nhị had not broken her vigil of tears for their fallen father since yesterday—and her freely flowing sorrow was enviable in its naked honesty. Phùng Thị Chính wore the countenance of shock, coupled with the steely resolve to enact revenge upon the Hán, which could be read upon the visage of their mother, Lady Man Thiện. The lady's only movement was the heaving of her breath, which she coaxed out of her with great effort like a stubborn calf. It seemed to Trưng Trắc as though her mother could simply vanish. She had been married to the lord since she was young and had scarcely known a life without him.

Mai took on the role of caretaker by default. She prepared tea and rice porridge, tidied the room, prepared furs for her guests to sleep on, and offered the physical comforts of a backrub or a hug if it was welcome. Phùng Thị Chính, a practitioner of the domestic arts herself, found it difficult to watch another woman cook and clean for her, but whenever she stood to help, Mai insisted that she rest and heal.

The night passed sleeplessly, day and night blending into a single dimness, during which hours Trưng Trắc pled silently with the Guardian Spirit to turn her nightmare into a mere illusion, and restore with the daylight her father and husband. Then, leaving off the possibility of bending the past to her will, she vowed to the Guardian Spirit that she would bring justice to Lạc Việt, to remove the Hán and free the Việt people from their oppression. Freedom was what Thi Sách had always wanted for her, after all.

By the first golden light of morning—the first day of sun since the dawn of the massacre—grief was a numb appendage, forever to remain, but functional and inseparable. Like a limb extending from her heart outward, it held the banner of revenge forever in her view.

Trưng Trắc put aside the mourning turban and wore a silk gown of a metallic sheen. Trưng Nhị wore an *áo dài* as green as the jungle. Once more in the public square—where Duy was beheaded—the Trưng Sisters now addressed a small crowd of women, nearly all peasants, for the tradeswomen and laborers had heard the news from Cung Điện Mê Linh and feared the retribution of the Hán.

"We have the numbers, and we have the will!" cried Trưng Trắc. The sparse group of villagers did not deter her. She knew that a revolution was built one body at a time and she intended to start here and now. "The Hán are a vine that clings to our branches and covers our bark, depriving us of the water we need to survive; then, if that were not enough, they make us believe that we *need* their protection in order to live! What have the Hán done for us that we could not do better for ourselves? They take everything from us, and they distort our lives and try to make Confucians of us. I made a vow in the mountains never to bend against my nature, even if it should mean my death. I am ready to reclaim my independence as a Việt, or to die in the name of freedom!"

Here was a speech of fire—the fiercest and truest words Trưng Trắc had ever spoken—yet it moved no one. The peasant women nodded agreeably, but shared none of the urgency or the volume of this call to war.

One wide-waisted woman on her way elsewhere, carrying a pack of goods, stopped briefly, listening to this appeal, then shouted back, "How can we think of going to war with the Hán, when all of our men are already off dying in Hán wars? You might be ready for war, your ladyship, but what about the rest of us, who aren't born and raised to fight? The women of Mê Linh can't even go out at night because of Răng the Tiger. How do you expect us to take up arms against the Hán?"

"What is your name?" said Trưng Trắc.

"Bát Nàn," she said.

"Well, Bát Nàn," said Trưng Trắc. "I need women like you, with loud voices and thoughtful minds, to help me lead our army."

"What army?" said Bát Nàn.

"You will see," said Trưng Trắc. "By the will of the Guardian Spirit, our Việt armies will rise, and the Hán will walk no more on our lands."

"I have to finish my delivery before nightfall," said Bát Nàn. "Otherwise, I might be mistaken for a revolutionary and get in trouble with the Hán!"

The sisters returned to Mai's home, their efforts unrewarded, yet their wills undeterred. They came barefoot, in defiance of the Hán custom, in their iridescent gowns.

"You should speak to the people," said Trưng Trắc to Trưng Nhị. "I am not an orator."

"You spoke with great power," said Trưng Nhị. "I could do no better. Yet the people are fearful."

"It's true. And there is reason to fear," said Mai, then abruptly stood as an idea struck her like a drum. "Listen:

Răng the Tiger has terrorized Mê Linh for more than ten years. You may be safe behind the walls of the palace, but for the women here in the village, he is their nightly curse."

"So what?" said Trưng Nhị. "Don't they realize that the Hán are a greater threat than a mere tiger?"

"They don't see Răng as a mere tiger. He is, to them, an avenging spirit," said Mai.

"Then our vengeance must be greater," said Trưng Trắc. "We will catch and kill the tiger, and when we do, we will have proven that we are more formidable than the fiercest enemy. So, too, with the Hán. They tire, they thirst, they piss, and God willing, they will bleed."

"It is not so easy," said Trưng Nhị, "to kill a tiger in his own jungle."

"Then we will draw him out of the jungle, and bring him to us," said Trưng Trắc.

"How can we?" said Trưng Nhị. "The tiger's only hunger is for a woman full with child."

Phùng Thị Chính stood up then. She parted her robe and placed her hands on her belly, which, now that it was bared, showed a convex curve that stretched her skin to the point where a dark line had begun to form down to the navel. "If you wish to catch the big fish," she said, "you need to have the proper bait."

CHAPTER 20

The Hunt

Crowded under the thatched roof of Mai's house, the Trưng Sisters listened to the patter of rain and the howling of wind, a cadence which brought up divergent associations: for Trưng Nhị, it recalled her innocence, when she and Phan Minh first explored each other's bodies in the gardener's longhouse during that monsoon long ago; as for Trưng Trắc, she remembered trying to light a fire in the wind and the rain atop the mountain, among the People. The passion of rain and the passion of fire. Both, Trưng Trắc reflected, have the power to cleanse, and the monsoon had a cathartic effect on the earth. As the day mourned, it took upon itself the heavy emotion that would otherwise have been overwhelming, if laid upon the shoulders of one woman.

As long as the rain persisted, they would not be able to lure Răng the Tiger by scent. So the women waited and plotted. With Phùng Thị Chính's help, they could surely bring the beast to them, but what happened then? How to capture or kill a natural hunter whose whole body was an instrument of death: his claws like spears, his teeth like knives, his weight like a boulder, and his speed like an arrow? Lady Man Thiện suggested a pit, in which Răng would be vulnerable to attack by long pikes from above; but how could they protect Phùng Thị Chính if she was trapped in a pit with Răng? The problem with bait was that it entailed a great risk, and the sisters were unwilling to give up even one more loyal Việt. Mai suggested adorning Phùng Thị Chính in layers of armor and hide, and dabbing the outer layer with poison, so that Răng would be frustrated, then sickened, by the effort of devouring her. Yet the threat to her and her baby's life was too great.

It was Trưng Trắc who strategized that the best way to keep Phùng Thị Chính safe was to elevate her above the tiger's range—to build a platform for her to perch upon atop the wooden pillar in the town square—and to cast a fishing net over the animal when he came near, weighted on its corners with heavy bronze bells, the sounds of which would further confuse the beast. Then, when it was caught up in the net, and confounded by the chaos, the other four women would emerge from surrounding buildings with spears and put an end to his legendary reign in the town of Mê Linh.

"Let's take a walk," said Lady Man Thiện to her daughters the next morning, after the rain had subsided. Looking upon the sisters now, Lady Man Thiện saw not only the fierce and intelligent women she had raised, but all that the lord had done by preparing them to fight for their people. She had watched her daughters grow from infants to young women, and with waves of pride, she understood that now they had become who they were meant to be. They may have never fought in a real war before, but they stood there with ready spirits as full of the will to victory as she had ever seen. She gained strength from her daughters and she knew a way to give them strength back. The three women left the neighborhood, passing the public square, the marketplace, and the game dens, until they were on the outskirts of Mê Linh.

"Where are we going?" said Trưng Nhị. For days they had been occupied with building the platform to hold Phùng Thị Chính and she saw this detour as a curious delay.

Lady Man Thiện did not answer. They were leaving town now, on the road toward Cung Điện Mê Linh. Even in their uncertainty, even in their grief, the sisters drew strength from the serene and authoritative presence of their mother. Whatever mischief or madness she was up to, she could not be said to lack a plan.

"We can't possibly be going home," said Trưng Trắc, slowing down a pace.

"No," said Lady Man Thiện, and she led them into the wood, until the women found themselves at an abandoned shed. The sisters stood outside the shed, bold but uncertain passengers on their mother's journey. Lady Man Thiện took a deep and deliberate breath. If she had been a different woman, then she would have spoken through a blur of tears; but as the Lady of Mê Linh, the only detectable emotion was the coarseness in her voice. "You know that this day is a day that your father has feared since you were young. He prepared you for this. You have become the women we always knew you would become: fierce and powerful and intelligent. Lord Trưng also prepared for this in other ways. Buried underneath the shed is another armory, one where we keep enough weapons to arm a village. We must use these to kill the tiger that is terrorizing the people, and then we must equip the people to defend Việt land."

"Does anyone else know of this armory?" said Trưng Nhị.

"No one knows of it but me and your father," said Lady Man Thiện, bowing her head at the invocation of the lord. Her heart heaved but she refused to let down the tears that threatened to break. "And now only the three of us."

Taking up farming tools, the women dug underneath the dirt floor of the shed. As they shoveled, the flat of their iron blades crossed, clinking and glinting until it revealed the buried cache. They dropped their tools, looking with marvel upon each other's dirtied faces and upon the mountain of weapons below. Then three pairs of hands pushed away the last of the soil. Underneath rested rows upon rows of swords, spears, shields, drums, and armor. For the purposes of hunting the hunter, they each took up long spears. To inspire and move the public, they each grabbed a bronze drum, ridged with patterns of sea birds and frogs. Beneath the crisscross of wood and bronze, a hint of gold gleamed. "What is that?" said Trưng Trắc.

"That," said Lady Man Thiện, "is for later."

Returning to Mai's home, the women, these survivors of the attack on Cung Điện Mê Linh, brought with them shields and spears from wars past, which they laid upon the floor. Wordlessly, a look passed from woman to woman. It acknowledged this new family that their shared grief had created. Did the Hán officers realize that by throwing these women into the fire, they were forging the very iron that would become their undoing? For the four survivors, that truth was as fixed as the stars and as inevitable as the sunrise.

Trưng Trắc's will propelled them all forward. In the many moments when each one was tempted to sink into the swamp of her own helplessness, Trưng Trắc was always there to channel their grief into rage, their pain into action. Phùng Thị Chính stared numbly at her hands, which had been useless to prevent the deaths of her children; Trưng Trắc put a spear into her hands and corrected her stance. When Trưng Nhị spoke mournfully of their dead father, Trưng Trắc invoked the names of their enemies: Commander Ho, Wan Fu, Governor Tô Định.

Lady Man Thiện had always seen her daughters this way: Trưng Trắc was obedient, prudent, and skilled; Trưng Nhị was passionate, foolhardy, and strong. But where had this reservoir of will within her elder daughter come from? It was as though destiny had chosen her, possessed her, and acted through her. Lady Man Thiện thought that she could die peacefully if she could live out her own fate as destiny's enabler.

Once built, the platform, braced against the wooden pole in the public square, was barely large enough to accommodate Phùng Thị Chính. She strapped herself in with rope, in case of a heavy wind, and wielded the fishing net, heavy with bronze bells on its corners so that handling it tired her, yet she would not protest or complain. Trưng Trắc, Trưng Nhị, Lady Man Thiện, and Mai waited within the surrounding buildings, listening for the chime of the bells. Everyone held to their position with great expectancy. Yet Phùng Thị Chính found that, several times throughout the day, she needed to descend the pole to relieve the muscles of her arms and legs, or her bladder. These intervals, however brief, were full of peril, for she had to leave the fishing net atop the platform, so she had no way to alert the other women should Răng the Tiger arrive at an inopportune moment, leaving her utterly alone and defenseless at such times.

It was upon just such an occasion that Răng finally appeared at the public square, his shaggy, filthy, and wild fur touched at the ends by the last rays of sun before it set on the horizon. He let his tongue in and out of his maw thirstily. Phùng Thị Chính stood immobilized, something in Răng's calm cat eyes hypnotizing her. When he began to trot forward, she awoke from his spell and realized the danger she was in, that if she did not act, she and the child she carried would become its next victims. Triangulating the distance between herself, the tiger, and the platform, she calculated that she just might be able to reach and climb the pole before Răng sprang. His speed, as he advanced and then leapt, was uncanny. She could not outrun him, and she was forced to use the wooden pillar as a barrier between her and the tiger. Her lateral movements were just swift enough to remain on the other side of the pole from her hunter. She cried out as loud as she could, but her voice vanished in the wind. If only the tiger would roar, then the women would hear and be alerted to his presence. Yet Răng was silent, patiently pacing, stalking her around the wooden pillar, behind which she barely maintained cover.

At that moment Trưng Nhị opened the door of her building and witnessed the chase: the pregnant woman desperately stepping from side to side behind a pillar, while the tiger prowled around her in slow, shrinking circles. A single false step would mean her death. Why wasn't she standing atop the platform? Why hadn't she thrown the fishing net and sounded the bells? The scene made little sense to her, yet Trưng Nhị had to act. She fought against every instinct for survival, against her ancestral fears, and charged out of the house with her long spear in hand.

With a primal scream, Trưng Nhị raced toward the tiger. The vision of his massive frame lurching over her helpless body years before shot up into her consciousness—she could not shake the memory of his face filling her sight, his jaw gaping as though to swallow her whole, and she could not help contemplating the ease with which the beast could have made a meal of her. Somehow she had thought that the single-minded Răng, with his appetite for the unborn, would stay fixed upon Phùng Thị Chính, and make an easy target for her attack from the side, yet he recognized her for the threat she presented, and Răng saw her hesitate, the fear enter as air enters the lungs, and charged Trưng Nhị with an echoing roar.

However fearsome the sight of the tiger stalking her, Trưng Nhị knew this sound was exactly what they needed—

Trưng Trắc, Lady Man Thiện, and Mai heard the roar and came out from their hidden places, and Phùng Thị Chính scaled the pole up to the platform, wielding the fishing net but finding the tiger now outside the range of her cast—and Trưng Nhị allowed the fear to leave her on the exhale, and calmly appraised her situation. She set the blunt end of the spear against the earth beneath her, so that if Răng leapt at her, the spear would puncture him with the exact force of his weight. But that beast—whether spirit or animal—knew exactly where to stop so that he did not fall upon the braced spear. He began to circle Trưng Nhị, and she knew that if she uprooted the spear from its notch in the earth, she lacked the strength to impale the tiger without the help of gravity.

When she followed the tiger's eyes, Trưng Nhị saw a calculated intelligence that knew how to outmaneuver a single spearpoint. She realized then what she had to do, and before she could second-guess her plan, she kicked down at her long spear, breaking it into two, then grabbed both pieces and used them to draw patterns in front of the tiger so that his eyes could not track, causing him to back away in confusion. Trưng Nhị maneuvered herself so that she stood in front of Phùng Thị Chính, then she backed up until she couldn't any farther, her body pressed against the pole. Răng approached her with the slow confidence of a creature that knows the inevitability of the hunt. Yet just as he roared and made his leap at the cornered prey, Phùng Thị Chính let the weighted fishing net go, which landed around the tiger and prevented his teeth from sinking into Trưng Nhị's flesh. Yet his body crushed her against the pillar, and Trưng Nhị collapsed. Trưng Trắc, Lady

Man Thiện, and Mai all rushed the struggling beast, and surrounding him, they drove their long spears into his hide until they clicked against bone. It was an injured Trưng Nhị who carefully located the beast's heart and mercifully quickened his death with a forceful thrust of her broken spear into his chest, and the thrashing body of Răng became forever still.

The next morning, the town of Mê Linh awoke to find the skinned carcass of a tiger in the public square. Word of Răng's death sang out from every corner of the town, from the market to the stables to the smithies, from the temples to the game dens to the houses of influence. Everyone celebrated the death of the beast who had menaced the village for more than a decade. It was never clearer than in the daylight of the public square that this rotting thing of muscle and tendon and bone was no supernatural terror, but an animal of earthly dimensions.

Trưng Nhị reveled in the victory, recounting the hunt with the closest thing any of them had felt to glee since her father's death. "Can you believe that we killed the beast with our own strength? We are mightier than anyone knows," she said. But for Trưng Trắc, the death of Răng was a mere necessity, and she spoke only of their imminent revenge. Phùng Thị Chính felt nothing, not even relief, yet allowed herself to be swept up in Trưng Trắc's plan.

In Mai's home, the tiger skin was stretched out on the floor, after having soaked in water overnight. Phùng Thị Chính dehaired the skin with alcohol, then oiled the hide until it became fibrous and dry enough to take ink. For it was Trưng Trắc's will that the skin of the tiger should be used as a parchment upon which to write their declaration of war. As a Việt woman, she could think of nothing more serious to the Hán than a proclamation of war written on tiger skin.

As they learned of Răng's death, the men and women of the village erupted in cheers and sought out those responsible for the deed. They found Mai's home and gathered around in celebration. For a decade, the women of Mê Linh had been afraid for their lives every day, afraid of their own fertility and the stories of the tiger who would consume them like a hungry spirit. But no more.

The Trưng Sisters' cadre of loyalists had grown ever since Răng's killing. The first woman to join them in their cause was Bát Nàn the fisherwoman. Bát Nàn was lean and dark-skinned from working out-of-doors all her life. Mai's house was too small to accommodate more bodies, so an assembly of women had begun to form outside her modest home. Inside the building, Trưng Trắc spoke to the three women whom she had dubbed her first generalcy—Lady Man Thiện, Phùng Thị Chính, and Mai—and to the new women whom she referred to as her second generalcy—including Bát Nàn.

Trưng Trắc said that it was not enough to kill Răng, it was not enough to proclaim the people free, and it was not even enough to bring the war to the governor's door. The people needed a sense of purpose that rallied them toward a common goal. Now, as the women huddled close in the tight quarters of Mai's simple home, Trưng Trắc hovered over the parchment, hoping somehow to employ the tiger skin toward this cause.

"As a symbol, the skin of this beast, whom the townsfolk once believed to be unkillable, has great meaning," Trưng Trắc said. "The words we use to declare our purpose as a people must be equally simple and powerful." She looked at Trưng Nhị.

Trưng Nhị responded, "We do not need eloquence, such as I or your late husband could have fashioned from a gemstone. This task calls for the rough ore of a common tongue."

Trưng Trắc stood poised with the bronze stylus, prepared to write the words that would launch a revolution. Nothing came to her immediately, and she closed her eyes momentarily to shut out the crowd of women gathered there. How can mere words animate a people to rise up and demand their freedoms? She needed to speak the truth, but the truth was vast and impossible to distill.

"Come," Phùng Thị Chính said to her fellow generals, "let us go and spread the word, that Lady Trắc and Lady Nhị are to make an address to the people tonight, after the day's work is over." The women all took their leave and dispersed into the village, accompanied by the crowd that waited out-of-doors.

"Thank goodness they are gone," said Trưng Nhị in solidarity with her sister. "Writing is not the labor of the many."

"Why is it so hard," said Trưng Trắc, "to say something so plain?"

"If Thi Sách were here, he would have answered your question with some proverb," said Trưng Nhị. She ventured to speak the name of the dead, though her sister permitted no expression of grief to temper her will for vengeance. Trưng Nhị worried that her sister might lash out at the merest reference to her husband, but now that it was just the two of them, Trưng Trắc looked up with tender eyes.

"According to Confucius," said Trưng Trắc, smiling at the memory of her husband's esoteric manner of speech, "clarity and sincerity are the preoccupations of the superior man."

"I've had about enough of the 'superior man,'" said Trưng Nhị with finality. "It is the common woman to whom we must make our appeal."

"And what kind of appeal would the common woman understand?" said Trưng Trắc.

Trưng Nhị squatted on the floor and encouraged Trưng Trắc to put down the stylus and squat with her in consultation. "Do you remember when you were younger, what kinds of things would you spend your time writing?" she said, placing a hand on her sister's arm.

"Do you mean my jokes?" said Trưng Trắc incredulously.

"No!" said Trưng Nhị, waving her hand. For a moment, it was as though they were girls again arguing in the halls of Cung Điện Mê Linh. "In the morning, after our bouts, you would always go directly to the writing room. What did you write, first thing in the morning?"

"Plans," said Trưng Trắc, "and lists." The mundanity of this memory, of when they were so carefree that they would spend days agonizing over the day's tasks, nearly broke her iron façade.

Trưng Nhị snapped and held her sister by the shoulders.

"*That* is something every woman understands. We are doers. It is the plain language of a list that has the power to motivate the people of Lạc Việt."

"A task list for revolution," Trưng Trắc said to herself, nodding with resolve and looking over Trưng Nhị's shoulder at the blank parchment that was once Răng's hide. She had been afraid in the tiger's presence, yet the fear that she would fail her people was greater still. Would her words ever be enough? The spirits of Lord Trưng and Thi Sách were restless for revenge, and to appease them was a duty unlike any Trưng Trắc had ever known.

Trưng Nhị left Trưng Trắc to compose the declaration in solitude. Out of habit, Trưng Nhị rolled her sleeve to the shoulder and looked at her tiger tattoo as she walked through Mê Linh. Though it was drawn as a symbol to commemorate her close encounter with death, it now represented many more things: her own ferocity of spirit, their successful conquest over the tiger Răng, the unjust death of her dear father. She marveled at the way that the tattoo accrued meaning as her life went on, like a living thing.

She returned to the public square as if drawn by an invisible force to the site of the hunt. The carcass of the tiger had since been removed, but the platform still stood as a monument to their task. Trưng Nhị found Lady Man Thiện standing there, drawn by the same impulse.

Standing side by side, without the indomitable Trưng Trắc to steer them, mother and daughter shared a still silence.

There was no monument to the lord, yet he remained every-where they went, as long as they stood together. Trưng Nhị wanted to reach out for her mother's hand, but to do so would have been to acknowledge the hole in their family, which would have overwhelmed them both and left them unfit for the task ahead.

"Have you made contact with your spies?" said Trưng Nhị.

"Yes," said Lady Man Thiện. "The Hán know nothing, and care nothing, about our activities in Mê Linh."

"Our men are dead," said Trưng Nhị, "so as far as these Confucians are concerned, the threat has passed."

"After tonight," Lady Man Thiện said, "it will not be long before the Hán are aware of our intentions. We need this speech to be decisive, and we need to strike tomorrow, before dawn, just as the Hán surprised us in our sleep."

"No," said Trưng Nhị. "Our movement is larger than us; it touches everyone in Lạc Việt. It is important that this, our first battle on the journey to independence, be a fair fight."

"That would mean the deaths of many women of Mê Linh," said Lady Man Thiện solemnly.

"This is a struggle that will be talked about for as long as there are Việts," said Trưng Nhị. "We must think larger than Mê Linh. After we take back our palace, we are going to raise an army from Chu Diên, Hợp Phố, Cửu Chân, Nhật Nam, and the rest of Lạc Việt, and we are going to march on Cổ Loa to remove the governor from power. To do so, we need not only to win, but to inspire."

"That is why I worry," said Lady Man Thiện. "Your sister knows how to win a war, but does she know how to inspire an army? We only have one skin of the tiger—why are you not the one writing our declaration of war?"

"You surprise me, Mother," said Trưng Nhị. "Was not Trưng Trắc always your best student?"

"What the Việts need now is not a great student, but a great leader," said Lady Man Thiện.

Trưng Nhị had always believed that her mother regarded obedience and leadership as one and the same. Where she demanded obedience, she spoke of duty. They were entwined. Yet now her mother appealed to her to lead because of her stubborn will. The temptation within Trưng Nhị to answer the appeal was powerful. Yet she herself saw a new Trưng Trắc, one whose will for vengeance was even stronger than her own. "Then we must trust," said Trưng Nhị, turning her thoughts to her sister's newfound determination, "that Trắc has what it takes to lead."

With that simple deflection, Trưng Nhị realized that she committed herself utterly to her sister's plan. She had been mistaken all those years when she judged Trưng Trắc harshly for her dull discipline. The people needed ferocity *and* discipline to prevail, she understood now. It was Trưng Trắc's discipline that buoyed them all.

"We will find out soon enough," said Lady Man Thiện.

When Trưng Trắc finally emerged from her sequestering, she held the tiger skin parchment in one hand, and the bronze stylus in the other, still wet with ink. Her heart thumped with the names of her lost loved ones and the names of the men responsible for the deaths. Their cadence matched her steps as she strode from the building. Her face grim with purpose. Her movements like a natural, inevitable force. The women who had crowded outside Mai's home dared not ask whether she had written the declaration. There was no need. Trưng Trắc moved past the gathering, walking purposefully through Mê Linh, taking the route that passed the market and the mills, the shops and the game dens, and upon every corner she amassed more of a crowd as each man and woman ceased their work to find out what the clamor was about, so that when she reached the public square, it was as though the whole town had assembled, minus all the young men who had been conscripted into war by the Hán.

Trưng Nhị and the women of the first generalcy were waiting at the public square. They wore their martial expressions like shields, yet underneath, each of them felt Trưng Trắc's gaze pierce through them. Each of them felt the momentousness of her march to the square. They hoisted Trưng Trắc up onto the platform, and there she stood above a sea of nón lá, surveying the population of Mê Linh like a commander preparing to lead an army. It was the golden hour of sunset, and the same light that fell upon Răng as he drew his last breath now landed upon Trưng Trắc's brow.

She raised the tiger skin parchment, and the din of the crowd subsided into an expectant hush. Standing in front of a sea of men and women, Trưng Trắc vowed she would not succumb to fear now. She had endured the worst and lived through it; what was the judgment of so many strangers to her? The air was still, and her voice carried in the windless day as though even the Guardian Spirit were listening in and had halted the weather to accommodate her words.

"By now you know that we have caught and killed the tiger who has terrorized Mê Linh for more than ten years. You have seen his dead body, you've smelled his reek, and now you know that the hunter can be hunted.

"Now that Răng is dead, you might think yourselves safe. But as long as the Hán maintain their hold upon our lands, upon our people, upon our goods, then you are not free. And just like the tiger, the Hán are an earthly threat, quite mortal and vulnerable to the thrust of a spear like every other breathing thing.

"Not long ago I took a vow to love and protect my husband, who is now dead at the hands of the enemy. But the vow I make today is even more sacred and solemn, because it enfolds the future of our people. Unlike my husband's, your blood still flows red in your veins, and I would not ask you to risk and sacrifice yourselves for anything short of victory.

"From this moment on, I will be called Trưng Vương, She-King of the Việts. And it is my holy burden to deliver Việt lands back into the hands of the Lạc Việts."

At this point Trưng Trắc—now Trưng Vương—unfurled the parchment, still tinted with the color of the tiger's skin, and read aloud the declaration. The words she had written expressed, for once, what her heart had cried out for so long: that if destiny had dealt this fate to her, then she would wrestle with destiny and make it submit to her will. Kingship was only a means to an end—the sword she would wield against the Hán enemy.

I swear first to avenge the nation;
second, to restore our lineage to its former position;
third, to have revenge for my husband;
fourth, to carry through to the end our common task.

A roar of approval came from the throng. Lady Man Thiện stood with the same iron expression she had worn ever since the death of her husband, but tears flowed down her cheeks as she reflected that her daughter had, with this declaration, made herself the foremost target of the Hán and its armies.

For Trưng Nhị, hearing the Hán condemned aloud was thrilling. Watching her sister's fiery oratory animate the crowd filled her with warmth. She herself was seized by the moment's grand inspiration. Trưng Nhị led the chant by crying out in a tiger's voice, "Take back Việt lands into Việt hands!"

PART THREE

SHE-KING OF THE VIỆTS

Lạc Việt Year 2738–2739
(40–41 CE)

CHAPTER 21

Homecoming

Trưng Vương led a silent march through the jungle, her eyes unblinking, her thoughts resolute. Feelings buried so deep within that they were no longer mental. Her stomach churned with the sorrow she hid from the surface. Grief had been buried so deep within her that it had become inextricable, like quartz in stone. Moments when she was alone, she could take it out and observe it at a distance, knowing that on the day the Hán were overthrown, she would bring it close again. The women wove between the trees and over the brambles and brush. For many, this would be their first sojourn into Cung Điện Mê Linh; others knew the palace only through the pleasures of the Spring Festival, and for them the gardens conjured memories of childhood play, adolescence courtships, and first loves.

But their first stop was a humble shed in a clearing in the woods. General Man Thiện went into the shed alone, down through the hole in the floor, and surfaced carrying a suit of golden armor carved with the elegantly plumed Mê Linh bird and a belt trimmed with golden bells. It seemed to glow in the dawn light, its reflections nearly blinding. This was, General Man Thiện declared, for Trưng Vương to wear into battle. There would be no mourning clothes.

General Man Thiện announced that each of the women gathered would enter the shed as a villager and emerge as a soldier. One by one, the women entered and then left equipped with bronze shields, straw sandals, and iron-tipped spears. The ritual of initiation was essential to banish the fear that stirred within every heart.

Trưng Nhị was the first to notice the giant gray body of an elephant coming down the horse trail, ludicrously outsized for its path, and another elephant behind it even larger than the first. Leading them was the Animal Acquirer, Keeper of the Names, and gardener's son, Minh the Dog, his smile broad and self-satisfied, showing off his dimples and the smile lines around his eyes. Trưng Nhị momentarily forgot the suffering and pain now deeply lodged in her heart and was brought back to that familiar sense of innocence and glee that radiated from Phan Minh's eyes when they caught her own.

"Trưng Nhị!" Phan Minh shouted. "I have been to the lowlands, and I have brought you a prize from afar."

"An elephant!" Trưng Nhị rushed ahead and stood in front of the massive beast. She stroked its trunk and looked into its sad goliath eyes. "What a beauty, and so well behaved," she said, turning to Phan Minh with a gaze of childlike abandon. Phan Minh returned the lingering look, fixing this brief joyous moment in his memory.

"She is called Xam," said Phan Minh, "and the other one

is Khong Lo. One for each of you." Then turning somber, he added, "I have heard of the tragedy that has befallen Cung Điện Mê Linh, and about the death of Lord Trưng. But now that you are coming to reclaim your homeland, the Hán will surely fall away in fear when you ride into the grounds on the back of such behemoths as these."

"And you are coming with us," said Trưng Nhị, turning back toward General Man Thiện to confirm it. General Man Thiện nodded.

"But I am banished," said Phan Minh.

"No longer," said Trưng Vương. "Just as the descendants of Lạc Long Quân will be restored to their rightful place, so will you be restored to your former position—an even greater one, as Elephant Handler in our army."

"Even Trắc is bestowing titles upon me now," joked Phan Minh.

Trưng Nhị said, "She is now known as Trưng Vương, She-King of the Việts."

Phan Minh nodded. "A worthy title," he said, then bowed before her. "My king."

"Please stand," said Trưng Vương, then looking up at the wrinkled gray wall of skin beside her, added, "and show us how to ride these things."

The stone borders of Cung Điện Mê Linh, which once seemed high, could have been stepped over or knocked down by the hulking elephants that led the charge. But this had once been their home, and would soon be their home again, and they did not wish to leave it a ruin. Instead, Trưng Vương, from atop the elephant Khong Lo, announced to the Hán who had gathered on the inside of the gate, bracing for an attack, that the King of the Việts had arrived, and would take back her ancestral home from the Hán. They could go willingly, or by force, but it was ordained by destiny that the Hán would soon cease to rule in Việt lands.

They responded with an attack as Trưng Vương had expected, and sent a volley of arrows over the wall, splintering against the bronze shields held in front of the villagers of Mê Linh.

But as a strategist, Trưng Vương had another play in mind. While the spectacle of their approach, riding on elephants and adorned with golden armor, bedecked with bells and the colorful banners of war, had distracted the Hán soldiers and drew them to the east gate, three separate platoons of Việt soldiers were at that moment entering from the unprotected north, west, and south gates, led by General Man Thiện, Mai, and Phùng Thị Chính.

Commander Ho, in the hours of the morning, had to accommodate several facts that contradicted his most deeply held lifelong notions: that here were thousands of women taking up arms in war against their superiors; that, after being shamed and thrown into mourning by the deaths of her father and husband, Trưng Trắc had returned to the home where her greatest grief had been endured; that her skill at war was such that he found himself and his soldiers overwhelmed before the battle had even begun. Yet Commander Ho still believed that even the strongest-willed enemy, when enacting her revenge, would want to shove the spear into her tormentor's heart herself. So as long as Trưng Trắc and Trưng Nhị stood on the other side of the gate, atop their gray monsters, he believed himself safe from harm. Up to the moment that he saw a Việt soldier up close—a woman named Nàng Quế, with hair cut in a neat line directly above her eyebrows—and felt the spear tip puncture his belly, twist inside him, and empty his viscera onto the dirt path, he believed himself safe from harm, and his last thought was utter surprise at how wrong he had been in his every calculation, and how unpredictable life had become.

Ever since Trưng Trắc had assumed the title "She-King of the Việts," she had become aware of how much distance there was between her and the people, and how that distance needed to be maintained in order to cultivate the myth of Trưng Vương. Whereas Trưng Nhị had been a mingler in the village, Trưng Trắc had always been the reclusive palace dweller, unknown to the mass of the people, and therefore infinite in her potential in the minds of the men and women of Mê Linh.

She crouched with Trưng Nhị by her side in the Great Hall, surrounded by her six generals. Each woman brought some concern to the king that she needed to address. Mai had witnessed great heroism and leadership on the part of two women in particular—Nàng Quế and Nàng Quỳnh—whom she believed worthy of elevating to the third generalcy. Phùng

Thị Chính insisted upon rituals for the dead. Bát Nàn asked for provisions for the living. The newest general requested that physicians should be sought from Chu Diên to treat the injured. Another suggested that the officers' tower should be cleared of any remaining Hán, and its resources and supplies used to equip the Việt soldiers.

It was General Man Thiện, however, who voiced the question underlying each woman's statement: "What is our next move, Trưng Vương?"

Trưng Vương knew that she could not say yes to everything. If you tried to ride four horses in four different directions, you wound up quartered. Although her impulse was to consent to all of their requests, she could not, in her first act as king, appease all; otherwise the impression that she was an indecisive, yielding leader would harden.

"First, we will clear Mê Linh of any remaining Hán, then we will make sure the healthy are kept healthy with supplies and provisions. The injured will remain here in Cung Điện Mê Linh, and I will seek the physician Thi Vũ to tend to them," said Trưng Vương. "But we will not hold rituals for the dead. We do not have the luxury to be idle in grief while the enemy amasses its armies."

"What of the heroes in the Battle of Cung Điện Mê Linh?" said Mai. "Nàng Quỳnh and Nàng Quê? Will they be made into generals?"

"If they are true leaders, as you say," said Trưng Vương, "then they can raise armies of their own, at which time we can call them generals."

General Man Thiện spoke again. "But what *next*, Trưng Vương?"

For a moment it seemed to Trưng Vương that she was being asked to pronounce a prophecy. But the astrologer was gone; her tutor and husband was gone; her father was gone. Days ago, it seemed unthinkable that the future could rest upon her slender shoulders. Now it was her duty to bend destiny. "We have a small, untrained army, and we must march on Cổ Loa within three months, lest we wait too long and the governor strike us first, in our homes," said Trưng Vương. "Trưng Nhị will train our soldiers in the martial arts, and I will personally go to Chu Diên, Nhật Nam, and Hợp Phố to raise an army from throughout all of Lạc Việt. General Man Thiện: you will oversee things here in Cung Điện Mê Linh. Phùng Thị Chính will be responsible for the defense of the village of Mê Linh. Meanwhile every other general is responsible for bringing in a thousand more soldiers from the surrounding countryside." She then divided Mai and the three women of the second generalcy into north, south, east, and west, and gave them enough copper from the treasury to fund their endeavors.

When Trưng Nhị and Trưng Vương were next alone, in the baths surrounded by stones, encroaching ferns, and the open moist air of night, the king confided her doubts. She believed that she had done the right thing, and had approached the situation thoughtfully, but in a way everything she had just declared felt random and capricious. How was she to know whether the governor would not strike back within three months? What effect would it have upon the people not to be given the opportunity to grieve their dead? And how did she expect to persuade the Lords and Ladies of Hợp Phố, Nhật Nam, and Chu Diên to rise up against the Hán, when her sister was the one who could convince the chickens to fly?

"It's true," said Trưng Nhị. "The future is unknown. But if it will take us three months to raise and train an army, it will surely take the governor longer, as practiced as he is in underestimating our people. And as far as your persuasive powers are concerned, convincing the people of Lạc Việt to rise up against the Hán should be more like convincing a rooster to crow. There isn't a Việt in the land who doesn't want to throw off the yoke of the Hán."

"What about the rituals for the dead?" said Trưng Vương.

Trưng Nhị turned her back to her sister, then stood up from the water and donned a robe. She paused before speaking, as she understood this would become their first kingly dispute. "I agree with Phùng Thị Chính. It might be in *your* nature to bury your own feelings alongside the bodies of the dead, Trưng Vương. But it is not in the rest of us to do so. If we deny our grief, how will we know what we are fighting for?"

"But we have no time for it," said Trưng Vương, standing, too, and dressing. "We can grieve properly when the Việt people once again reign in Lạc Việt. Until then, there is too much to do. How can the indulgence of sorrows coexist with the hard duty of vengeance?" Trưng Vương could not hide her frustration at what appeared to her the most obvious choice among choices: you either mourn or wage war; you cannot do both. To Trưng Nhị, to deny the spirits of the dead was to invite an even greater tragedy. Although in their opposition to the Hán, their feet were firmly planted together, their emotional truths stood wide apart.

"Trưng Vương," said Trưng Nhị in an entreating tone. She abandoned the persuasive rhetoric and simply spoke as sister to sister. "We grieve differently. You throw yourself into action, but I need to linger on the memory of our father, to keep him in the center of my mind, so that I know with every thrust of my spear that I'm fighting for his legacy, and his memory."

"Our father lived a complicated life," said Trưng Vương, "and we honor him by taking revenge on the men who brought about his death." Trưng Vương's true feelings were that, as the filial one, her grief was greater than her sister's.

"And what about the children of Phùng Thị Chính? Can you make an exception for a mother who lost five children?" Trưng Nhị looked intently at Trưng Vương but saw blankness.

"Their souls will not be at peace until the men responsible are killed." Even Trưng Vương knew how hollow her words sounded. Yet she could not acknowledge the conflict within her. It risked weakness. "That is enough consultation for now."

Trưng Nhị and Trưng Vương retired to their separate chambers, where Trưng Nhị was greeted by Phan Minh and the dog Xấu—a family unto their own and a refuge from all the talk of war—and where Trưng Vương was met by no one.

Next day, Trưng Vương prepared for her departure. She brought with her Nàng Quỳnh and Nàng Quế, sisters and heroes of the Battle of Cung Điện Mê Linh, as well as a handful of servants and bodyguards, all of whom were women. She bade farewell to each of the four generals whose mission was to recruit soldiers from the surrounding countryside, then visited with the injured and promised them retribution for the fallen. Lastly, she said good-bye to General Man Thiện.

"The men are wondering," said General Man Thiện, "how they can help in this war. It is not only the women who have been living under the oppression of the Hán."

"Even when war rages, village life continues," said Trưng Vương. "We need fishermen and farmers and merchants and metal workers and carpenters and tanners and cooks and servants. Nothing at all could be done without *their* noble work."

"But surely *some* men," said General Man Thiện, "are fit for our purposes. War is in their nature."

"That is precisely why I do not want them fighting alongside us," said Trưng Vương. She reflected on the fear and stupidity of Commander Ho and Wan Fu. They so disgusted her that she wanted no one so thoughtless and cowardly—not just in her army, but in her presence. "Ours is not a war for bloodthirsty men to tear each other apart. Ours is a war to restore justice. No woman would fight for the sake of the fight, and every one of us is in it for the cause."

"I think you are being too generous to the character of women," said General Man Thiện. "Your noble sentiments are not universally shared. Women *and* men have the capacity for great evil, and for great heroism."

"I am much more acquainted with the evil that men do," said Trưng Vương.

"Please, just think about allowing the men to fight," said General Man Thiện. "Our leadership will remain a generalcy of women, but if a man wishes to be infantry, cavalry, or archer, it would be folly to deny him."

"Yet all the healthy young men are already fighting for the Hán," said Trưng Vương. "No. This war will be our war, and it will be won by women who wish to be free."

Trưng Vương mounted her horse and led her retinue east to Chu Diên, to beseech the Lord Đặng Vũ to give the women of his village an opportunity to avenge their stolen men.

CHAPTER 22

Journey to Chu Diên

Trưng Vương had never taken the road to Chu Diên. Famous for its temples and scriptoria, Chu Diên was known for both its institutions of learning and the piety of its people. It was also home to her husband's family, whom she had met at the wedding, and to whom she was now burdened with reporting the news of his death. Though she found herself hesitating every step closer to the village of Chu Diên, she could not let the task weigh on her spirit, for hers was a mission of hope: to bring a message of imminent victory over the Hán oppressors. Congruent with Trưng Vương's goal to elevate her name to the status of myth—the better to inspire the common people—she sent ahead a herald to announce the king's arrival in Chu Diên.

When Trưng Vương rode into Chu Diên that evening, she was met by a crowd of curious citizens. She appeared, not adorned in golden armor or riding on an elephant, as she had when marching into battle, but with a broad *nón lá* shading her eyes and a blue-and-green *áo dài* that draped all the way to her feet. She balanced her common apparel with a noble bearing, at once accessible and aloof, of-the-people and of-greatness, suggesting to all the possibility that such nobility and greatness resided in everyone. Such was the promise of a king, that she could inspire the people through the embodiment of their innermost yearnings for strength and pride.

Her meeting with the Lord of Chu Diên, Đặng Vũ, was a mere formality. Her presence in Chu Diên was, by itself, enough to galvanize an army. For their intellectual traditions had been assailed by the Hán for years, and all this time they awaited a leader with the audacity to defy their oppressors. When Trưng Vương passed by the temple grounds, the nuns bowed, and the monks clasped their hands together in prayer to the Guardian Spirit.

Trưng Vương did not ride straight to the palace, but made a stop at the home of Thi Vũ. The physician who had cared for her as a child—who had delivered her into this world—had not joined the crowds to greet her, but lay listless and leaden in his bed. For he had heard the news of his son's death, and he chose to disbelieve it, until the moment that it was announced that the daughter of Lord Trưng, called She-King of the Việts, was to arrive in Chu Diên without her husband.

A young woman, his caretaker, greeted Trưng Vương at the door, welcoming the king as she entered the physician's home without her retinue. As soon as they were alone, Trưng Vương let her visage of stone fall away, and threw herself on the floor at the feet of her father-in-law and begged his forgiveness for failing to safeguard his son. The tears that she had refused to shed, even on her day of mourning, rose to her eyes now that she was in the presence of one who shared her unceasing love for the fallen Thi Sách. The grief was no longer her own; it belonged to both of them, and the memory of her words to Thi Sách at their wedding repeated over and over in her mind: "I promise to protect you." Her chest heaved, yet she wept silently so that the caretaker and her retinue would not hear her just outside the door.

"I do not blame you," said Thi Vũ softly, "but I cannot comfort you. My wound is too new to tend to the injuries of others."

Trưng Vương rose to a crouch and rubbed away the tears from her eyes with a silk sleeve. She withheld, for now, the fact that she had come to Chu Diên partly to recruit the old physician to tend to the injured soldiers in her army. She rebuked herself for this lapse in strength. It was for a purpose that she came to see Thi Vũ and that purpose was not sentimental.

"I won't ask you if my son died peacefully," said Thi Vũ, for whom the slightest movement provoked an unbearable dizziness, "because I don't want to know the answer." His stillness, prone in his chambers, transcended these humble surroundings with a father's grief that was almost holy.

"He died nobly," said Trưng Vương, "with a prophecy on his lips—that his executioners would soon be put to justice—a prophecy that I will bring to fruition. He begged not for his own life, but for my life to be spared. There has never been a more honorable man, and though I only knew him as husband for one month, that month had more life in it than generations of men."

Thi Vũ struggled to his feet. Now he took Trưng Vương's hand in his and said, "I have heard the declaration. It is heard throughout all of Lạc Việt and the story of your campaign has inspired the people so that the Hán are already beginning their retreat to Cổ Loa, where they believe themselves safe. May I ask why avenging your husband is *third* in priority on your list of proclamations?"

"Because such is my love for our country and our people, that it surpasses even my highest personal attachment. It was Thi Sách who taught me to be a patriot," said Trưng Vương, "and it was Thi Sách who taught me that the greatest love begins with gratitude to our ancestors."

"He was always a filial son," said Thi Vũ.

Trưng Vương now held both of Thi Vũ's hands, and beheld him, imagining that this was her husband Thi Sách as an old man, having lived out the rest of his life undisturbed and idle. It brought her a momentary joy that was startling in its intensity. She reminded herself once again why she had come. "There is something else," said Trưng Vương, resuming her kingly aspect. "The physician employed by the Trưngs was murdered by the Hán, along with every other man in our clan, and we are in need of a doctor to care for the injured from the Battle of Cung Điện Mê Linh. Would you—"

"Wife of my son," said Thi Vũ, "not only will I go to Cung Điện Mê Linh to tend to your injured, but I will bring my fellow younger, and more able, doctors to aid us."

In the court of Lord Đặng Vũ there were lacquer paintings on every wall, spanning the many rooms and even the outer walls of the palace. When Trưng Vương arrived, the lord wasted no time before treating her to a tour of his palace, with the most precious detail put into his account for each of his art objects. After indulgently listening to his discourses—however idle— the king thanked the lord and praised his collection, then asked if they could discuss business at last.

"What is there to discuss?" said Lord Đặng Vũ. "My people are in full support of the revolution, and we will join you in arms to cast out the Hán from our lands once and for all."

"Is it as easy as that?" said Trưng Vương. "Have you no demands or conditions upon your support for our cause?"

"May I deign to hope," said Lord Đặng Vũ, "that my son Đặng Thảo be given a place in your generalcy? Though he has no experience of war, he is wise beyond his years, and noble of heart."

Trưng Vương managed to maintain an aloof and confident expression. This would be the first of many such appeals and she needed to hold on to her composure. "I regret that he cannot," she said. "Though I know Đặng Thảo to be worthy, this is a revolution of women."

Lord Đặng Vũ frowned, and asked whether his son might have a place in the cavalry, as he was a capable horse rider.

Trưng Vương was silent. She had been so determined to make theirs an army of women, she had never considered the impossibility of galvanizing support from her allies without the involvement of a few noblemen. She thought of Trưng Nhị and General Man Thiện, her proud sister and mother who nevertheless advocated for compromise, which softened her resolve.

"If he is determined to fight the Hán," said Trưng Vương, her back stiffening and her visage blank, "then he is welcome to do so alongside us."

When Đặng Thảo was summoned to the court, he would not agree to a position as a mere cavalryman. It was not enough to fight, he said. He had been groomed all his life to be a leader, and anything else would be an insult to the future Lord of Chu Diên.

Lord Đặng Vũ said, "Our generation of men had to fight in wars for which there was no cause other than serving the will of the Hán. Now we have a king who will unite us *against* the Hán—the only righteous war in a hundred years—yet you hedge and argue."

"No hedging," said Đặng Thảo. "I am adamant that I will not fight in this war unless I am given a title."

Then Trưng Vương spoke, saying, "I understand your reluctance. I am sorry that we cannot accommodate you. You will do us a greater service by speaking to the people of Chu Diên and helping us raise an army from among them." Practical down to her bones, Trưng Vương now began to see the role Đặng Thảo must play in the drama: a diplomat. "We are past conferring titles now. Everyone in the army must love the cause, and none shall seek glory in this war."

Trưng Nhị had never been a teacher, yet she intuited that a warrior's education would not consist of the sorts of games and lessons upon which she was weaned. Nor would it be a simple matter of sparring, for the tools of war were precious, and could not be wasted in practice: there were barely enough swords, spears, axes, and shields for the army as it was. Instead, they would have to learn how to cohere as a unit, and to act in perfect coordination. Therefore, each day brought a new configuration, as Trưng Nhị, the Second King, trained the villagers of Mê Linh in formations such as "the shell," "the spearhead," "the pincer," and "the lattice."

Only those women with a sense of rhythm were given the job of drummer, and this would become the most important role, as each rhythm corresponded to a different formation, and gave the entire army its shape. If Trưng Nhị conceived of the army as a single instrument, rather than as an assemblage of disparate individuals, then it became possible to wield that instrument. It was the bronze drums that instructed the army in what kind of instrument it was.

The volume of her voice, which as a child had filled the halls and gardens of Cung Điện Mê Linh, now lent itself to the command of so many units of an army. "We have much work to do." She spoke under her breath between her confident shouts of discipline.

Out of the corner of her eye, she took notice of a flock of wild geese flying in perfect formation in the sky above the palace.

Unlike Cung Điện Mê Linh, the palace at Chu Diên was a gathering place for villagers, and the ringing of the great bell meant an assembly of the people. What was, at Cung Điện Mê Linh, only an annual privilege granted with the coming of the Spring Festival, in Chu Diên became a monthly occurrence, as the people had been afforded participation in leadership, due to their superior learning. Here were so many monks, nuns, scholars, and scribes such as would have fit a pilgrimage. Yet each man and woman had showed up for the cause of revolution. This was a crowd of idle Việts, soft-handed and pale of cheek—a people for whom the realities ahead were still but an appealing abstraction.

Although she had spent her entire life studying war, Trưng Vương had never seen an army in person before, other than the one she had lately led into victory. All was potential, and potential is infinite.

CHAPTER 23

The Persuasion of Võ Quan

As an iron- and bronze-working town, Nhật Nam was the main stage for recruitment on the king's expedition. If she did not secure the support of the dutiful and boorish Võ Quan, now the Lord of Nhật Nam, then there would be few weapons with which to equip the army, and the revolution might wilt before its stem could bear leaves. Trưng Vương approached the town with a sense of unease. The larger the army became, the greater their chances, but greater, too, became the burden of victory. What evil punishment awaited them at the hands of the Hán should they amass such an army and then be routed by the enemy? Yet she could not entertain every terror that entered her heart; her resolve was too great. The herald had preceded the arrival of the king, just as she had done at Chu Diên, but in Nhật Nam there were no crowds gathered to receive the procession.

Instead, the laborers in their workshops continued their smelting and smithing, indifferent to the legend in their midst. Word of Trưng Vương's victory over the local Hán officials of Mê Linh had reached Nhật Nam, but the villagers were distant and prosperous enough to think of the victory as local, and having little to do with the affairs of Nhật Nam. Matters of state, in fact, had always been a burden and intrusion to the workers of that city. The only occasions when the Hán presence came into play for the people of Nhật Nam was when they had to yield their taxes and follow their laws— and unlike the unruly farming and fishing community of Mê Linh, the workers of Nhật Nam scarcely made trouble, and looked unsympathetically upon those who did. The marriage of aristocrats, too, was congruent with their history, and the Confucian family order suited the lifestyle of the industrious men and women of that town.

"I have only lately become Lord of Nhật Nam," said Lord Võ Quan. "Should my first act as lord be to send my people to fight and die against the Hán?"

They sat on the floor, but there were no cups of tea or pleasantries exchanged.

"When we remove the Hán from Việt lands, it will be because of Nhật Nam, and because of your leadership," said Trưng Vương.

"You seem confident of my support," said Lord Võ Quan. "There was a time when you had the chance to unite Mê Linh with Nhật Nam, but that time has passed. You chose instead to marry a peasant from Chu Diên."

Trưng Vương suppressed an angry impulse, and her visage conveyed only dissension. *This oaf's bitterness matters nothing*, she reminded herself. *It is only his smithies that I need.*

"I know this much about you, Lord Võ Quan: that you

care deeply about duty, and I know that if you consider how our ancestors suffered from the abuse of the Hán—how we continue to suffer—you will realize our cause is righteous. As She-King of the Việts, it is my sacred obligation to repel the Hán from this country and to once again bring the rule of Lạc Việt into the descendants of the Dragon Lord."

Lord Võ Quan looked up from beneath his lowered brow and planted his hands on his knees. "You speak impressively," he said. "If only you were so eloquent when it most mattered. Now it is too late. If we lend our support to your cause, we risk our livelihoods. Where will the Hán strike first? Surely it will be against our ironworkers and bronzeworkers. No, I think we will try to increase our productivity to appease the Hán, and pretend this conversation never happened. You will no doubt be deemed an insurrectionist by the governor."

"The governor will be dead in two months," Trưng Vương insisted. "Suppose you *can* appease the Hán, and give up your able young men to fight in their wars, and allow your noblemen and noblewomen to be forced into marriage…What of worshipping Hán gods, obeying Hán customs and laws, and dressing and speaking as the Hán do? Will the noble men and women of Nhật Nam succumb to these dictates?"

"It is possible," said Lord Võ Quan, looking away, "to speak one way with your tongue, and speak another way with your heart."

In the Lord of Nhật Nam's sad look of resignation, Trưng Vương could see her victory, her vengeance and her iron conviction slipping away. *But my will is stronger,* she thought to herself, *than any man's.*

"Will you at least introduce me to your people as Trưng Vương, She-King of the Việts?" she said with barely concealed frustration. "If you acknowledge me in public, that is enough."

"Impossible," said Lord Võ Quan. "I cannot, unless I wish to be exposed as an insurrectionist by Hán spies."

Trưng Vương thought about the military game of shells, stones, and coins they played as children, and how Trưng Nhị had always tried to compel the innocents to become allies by force. She considered Trưng Nhị's method of conquering Nhật Nam and conscripting its women, but she tossed aside this thought as unworthy of a Việt king. She did not want to sow discord among the Việt people before the fight against the Hán had even begun.

Trưng Vương stood up. "You may not join our army, and you may not endorse our cause, but I ask of you only this, Lord Võ Quan: do not stand in our way. For we will vanquish the Hán despite you, and your loyalty to their distant and brittle empire will count for nothing in the end."

As she stepped outside of the squat stone palace of Nhật Nam, Trưng Vương wished that Trưng Nhị were there to ply her art of persuasion directly to the women of the village. Trưng Vương couldn't even convince one stubborn lord, and here she was about to take her appeal to the streets. But she banished the thought almost as soon as it occurred to her. A king could not hide behind anyone, not even another king.

"I despise the Hán," said the smith, "but not so much that I would face death to expel them from our country."

Without the Lord of Nhật Nam to gather the people, Trưng Vương had to approach the villagers one by one and ingratiate herself with them. She could not simply march aloofly through the streets and expect a following. She had to earn every woman's loyalty.

Walking into a smithy, she found herself with none of the formalities of introduction that accompanied a meeting of aristocrats. There were three women and two old men, sweating in the heat of the workshop, and they wore scarcely any clothing. Yet they were unembarrassed by the intrusion of a king. One of the women quit her task of feeding the furnace and approached the awkward royal. Trưng Vương inclined her head, not quite a bow but a discernible gesture, nonetheless. "What do you need?" the woman said.

"I need…," Trưng Vương began, nervously at first, then, remembering her status and regaining some of her confidence, said in a flurry, "I need you to come join our revolution, and I need your menfolk to stay in Nhật Nam and make weapons for us to vanquish the Hán."

The woman smirked, then grimaced. "I have worked this smithy since before I was old enough to speak. Do you think you can change my whole life just by asking nicely?"

"The Hán have changed all of our lives, and they haven't even asked nicely," said Trưng Vương.

"Then what can I do to persuade you?" said Trưng Vương, her voice taking on a plea of desperation that she never had before. How could it be that the fate of a nation rested on the back, not of the king, but of the common worker?

"The armies of Lạc Việt will be fed," Trưng Vương said. "But if you remain here in Nhật Nam, soon your food will run out, and Mê Linh will have nothing to provide you. Once we rout the Hán, then we will return to our paddies and streams. Until then, revolution is both the sowing and the harvest."

The woman broke into tears. "I work all day and my family goes hungry," she said. "I would do anything to feed them."

"Go and tell your family that they will soon be fed," Trưng Vương said, wondering whether they indeed had the capacity to feed all of Lạc Việt, "then go and tell your neighbors that there will be food enough for those who support the revolution."

By the end of the first month, an influx of women from Chu Diên and from the surrounding countryside flooded into Mê Linh, full of revolutionary fervor. Soon, there were too many soldiers for Trưng Nhị alone to train. The Second King had to make her first choice as a leader in Trưng Vương's absence, and she decided to appoint more generals to handle the surge of recruits to their cause. She had, by then, learned well which of the women possessed the canniest and most capable minds, and the hardiness of spirit that would make them superior leaders, and she named nine of these to the fourth generalcy.

Their number now stood at thirty thousand. Each general, as well as the Second King herself, was responsible for training three thousand soldiers. There were enough horses for half of the legions to train as cavalry, but not enough weapons or shields to supply the whole company. Instead, the women took up broomsticks, farming hoes, cattle prods, awls, and pot lids. They went barefoot, and they wore woolen sashes, and although they did not look the part of an army, they trained with the spirit of warriors.

Trưng Nhị met with her nine generals and dozens of lieutenants every night to discuss the progress and challenges facing the soldiery. At first, these challenges were logistical—how to make do without enough food and without enough resources in the treasury or the armory; but with time, morale would become the foremost issue. The march on Cổ Loa was still months away, and already the cause of independence felt remote to the infantrywomen. The wickedness and cruelty of the Hán, now that they had been removed from the village of Mê Linh, had become abstract. They seemed to have forgotten even the fate of their beloved men, conscripted to fight in distant wars for the whim of the emperor. It was time, the generals said, for another address to the army.

Next morning, the beating of the bronze drum signaled a general gathering of the troops—one strike on the side and three on the wide surface of the tympanum: *Shuk-rum-rum-rum, shuck-rum-rum-rum, shuck-rum-rum-rum, shuck-rum-rum-rum.* Their training grounds stood to the south of the city, in the same valley overlooking the rice paddies where Trưng Nhị and Phan Minh had once ridden as children. Sitting astride the elephant Xam afforded the best vantage from which to survey the army. Once the drummers' rhythms subsided, criers were tasked with repeating the words of the Second King as she shouted from atop the howdah.

Now, as she considered how to rekindle the fire of revolution in this army, Trưng Nhị fell back upon her lessons under the tutor Thi Sách. As it turned out, there was a reason for these short aphorisms for which her tutor became justly famous. When speaking to the masses, you could not communicate in speeches. You needed language that was quick and catchy and easy to repeat.

"What do the Hán want? Our blood!"

The criers shouted the chorus to the rest of the company: *What do the Hán want? Our blood!*

"What do the Việts want? Freedom!"

Again, their cries sounded over the field: *What do the Việts want? Freedom!*

"How do we achieve freedom? Revolution!"

How do we achieve freedom? Revolution!

"Who will stand in our way? No one!"

Who will stand in our way? No one!

CHAPTER 24

The Persistent Suitor

The men and women of Hợp Phố were known for their prowess in building, and as the king and her retinue entered the village, they understood why the people had earned such a reputation: Instead of longhouses with straw roofs, even the commoners boasted of ceramic tile roofs and elaborately carved wooden doors. The homes were all similarly constructed, and although the quality of each building was high, a visitor would have difficulty differentiating them. In Hợp Phố, order prevailed.

The king's company wended its way through the village to the palace—an even grander specimen of building than could be found in the temples of Chu Diên. They were warmly greeted by the Lord and Lady of Hợp Phố, who had gotten word about their mission to recruit armies from throughout all of Lạc Việt, and therefore had been expecting a visit from the She-King of the Việts. Trưng Vương was surprised to find the Lord of Hợp Phố bowing obsequiously at her feet, and as he bowed, the revelation that she was now the protector of the people strummed her nerves.

"Please stand," she said to the Lord of Hợp Phố. "What news do you have from Mê Linh?"

The lord kept smiling but appeared confused. "We have heard nothing from Mê Linh," he said.

"I thought," said Trưng Vương, still disoriented by the lord's sudden fealty, "because you kowtowed...you had been privy to a threat from the Hán." A part of her heart would always reside in Mê Linh, where the armies gathered and her sister awaited her return. She prayed to the Guardian Spirit that the governor's forces would not march on the village before then.

"I am paying obeisance to my king," said the lord, bowing low again.

"You must get used to this mode of address," said the Lady of Hợp Phố, bowing beside him.

"Please stand," said Trưng Vương, and the lord and lady complied. It was this same lord and lady who had seemed so august, so unflappable and regal, from their style of dress to their manners to their demeanor, just three short years ago.

"It is our honor to welcome Trưng Vương, She-King of the Việts, into our palace," said the lord. "Please join us for a feast in your honor."

Trưng Vương consented, but she could not help thinking about all the hungry families in Nhật Nam, from which she had lately arrived, and how she had been forced to use their desperation to fuel her mission. Without Nhật Nam, there would be no revolution. And now, the people of Hợp Phố were ready to empty their scarce resources to court her favor. She would sit for a feast, and enjoy the company of her fellow aristocrats, but she would not forget the struggles of the people, and she would one day repay them in plenitude, just as surely as she would avenge her husband.

"They have entertainments planned after the feast. You might want to partake of the wine to, you know, unbridle your festive self," said Trinh Sang.

"Don't get the wrong idea," said Trưng Vương. "My solemnity comes from the burden I carry as king."

"Well, the Lord and Lady of Hợp Phố have the wrong idea—and it is solely *their* idea—that you have come to Hợp Phố not just to recruit another army, but to unite our clans in a more permanent way," said Trinh Sang.

"They believe I'm after marriage?" said Trưng Vương. The Lord and Lady of Hợp Phố showed none of the pettiness of Đặng Thảo, nor the bitterness of Võ Quan, but like the rest, they assumed that she needed a husband. "But I am already married."

"Married to a ghost?" said Trinh Sang. "Is it such a wild idea, that you might need the comfort of a husband to keep you balanced?"

"The passion of the fire and the passion of the rain do not *need* each other," said Trưng Vương.

It was Trinh Sang's turn to appear empty of expression. "What?" he said.

Trưng Vương patted his fuzzy cheek. "Why don't you court the Second King when you see her next? Ask her to marry? I confess that *that* would bring me amusement." Then her expression turned affronted, and Trinh Sang felt it like a sudden change of weather. "If you insist upon the matter of marriage again, it will be received as an insult to my husband."

The two had been left alone now with the untouched feast laid out in front of them.

"Do you think I would ever entertain a rival to my status as king? A husband would so confuse the people that it would dampen the fire of revolution before the first flame is lit." Now Trưng Vương stood, and Trinh Sang felt the rousing of her ire, and kowtowed with head upon the floor, like a Hán. Unlike the Lord of Nhật Nam, she sensed that Trinh Sang could be compelled by her authority. "I want the armies of Hợp Phố, and I want to hear no more talk of marriage."

Trinh Sang stayed bowed, waiting until he could speak without a shake in his voice, when he finally said, "Your wish is my command, my king."

The Second King and the Lady of Cửu Chân walked amid this body of new soldiers, inquiring from the lieutenants about the progress of each troop. Recruits had been arriving from all throughout Lạc Việt, and such a simple fact as the number of soldiers in the army's population was ever in flux. Who knew whether Hán spies could have infiltrated their rank? This threat would become the obsession of General Man Thiện, who, though a general, had been tasked with running the affairs at Cung Điện Mê Linh. For the mother of kings, this meant rooting out any possible threat against her daughters and their mission.

No one but the Trưng family itself was exempt from suspicion. Even the generals could be called in to be interrogated by the mother of the king. Of particular interest to General Man Thiện was General Mai who, though she had proven her loyalty by consoling the grieving family after their tragedy, was suspect because of her mercenary profession. Could she be bought by the Hán? She certainly had shared a bed with the same commander responsible for the death of General Man Thiện's husband.

"My loyalty is absolute," said Mai of the first generalcy. "I am willing to die to prove it. My seduction of the commander was in service of protecting your daughters from his wrath, if you remember."

"But surely the commander revealed something of his intention to you, his bedmate, before he sneaked into Cung Điện Mê Linh and massacred our people," said General Man Thiện. "You do not need to lie to me, General Mai. It is wasteful to do so, as I can see through a lie as a gull can see a fish through clear water."

"I needn't resort to lies," said Mai. "I have ever been loyal to her ladyship, and on those occasions when I took a Hán devil to my bed, it was always to serve as a spy on *your* behalf, and not to the benefit of the enemy."

"I simply cannot believe—" General Man Thiện began.

"In sex without attachment?" said General Mai. "It is the luxury of your love with Lord Trưng that allows you to say so. I do not have this luxury, as a mere prostitute."

At the invocation of her husband's name, General Man Thiện's steel expression broke, but rather than shed tears, her shoulders heaved as though in a spasm, and she held out her hands to brace herself on the earth. "You are not a mere prostitute. You are a general," she said.

"And you are a general," said Mai, "in grief. You are entitled to feel whatever you feel. But I am not your enemy."

CHAPTER 25

Upon the Mountains

Trưng Vương returned to Mê Linh one morning during the dry season, triumphant, her kingdom unified. More than two months had passed, and the newly forged weapons had begun to arrive from Nhật Nam, so that the soldiery felt, for the first time, like true warriors of the Việt army.

Her first visit was to the elephant Khong Lo, to renew the bond she had begun to form with the beast. Xam and Khong Lo roamed freely because their range was limited by the thickness of the surrounding woods. Military tents littered the landscape, and out of one of these makeshift shelters came Trưng Nhị and Phan Minh the elephant handler. They had heard the commotion of the king's arrival, and now stood face-to-face with the monarch. Phan Minh and Trưng Nhị felt abashed for having been discovered sharing a tent, for they knew that Trưng Vương had no such comfort awaiting her, but their awkwardness was not returned by the king, who embraced them.

Second King approached Trưng Vương and, putting a

hand on her shoulder gently, said that there was much that needed to be discussed. General Man Thiện had been imprisoning and punishing loyal lieutenants for the slightest shade of dissent, for fear of infiltration by Hán spies.

"You are King of the Việts," said Trưng Vương to her sister. For all the good that Trưng Nhị had done in her absence, she had not been able to keep their mother in check. "Why did you not stop General Man Thiện?"

"She and I are too much alike," said Trưng Nhị. "I confess that I did not want to contradict her, because perhaps she can indeed see what is unseen to me."

Trưng Vương looked askance at Trưng Nhị. This was no longer a sparring match between sisters. No self-restraint was necessary. She wished she could communicate the solemnity of duty to Trưng Nhị but she knew her sister would never understand. "General Man Thiện is right. There are almost certainly Hán spies among our leadership. But we must not be driven by fear. We must act consistent with our truth: we know our victory to be inevitable. No number of spies can squelch the spirit of our revolution. Therefore, it is more important to betray no fear than it is to catch every infiltrator."

"You must deal with our mother," said Trưng Nhị, stung and startled by the king's sudden departure so soon after her triumphant return.

"No," said Trưng Vương firmly. "I must embark upon a secret mission: to go up into the mountains and recruit the greatest archers in the land. It is *you* who must deal with General Man Thiện." She believed in Trưng Nhị's powers of persuasion. It had been Trưng Nhị, after all, who had always challenged their mother throughout their youth. "I am counting on you." With that, the king clasped the hands of the Second King, then pivoted to prepare her voyage into the mountains.

In the court of the governor, Tô Định's inner circle awaited the latest report from the spymaster. In Cổ Loa, they counted down the days to the siege. Once the scale of the problem amassing to the south became clear, it was decided that their most judicious course would be for the Hán to gather its own army, and wait to fight on home territory, rather than to launch an attack upon Mê Linh, which comprised the base of operations for the enemy.

Each of the cities of Lạc Việt had expelled their Hán officials, and one by one they fell under the influence of this self-declared girl-king. The governor Tô Định had misunderstood their threat all along, he realized. How could he have supposed that all the men and women in his region would decide to throw their nets into the muddy river, where the yield is yet unknown, rather than fishing in the clear waters of the familiar? And that they would unite under a woman, in defiance of the powerful governor, whom they should have learned by now to fear?

The Hán would show their strength, but they would do so in proper time, not rushing the defeat of the Việts, who would prove themselves obedient in the end. Cổ Loa had once been used as a fortress from which the conquest of Lạc Việt was launched, and its high walls and elevated position on a plateau surrounded by prairie made it ideal for defense. The citadel was vast enough to accommodate an army, and these were all men, superior in strength and training to the mob of Việt women that gathered in the south.

The spymaster reported that the day of the attack was imminent. In fact, only three days would be gone before the army mobilized. Yet the army idled without a queen. No one knew the whereabouts of the "she-king," and in her absence, there was dissent in the ranks. It was time to strike, while the leadership was in disarray.

Trưng Vương saddled a horse, and brought along a lone servant, a loyal woman whose family had served the Trưngs for generations, and whose purpose now was to feed and tend the horse while the king climbed up the mountain to seek a village where she had never set foot. As soon as the rocky climb became too steep for the horse, Trưng Vương climbed the rest of the way by hand and foot. She soon came to the plateau where she had first encountered the People, now just a verdant outcropping with a view of the treetops and two adjacent mountains; then she undertook the climb where she had once given up and nearly fallen to her death, swinging into the rock chimney that made the ascent easy and led to the cave where she had once lit a fire in the slanting rain. It was there that she looked around and wondered in which direction she would find the home of the People. She tried crying out to the empty and indifferent air, and she tried banging a drum until it left a ringing in her ears, but there came no reply.

She was no hunter, and no tracker, but Trưng Vương studied the cave for clues anyway. The burnt remnants of her husband's book had been swept away by the wind, and the only marking it left was a hint of char a few feet into the recess. It stood as a reminder of what little was left of us when we are gone and this drove Trưng Vương deeper into her conviction to fight for what was enduring—the honor of the Việts. Like her husband, Trưng Vương, too, would become a ghost one day, but she vowed that she would choose the manner of her own death.

Trưng Vương decided that the village of the People would be found at the highest precipice. So she continued climbing. When she came to a resting place where a hardy tree rose out of the rock, she was forced to recline against it, lest her limbs give up completely and leave her at the mercy of gravity.

She wore the bronze drum on a rope around her neck, and she tapped it a few times to restore the feeling to her fingers. Looking out upon the realm from the highest vista from which she had ever peered, Trưng Vương felt immense pride at the richness and verdancy of her kingdom. At this height, one could see the river delta meeting the ocean, and the sister mountains, and the nearby jungles and distant green fields. It was no wonder that the Hán coveted these lands, so teeming with life as far as the eye could see. Yet she had to keep climbing.

The next plateau led to a steep incline; ignoring the strain in her calves, the burn of her thighs, she continued the ascent. Suddenly she felt a thump on her chest, pushing her back and knocking her down where she clambered back to her feet. An arrow had struck the bronze drum around her neck and splintered. She feared that another arrow would soon follow it. The dented drum hovered over her heart.

From behind a rock formation, about sixty feet away, stepped a woman wielding a straight bow with an arrow nocked and ready to fire.

"Please don't!" said the king, holding out her hands. "I am looking for Ly Chau."

"Go back to the prairie," said the mountain woman. "I could have pierced your neck with that arrow."

"I know it," said the king, remembering the fate that nearly was. "I once spent three days among the People, and tried to join your tribe. I failed."

"Then why," said the mountain woman, "have you returned?"

"Because the Việt revolution has begun, and the Hán will soon overwhelm us, as they did generations ago," said Trưng Vương, "and because I have been declared She-King of the Việts, and have raised an army of women to drive out the Hán from Lạc Việt forever. Yet we have no elite archers. The mountain folk are our only way to win this war. Spies from our army have been reporting to the Hán our every movement, each new recruit, yet none but I and the Second King know of the plan to bring the People into our fold."

The mountain woman paused, lowered her bow, and laughed. "You are the King of the Việts?"

"Yes, well," said Trưng Vương apologetically, "I am filthy and weary from the climb. I couldn't exactly wear my golden armor and come riding on an elephant into the mountains.

But I come to you not just as a king, but once again as an aspirant to join the People."

The mountain woman scoffed. "I don't believe that you could even pass the trial of entry into our tribe that our children undertake."

"I'm not afraid to fail," said Trưng Vương. "Only let me into your village to petition your lord for an alliance."

"No," said the mountain woman. "You will come with me to the kites' landing, and if you can prove yourself, only then can you be admitted."

Three days had elapsed, and the governor's army lay in wait for the siege. Archers huddled behind each parapet of the battlements. Infantrymen stood armored and at the ready, row by row, in the bailey. Cavalrymen ran routes inside and outside the ramparts.

In the war room, the governor and his advisors conferred around a map of Cổ Loa. The Việts would not infiltrate their defenses, but should they somehow make it into the citadel, they would find themselves stuck in a spider's web, surrounded by the governor's elite forces, vulnerable to attack from all sides. The haste of the Việt army would be its undoing. The Hán, like the spider, would practice patience.

The king and the mountain woman stood side by side across from the kites' landing, awaiting the dusk, when the raptors would gather.

"I do not know whether we can win this war without you," said Trưng Vương, accepting the straight bow from the mountain woman. "But I know that your elite archers would ensure the safety and survival of many Việt women who would otherwise die at the hands of the Hán."

"Focus on the task ahead of you," said the mountain woman. "Every war is a series of battles, and every battle is a series of skirmishes, and every skirmish is a series of melees. Needless to say, a melee is won one strike at a time. Put all of your will into each strike, and you are sure to win the war. Now..." She passed two arrows to the king.

Since her last failure to down the kite, Trưng Vương had practiced archery, but she doubted her own mastery. Instead of falling back on habit, she would need complete focus, complete calm. She breathed in, concentrated on her moving target and the target's potential destination as it jinked and swerved in the air, the saccading of her eyes matching the unpredictability of the prey. Patiently, she allowed the kite to land, but she would not fire upon the stationary bird. She felt the wind on her cheek, and aimed slightly leftward, then awaited its launch. There was a chance that she had judged correctly, and that when the kite alit, it would soar to the left, but she had to trust in this instinct, because she had no instinct to trust but her own.

The kite sprung, and before she could gauge its angle and direction, Trưng Vương let fly the first arrow to its left, and immediately nocked the second arrow and fired without thought. It was the second arrow that landed true, as though some faculty buried far beneath her conscious mind knew the kite would dip rather than rise, and when the arrow struck, the kite tumbled onto a dusty ledge below.

The king and the mountain woman exhaled at the same moment, and the mountain woman put her hand on Trưng Vương's shoulder and gave her a solemn look as though to say, simply, it was what it was. Celebration at that moment might have been unbefitting a king, but her heart swelled at this small victory for the first time in months. Joy felt like a muscle long disused abruptly employed to hold weight.

As proof of Trưng Vương's worthiness, the mountain woman nimbly scaled down, then leapt from one ridge to another, to retrieve the arrow-pierced kite.

General Man Thiện's steely expression was gone. In its place was a different mask, fragile and torn, like a young girl who had spent all her tears and had no more in her to shed. When Trưng Nhị approached her, General Man Thiện scowled and peered bitterly in her direction, through a mess of hair that had not seen a comb for days.

"Am I the next to be accused?" said Trưng Nhị.

General Man Thiện laughed a manic laugh. "You would not be so scornful if you saw what I see among our generalcy. They believe that it will be impossible to drive out the Hán, so they are conspiring with the Hán to curry favor in advance of our anticipated defeat."

"*Who* believes it will be impossible to drive out the Hán?" said Trưng Nhị. She prayed that her mother had not succumbed to madness. "Are you sure it isn't *you* who believe that? You are the only one saying it."

"My love for my daughters crowds out any doubt," said General Man Thiện.

"I come to you not as a daughter to her mother, but as a king to her general," said Trưng Nhị. She thought of what her sister would say, what her elder would do. "Morale is more important than discretion. Trưng Vương and I are working in secret on a strategy that will ensure our success against the Hán. No one but we two kings are privy to this plan, so it doesn't matter what the Hán think they know. In the meantime, you are poisoning the stream by accusing your fellow generals. The will of our leadership is waning."

"You want me to ignore spies in our midst?" said General Man Thiện, a clarity coming in her eyes.

"Yes," said Trưng Nhị. "If there are spies in our ranks, then they can only misinform the Hán, which is to our ultimate benefit."

"But what if they are not spies, but assassins, too?" said General Man Thiện.

Trưng Nhị paused. She had to admit that she had never considered for a second that another Việt woman would be so treacherous as to slay a fellow Việt. Now that the thought was uttered, it hit with the force of revelation—that she possessed the courage that came from a woman who had slain a tiger and led an army and survived a long isolation; that she would die if she had to. "Then let's give thanks to the Guardian Spirit that I am not the only king."

In the village, the king drew stares from the mountain folk, which alternated between the angry and the curious. If Trưng Vương were to persuade the archers of the mountains to join her, first she had to survive. To survive among the People meant to show no fear. So as she paraded alone among strangers, she spoke these words to herself: *I am King of the Việts, and these are my subjects.*

Somehow, she had always pictured the homes of the mountain folk to be unclean caves, either dusty and dry or lichen-covered, not these modest stone structures reminiscent in their construction to the walls of Cung Điện Mê Linh. On their march, they passed the girl Ly Anh, who, recognizing the stranger, ran to fetch Ly Chau the huntress. The mountain woman led Trưng Vương to a natural amphitheater, a circle surrounded by ridges of stone at a comfortable level for seating. Once there, the mountain woman nudged the king to the middle of the circle. There was a redness to the earth here that was lovely and disconcerting.

Ly Chau the huntress appeared, and though Trưng Vương was pleased to see a familiar face, Ly Chau's expression did not return the pleasure. Beside her stood a tattooed man with hair tucked back and a short beard pulled into a tight point. It was apparent from their bearing that these two led the village.

"You should not have returned to our mountain home, prairie dweller," said Ly Chau.

"I have succeeded in the trials of the People," said Trưng Vương defiantly, "and downed the black-winged kite. I have the right to be here."

"Is this true?" Ly Chau asked the mountain woman who stood beside the king.

The mountain woman nodded. A crowd had already begun to gather in the natural amphitheater, but now their curiosity was piqued.

"But you already failed in the trials," said Ly Chau with finality. "It is not a game of bamboo toss, where you get to try and try again until you get the result you want."

"If I have not earned a place among the People, then surely I have earned the right to speak to you, as King of the Việts."

"You are no king," pronounced Ly Chau. "You are a silly and desperate girl chasing after her own death."

"I *was* a silly and desperate girl chasing after her own death," Trưng Vương corrected her, lifting her arms as though to encompass the landscape. "I now command an army of seventy thousand women, and we are preparing to drive the Hán out of Lạc Việt forever, and we need your archers to lead us to victory."

"What are the Hán to us? They dare not infiltrate our mountain home, whereas *you* have disturbed our affairs twice."

"If you have had no dealings with the Hán, then let me tell you about them," Trưng Vương appealed.

"It is not I alone who makes decisions for the village. I may carry the passion of the fire," said Ly Chau, then she gestured to the man beside her, "but there is also the passion of the rain."

The tattooed man then spoke, saying, "You must give us two reasons, and two reasons only, why we should join the prairie folk in its war on the Hán. Then we will decide whether your reasons are sufficient to risk our lives for your cause."

What could Trưng Vương say? Her proclamation on the skin of the tiger would not move these hardened mountain folk. What was the Trưng name to them? What was nation-hood to them? What was her burning need for revenge to them?

The king, her open mouth silent, stood across from this pair and wondered how much time she had to gather her thoughts and devise a reply before they would give up on her. She had no time for oratorical flourish or rhetorical strategy. She simply had to give her most earnest plea and hope it was sufficient.

"This is how it is among the prairie dwellers: the Hán will kill us for saying the wrong things, they will kill us for believing the wrong things, they take our men, and murder our children if we stand against them. They will do the same to you, unless we all stand together," pleaded Trưng Vương. "And my second reason is this: that though we live separately, we share ancestors. We are sisters and brothers, and if ever a threat imperiled your People, I would do anything to protect you from extinction." Her strategy to defeat the Hán depended on the superior archery of the Degar. Without them, she feared that all her plans would amount to nothing. Yet she could not let on how desperate and tenuous their cause truly was.

Ly Chau and the tattooed man conferred, while the gathered crowd chattered and stirred uneasily. Eventually the tattooed man spoke again. "How is the King of the Việts sending our men to fight in their war any different from the emperor of the Hán sending *your* men to fight in their wars?"

Trưng Vương smiled for the first time, because she knew with marrow-deep certainty that she had already won their support. "It is different, first," she began, "because I am not asking you to send your *men*."

CHAPTER 26

The Army Assembles

The armies under the command of the Second King were ordered to remain ready during the king's absence. The Second King could not afford an idle army, for on the day that the king arrived from the mountains, they would start the march to Cổ Loa. Six days had now passed. They had missed the appointed hour upon which the astrologers had predicted a most fortuitous outcome.

In the camp of the Việts, outside the village of Mê Linh, the hero Nàng Quỳnh had raised an army of her own and become a respected general. The hero Nàng Quế would have been her lieutenant, as she was the most celebrated warrior in all of the army, rumored to be superior in martial skill to even the Second King. Yet Nàng Quế did not possess the ambition of a leader, nor did she care for any pursuit other than to fight as a cavalrywoman. Her horse, named Thuan, was legendary for its speed and endurance, and together the horse and rider inspired the nation.

On the seventh day of waiting in a state of battle-readiness, the hero Nàng Quế came to Cung Điện Mê Linh to address the thirty-five generals and the Second King. Rather than meeting in the Great Hall, Nàng Quế asked that the thirty-five generals come to meet her in the gardens, where she could sit astride Thuan. Once Trưng Nhị and the generalcy were gathered, Nàng Quế proclaimed that it was time to fight the Hán, with or without the king. Needless delay could only bring about discord. The soldiers began to believe that the generals did not order the march on Cổ Loa out of fear, rather than out of strategy. That fear was spreading to the rank and file, and they suspected that the Hán armies were amassing and preparing to descend upon Mê Linh at any moment.

"None of that is true," said the Second King, concealing a frustration that, in a leader, would too closely resemble petulance. "We only need patience in order to be victorious. Is it time for another speech to inspire the army?"

"No more speeches," said the hero Nàng Quế. "The army is inspired enough as it is; they are so inspired that they want to finish this war—to drive out the Hán *now*, rather than await a less fortuitous hour."

"The stars will not decide our fate," said the Second King defiantly. "Strategy will."

"One more day of battle-readiness," said Nàng Quế. "We will give you until sunset tomorrow, then you must either send us to war, or send us home to our families."

The mountain folk needed seven days to make enough arrows to equip an army. They sent messengers to surrounding villages, carrying the call to arms among the Degar of the highlands. The king resisted the urge to hasten the preparations; she knew that the loyalty of the People was as breakable as an arrow, and needed patience to fly true to its target without shattering against authority's wall. So she bided her time, knowing her servant had brought enough provisions to survive the wait at the foot of the mountain, knowing her sister had strength enough to lead an idle army, and knowing the fierce will of the Việt people would not abate with time. What she did not know were the plans of the Hán, and she prayed to the Guardian Spirit that they did not launch an attack in her absence. Trưng Vương surmised that it was past the time when the governor could have made an effective demonstration by an attack on Mê Linh. Soon they would be eighty thousand strong, skilled in horsemanship and in the discipline of combat, with the best archers in the land. She felt assured of their victory, though it would not be without sacrifice. Only, she prayed the Hán would not dare attack the Việts on their home territory before she could be there to command the army to its ultimate victory.

While out surveying the training women in the village, Trưng Vương noticed several children practicing bowmanship, and going through training drills. When she returned to the home where she was staying as a guest of Ly Chau the huntress, Trưng Vương asked her, "Are the children of the village playing at war, and mimicking their parents?"

"No, my king," said Ly Chau. "They, too, are preparing for battle. In the mountains, our sons and daughters fight alongside the men and women. We do everything together: we hunt together, we feast together, we fight together, and we die together."

"But," said Trưng Vương, "it will be hard for the women of the prairie to fight alongside children. We would feel too protective of them; but in battle, sometimes soldiers must sacrifice themselves in order to achieve our mission."

"Only the children who have gone through the trials will join us," said Ly Chau. "I would rather fight alongside a Degar child than a grown woman of the prairie. *You* should be more concerned about the others in your army. How long have your archers been training? If they have not been surviving on the skill of their bow all of their lives, we do not want them in our division. Their clumsy bowmanship would interfere with the trajectory of our arrows."

"I will make you a deal," said the king, imagining her army dissipating with the whiff of the suggestion that this war would lead children to their deaths. "I will weed out the archers who aren't masters of bowmanship, if you will promise to leave the children at home."

Ly Chau looked pensive and studied the face of the king. "Is this an absolute condition? Would you not accept the help of the Degar if we brought our children to war, as is our tradition?"

The king weighed the morale of her army against the necessity of recruiting the greatest archers in the land. Her face reflected back to Ly Chau the huntress the same pained expression of a thought being stretched to its limit. "I would not," Trưng Vương said at last.

Dusk approached the camp of Mê Linh, and the generals, in the Great Hall of Cung Điện Mê Linh, debated what was to be done if the sun set without the arrival of the king. Several of the newest generals sided with Nàng Quế, and favored launching an attack on Cổ Loa without Trưng Vương and her secret strategy. Bát Nàn, of the second generalcy, wished to pacify the hero Nàng Quế by offering her a position as the thirty-sixth general, though she had not raised an army of her own. Her influence was so great among all the armies that she was much like a general already. Mai and Phùng Thị Chính doubted that this strategy would work—Nàng Quế had great integrity, and was not the sort to be tempted by titles. Her only ambition was the revolution.

General Man Thiện suggested punishing Nàng Quế severely, if not by execution then by a public flogging. Her defiance could not be countenanced if order was to be maintained. A demonstration must be made of the cavalrywoman who issued an ultimatum to the Second King.

Trưng Nhị had remained silent during these deliberations, until General Man Thiện's fervor became impossible to ignore. "Trưng Vương will come. I know it. We must reckon with Nàng Quế's demand, but we cannot give up on the king."

"But how do we reckon with Nàng Quế's demand if she insists that we do not wait a moment longer for the king?" said Phùng Thị Chính.

Trưng Nhị's impulse was to meet one-on-one with the hero Nàng Quế and to persuade her through her charm and clever argumentation, but she sensed rightly that Nàng Quế was not one to waver, nor to succumb to persuasion. "If we march on Cổ Loa, we would wait until the morning anyway. Tell Nàng Quế that we will leave at sunrise, unless the king arrives before then to lead us." She believed, if nothing else, in her sister's reliability and consistency. The last time she disappeared into the mountains, Trưng Vương had returned in three days and now three days were almost gone.

Her decree was carried to Nàng Quế, and subsequently to the army, and their excitement over the imminent victory was palpable in the camps. Everyone felt the lifted spirits, and Trưng Nhị began to wonder if she would indeed have to lead the army into Cổ Loa without her sister. Could Trưng Vương have died in the mountains, or been held prisoner there? She could not risk sending a scout to find out, on the chance that their secret strategy would be passed along to the Hán.

Having bought some time before she must lead the army into battle as king, Trưng Nhị could not rest at all, and decided instead to take the dog for a walk in the camps in the middle of the night. Trưng Nhị herself wished that she could whisper into the ear of the governor and tell him vengeance was on its way, and that the Hán should flee before the army even reached their citadel. His cowardice would save lives.

Trưng Nhị found the sentinel at the west gate and stood beside her. Xấu rubbed himself against their knees, wagging his tail expectantly. He was unsure why they kept this vigil, but sensed somehow its import.

When the hour of dawn arrived, the sun was hidden behind a heavy layer of clouds, and therefore the sun could not be said to have risen. Trưng Nhị prolonged her hope that, as long as the sun remained hidden, she still held the title of Second King. A fog came in that morning, further obscuring the sunrise, and Trưng Nhị was about to return to the palace when Xấu dashed off into the mist. "Xấu! Come back!" called Trưng Nhị, but she did not follow him.

Then she heard the clop of hooves approaching; the sentinel raised her stick to strike the drum, but Trưng Nhị stayed her hand. It was Trưng Vương and her servant coming in on horseback, followed by an excited Xấu. But there was no Degar army behind her. She had come alone.

The Second King slept easily now that Trưng Vương had returned. After they conferred briefly, Trưng Nhị felt right with the world again, enough to retire to her own bed. The hero Nàng Quế met with the king; Trưng Vương poured the tea in the receiving room. "I understand that you wish to march on Cổ Loa this morning," said Trưng Vương.

"This was promised by the Second King," said Nàng Quế.

"Upon the condition that I did not arrive before sunrise," said Trưng Vương.

"The day arrived before you did," said Nàng Quế, "and the army is ready."

"But the sun did not rise. It was obscured by the clouds and the mist. Technically, the sun still has not yet risen," said Trưng Vương. In a former incarnation, she would not have approved resorting to ruses and technicalities, but *this* self was an instrument, and the king would have her will obeyed.

Nàng Quế frowned.

"If you would have enough patience to wait until the end of the day, then we could implement a strategy that is sure to bring us victory, and with the least amount of Việt casualties," said Trưng Vương.

"Our women are not afraid to die," said Nàng Quế, raising her chin.

"I know it. But each of them is valuable," said Trưng Vương. "This is why you are a hero and not a general. A leader must think about such things as protecting our soldiers from unnecessary harm. It is the luxury of the hero to sacrifice herself nobly for a cause—an admirable feat, but one without consequences."

Nàng Quế didn't know whether to feel insulted or complimented. In the end, she did not care for flattery. "It would help greatly if you would tell me this secret strategy of yours," said Nàng Quế.

Trưng Vương smoothed the silk of her robe with her hands. She weighed the risks of revealing or concealing her plans, and decided that Nàng Quế possessed a will that was equal to her own. "I will tell you our strategy this once, because there is no spy so swift that they could warn the Hán in time so that they can prepare for what is about to unfold. A Degar army approaches from the west, archers so deadly and so accurate that they can neutralize the Hán's long-range advantage as a defensive force."

"If that is so, then why did you come alone?" said Nàng Quế.

"Because I came on a horse, and the Degar do not ride on horseback," said Trưng Vương. "And I needed to arrive first to declare an archery contest, to prove that any archers in our army from the prairie are masters in bowmanship. It was a condition of the leader Ly Chau, on whom I have conferred the title of general, the thirty-sixth of our army."

"We barely have enough arrows now to do battle as it is," said Nàng Quế, "much less a surplus to spend on war games."

"The Degar bring enough arrows for every head and heart in the Hán army, and the skill to deliver them unto their targets."

The new arrivals did not mingle well with the prairie folk. The first night, especially, presented a conundrum for the Degar, who had traded in their stone homes set in the mountain-side for tents on the open prairie. Trưng Vương planned only two days of training before the march to Cổ Loa, and most of that time was devoted to learning the meaning of the different rhythms played upon the bronze drum. The soldiers had already been well trained in the art of combat, and if they hadn't, then they were not about to acquire that training in the remaining hours; yet they *must* know the rhythms of the bronze drum, else they would not be an army at all.

CHAPTER 27

The Informant

Kha the guardsman paced, the governor standing nearby. His ruse of betraying the Trưng clan may have worked *too* well. He found himself always within shouting range of his employer, and had not had a break in the year since he'd joined the ranks of the Hán. His consolation was that he now ate meat every day—a luxury of being within the governor's inner circle. His rivals within the court—those ambitious men who sought the perks of a higher appointment—resented the favor with which the Việt was treated, but they lacked his pedigree: that he had intimate knowledge of the governor's principal enemies.

When the governor's spies among the enemy army failed to report the date of the siege accurately, Tô Định turned to Kha for an explanation.

"Those girls are always running late," said Kha. "And always disappearing from view when you are supposed to know where they are."

The governor's advisor, Li Hong, inserted himself into the

conversation. "The Trưng clan is afraid, and rightly so," he said.

"Have they finally learned to be afraid?" said Tô Định to Kha the guardsman.

"No," said Kha, "the Trưngs are foolishly unafraid. They will arrive at our gates soon, but not when we expect it."

"They think they can win a war by frustrating us to death?" said Tô Định.

Li Hong spoke up again, saying, "The Việt armies did not attack at the appointed hour. Trust me when I say that they will not strike us, so we need to take the fight *to them*, to demonstrate once and for all the superiority of the Hán's might."

"I don't think the governor has anything to fear from these women," said Kha, ignoring the advisor. "They are untrained, inexperienced, and distracted."

Tô Định scowled. "I don't fear the Trưng Sisters, or the army of the Việts."

"Of course," said Kha, though he noticed that the governor blinked fiercely when he made this declaration.

It was that night that a scout reported an army approaching from the south. The Việts would arrive at Cổ Loa by daybreak. The governor instructed Kha to raise the alarm, and scolded his advisor Li Hong for his poor foresight. "If I had listened to the guardsman," said the governor, "our armies would now be ready."

Kha rang the bell alerting the Hán army to the threat, and the soldiers dressed, armed themselves, and took up positions. Observing the predawn bustle of the Hán, Kha had to admit that there was an admirable discipline in this army, a habit of obedience that translated well into the sphere of war making. The last he had seen of Trưng Trắc and Trưng Nhị, they were not kings; and the last he had seen of his fellow Việts in Mê Linh, they were the farthest thing from an army that he could have imagined. He wished he could halt the boulder's tumble toward war; he wished he could unmask and beg the governor to have mercy on these innocent women. They were not ready, he thought; how could they ever be ready to face the unscrupulous, unyielding governor's armies?

Cổ Loa stood on a high plain overlooking rich farmland. Approaching a walled city on high ground presented a risk to the Việt army, but the fertility of the landscape was an asset to the invading forces. Scouts had reported a small entrance to the rear of the citadel, and Trưng Vương instructed the drummers to play the rhythm for a "pincer" formation, and the army formed a U-shape, so that if the enemy should flee, they would have no choice but to do so through the small northern entrance. That way, their flight could be slowed, to trap the governor, who, more than anyone else, was responsible for the deaths of thousands of Việts.

Two shieldswomen flanked each elite archer, and hundreds of these trinities advanced to within firing range of the wall's ramparts. The Hán archers fired through the embrasures, while the Việts formed embrasures of their own between the shieldswomen. The superior archery of the Degar would be the key to a Việt victory, and this first stage of the assault on Cổ Loa was critical. If they could not neutralize the Hán archers, then an army advancing on a castle from a low prairie would be vulnerable.

Out of range of the Hán archers were the Trưng Sisters atop their elephants, Trưng Vương in the golden armor with the Mê Linh bird, Trưng Nhị in a suit of bronze, the colorful banner of the Việt army flapping in the morning wind. One sister felt equal to the moment, her thirst for vengeance even larger than the gathered armies and the citadel itself; the other saw this war as a terrible necessity, the lesser of two evils. Both women held swords at the ready, and conducted the drummers by signaling with the position of their weapons. At the center joint of this "pincer," the Trưng Sisters sent forth the Degar archers into the open field.

General Ly Chau proved the worth of her people. These expert huntresses fired into the embrasures, removing one by one the archers who hid behind the parapets. Knowing their deadliest range, the Degar archers stopped precisely at the point where they could fire consistently into the embrasures without fearing similar accuracy from the enemy. Yet although the volleys of arrows from the ramparts of the wall were not perfectly aimed, their sheer volume battered the shields of the women who stood protecting the archers and were driven into the feet of many women who were otherwise fully protected.

Even this—being shieldless and vulnerable, with an arrow piercing a limb—did not deter these mountain women, who, though their own bodies would soon be separated from their life-force, knew that, with a few more shots, they could take the Hán's advance guard down with them. The drum beat on,

and the women emptied their quivers into the chests and arms
of the relentless enemy.

The field below the citadel, covered with arrows, fell quiet.
Both armies were depleted, but for every Degar woman who
died, there were multiple Hán archers who would never take
another breath. Finally, the drum beat changed, and the
remaining Degar archers and arrow gatherers retreated.

Watching from the ramparts beside the governor, it was not
difficult for Kha to hide his glee at the Việt victory. For all the
pride he felt on behalf of his people, his surprise was so much
greater that it overwhelmed the former feeling. Tô Định mis-
read the guardsman's shock as sympathy for the fallen, and
instructed Kha to fetch Wu Sheng, the most skilled warrior
in the army.

Kha ran with a waddle—his clothes always seemed ill-
fitting and irksome to him—and once he reached the garrison,
asked for Wu Sheng. Kha was impressed by the composure of
the champion Wu Sheng, whose every movement appeared
both flowing yet solid, like a rushing river. *This is no good*, he
thought as he carried the armor to the chambers of Wu Sheng.
*I am no great warrior, but I know a great warrior when I see one.
This Wu Sheng will be the end of us.* By the time they'd reached
the residence, Kha knew he had to do something.

Kha looked around desperately until his eyes landed on a
statue of the emperor beside the chamber door. As soon as Wu
Sheng entered the chamber, Kha said that modesty compelled
him to wait outside while the noble dressed in his gambeson,

and once the nobleman was covered in padding and mail, Kha would bring in the armor and help him into it. But as soon as the chamber door was closed, seizing his opportunity, Kha went around to the other side of the emperor statue and leaned on it with all his strength, straining even the muscles of his face, so that the great stone figure landed in front of the chamber door, blocking the nobleman's exit. Kha waddled away at full speed, with the cries of the nobleman sounding in his ear—"What's going on?"—then louder as he banged on the immobile door.

Dressing in Wu Sheng's imperial armor, which was so tight on his body that it chafed his thighs and waist, and a helm that masked his face, Kha wordlessly went to the stables, where a footman showed him to his horse, and supported him as he mounted it. He grunted in approval, and the footman tried to peek under his mask, but Kha dashed away.

Marching through the citadel of Cổ Loa, Kha prayed to the Guardian Spirit that no one should stop him before he reached the gate. But he had not yet attained the goal when the din and uproar of outrage rose from behind. He picked up the pace, and waved confidently at the sentinels, who, seeing him adorned in the imperial armor, unlocked the gate.

Once the gate was cracked, Kha did not wait for it to fully open, but charged through as narrow an aperture as he could, with the sounds of screaming behind him. "Stop! Traitor!"

As soon as he broke free from the gates of Cổ Loa, Kha saw the Việt soldiers ready to meet his charge with swords and spears. For the Việt army knew not who he was. To them, he appeared as another fierce warrior ready to shed Việt blood.

Nàng Quế prepared for his charge, but when he ran right past her toward the Việt army, she tilted her head in confusion.

"I am not a Hán! I have no weapons!" Kha shouted as he charged straight into the pincer formation. The Hán, he knew, had precious few archers left to pose a threat, but as soon as he came into range of the Việts, they could have easily toppled him with a single arrow. He started to shed his armor as he rode, and as soon as his belly came free of the clothes that contained it, the Second King cried out his name, and ordered the drummers to play the rhythm for idling: *thum-thum, thum-thum, thum-thum*.

Once the governor understood what was happening, inflamed with anger, he shouted "Seize the traitor!" Taking this as an official command, the general ordered the army to attack, and the Hán soldiers emptied out of the open gate onto the prairie, pursuing the renegade guardsman. This was precisely the opposite of what the governor had wanted, which was to trap the Việts within the "spider's nest" of Cổ Loa, but ordering a retreat moments after accidentally ordering an attack would be fatal. The Hán army marched straight into the "pincer" formation, and the flanks of the Việt army charged from opposing sides, and the arms of the pincer closed upon the Hán.

CHAPTER 28

The Prairie War

Phật Nguyệt from Nhật Nam, of the sixth generalcy, wore her hair in a short line across her forehead, and had sleepy eyes and a knobbed nose, qualities associated with nobility and the descendants of Lạc Long Quân. Her soldiers comprised the outermost layer of the eastern flank, and it was her army's task to close off the stream of Hán soldiers pouring out of Cổ Loa's southern gate, so that the Hán army would be split in two, half of which would be stuck within the high walls of the citadel, and half of which would become fully surrounded by the Việt army.

Her army's task was one requiring great precision. So far, the technique of wedging a line of Việt soldiers into the midst of the outpour of the Hán through the gate of Cổ Loa had failed. The width of the ranks of the disciplined Hán, shoulder to shoulder as they marched, repelled the interference of single sacrificial soldiers throwing themselves one at a time into the fray. Furthermore, even though the Hán archers had been neutralized, Phật Nguyệt's army was so close to the wall that the Hán were emptying hot oil onto the women from between the parapets. Their soldiers instinctively covered their heads with their shields, leaving them vulnerable to attack from the front.

Recalling how the pincer closed in on the Hán, Phật Nguyệt had an epiphany that what she needed now was a wedge to open them up. She ordered her women to form a spearhead, to attack the Hán ranks diagonally, to avoid the pouring oil and to break up the Hán line with maximum efficiency, like the felling of a tree. The clash with the Hán ranks failed to break the line, but succeeded in creating chaos, as the slain soldiers near the gate now represented a new kind of hill to surmount. *If only*, thought Phật Nguyệt, *another spearhead formation attacked from the western flank, then we would have broken the line.* Belatedly, almost too late for action, Phật Nguyệt remembered her own bronze drum, which she now struck as loudly as she could to ring over the din of the fight. *Ka-shuick-a-thum-thum, ka-shuick-a-thum-thum, ka-shuick-a-thum-thum.* This rhythm meant a spearhead formation from the west, which at first confused her army, approaching as they did from the east; but soon a drummer from the western flank picked up the rhythm, and a wedge of soldiers attacked from the other side. When the eastern and the western flanks of the Việt army finally met at the middle, they thrust themselves northward, at considerable sacrifice to the women at the front. Lives were lost but ground was gained, and the two halves of the Hán army were cut off from each other.

It was Phật Nguyệt who reported the Hán's strategy to Trưng Vương, that the Hán army would avoid engagement in a thousand skirmishes, to be overwhelmed by the superior numbers of the Việts, but would instead charge forward to strike at the leadership, even if it cost them half of their army. They had already succeeded in puncturing the joint of the pincer, at a considerable loss to their men, and moved closer and closer to where they now stood: the short, and short-haired, Phật Nguyệt on horseback, Trưng Vương on her howdah.

"Phật Nguyệt," said Trưng Vương. "You have proven yourself steadfast and faithful. I will therefore entrust this task to you. Find the Hán generalcy and strike at their leadership before they can strike at us. Meanwhile, the Second King and I will not hide behind our cavalry, nor will we wait for the Hán to trap us in close combat. We will separate and join the western and eastern flanks; with two kings as targets, the Hán army will be divided yet again and vulnerable to our assaults."

"I will find and slay the Hán generals, though they carry no banner and hide among the infantry like cowards," said Phật Nguyệt.

Freed from his constrictive armor, Kha sat nearly naked atop the horse of Wu Sheng, breathing heavily from the exertion of the chase.

"Why are you all out of breath?" said Trưng Nhị from high upon the elephant's peaked back. "It's your horse who did all the work." She concealed her joy and relief at seeing the bumbling guardsman again. Kha's well-being was as welcome to her as the familiar halls of Cung Điện Mê Linh itself.

"The excitement is more than I can take," said Kha. "I'm not built for war."

Kha and Trưng Nhị moved behind the western flank, while Trưng Vương was headed east, now that the pincer formation had started to dissolve. The current challenge came from the chance that they could issue contradictory commands from opposing ends of the battlefront.

"You are a guardsman!" said Trưng Nhị, grateful to be back in his presence and lobbing insults at him. "Shouldn't you be prepared for anything?"

Kha waved his hand in front of his face as though to fan away an odor. "I look forward to a time when we are all back in Cung Điện Mê Linh, as though none of this had ever happened."

"The time will come when we return, triumphant, to our homeland," said Trưng Nhị, "but much has changed." Her mischievous smile faded, and her voice took on its kingly resonance. "When the Hán came to behead our men, shame our women, and claim Cung Điện Mê Linh for their own, you were not there to protect us. You stood at the governor's side while he made plans for our undoing."

"The siege of Cung Điện Mê Linh was hidden from me," said Kha sadly. "Yet even when it happened, I did not regret my choice. I knew I could do more to protect the Trưng clan from Cổ Loa than I ever could from Mê Linh. I just needed to bide my time for the right moment. Even now, I can report useful news to you: the governor plans to draw you into the citadel, then to abandon Cổ Loa through the northern gate, setting fire to the houses within, and leaving you trapped within its walls to be incinerated in the conflagration."

"Out here on the prairie, we have every advantage," said Trưng Nhị. "I suppose I should thank you for drawing out the enemy army."

"Whatever you may think," said Kha, "I have only ever done my duty to the Trưng clan."

From her high perch, Trưng Nhị looked over the battlefield and saw, in the far distance, her sister reaching the easternmost end. The Hán soldiers who had been plowing through the hinge of the pincer were thrown into chaos briefly, until their generals ordered them to split up and work their way toward the two kings.

"This elephant of yours is impressive," said Kha. "Nothing on earth could stand in its way, wherever it chooses to roam."

"Why do I get the feeling that you are trying to flatter me?" said Trưng Nhị.

"Because deep down you know that you are an unstoppable force, like this elephant," said Kha.

"If I believed that," said Trưng Nhị, "then we would all be sacrificed at the altar of my vanity."

Looking behind him at the elephant's droppings in the grass, Kha said, "And what she leaves behind is as impressive as what she carries on her back."

Scouts reported that the Hán general could be distinguished by the markings on his imperial armor: a fan of long black diamonds like pointed fingers reaching downward from his chestplate. To slay the Hán general, General Phật Nguyệt would have to fight her way to the center of the army of twenty thousand troops, and get close enough to stare each soldier in the chest.

She gathered her elite guards around her. Nearby stood Phùng Thị Chính, whose belly had by now bloomed into a sphere. The storm of war raged nearby, but the two generals stood head-to-head and conferred, shouting to be heard over the din. "Trưng Vương has ordered me to kill the Hán general, who wears a chestplate marked with black diamonds," said Phật Nguyệt. "Lend me your army, and I will go forth, perhaps to my death, in order to bring down the enemy from within."

"I will take up the rear of the advance army, so that, should you fail, I can fulfill your mission," said Phùng Thị Chính.

It was not long before Phật Nguyệt's banner fell. The Hán let out a cheer, and just as suddenly, Phùng Thị Chính felt a powerful cramp radiate throughout her body, starting in the belly then traveling to her back, where she felt a tight strain, a tingling and stinging like a sleeping limb.

The feel of the hilts of two swords in her hands rooted her in the battle. The presence of a tremendously pregnant woman in the field of combat, wandering about and staring at the armor of the passing enemy, confounded the Hán soldiers, and she walked unaccosted deeper into their ranks. Another contraction cut like a blade, and the pressure did not abate before another wave of pain came. They arrived closer and closer together now, so that she stood immobile, vulnerable in the field of battle. But then, like a bird darting from a branch, Phùng Thị Chính's eyes lit upon the black diamond pattern on a chestplate not far away. She kept him in her sight; now that she had spotted the general, he was easy to identify for the cadre of soldiers who surrounded and protected him.

The Hán soldiers, realizing that this fierce, raw, and frenzied warrior woman stalked their leader, charged at her with their polearms. But Phùng Thị Chính dove at the feet of the general, the polearms swinging in the space where she had been only moments before, and she sliced at the loose cloth at his calf, just above the boot. He fell next to Phùng Thị Chính, the Hán general and the Việt general momentarily side by side on the grass. Phùng Thị Chính quickly wrapped her arms around his neck from the rear, using his body as a shield, and put the gutting knife to his throat. The Hán soldiers pointed their polearms but dared not approach.

Phùng Thị Chính's army from Mê Linh fought their way to the line of Hán soldiers that surrounded the fallen generals. It was the epicenter of the battle, and the circle of Hán surrounding her was now engaged in combat with an outer layer of Việts. Phùng Thị Chính saw her opportunity and, slitting the throat of the enemy general, shoved his body aside. The spray from the Hán general's neck coated not just the ample body of Phùng Thị Chính herself, but the surrounding Hán. Phùng Thị Chính seized the general's halberd, which she used to create an opening in the circle, impaling a Hán soldier from behind, then clambering over his body to break away into the Việt territory, lumbering toward Trưng Vương to report the death of the Hán's commanding general, who led this half of the diminishing army.

Now surrounded by her own women, Phùng Thị Chính took two more steps before she felt her legs wobble, and the swords fell from her limp hands. The fire of birth, it seemed, would rage on despite the war. She instinctively freed her legs from their armor and padding. The modest among them kept their distance, and the immodest were horrified by the intimate scene and gave the Việt general a wide berth.

She breathed heavily, pushed, and bore down with the muscles of her abdomen until this, her sixth and only living child, came into the world, and into her own arms with a squeal. The cry of an infant is a terrifying sound on the battlefield, and the Hán were repelled from it. But to Phùng Thị Chính the voice of new life announcing itself into a world at war connected her to her life before when, surrounded by her children, she would prepare the daily meals thinking only of them. The sound of the infant's scream brought the promise of peace, but first there was the enemy at hand.

She reached behind her back with one arm, emptying her leather quiver of arrows, then lifted the infant—a girl, she noticed, aglow like a moon in the waning light—and slotted her into the empty quiver. She pulled out a gutting knife and cut the umbilical cord, tying it off with a knot, then limping forward until she reentered the fray.

When the eastern and the western flanks had closed in upon the enemy, and the Hán were captured and bound by the victors, Trưng Vương and Trưng Nhị met in the middle. As they descended from their elephants, they embraced. The elder sister thanked the Guardian Spirit for protecting them both, while the younger could only stand in awe and admiration for Trưng Vương, whose strategies seemed almost prophetic. Phan Minh took Xam and Khong Lo in hand while the kings exchanged intelligence gathered from spies and reported to their lieutenants, and through the leadership, delivered unto the kings. But it was Kha's access to the governor's inner circle that yielded the most valuable knowledge. To lay siege to Cổ Loa would be to stumble straight into the enemy's trap; to forgo a siege would leave the Việt army adrift with no mission.

CHAPTER 29

The Siege of Cổ Loa

The bodies of the fallen crisscrossed the field of battle. The writhing wounded men and women had little relief. The prairie was painted with the color of dried blood and the tones of piercing wails of horror and desperation.

The leadership assembled in the tent as rain began to thrum on the roof and the field, rinsing the dead. In the corner, Phùng Thị Chính nursed her new daughter, Triệu Ẩu, whose home in the quiver was now swaddled with fur. Trưng Vương and Trưng Nhị sat side by side, legs folded, listening to the reports of the generals and their calls to action. Despite their early triumphs, the citadel remained unsieged and it might be a long time before they penetrated its walls, yet they wore their confidence in victory for the sake of the command.

"We have access to the fertile fields surrounding Cổ Loa," said Mai. "Let them starve while we feast. Eventually they must bring the war to us."

"If they are determined to set Cổ Loa aflame, let us do

them the courtesy of starting the fire," said General Man Thiện. "We have the archers and we have the ammunition to send incendiary arrows into their citadel, so that they must either flee or perish."

Bát Nàn suggested blocking the north and south entrances, and laying siege from both, so that the Hán could not set the citadel afire without trapping themselves in.

"The time to strike is now," said Phùng Thị Chính from the corner where she swayed with her infant daughter. "When the rain is heavy, the fire cannot catch."

"Whatever we do, we need to be thoughtful and deliberate in action," said Nàng Quỳnh, "and not to be rash."

"Before we do anything else," said Trưng Nhị, "we must tend to the wounded and bury the dead. They fought valiantly to the end in order to accomplish our victory, and some still suffer from injury, without food or drink, as we speak."

"They have the rain to drink," said Trưng Vương, and Trưng Nhị cast her sister a horrified look. "Are we meant to build altars and light incense and make sacrifices to the dead, all while the war rages on?"

"At least we could save many infantry women who fought on the front lines and still live, yet cannot help themselves," said Trưng Nhị.

A tense stillness entered the tent as the kings laid bare their rift to the rest of the leadership.

"Let us not take sides," said Trưng Vương, seeing how the generals were about to chime in. "Let us instead seek compromise. We will bury General Phật Nguyệt, as she was critical to our victory and must be honored appropriately. As for the wounded, your lieutenants may go among the dead and dying and decide who can be saved and who cannot. For those whose injuries are not fatal, we will do our best to treat them. But for those who will not survive, we cannot waste our medicine, and we will let them decide whether they want a merciful death."

Trưng Nhị, whose great weakness was that her face, unlike that of her sister's, showed every emotion that passed through her head and heart, somehow managed to appear neutral to this declaration. The fate of their clan and their people depended upon it. "It must be the lieutenants," said Trưng Nhị. "Soldiers should not kill their sisters-in-arms, and generals should not kill those under their command, no matter if it is an act of mercy."

General Phùng Thị Chính spoke from the corner, where Triệu Ẩu suckled hungrily and breathed loudly through her nose. "After we bury Phật Nguyệt, and take care of the injured, what is next?"

All eyes turned to the King of the Việts, who smiled with half of her face and planted her hands on her folded knees. "It is Bát Nàn whose strategy is the most sound," said Trưng Vương, and Bát Nàn nodded with pride. "But we won't do it. Nor will we depend on the wild elements to decide the fortunes of our people."

"Then what will we do?" asked General Man Thiện. The same question echoed in the tightly knit brows and open mouths of the generals. Once again the answer was hidden in Trưng Vương's mind, who did not speak her thoughts lest they reach the ears of the Hán.

The nobles who had once advised the governor, and whose counsel had never broken through to his inner circle, were now in revolt.

"The greatest threat now is not the Việts themselves," said the governor. "If it were simply an assembly of women from Lạc Việt, then we would have nothing at all to fear."

"It is exactly so," said Li Hong. "What we need now, more than victory itself, is to strengthen the will of our armies."

"But we have lost Wu Sheng, our greatest champion, who might have challenged ten Việts and won." The governor looked at his advisor darkly, as though already in the throes of defeat.

"And the Việts have lost their champion as well," said Li Hong. "We must send word to our spies: that the head of the hero Nàng Quế is to be taken and set upon a pike, to be paraded among the Hán armies as proof of our victory."

The governor smacked the table with the flat of his hand. "It shall be done."

General Lê Chân, a slight, pale woman who hailed from a remote farm, had risen to the position of general based on her superior horsemanship; she now oversaw more than two thousand cavalrywomen. But it was her formidable mind that had led her into Trưng Vương's circle, so that the two women conferred on a plan so secret that even the Second King had to wait to learn how it would unfold.

When Lê Chân and the king were finally separated, Trưng Nhị approached Trưng Vương and took her aside, into a tent, and spoke softly.

"Sister," said Trưng Nhị with concern. "You risk alienating the leadership by keeping your plans to yourself. Lê Chân is wise, but inexperienced. By not heeding the women of the first generalcy, who have been with us from the beginning, you are sowing distrust in our ranks."

"Our secret need not last long," said Trưng Vương, understanding the risk but believing in General Lê Chân's designs, which would determine the fate of this war fully. "I only ask that you give us until tomorrow to bring this plan to fruition."

Trưng Nhị looked skeptical, but nodded her assent. "Yet at least speak to General Man Thiện and reassure her, for she believes Lê Chân to be a Hán spy."

Trưng Vương knew her mother suspected Lê Chân, who reported to the enemy and acted as a double agent on behalf of the Việts. She took on a distant look, and she recited an aphorism that she had undoubtedly learned from Thi Sách: "The eyes can see only one side of the ox at a time."

"If you ask for absolute faith from our mother," said Trưng Nhị, "then you ask too much."

Trưng Vương put her hand on Trưng Nhị's shoulder. "I have one more thing to ask," she said. "For our plan to work, we need to allow the head of the hero Nàng Quế to be set upon a pike and paraded through Cổ Loa."

The expression on Trưng Nhị's face was like nothing Trưng Vương had seen before: a swirl of emotion, encompassing doubt, horror, surprise, marbled with veins of sisterly duty and the bedrock of a long-standing trust. Trưng Vương beckoned her sister forward, and Trưng Nhị leaned in to her whispers.

General Lê Chân could not enter the citadel herself, which would have been too transparent a ploy. Instead she sent her lieutenant Quách A, who sneaked into the citadel by the north entrance, at night, with the help of stealthy Hán spies. Quách A had a long neck and a smile that was all gums, which she wore perpetually, even in the middle of a war. She brought with her a large clay pot, and the occasional clink of the jar was the only sound one could hear within the walls in the nighttime.

"What is in there?" a guardsman asked Quách A, pointing at the large clay pot.

"The head of the hero Nàng Quế," said the lieutenant and spy, showing her unmistakable smile.

"Why did you bring it in a clay pot?" the guardsman asked.

"Việts are not accustomed to carrying heads around," apologized the lieutenant. "We had no box of the right size, so I had to improvise."

The guardsman eyed the large clay pot dubiously.

"Would you like to see?" Quách A said, lifting the lid and letting the rank odor of the severed head waft into the night air.

"Shut it," said the guardsman, turning away, and led Quách A to the governor's receiving room.

That morning, the Hán army had its first celebration since

its engagement with the enemy. The streets were thronged with cheering men. Hero Nàng Quê's head was impaled, horribly disfigured into an expression of agony, and raised above the crowd. Those who carried the pikes paraded through the bailey, moving slowly through a bustle of activity. The mood among the army was, for once, electric. They felt powerful and ready for war making. If the Việts had laid siege at that moment, it seemed, they would be vanquished by the borrowed will from the humiliation of the Việts. The men cried out, "Bring on the war!" and "Death to the Việts!" and roared so that the vast army that surrounded their citadel would quake with fear at their newfound spirit.

Settling down near the crowd, Lieutenant Quách A took out a spearhead and chert, held it above the open clay pot, and struck them together several times until a spark lit, igniting the compact crush of charcoal, sulphur, and saltpeter inside. These were materials for cooking, gathered by General Lê Chân, which, taken together, produced such an explosion of noise, rising and rising as the ignition of the clay pot lit the air, that the Hán trampled over each other to leave the citadel, believing the city to be crumbling all around them. The gates were opened, and the Hán soldiers poured out into the field. The celebration of their own power, and the boost to the morale that it gave them to make war on the enemy, dissipated with the fear of finding themselves suddenly engaged in the battle that they had been crying out for.

From the moment the fireworks sounded over the prairie, and the boastful cries of the Hán turned into cries of desperation and fear, the Việt army was poised to strike, hidden among the dead of the field. In the night, they had slept among the reek of death, biding their time for just that moment to rise as one, bearing sword and shield to face the onrushing Hán army. The drums thundered now for them to advance. The wind was at their backs, and even the generals stormed the enemy. Trưng Vương and Trưng Nhị rode their elephants into the sprawling and scattering enemy soldiers, adding to the sense of chaos afflicting the Hán. But this was more than strategic. Trưng Vương needed to kill Tô Định, and she knew that the governor would never leave the safety of his citadel except to flee, and she vowed not to allow it. The metal of her grief was of his forge. The governor was the smelter and smith of her woes. Her life might otherwise have been a garden, a gentle river, a fertile field; yet by his design, it was, instead, an iron veil.

Once they had reached the south gate, Generals Mai, Phùng Thị Chính, Lê Chân, and Lê Ngọc Trinh led their armies inside the citadel, but the kings went their separate ways, astride their great gray elephants, and navigated the wall so that they could flank the enemy at the north gate.

Once inside, the generals came upon a scene scarcely less chaotic than that upon the field. The proximity to the ramparts, though, meant that the Việts were vulnerable to attacks from above, which the surviving Hán generals tried to exploit. General Lê Ngọc Trinh charged up a flight of steps to attack a Hán general giving orders to men to pour boiling oil upon the invading army. Yet in her haste to storm the ramparts, General Lê Ngọc Trinh left her army behind. She faced the Hán general alone, and he unsheathed his sword. She swung at him, and the Hán general shrugged off the attack with his shield, and jabbed with his own blade, which nearly found its mark as General Lê Ngọc Trinh backed away. She swung again, with the same arc and, anticipating this strike, the Hán general lifted up his own sword and brought it down upon her hilt, so that she was forced to let go of the weapon. It clanged down into the bailey. General Lê Ngọc Trinh, weaponless, backed down the steps; desperate now, as the Hán general charged her, she reached down to pick up rocks and hurl them at her attacker. He held his shield in front of him, giving General Lê Ngọc Trinh enough time to improvise a weapon. She took a heavy rock, placed it in her silk sash, and swung it over her head like a whip. When the Hán general let down the shield and began to charge with his sword, she let fly the silk sash with the heavy rock within, crushing her foe's head with a single blow. Her army approaching from behind her now, General Lê Ngọc Trinh did not fetch her sword to charge the ramparts, but wielded instead the silk sash with the rock that had crushed the head of the Hán general.

Trưng Vương found herself at the north gate alone; Trưng Nhị must have been waylaid by another skirmish to the west of the citadel. So the fate of the battle depended upon her instinct: that the governor would try to flee stealthily through the unguarded back door. If he followed through with his plan to set fire to the citadel, he would have failed to trap the Việt army; if he brought with him a legion to protect him as he departed through the north gate, he would have been conspicuous, and prone to attack; it is only by leaving surreptitiously with a small retinue that Tô Định stood any chance of survival. The king waited outside the north gate, anticipating an imminent victory but fearing the possibility of ambush, for she and Khong Lo the elephant were alone.

The vines of doubt that clung to Trưng Vương only choked the branches of her intellect. She knew that her trunk and roots—the will and determination that animated her—were nourished by grief's rain. Yet it was still possible that she would fail, that one poor calculation or misstep would end their revolution on the verge of victory.

The gate finally creaked open, and out shuffled three men: Tô Định the governor, Li Hong the advisor, and a bodyguard. "Go back!" called Li Hong when he saw the monstrous elephant waiting in his path.

"No!" said the bodyguard. "Inside the citadel is an army of Việts. She is but one woman. She can do us no harm."

"I wish to talk to the lord's daughter," said the governor, stepping out from behind the bodyguard and the advisor.

Trưng Vương said nothing, but clanged her sword against her golden armor, letting the metal ringing echo in the ears of the Hán governor. In her blood she vacillated between the cold duty of leadership and the hot pulse of vengeance.

The governor proceeded to step forward, saying, "You would not have come alone unless a part of you wished to negotiate a surrender. I believe in rational decision making, not in indulging our emotions. And I believe that the best way to end this war—to save the lives of Việts and Hán alike—is for us to become your prisoners." He held up his hands to be tied, dangerously close to Khong Lo the elephant, who stood unmoved by this gesture. It blinked its massive eyes.

"Once, you told my father that I was unfit to lead, that I was unfit to speak in your presence, that what I needed was a husband to rule over me." Trưng Vương spoke without wavering, without for a moment betraying the stampede of emotions that galloped through her upon the threshold of her vengeance. "I found a worthy husband, and you had him killed, and now I am here for your head." Trưng Vương threw a bladder of water to the dusty ground in front of him, and said, "Here is some water. Wash your neck for my blade."

The governor tried and failed to smirk. "I told you that I am a rational man, and I do not succumb to displays of emotion. You will never hear me beg, yet I appeal to your self-interest: make me a prisoner, then send a message to the emperor. If I am ransomed, I think you will find the terms quite generous."

"With this sword," said Trưng Vương, holding aloft a broad blade, "I will send *your head* as a message to the emperor." She brandished, in her other hand, a polearm. The heat of her anger was almost too much to bear. She tried to calm herself with thoughts of Thi Sách's peaceful presence, yet it only enraged her further. "But first I will march it through the battlefields on a pike. Barbarism is what the Hán understand best."

Tô Định shook his head. "You are making a mistake, King of the Việts," he said. "Do you think the emperor will abide such an insult to the throne? That His Illustriousness will simply give up Lạc Việt to the Việts? Your insurrection is a minor setback in a conquest that will last as long as the empire is large."

By then the governor had come so close that he stood directly below Trưng Vương's leg, and he unsheathed a jade-gilt dagger, driving it into the king's calf. She had allowed herself to be stirred into a rage from which there was no exit but through the heart of the enemy. Her sword, sharpened to the width of a blade of grass, fell upon the neck of Tô Định, leaving the headless governor to stumble and sink beside himself. She had pictured this scene a thousand times before and never in all her imaginings did the governor have the honor of fighting back. She wanted to restore his head to his body so that she could dominate his will, to make him grovel and beg and to refuse him the way he had refused mercy on the Việts. It was only just.

Watching his leader fall to the king's blade, the governor's bodyguard jabbed at Khong Lo with his polearm, agitating the elephant, which reared back and trumpeted but did not throw its rider. Trưng Vương let go of the sword so that she could engage the bodyguard with her own polearm two-handed.

Meanwhile, Li Hong fled into the woods, his yellow robe flapping in his wake, the soft earth muting the clop of his boots. Trưng Vương was dimly aware of the pain in her leg and the escape of the advisor, who according to Kha deserved as much blame for the tragedies that befell them as the governor himself. But she was too preoccupied with the task of straddling the elephant as it charged the bodyguard, and parrying the bodyguard's attack before boring through his chest with her awl. Sometimes the wicked live to thrive, she concluded. Sometimes evil goes unpunished by man or woman or god.

By the time she withdrew her polearm from the corpse of the bodyguard, she turned around and saw a dark and empty woods. As the immediacy of the fight faded into memory, the throbbing pain in her leg increased until she was forced to tear at the decorative cloth draped over the back of the elephant, and use it to bandage the wound and stanch the flow of blood. She then played the rhythm on the drum that signaled help was needed: *thum-ka-thum-ka-thum-ka-ka-ka, thum-ka-ka.*

To her surprise, when Trưng Vương stopped beating the bronze drum, the figures that approached came not from the battlefield, nor from the citadel, but from the north woods. Her face had gone pale, and she felt feverish and weary. She leaned all the way forward, lying atop the elephant's humped back. If the figures approaching were Hán, then she didn't know whether she possessed the strength to continue the fight.

As her eyes cleared, she saw the yellow robe of the advisor, yet behind him, with a spearpoint at Li Hong's back, walked Trưng Nhị.

It was the sight of the governor's head paraded on the field that subdued the generals and hastened the battle's end. For those few Hán who refused to surrender, the advisor Li Hong begged them to let down their arms. The fighting ceased, and a wind carried the scent of death southward.

The surviving soldiers showed defeat in their sagging limbs and empty eyes. Some men wept, fearing the consequences of their failure, at the hands of either the Việt or the Hán.

Trưng Vương, adorned in the golden armor that shone into the eyes of the former Hán army, shouted her message to the Việt heralds, who repeated the speech, sentence by sentence, to the defeated prisoners, among whom she strode on horseback.

"You have come from far-flung lands," she began. "You owe no loyalty to the Hán. You are from the frontier regions—Jiuquan, Zhangyi, Dunhuang, and Wuwei—and have been conscripted into war just as our husbands and brothers have been." She trotted down the aisle of men upon their knees, behind whom stood rows of armored Việt women. "Lạc Việt is its own country, a country of Việts, separate and independent from the Hán. You may go home to your frontier lands, or you may retreat to the capitol region, or you may stay in Việt lands, but any man who tries to establish a society within Lạc Việt that is loyal to the Hán emperor will be dealt with, as we will now deal with the poisonous advisor, Li Hong." Trưng Vương then signaled the drummers to play their rhythm for a formal execution: *tak-tak-tak-tak, tak-tak-tak-tak, tak-tak-tak-tak*.

The advisor was brought out into the aisle of men, across from the Việt king. The piteous and thin-bearded Li Hong bowed and begged and sobbed, but the fate set in motion by his words crashed upon him now, down upon his head, caving it in with an ax blow. Trưng Vương then signaled for the rhythm to cease, and allowed the ten thousand ensuing silences to speak for her.

CHAPTER 30

A Time of Peace

In a time of prosperity and peace, the greatest adversity that Trưng Vương contended with concerned perceptions of her own favoritism toward the people of Mê Linh and Chu Diên, her late husband's city of origin. Free at last from the yoke of the Hán, the men and women of Lạc Việt began to see oppression in the subtlest of signals of their new rulers. Politics exhausted her more than war ever could. Võ Quan from Nhật Nam, in particular, struggled with the proclaimed neutrality of the new regime. Though his people were no longer poor or hungry, he wondered if, by providing the weaponry that won the war for the Việts, Nhật Nam shouldn't be given more than an equal share under the new government. Trưng Vương insisted, through the lord's herald, that Nhật Nam would not be treated differently from the other towns in Lạc Việt, despite the fact that it had only participated in the war through compulsion. *What more does he expect?* Trưng Vương said to the ghost of her husband. *His people are no longer starving and they are prosperous and free. Are men never satisfied?*

To reassure herself of the glory of her people's liberation, Trưng Vương turned her attention to Trịnh Sang, now Lord of Hợp Phố, who commissioned statues of the sister-kings to be built in his city, where they were beloved heroes as well as heads of state. The Trưng Sisters visited the town to witness their icons worshiped like gods. To Trưng Vương, this was further proof of the righteousness of their cause. Yet Trưng Nhị could not help but feel a deep discomfort at beholding herself, twelve feet high and perpetually armed for war. Drummers played the bronze drums as a reminder of the Trưng Sisters' great victory, and Việts came from throughout Lạc Việt to dance around the likenesses of the kings.

Trưng Vương took particular interest in Đặng Thảo, who was charged with easing the army's transition to peace-time. Many women, especially from Chu Diên, wished to liberate their men from the Hán armies, and brashly demanded to march north until they were face-to-face with the Hán emperor. It was Đặng Thảo who reasoned with the reckless lieutenants, and answered their impassioned pleas with sober argument. *Marching upon the Hán in their own territory would be suicide for our armies*, explained Đặng Thảo, *and it should be enough that the Hán will not conscript any more of our men for their wars*. Now a lord himself, Đặng Thảo had already sacrificed his reputation as a leader for the good of the nation, and Trưng Vương rewarded him by conferring upon him the title Champion of the Peace. The Lord of Chu Diên was the only man in power, it seemed, who did not wish to cage or subdue the king. Therefore, she indulged the lord's company, as a friend and confidant, risking the appearance of favoritism.

Trưng Vương only wanted peace. Her conviction grew that politics and peace were one and the same; like her mother before her, she yearned at such times for the simplicity of war.

One morning, the dawn bell went unrung, and it was Trưng Nhị and Phan Minh who, rising from their furs, saw through the open slats of the window the guardsman lying belly-up in the garden path. They rushed out to find him delirious, lips quivering, dried blood on his chest from a series of cuts made by the spearhead, still clutched in his hands. Trưng Nhị snatched the spearhead from Kha's hands, wresting it away with a twist of the thumb, while Phan Minh supported his head and asked, "What happened? Are you okay? Was there an attack?"

"Duy did this," said Kha, fixing his eyes on Phan Minh. "It was Duy."

"Duy the beggar?" said Phan Minh, turning instantly pale with fright, then slowly adjusted to the realization that Kha had harmed himself. "Duy is dead."

"Nothing dies," said Kha. "Nothing dies."

The guardsman's words haunted the gardener's son, who turned cold, then stood up wearing a solemn expression. To Trưng Nhị, he said, "Kha must be sent away, to a place where he can be helped. He is no good to us in this state." Kha had been suffering from bleak visions for months, and his condition had worsened of late. Trưng Nhị wondered if he had been possessed by an itinerant spirit, the same demon that had afflicted her father.

"He needs to see the physician," said Trưng Nhị urgently.

"We *all* need to go to a new place," said Kha, doing his best to appear lucid. "Maybe in the mountains. It isn't safe here."

"Poor, dear Kha," said Trưng Nhị, embracing the troubled guardsman. He had always been a big man, but she thought at that moment how impossibly large he had seemed when she was a little girl, and how diminished he seemed at that moment. She and Phan Minh lifted him into a standing position, and took him, one underneath each armpit, to see the many physicians employed at the palace. A row of guardsmen who had come to help all looked away, unsure, if they were to meet Kha's eyes, what kind of horrible prophecy they would find there.

"I don't have the time to dedicate to the problems of one guardsman," said Trưng Vương when the Second King approached her about Kha's sufferings. "I have the troubles of all of Lạc Việt to attend to."

It hurt Trưng Nhị's heart that her sister saw Kha as a mere guardsman. "What troubles? Peace reigns, and the petty petitions of these regional lords are the dove cry that comes every morning. It won't spoil. But that *one guardsman* kept us safe for all our lives, and helped win the war for us with his act of espionage."

"It was his wish not to become a man of title and worth," said Trưng Vương coldly, stepping gingerly on her leg, which had healed from the battle so many months ago, but which she still favored out of habit. It was a simple matter to the king; much simpler than the problems that vexed her daily. "He always said he would die a guardsman in Cung Điện Mê Linh."

"But not today!" Trưng Nhị raised a fist defiantly. The

king's advisors rushed out of the Great Hall, ceding the room to the embattled monarchs.

Trưng Vương stared at her sister's clenched fist. She felt, for a brief moment, a sting on her cheek as though struck, a memory of their sparring days. Trưng Vương returned just as quickly to the memory of her own kingliness. "How am I to read the riddle of your hand, lifted against me?" she said.

Trưng Nhị lowered her hand and unflexed her fingers. "Our power—yours and mine—is earthly, temporal. What is a title and property worth? Nothing, when compared to our integrity."

"I simply have no time," said Trưng Vương wearily, "to reassure you. Get to your point."

Trưng Nhị spoke quickly, trusting in the art of persuasion but stymied by her sister's uncompromising stare. "Phan Minh wishes to send Kha away to Chu Diên, where he will live a peaceful life in the Temple of the Guardian Spirit, and be unburdened by the duties that have undone him here in Cung Điện Mê Linh. But I wonder if we should heed the guardsman's warning. By the mere act of execution, we may have pushed down the hill the wagon of our own destruction."

"The governor would have killed me," said Trưng Vương indignantly. "Tô Định deserved a worse fate than a beheading."

"I'm talking," said Trưng Nhị, "about Duy the beggar."

"Duy the beggar has nothing to do with this," said Trưng Vương, curling her lip. "You sound like our father, with these dreams and superstitions."

"And you sound like a Hán bureaucrat," said Trưng Nhị, with bitterness and sorrow marbling her voice, "forever preoccupied with the petty disputes of lords, the sum in the treasury, and the pomp and ceremony of the court." She wished to remind Trưng Vương that she, too, was a king.

"This is my final word on this matter," said Trưng Vương. "Kha is to be taken to the Temple of the Guardian Spirit in Chu Diên, where he will be cared for by the monks and live out the rest of his life in peace, free of any duty but to care for himself. Now, let's move on." She clapped her hands to summon the advisors into the room, and Trưng Nhị lingered for only a moment before she left the Great Hall.

The Hán who remained in Lạc Việt lived uneasily as neighbors to those once oppressed by their countrymen. The officers' towers and barracks and prisons were seized by the regional lords, and some of the Hán who had once commanded these towers now sat in its prisons. The edict of the land forbade the lords from punishing Hán simply for being Hán. But individuals did not operate under the same law, and many Hán would become scapegoats for the greater troubles brought upon by a governor now dead for more than a year. These found themselves ostracized, shoved around at the market, sometimes beaten in the game dens at night, and in the most extreme situations, victims of mob violence.

Then there were Hán who were men of worth, as demonstrated through their generous and compassionate natures, which in some cases were undeniable. They married Việt women, and raised Việt children, and lived their lives in every other way as Việts themselves. But even these men longed for a time when they would not have to prove themselves as fully human—when Hán and Việts no longer sought to conquer or oppress their kin.

PART FOUR

THE STORY OF MA YUAN

Lạc Việt Year 2740–2741
(42–43 CE)

CHAPTER 31

The Exodus

Upon the stone terrace of their palatial home in Xingping, overlooking the peach orchard in bloom, General Ma Yuan and Lady Lin stood at arm's length, awkward like new lovers, though they had wed nine years before. Their soft words died in the gusty spring air, and the gardeners below and the servants of the house heard only the chime of a hanging bell and the birdsong.

He calmly explained to his wife, Lady Lin, that he would leave in one week, not to return for more than a year.

"You have a baby now," she said. "Fen barely knows you as it is." Lady Lin did not live by the axiom that she should humbly indulge a husband's every command.

Ma Yuan lived by one rule: duty to others. When his duty to the Hán abraded his duty to family, he felt a depth of regret that took nothing away from his absolute devotion to his country. When he contemplated the dangers that awaited his men in the southlands—jungles of poisonous snakes, miasmas that spread disease on the wind, treacherous paths that could cripple horses, Việt armies said to be eighty thousand strong and hardened by rebellion—these threats intrigued him with their seeming intractability.

"All of this"—he gestured to their well-appointed home and the grounds beyond—"we owe to Emperor Guangwu. Without war, we would have nothing."

Lady Lin tightened the coil of her robe around her shoulders, as though bracing for a sudden wind. "I'd rather have nothing." She fell into her husband's chest, letting him embrace her in such a way that her fists pressed against his torso, though she rested her cheek against his neck. She felt the throb of his pulse through the skin and allowed the moment to unfold to encompass the next, and the next, until her silence could be construed as yielding. "I'm not finished punishing you for leaving us," she said.

"I expect no less," said Ma Yuan.

Outside, peach blossoms gently fell to the orchard floor, one at a time, like children at a lake awaiting their turn to dive into the water. "The peacock pheasants will miss you," said Lady Lin.

"Should I fail to answer the emperor's call, and the call of my country, because I will leave the peacock pheasants without my good company?"

Lady Lin gestured toward the gardens. "The peach trees will miss you," she said, turning her chin up to look him intensely in the eyes.

"They will be blooming again the next time we see each other," Ma Yuan promised.

Ma Yuan and his men rode without their armor. The journey would be long, and Ma Yuan had no wish to punish his men beyond the pain they would all endure at the hands of nature and the elements. At the start of the trek, they were one hundred thousand strong. By the time they reached Jiaozhi, Ma Yuan knew, they would be diminished. The first juncture at which they turned to the south, away from Xingping or any path that led to the realm of the familiar, Ma Yuan steeled himself for this imminent reality.

Ma Yuan's lieutenants served him with absolute devotion. He had saved their lives and made them fortunes and titles such that they could only repay that debt with the meagerest of remittances: their obedience. He surprised them all that day by singing a fisherman's song:

> Fish are swimming, swimming up the Li River,
> Toward the current they toss their silvery tails,
> It's like an idle game, they could do this forever,
> But we catch them, gut them, and peel off their
>   scales...then eat!

Soon all of the army was singing along with the tune. If Ma Yuan was correct, and the journey ahead was as perilous as he believed, then this would be their last chance for cheer.

In the second year of their reign in Lạc Việt, Trưng Vương and Trưng Nhị barely spoke, though they dwelled in the same palace. This was not a shunning but simply that Trưng Vương occupied herself solemnly with affairs of Lạc Việt, and did not indulge in idle conversation. Even her habit of writing out lists, riddles, and records of the day's events fell away, in favor of writing letters, laws, and decrees. And whenever she found a free moment, she would court the ghost of Thi Sách with the flute's melody.

Done with the day's work, Trưng Vương visited neither the meditation room nor the altar to the Guardian Spirit, but returned to her humble chambers and the comfort of her husband's ghost. "Never has there been greater prosperity, freedom, and equality in the land of Lạc Việt, yet the Lạc lords are dissatisfied," she told the absent Thi Sách. "If I reward any lord for his loyalty and service, the others become jealous like insecure lovers."

Without his book, Trưng Vương had to imagine the responses of Thi Sách. If she had only known that the words he'd left behind would be the sum remnants of his life, she would never have reduced the book to ash, even to win the support of the Degar. As king, her will would be obeyed, but nothing would bring back her husband. *If only I could hear his voice once more*, she thought. Yet she understood that one utterance would never be enough.

Wealth and independence do not make happiness, as long as that happiness can be measured against one's neighbor's.

"That may be so," said Trưng Vương, "but as king, what have I to do with their happiness? My duty is to provide for the people and to protect their lives. Happiness is not my realm of influence."

Victory made them happy. Now that the Hán oppressors are but a bad memory, the Lạc lords will measure the height of their happiness according to that peak of triumph, and will find that they stand forever below the threshold.

These motes of wisdom, drawn from Trưng Vương's subconscious, where her husband now resided, were oceans apart from the obscure aphorisms for which Thi Sách was known. She wanted to puzzle through his words, to live with the uncertainty, then to wrestle with multiple possibilities and finally to settle on the conclusion that every impenetrable phrase carried the enigma of love.

The weeks-long journey through Guangxi lulled the army into a false sense of ease. This part of the southward march felt more like a parade, as they passed through town after town of loyal Hán men and women who cheered them on. All was familiar and friendly. But soon the path would become strange. The very air would become hostile.

In one of these forgettable towns, a boy holding a home-made wooden sword ran alongside the cavalcade. He shouted, "Let me join you! I am strong and I am ready! The enemy has no chance against me!"

The soldiers proceeded indifferently, but when Ma Yuan saw the boy, he dismounted and patted him on the shoulder. Admiring the boy's unused sword, he said, "Unlike the rebel Việts, the Hán army uses only trained soldiers to fight in their wars. You may yet become a great soldier, or even a great general, if you keep that spirit alive. For now, you must keep practicing with that sword until it has more than a thousand nicks and gouges, indeed, until it has turned to kindling from so much use. Then, come and visit me in Xingping, and I will make you into a soldier."

The boy looked at General Ma Yuan solemnly. The procession of soldiers continued behind them—a seemingly endless line of men and horses and the scent of a hundred thousand unwashed bodies—until the boy nodded with purpose, and the general mounted his horse and trotted beside them.

CHAPTER 32

Ghost Gate Pass

There were so many horses fording the river that the muddy waters rose around them. Their muzzles strained upward and their wide black eyes seemed to appeal for relief from man or god. The only answer was the master's heel urging them forward, where they stepped from rock to slippery rock, barely keeping their riders' shoulders above the surface of the stream.

Once they had reached the other side, they followed the river upstream as it bent to the south. A layer of silt rested on their saddles, packs, and clothes. A vision of indigo mountains splayed out in front of them would have induced awe at the beauty of this country if it were not the only path ahead—if they would not soon be traversing those very cliffs that created a corrugated pattern against the blank white sky and, approaching their peaks, faded into mist.

As the first signs of hardship were revealed to the army, it became necessary for Ma Yuan to lead. Where he had ridden comfortably toward the middle of this vast wave of horses and men up until the Yu river, once they approached Ghost Gate

Pass, he took up the forward position: the first to bend the tall grass at the foothills, the first to pass through every spiderweb on the path, and the first to endure the rocky climb.

Many horses, unfit for the ascent because of a cracked hoof, skin infection, or mud fever, were mercifully left behind. The road ahead was cruel.

Safe passage upon the mountain meant walking single-file with both horse and rider staring straight ahead, to conquer the fear of falling. Now and then a rider would be afflicted by curiosity, looking down to assess the risk, and find himself tilting unconsciously toward the void. Many times it was the horse that refused this shift toward the left, and into oblivion. But the most trusting horses felt their rider incline leftward and would step only slightly in that direction, and plummet. At other times, by no fault of horse or rider, a loose rock below or above would dislodge the ground beneath them, and another one tumbled down the cliff.

Ghost Gate Pass was named for the mists that obscured the path, the sky, and the rider in front of you. Nothing was quite visible except for the plunge below and the corpses of the fallen. Even where the passage was wide, the lack of sight created a sense of panic. Then the mist started to reek of a foul odor. Pestilential emanations from the deathly river below rose and joined with the fog. Every soldier in the army succumbed to the reflexive impulse to cover his face, trusting in his steed to navigate the road ahead.

At the front of the army, Ma Yuan witnessed something

he would remember for the rest of his days, a thing that would form his most concrete recollection of the journey: a bird passed over the river below, and once it entered the miasma, died mid-flight and sank soundlessly to the bank. He could not have known, at the time, exactly what this foretold.

Ma Yuan would witness, thousands of times over, the slow deaths of his men, lips turned dark, breathing labored, eyes glazed with what appeared to be confusion, but was in fact the dread clarity of death's acceptance. When so many die in so short a span, death is an embodiment, there in the crowd, a physical fact as real as a stubbed toe.

A spy from Giaozhou reported to Trưng Nhị that a massive Hán army was on the march to Lạc Việt, and would reach Cổ Loa in little more than a fortnight. The comfort of her life with Phan Minh in Cung Điện Mê Linh—a life about which she had long dreamt—led her to consider for a brief moment fleeing for the jungles of the south, where they would live beyond the reach of the Hán. This first reaction was not one befitting a king, and was quickly supplanted with nobler notions of duty to and solidarity with her Việt sisters.

Yet Trưng Nhị did not immediately report this intelligence to Trưng Vương. She told Xấu, the dog, that war was coming once again, like an unwelcome guest at Cổ Loa, the front door of Lạc Việt, before long. Xấu panted and lifted his head eagerly. Trưng Nhị sank back into the furs formerly belonging to her mother and father. She could understand, for the first time, the despair and torpor of Lord Trưng. The alternative was a constant vigilance against enemies, or betrayals among allies, that was indistinguishable from paranoia.

When Phan Minh returned to their chambers, he saw his beloved sprawled languorously on the furs and mistook the scene for a prelude to intimacy. He playfully crawled toward her on all fours, sneering like a charging bull, pawing at the floor. Taking on the roles of animals of the wilderness, or the field, was a familiar pretense to Trưng Nhị, yet she did not respond in kind.

"What troubles you, Nhị-*ơi*?" asked Phan Minh.

"When I was growing up, every now and then my father would wake us up in the middle of the night and tell us *today is the day*, and we were told to be prepared to disguise ourselves as a family of peasants, and to flee Cung Điện Mê Linh to become anonymous beggars in a distant city," said Trưng Nhị. "Deep down, he wished to abdicate his lordship and live a carefree life. He and I are more alike than I ever knew."

Phan Minh listened. There were questions in his eyes, but he did not wish to interrupt Trưng Nhị's flow of thought. He understood that she sought a receptive ear, not advisement or consolation.

"The Hán army is on its way," said Trưng Nhị, "and we will need to go to Cổ Loa, or farther north, to stop the second wave of the enemy before it gathers into a surging tide."

"When?" said Phan Minh.

"Now," said Trưng Nhị. "We must act now."

Phan Minh held Trưng Nhị in his arms, and while they embraced, the peacocks called and the wind moved through the trees. For as soon as they separated, they knew, imminent war would have to be faced. And they secretly wished that they could live the rest of their lives without hearing the beating of the bronze drum again.

Past the Ghost Gate Pass—past the rocky terrain that had caused their horses' hooves to crack, and the miasmas that spread disease among the men—the Hán army now waded through a swamp. Vines draped all around and dead trees reached their naked limbs toward the path. Occasionally, when a soldier reached up to push a vine away, that vine would lash out and bite, revealing itself as a viper, and the unarmored victim would suffer a sting that turned to a throb, which slowly grew into a mortal pang, as the flesh around the bite turned blue-black.

The land of Jiaozhi was near, yet felt more distant than ever. Their passage was slowed by swamps and vines and snakes, as though the terrain were a hostile enemy. There was nothing General Ma Yuan could do to improve the morale of the army until they won their first victory against nature, which was to survive the journey.

But when the path ahead opened into green fields, the promise of fertile lands offered the hope of society, and even though it was the men's burden to do battle with and eventually conquer that society, they welcomed the companionship of war, which was preferable to dying one precipitous fall, one pestilential breath, one snakebite at a time.

"Now," said General Ma Yuan, leading the cavalcade out of the swamp and into the open prairie. "Spread the word to the army. We will don our armor for the remainder of the voyage."

Trưng Vương seemed to have inherited none of her father's ambivalence about leadership. As different as she was from her mother in ferocity of spirit, she possessed Lady Man Thiện's clear resolve. This confidence had served her well in the Batttle of Cổ Loa; if the Guardian Spirit allowed it, it would serve her well now. As soon as Trưng Nhị reported the advance of the enemy's army upon Cổ Loa, Trưng Vương ordered more than a dozen heralds to fan out across Lạc Việt and to rally the Lạc lords to unite at Cổ Loa and protect the city from reoccupation by the Hán. From there, the Việt armies would head north and confront the Hán at Lãng Bạc, where two armies from Nhật Nam and Hợp Phố would flank the enemy, cutting them off from the fertile lands and forcing them to retreat. Unlike the Battle of Cổ Loa, the Battle of Lãng Bạc would not be won in a matter of days. It must be a war of attrition, in which the enemy is compelled to disperse or flee because it is the only way to survive.

"This is what we have been waiting for," said Trưng Vương to the court. Had they not been victorious against the Hán before? Was her strategy not perfect during the Battle of Cổ Loa? "We knew this was coming. We have prepared for this."

Trưng Nhị felt less certain of victory; her guts roiled at the prospect of fighting in another war. Yet she could not voice her doubts. Perhaps Trưng Vương's will would be strong enough to vanquish the enemy, this time in greater numbers and with firmer resolve.

Many members of the court took strength from these words, believing in the legend and the leadership of Trưng Vương, She-King of the Việts. But there were others in attendance who looked down at the floor and dared not reveal their faces, for they had not seen a Việt army practicing on the training fields for more than a year, and doubted that the same women who fought so fiercely to gain their independence, once they had known prosperity and luxury, could fight as passionately to keep it.

CHAPTER 33

An Assembly of Lords

At Tay Vu, the Lạc lords met in the palace of Lord Dũ Chí, who had remained neutral during the uprising. Lord Dũ Chí took pride in the harmonious relations between Việts and Hán in his protectorate, and his province was one of the few with Hán officials. Absent from this gathering were Trưng Vương and Trưng Nhị, as well as the many princesses, generals, and ladies of the court.

"What intelligence have we gathered on the threat from the north?" asked Trinh Sang, the bearded, dissipated Lord of Hợp Phố, who was the last to arrive at this gathering.

"How can we call it a threat before we know the army's intention?" said Dũ Chí. He looked out upon the assembled lords from underneath a single connected eyebrow.

"Do armies usually come to scatter flowers and make merry?" said Trinh Sang. This elicited a hearty chuckle from the other lords.

"*You* may feel the luxury to laugh," said Dũ Chí. "The women of Hợp Phố fought side by side with the Trưngs in the rebellion and you have been rewarded handsomely for your loyalty."

The lords turned quiet, and Trinh Sang turned quiet with them, understanding now the hazard of his late arrival. The tide of the conversation had turned against the Trưng Sisters.

"We were never truly independent of the Hán," said Dũ Chí. "It was always an illusion, an idle dream woven by the witchery of angry women. They do not speak for us."

"Are you suggesting there is no possibility of winning?" said Đặng Thảo, Lord of Chu Diên.

"What does it mean to 'win' when you were never allowed in the fight? Our men were never welcome on the battlefield, and now our women are filled with ideas of liberation and would challenge our authority as leaders and as men," said Dũ Chí.

"I must disagree," said Đặng Thảo. To him, the glory of their victory still glowed with campfire light. "The Trưng Sisters are heroes of the people, and beloved across all of Lạc Việt."

"But does anyone believe that these women can overwhelm the Hán's fiercest general and an army of elite soldiers coming with the sole purpose of subduing a rebellion? No, they are not heroes. They are illusionists."

Trinh Sang stood up, saying, "It appears that the Lạc lords have already decided to remain neutral, and to make peace with the victor, whoever it should be."

"But to remain neutral is the same as condemning the kings to death," said Đặng Thảo.

"They seemed content to fight without the help of men the

last time," said Dũ Chí. "If we do nothing, how is it any different from remaining idle, as we did during the rebellion?"

"But," said Đặng Thảo, "surely we must tell the kings that they will receive no support?"

"Fellow lords," Dũ Chí said, "history will judge us by our prescience, not by our passions. If we choose to sidestep the danger of engaging with the Hán army, surely it follows that we would reconcile with the Hán afterward. How can we reconcile in good faith when we have warned their enemy of our every intention beforehand? Let the Trưngs suffer a necessary defeat at the hands of the Hán that will teach them obedience."

There was no time for marshaling support among the cities of Lạc Việt. Trưng Vương merely sent word to all the Lạc lords of their orders: for every army to travel north of Cổ Loa and meet the Hán army before it claims the conch-shaped citadel. Once again, the armies would clash in the open, but this time they would have nowhere to retreat, and no access to the fertile lands that would replenish them. The trek would be a three-day journey, in order to meet the enemy at Lãng Bạc.

It was in the armory, while Trưng Vương adorned herself in golden mail—a vision to inspire the Việts—that Trưng Nhị confronted her sister.

"We need the help of the Degar," said Trưng Nhị. "We would have lost the Battle of Cổ Loa without their archers."

"The People were clear. They will not answer our call a second time. Our heralds could not even find their mountain refuge."

"Then you must go and make the appeal once again." Trưng Nhị clasped her hands together, making her own desperate appeal to the king. "You have been to the city in the mountains."

"We have no time." Trưng Vương struggled to adjust the ties of her armor. "Help me with this lamellar."

Despite herself, Trưng Nhị helped her sister affix the woven golden breastplate in its place, lacing it to the back.

"After all," said Trưng Vương, "the coming war is a battle of resources, and will not be won one arrow at a time."

But while we wait to outlast the stamina of the enemy, thought Trưng Nhị, *our own soldiers will suffer, good women will die, and the morale of the army will fade.*

Observing Trưng Nhị's back-leaning posture and flat expression, sensing her skepticism, Trưng Vương planted her hands upon Trưng Nhị's shoulders and said, "Do not worry, my sister. Our feats on the battlefield are now legend."

Fully armored, Trưng Vương tromped out of the room with a clanging that receded with distance. Into the emptiness, Trưng Nhị released a held breath. She thought of all the training of their youth and wondered for a moment if they could abandon it all. *Are human beings made for war?* Trưng Nhị asked herself. Even Trưng Vương did not think so while her husband lived. "Becoming a legend," said Trưng Nhị to no one, "is the thing I'm afraid of."

The distance to his goal narrowing, General Ma Yuan revived the chants and songs that he'd begun at the outset of the journey. To the usual refrains of the fisherman's song he now added the number of days left in the journey.

> Seven fish swimming, swimming up the Li River,
> Toward the current they toss their silvery tails,
> It's like an idle game, they could do this forever,
> But we catch them, gut them, and peel off their
>   scales...then eat!

Next day the same refrain would flow from their lips with greater urgency and spirit, as the knowledge that another day of trudging was behind them:

> Six fish swimming, swimming up the Li River,
> Toward the current they toss their silver tails,
> It's like an idle game, they could do this forever,
> But we catch them, gut them, and peel off their
>   scales...then eat!

In the final stretch, General Ma Yuan varied the song to prepare his men for the fight ahead:

> Five Việts marching, marching up the Yu River,
> Toward Cổ Loa they step with crooked feet,

It's like an idle game, they could do this forever,
But we catch them, gut them, and peel off their
      scales . . . then eat!

It was three days out from Cổ Loa that a Hán scout reported an army approaching from the south. They would clash next day. He estimated their number at twenty thousand—less than half the size of the remaining Hán army—and all women.

"Only one army?" said General Ma Yuan. He spoke as much to himself as to the lieutenants. "If I were the King of the Việts, I would have tried to flank us from both sides, and to cut off our access to the farmland. I wonder what she means by sending such a meager army."

"Is she underestimating us?" volunteered one of the lieutenants.

"No," said General Ma Yuan. "She is too clever for that, and she must know my reputation throughout all of the Hán Empire and the provinces."

"She must be losing support among the Việts," spoke another lieutenant.

"Yes," said General Ma Yuan. "So why not take a defensive position? Surely she knows they have a better chance of defending Cổ Loa than of overwhelming us on the open field of Lãng Bạc." Then his eyes lit up and his lips formed an upward curl at the corners. "The King of the Việts *does not know* she has lost the support of her armies. She charges on alone."

The first lieutenant puffed up with pride, and exhaled in audible relief. "This will be our moment of triumph. They will surrender themselves once they realize the inevitability of their loss."

"If only I could call this a triumph, rather than a massacre. Having heard the tales from the Battle of Cổ Loa, and how these women disciplined themselves to respond to the subtle changes in the rhythms of the drums, I had hoped to test myself against a formidable enemy."

CHAPTER 34

The Battle of Lãng Bạc

At Lãng Bạc, the morning sky seeped yellow and red like an infected wound. To build energy for the fight, the Hán army gathered provisions from the fertile farmland around them. This, the day upon which they would confront the Việt army, ushered in a startling change in General Ma Yuan. Gone were his songs and his sentimentality and talk of family. In their stead, in his aspect one could read only the story that his reputation told: the Hán butcher, who left entire armies headless, who spared no living thing that stood against him, not even the horses.

For the lieutenants, General Ma Yuan shouted: "Today is the day for which we have fought time and the elements and our own demons, to meet destiny. Although we have lost many men, and although our spirits have been lashed by heaven's whip, our endurance has been tested; we complete our journey as victors in a struggle against nature, and we will soon conquer a far less formidable foe: an army of women emboldened by a revolution that it is our duty to end, here and forever."

Ma Yuan ordered his soldiers to crouch in the tall grass of the field, to hide their number. Upon the first blow of the horn, the archers would let launch their arrows. Upon the horn's second blow, they would raise their shields. Upon the third, the infantry would set their spears; and upon the fourth, a cavalry charge. Yet the elite guard were instructed, on the horn's fourth blow, to take a long route around the western edge of the enemy army to pursue the Việt kings and give chase.

The armies from Mê Linh and Chu Diên were the first to reach Lãng Bạc. The lords and armies from Hợp Phố, Nhật Nam, and Cửu Chân were late for the rendezvous, Trưng Vương thought. Yet it would be enough, today, to show their power with a frontal attack, as long as the eastern and western flanks arrived by nightfall. They would make do with their inept archers and arbalists because they would maintain a distance where the volume of bolts and arrows mattered more than their deadly accuracy.

By the time Trưng Vương and her army realized that the Hán were hiding in the tall grass, they were closer to the enemy than they had strategized, and at the first blow of the horn, a rain of enemy arrows whistled on the wind, pouring down from above. By the time Trưng Vương gave the order to the drummers to play the rhythm for their own arrow volley, many of the drummers had already been struck down by the onslaught. The enemy was targeting the players, and the Việt army had had no time for defensive maneuvers.

A second blow of the horn, and it was as though the Hán army appeared out of the earth behind a gentle green hill, their broad shields suddenly visible as it formed a protective layer over them all. Then, a small group of archers and arbalists among the Việts let fly their own missiles, which inflicted little damage upon the Hán's defenses. Many archers stood idle, for the Việt army advanced in a wide line, to appear more numerous, so that those on the extreme ends could scarcely hear the drum song.

Before the Hán could return another volley of arrows, Trưng Vương ordered the drummers to play the rhythm for a charge: *shuck-rum, shuck-rum-rum, shuck-rum, shuck-rum-rum*. The front line of the Việt army ran forward to surround the enemy. Yet this order had an answer, as the horn blew a third time, and the Hán infantry set their spears for a charge. When the front line of women arrived for a skirmish with the enemy soldiers, many of their horses were skewered on the ends of the polearms. Others leapt over the shields of the enemy and attempted to disrupt their discipline by their wild swipes, to engage the Hán in a wild exchange, to throw them off their preparation. Yet others retreated or maneuvered their horses away from the phalanx.

The success of the Hán army depended entirely upon their ability to anticipate and react to the movements of the Việt army, Trưng Vương realized. Her strategy had been too predictable. The advantage of the drummers was that they could change their strategy at any moment—with the soldiers' memorization of the nineteen rhythms, they had the nimbleness and agility to reformulate on the spot. But where were the other Việt armies? Surely the women of the northlands were arriving at any moment? There was no way their desperate pleas could have been ignored in the palaces of Hợp Phố, Nhật Nam, and Cửu Chân?

In the absence of reinforcements, Trưng Vương ordered the drummers to change their rhythm to flank the enemy anyway. Even without all eighty thousand women under her command, each of this dedicated group of twenty thousand soldiers would do the labor of four. "The war of attrition has begun," she declared. And the drummers let out the song for a tripartite army: *shuck-shuick-rum, shuck-shuick-rum, shuck-shuik-rum.*

Remaining with the central army, the Trưng Sisters waited while the army reconfigured itself. Meanwhile, the Hán horn blew a fourth time, and their army charged forward, oblivious to the Việt's flanking maneuver.

Just over the crest of the hill marching toward them were wave upon wave of Hán soldiers. They could barely be seen in the tall grass, although the sun shone directly on their faces. Their helmets looked like so many dark-shelled beetles infesting the plain.

"They are more than twice our number," said Trưng Nhị, appealing to her sister's reason. She could not deny the creeping forebodings of doom, which had grown inside her like a strangling vine. Trưng Nhị desperately wished to make Trưng Vương understand, yet the king would not support a single misgiving, nor any disquiet that threatened to sway the resolve of the leadership.

"But we have the righteousness of our cause," said Trưng Vương, unblinking and perched upon her elephant, Khong Lo. "And we have the fire of womanhood, in which all mankind is forged." *This is what it means to be a king*, thought Trưng Vương before the charge, quenching the seeds of anticipation before they could sprout into fears and doubts, the roots of which were strong enough to puncture the hardest clay.

"Yet they are better equipped, and better trained," said Trưng Nhị, more desperate now for her warnings to be heard.

"Against this fire," said Trưng Vương, "the Hán must eventually recoil or suffer the burns of labor, which their mothers felt upon their births, returned upon them tenfold."

The Battle of Lãng Bạc, through the eyes of General Ma Yuan, was like witnessing the crumbling of a cliff face after years of erosion—the cause felt remote, and the effects seemed inevitable. There was nowhere for the falling rocks to go but to follow the direction of gravity. He fulfilled a natural order, a mission that may as well have come from the dictates of heaven. And just as the tide rises to encompass the sand, to touch the dry bank and do the slow work of destruction, so would the Hán conquer the Việts and return them to their natural state.

"When this is all over," Ma Yuan said to a lieutenant, "we will owe no debt to the cowardly Việts who did not rise up to defend their homeland. They could have come out in force, to the last one, and the Hán tide would still have claimed the land. They are ours."

"When this is all over," said the lieutenant, "no Việt will ever challenge us again."

"We can end this war," said Ma Yuan, "if we strike them at the source of their strength."

"The Trưngs!" said the lieutenant.

"No," said Ma Yuan. "The drums."

The thin line of Việt soldiers, which had tried and failed to surround the larger army, dwindled into chaos as the Hán pushed forward, into the ranks of the leadership. It happened so fast that Trưng Vương scarcely had the time to execute a last order before the drummers were slaughtered in front of her. The king had never seen so many throats opened, so many limbs severed; the horror of watching her sisters-in-arms cut apart overwhelmed her, thrusting Trưng Vương into an unfamiliar state of inaction. So Trưng Nhị took up her own bronze drum and played the rhythm that had never been used before, for a retreat: *thum-thum-ka-ka, thum-thum-ka-ka, thum-thum-ka-ka, thum-thum-ka-ka.*

It signaled to the leadership what they already knew in their hearts—the hopelessness of the struggle. The elephants stomped toward Cổ Loa, with a vee of horses in their wake, only to encounter more Hán soldiers approaching from the south. These were the elite guard who had circled around the battlefield at the fourth sounding of the horn.

The stampede of the elephants, Xam and Khong Lo, was enough to split the elite guard, and the sisters broke through the line, although they suffered the swipe of many swords and the jab of spears as they trod through the ranks of the enemy. Committed to defending the Trưng kings at any cost, some of the generals continued on to guard them, while others stayed behind to battle the elite guard, knowing their deaths would spare Trưng Vương and Trưng Nhị so that they could live.

They had gone fifteen *li* before they stopped to take stock of the survivors. Seven generals, including Phùng Thị Chính, Mai, and Nàng Quỳnh; twenty-one lieutenants; less than one thousand soldiers. They could only hope that the rest had taken flight to the west, even if their other routes were cut off by the enemy. Trưng Nhị's lips moved but she said nothing. This despair was unrecognizable—nothing like the disappointment of losing a spar, or the frustration of being imprisoned for months—a new depth that stunned her into incomprehensible and silent muttering.

Xam had suffered greater than Khong Lo, and Trưng Nhị was forced to give up her beloved mount and ride with Trưng Vương on the larger elephant.

CHAPTER 35

Retreat to Mê Linh

Trưng Vương thought she understood ghosts. But now, as the surviving women of the Việt army returned to Mê Linh, wandering from place to place in search of someone to restore a sense of the familiar, she realized that she never truly had. These were not solitary spirits come to bless or haunt the living in cursed spaces. These were communities, nations, armies, packed into a world that no longer wanted them, and they could not possess the living, but could only inhabit a thought for long enough to imprint the faintest sense of their vestigial loss. When they arose all at once, however, they could drive the living to madness.

Khong Lo the elephant had not survived the trip from Cổ Loa, and Trưng Vương and Trưng Nhị walked into the town like lost strangers. A few men stared blankly out of their windows, and if they recognized their kings, they gave no sign of it, as each one calculated the tax of loyalty.

Trưng Vương had lost the aura, her sister observed—that air of invincibility, of faith in the future—the aura that had once emanated so thick that it encompassed an army. Seeing her elder sister so diminished, Trưng Nhị knew it must be the end of their noble cause.

A beggar on the street, seeing the golden-armored Trưng Vương approaching, asked for a copper coin to purchase food for his family. Observing the shock on their faces, the beggar said that he would settle instead for a bowl of rice.

"You had better leave town," said Trưng Nhị. "The Hán are coming, and there is no one left to save you."

As they passed, the beggar called out, "Is it true that the Trưng Sisters have been beheaded by the Hán armies?"

"Is that what you have heard?" said Trưng Vương.

"That's what they're saying," said the beggar. "A deserter passed through here yesterday and he saw the deaths of the Trưng Sisters with his own eyes."

"And now you can say," said Trưng Vương, "that you have seen the ghosts of the Trưng Sisters with your own eyes."

General Ma Yuan was the only one not celebrating his victory. In the Hán camp, men feasted on the freely available rice and vegetables, planted by local Việts. They became as boisterous as drinkers, and one could even hear the strains of song: the bronze drums had been seized and were being played by Hán soldiers, who sang their loudest, as though to do so were to reclaim the night. The general could scarcely stand the sound, and told his lieutenants that, come morning, the bronze drums were no longer to be played.

As far as Ma Yuan was concerned, the mission remained

unfinished. Though the Việt kings would never pose a threat again, he would not be satisfied until he delivered their heads to the emperor. To merely win the war was an insufficient compromise. To truly quell the rebellion, they needed two bloody trophies.

They sent troops to round up the Việts who fled. They sent troops to warn the Lạc lords not to join in this reckless campaign. And they sent troops back to Hán territory to report on their progress. But most of the soldiers remained in Cổ Loa, while General Ma Yuan himself proceeded with his elite guard to Mê Linh to finish off the last of the rebels.

At Cung Điện Mê Linh, the palace was as empty as the town. The servants and guardsmen had fled, leaving only the caretaker of Phùng Thị Chính's daughter, who refused to abandon the palace on a rumor. "I knew you were alive," she said to the Trưng Sisters, then handed the girl Triệu Ẩu over to her mother, who cradled her to her chest, eyes wet with tears she refused to shed.

"Minh-*ơi*!" called Trưng Nhị, dismounting to search the palace.

"Wait!" called out the caretaker.

Although the royal chambers were empty, Trưng Nhị explored the building until she came to the courtyard, where Phan Minh lay shivering and deathly white. Near him, Xấu sat on his hind legs with sad eyes.

"Minh-*ơi*," said Trưng Nhị, cradling his head and pressing his sickly cheek against her cheek. "What happened to you?"

"The heartbreak grass," he said with a wan smile.

When they were younger, Phan Minh had always told Trưng Nhị which plants to eat, and which to avoid. He was the gardener's son, and knew as much about the flora of the field as he did about the fauna of the wild.

"Why didn't you wait for me?" she said. Trưng Nhị had begun to think of tragedy upon tragedy as the sinking of a body into water of unknown depths. Surely the body could sink no deeper than *this*, she thought. Then it dropped further, and the lake of her sorrow was revealed to be an ocean.

"You died," said Phan Minh incredulously. Though his body was failing, he felt delirious with joy in her presence.

Trưng Nhị shook her head. She wished to scold him, to shout at his frailty and the Hán and the evil poison within him. But the heartbreak grass would not be slowed by her rage. "You should not have believed it. Even if I had died, you should have lived a long and happy life...as a eunuch."

Phan Minh tried to laugh, but it came up as a wheeze. His throat had already started to close, and he breathed slower and slower until his body grew still.

Trưng Nhị crouched close to Phan Minh, eye to closed eye.

This was how Trưng Vương found them, cradled like lovers on the moss, one dead and one living, under the shadow of the elephant statue.

"What of our vengeance?" cried Trưng Nhị. "What of our mourning?"

"We cannot do both," said Trưng Vương. She offered no consolation, no sympathy, though the desire to comfort her sister from this loss was powerful. Trưng Vương may have lost the aura, but she maintained the conviction that one could not be strong while mourning. She needed her sister's strength at that moment. Now she, too, had lost everything.

"We cannot do either!" Trưng Nhị shouted accusingly. "Not as long as the Hán devour all that they cannot control."

"While he lived, he lived free," said Trưng Vương, and even as she spoke, she realized the insufficiency of words.

"Is that what they will say of us?" said Trưng Nhị, rising now as though lifted by a gust of wind. "Is that a worthy epitaph?"

"They will say, not that we set the Lạc Việts free, but that we *realized* their freedom, and showed them how." Trưng Vương reached out for her sister's hand, which she tearfully accepted.

General Ma Yuan and his elite guard carried lit torches into Cung Điện Mê Linh. The palace was built of clay, and could not be burned, but the longhouses with their thatched roofs were set aflame. The peacocks made their desperate calls and, for all their frenzy, were hunted by bow and arrow. Xấu, no longer a puppy, tried to protect his territory by growling at the invading army. But General Ma Yuan approached the dog with his palm up, and in a few moments, the disobedient dog was licking salty blood and ash from the general's fingers. The turtle Kim Quy waddled into the fish pond, determined to survive another generation of men.

When trackers found fresh hoofprints heading west, the

guard took off in pursuit of the fallen kings. The path led toward the mountains, and the horses slowed on the incline. They passed under a peach tree, and Ma Yuan thought of his orchard at home—how he would return to his domestic paradise before long. But in front of him, this last task.

Trưng Vương guided her sister past the eagle's landing, up the rock chimney, and alongside the caves where she had endured the trials of the People. Trưng Nhị's arms and legs burned from the exertion, for this was her first climb. So that when they were met by three Degar women aiming their nocked bows in her direction, she had no energy in her left to resist.

"The Hán are coming," begged Trưng Vương, "and you must give us sanctuary and protect us."

"The Hán are coming," said one of the women, "and it was you who led them here."

"We fought side by side in the Battle of Cổ Loa. Surely our history as sisters-in-arms counts for something."

"We have known of the Hán's invasion for some time, and the council has decided: we are forbidden from making enemies of the Hán," said another Degar woman.

"You mean *the men* have decided," said Trưng Vương. "General Ly Chau would never betray her kings for a position at the feet of the Hán Empire."

"The People are united," said the woman. "Go back the way you came, or we will fire and we will not miss."

Seven men of the elite guard abandoned their armor for the climb. The general would continue on, accompanied by his most elite men, to capture and behead the Việt kings. Yet the path upward was more treacherous, and less certain, than it had appeared at first. The Trưng Sisters left no footprint on solid rock, and there were stretches where there was no path at all, just a vertical rock face. One of the seven—a legendary soldier in his country, who had faced off with three barbarians at once, and through stealth and skill emerged victorious—relied too much on his upper body, and reaching the arms' natural limit, he could do nothing but fall; and Ma Yuan and his men could do nothing but watch.

When they passed the shallow caves, they did not investigate, where keener eyes would have seen the shadows of the People, hidden and huddled where they could spring into action if threatened. And on the incline, surrounded by young trees, there were many arrows pointed at them that never fired. Here they found stepped-on grass, so that they believed themselves on the Trưng Sisters' trail, where they were, in fact, approaching a Degar village.

From a rocky outcropping appeared a man from the village who held his empty hands in front of him, to show that he carried no weapon. The soldiers drew their swords and walked forward. This stranger put his fingers to his lips, and in the ensuing silence they could all hear the melody of a flute in the distance.

One of the elite guard—a brash, impulsive, but heroic soul who was known for always charging forward fearlessly—sped up to attack the stranger while the others held back. He was immediately pierced by three arrows in his exposed torso, and landed in front of the stranger. General Ma Yuan merely nodded, guiding his men north up another treacherous climb. And now there were five.

In the distance, storms. All around them, warmth and sunlight. Trưng Vương and Trưng Nhị stood on a high precipice overlooking the kingdom as the clash of dark clouds turned day into night upon the horizon. But there, where the Trưng Sisters stood, the perfect weather mocked their despair. They looked upon each other's faces. In the other's eyes, they detected no more presence, no more soul than was necessary to sustain life. For as long as she could remember, Trưng Nhị had wanted to look into her sister's eyes and see something of her self reflected back. Now, as she gazed upon the same emptiness within Trưng Vương that she harbored in her own heart, the horror of the gaze overwhelmed her.

They thought of many superfluous words, but left them unuttered, for their shared understanding as their eyes cast downward was profound. It was failure, yes, and loss, yes, and tragic apprehension. But among the predictable upheavals they stood upon an edifice of relief—that the worst imaginable fate was manifested, and there was nothing more to fear from the world. To leap from this edifice felt as natural and necessary as the configuration of the stars.

Trưng Vương lowered the flute from her lips, and thought of the myth songs they used to sing in the courtyard of Cung

Điện Mê Linh, and the words that were now lost to the oblivion of time.

From behind them, the rhythmic steps of soldiers announced the end.

"Surrender to us now, and we will bring you safely to Hán territory, to face justice at the court of the emperor," said Ma Yuan, calmly, as though he had not come lately from the war front.

"You are better at war making than you are at lying," said Trưng Vương.

"All right then," said Ma Yuan. "We will be honest with one another, because I respect you as a strategist. Surrender your lives willingly, so that we do not have to fetch your heads from the canyon below. If you do us this favor, we will spare the lives of your families."

"Our families," said Trưng Nhị, "are already gone." She thought of Lord Trưng, who lived in fear but prepared his daughters to face the future. She thought of Thi Sách, who lived for knowledge and ideals until one day he lived for love. She thought of Phan Minh, who lived to serve but whose short life was one of absolute devotion. Then she thought of Lady Man Thiện and wondered whether she had survived. If her mother lived, then the deaths of her daughters would surely kill her.

"The Hán are nothing," said Trưng Vương, "if not thorough."

Ma Yuan stood at a lower plane than the Trưng Sisters, though he took a step upward when he said, "I can share in your tragedy, even as I am its harbinger. You may think it cruel and barbaric, but there is no swifter way to die than by a beheading."

"We will not be bargained for," said Trưng Vương. "We did not come this far in opposing the Hán just to abandon our bodies to you."

A gust rippled the fabric of their *áo dài*. They had given up their armor in order to make the climb, and now the chill brought gooseflesh to their arms. The distant storm made itself known by each sudden and powerful zephyr.

"Can I interest you in a fair fight?" said Trưng Nhị. "You and me? A bout to the death?"

"I thought we were past bargaining," said Ma Yuan.

"I had to try," she said.

The bowmen of the guard nocked their arrows, careful not to aim at the precious heads of the kings.

"How, then, do you wish to die?" said Ma Yuan.

Trưng Nhị clasped her sister's hand and said, "Nothing ever dies." Then the Việt kings leapt like seabirds diving into the ocean's swell, so that the fall would crush their skulls, and give the enemy no prize to present to the emperor.

The horses dragged fishing nets full of bronze drums, collected from throughout the province, which would ping each time the bundle knocked against a rock in the path or the pace of the horses would speed up. The arrhythmic sound was a reminder, to the women of Nhật Nam, of what was and what might have been, as hundreds of horses paraded into their town, towing more than two thousand instruments that had been pulled from the arms, living and dead, of as many faithful Việts.

Led by Ma Yuan himself, this convoy marched to the squat stone palace of Võ Quan. The Lord of Nhật Nam welcomed the Hán general, inviting him into his halls. But Ma Yuan, wary of being stuck in close quarters with Việts, declined the offer. Instead, he pronounced to the Lord of Nhật Nam that every last bronze drum would be smelted, and the resulting ore used to construct two vast columns at the southernmost limit of the Hán territory, in Tượng Lâm. The Việts of Lạc Việt had been conquered, and these bronze columns served as a reminder to any visitor from the southlands that this land was now under the control of the Hán Empire.

Then, lifting his voice with a surprising fullness, Ma Yuan proclaimed to the citizens of Nhật Nam that it was forbidden to forge new bronze drums. No matter whether they were intended for war making, or for ritual, or for music, these artifacts were now a relic of the past, of the old order, one day to be forgotten and never even mentioned in story or song so that their children would never know the sound of struck metal except in the forges, which now served the needs of the Hán.

As though to impress upon the Việts their condition as a subjugated people, Ma Yuan ordered that the bronze columns be carried on the backs of one hundred women each, all the way to Tượng Lâm. Even though the Lord of Nhật Nam had remained neutral during the war, many women of that city had joined in the fight for independence, and now faced the consequences of their impetuosity.

Whenever one woman would succumb to fatigue, she would be whipped until she found the energy to continue. When such a woman would collapse, and fall unconscious, she would be replaced by another. So that by the time the columns arrived in Tượng Lâm, the women of Nhật Nam were broken, made to walk with crooked backs. And although the bronze columns themselves were erected with pulleys, a feat of Hán engineering, this symbol of their power bore the irony of having never been touched by Hán hands.

After learning of the deaths of her daughters, and the fall of Lạc Việt to the Hán, Lady Man Thiện leapt into the Red River after Trưng Vương and Trưng Nhị. Her life had always been one of absolute control. She had worked hard in the years of Việt independence to undo the stranglehold in which the need for total control had held her. Yet by forfeiting control, Lady Man Thiện had let in the chaos, and it ate away at her, step by gentle step, as she approached the edge of the Red River, then, looking down into the rapid current that flowed toward a waterfall, tumbled into it.

Lạc Việt Year 2749 (51 CE)

At the Temple of the Guardian Spirit, in the city of Chu Diên, the monks treated Kha with a solicitude born of pity, and he played the part of the mental invalid, speaking in cryptic and irrelevant digressions, scratching himself inappropriately and indulging in emotional outbursts like a baby. He was the pet of the nuns as well, and acted as a surrogate child, with all of a child's tempers and moods. The keepers of the Temple would cradle him and soothe him until, at the end of the day, this giant man-child would reach exhaustion and retire to his solitary chamber.

One of Kha's caretakers, a young girl with long hair and a silk headband named Triệu Ẩu, brought hot water and oil to his chambers for him to soak his feet in. "I am onto you," she told him one night, after laying the bowl at the side of his bed. "You aren't crazy; you are just too lazy to take care of yourself."

Kha looked amusedly at the precocious young girl. "How can you be so sure?"

"I've seen you planting seeds. In the garden," Triệu Ẩu said.

"Maybe I am uprooting the seeds," said Kha.

"You aren't the first man to act the invalid just to be cared for by women." Triệu Ẩu stood up.

"What do you suppose I am growing in the garden?" said Kha.

"Food?" said Triệu Ẩu with a shrug.

"You think I'm growing vegetables?" said Kha, looking hurt.

"What else?" said Triệu Ẩu.

"I will show you," said Kha, "if you promise not to reveal my secret."

Triệu Ẩu leveled a look at the guardsman that said, *I make no promises.*

Then, when all the monks were abed, Kha and Triệu Ẩu ventured into the garden at night, stepping carefully to avoid trampling the budding plants, and dug up a pair of young orchids. Underneath the soil, which he sifted through his fingers, there was a bronze drum. He tapped it once, so gently that only the two of them could hear its resonance, then returned it to its place under the orchids of the garden, hidden safely in a corner of the kingdom where it would remain, under the care of the Guardian Spirit, for two thousand years.

ACKNOWLEDGMENTS

This book would never have been written without the wisdom of my father, Hien Nguyen, who first told me the story of the Trung Sisters. He also provided feedback on the manuscript and helped me with the use of diacritical marks on places and names. He wants me to let you know that this book is a work of fiction.

Thanks also to my mother, Emily Nguyen, who encouraged the creation of this book every step of the way.

The anthropological archaeologist Nam C. Kim provided invaluable insights on the artifacts, materials, cultural practices, and technologies of the Bronze Age in Ancient Vietnam. His book *The Origins of Ancient Vietnam* was an essential resource in the writing of this novel. Dr. Kim heroically answered every e-mail in minute detail, knowing that as a storyteller, I would have to ignore his good counsel and insert anachronisms into the book (such as the presence of *áo dài*, *nón lá*, etc.). Any such anachronism is my doing, and not an error on the part of the anthropological archaeologist who advised me.

Many thanks to my writing group—Trudy Lewis,

Evelyn Rogers, and Michael Pritchett, who read the book as it developed—and to early readers Steve Paul, Gail Crump, Abby Manzella, Tom Dillingham, Carolyn McCarthy, Christina Clancy, Whitney Terrill, Natalia Sylvester, Martin Seay, Liam Callanan, and Zachary Mason.

Thanks to Richard G. Miller for creating and supporting the position of Miller Family Endowed Chair in Literature and Writing at the University of Missouri. Thanks to my colleagues at the University of Missouri and to fellow summer faculty at Martha's Vineyard Institute of Creative Writing. Appreciation for Art Ozias, owner of Java Junction in Warrensburg, Missouri, where much of the book was written.

With gratitude to Nat Sobel, Sara Paolozzi, and to everyone at Sobel-Weber Associates; and to editors Beth deGuzman, Seema Mahanian, and Kirsiah McNamara, and the rest of the team at Grand Central Publishing.

Enduring love to my wife, Sarah, whose tenacity as an artist and as a woman has inspired me for a quarter century.

An Dương Vương—mythological king who wielded a turtle's claw crossbow that rendered his army invincible (mythical).

áo dài—the long silk dresses that are often worn by contemporary Vietnamese women (a deliberate anachronism).

Âu Cơ—the princess who married and had one hundred children from the Dragon Lord, then divorced the Dragon Lord and took fifty of her children to the mountains (mythical).

bạc hà—a long-haired dog native to Vietnam that is known for being quiet and docile.

Bác Huy Vũ—the astrologer employed by Lord Trưng and Lady Man Thiện at Cung Điện Mê Linh (fictional).

Chu Diên—a city of temples, schools, and scriptoria.

Cổ Loa—a citadel in the shape of a conch shell, from which the governor governs.

Confucius (Khổng Tử)—an influential Chinese philosopher.

Cung Điện—"a palace."

Cung Điện Mê Linh—the palace at Mê Linh.

Cửu Chân—the southern city in Lạc Việt.

Đặng Quốc—ancient scholar (fictional).

Đặng Thảo—son of Đặng Vũ, the Lord of Chu Diên. Later, the Lord of Chu Diên.

Đặng Vũ—Lord of Chu Diên.

Degar—title for those who live in the mountains.

Dũ Chí—Lord of Tay Vu.

Dunhuang (Chinese)—frontier region and colony of the Hán.

Duy—beggar who lives outside Cung Điện Mê Linh (fictional).

Giaozhou (Vietnamese: Giao Châu)—Chinese name for a region in northern Lạc Việt.

Guangwu (Chinese)—Emperor of China from 25 to 57 CE (historical).

Guangxi (Vietnamese: Quảng Tây)—a southern province in modern China.

Hán—the Chinese dynasty during the time of the Trưng Sisters.

Ho (Chinese)—commander of the officers of Mê Linh (fictional).

Hoàng Tâm—a girl who hangs herself with a rope made of her own hair.

Hợp Phố—a city that is known for its architecture.

Huỳnh Quyền—the master of spies employed by Lord Trưng (fictional).

jen (Chinese)—Confucian virtue meaning *benevolence*.

Jiaozhi (Chinese) (Giao Chỉ in Vietnamese)—the Chinese name for the region of Lạc Việt.

Jiuquan—frontier region and colony of ancient China.

Kha—guardsman of Cung Điện Mê Linh (fictional).

Khong Lo—Trưng Vương's elephant.

Kim Quy—golden turtle. Both the name of the painted turtle in the gardens of Cung Điện Mê Linh and the subject of myth.

lá ngón—the "heartbreak grass," which kills by closing the throat of those who eat it.

Lạc Long Quân—the Dragon Lord, ancestor of the Trưngs and the subject of myth. Married Princess Âu Cơ, had one hundred children, then divorced, after which Âu Cơ led fifty of his children to live by the mountains, leaving him and the remaining fifty children to live in the plains by the sea.

Lạc Việt—name for the Red River Delta during the Bronze Age.

Lãng Bạc—site of the Battle of Lang Bac, between the Hán army led by Ma Yuan and the Việt army led by the Trưng Sisters.

Laozi (Chinese)—ancient Chinese philosopher.

Lê Chân—a former farmer turned princess and general in the Trưng Sisters' army.

Lê Ngọc Trinh—a famous general in the Trưng Sisters' army (historical).

li (Chinese)—a unit of measurement (about one-third of a mile).

li (Chinese)—a Confucian virtue meaning "propriety."

Li Hong (Chinese)—advisor to the governor, Tô Định.

Lin (Chinese)—wife of General Ma Yuan.

Lồng—Trưng Nhị's parakeet.

Ly Anh—young Degar girl, a hunter (fictional).

Ly Chau—leader of the Degar, a woman of the mountains (fictional).

Ma Yuan (Mã Viện)—Chinese general who eventually defeated the Trưng Sisters (historical).

Mai—a prostitute in Mê Linh and spy for Lady Man Thiện, later a general in the Việt army.

Man Thiện, Lady—mother of the Trưng Sisters (historical).

Mê Linh—the city where the Trưng Sisters lived.

Mencius (Mạnh Tử)—ancient Chinese philosopher.

Mo—name of the kingfisher at Cung Điện Mê Linh.

Mozi (Chinese)—ancient Chinese philosopher.

Mực—"black." The name of Trưng Nhị's horse.

Nàng Quế—a Việt general (historical).

Nàng Quỳnh—a Việt general (historical).

Ngô Cầm—a tattooed man from the mountains (fictional).

Ngoan—the initial name of Trưng Nhị's pet dog, whose name changes to Xấu.

Ngốc—a snail.

Nhật Nam—a bronze- and iron-working city under Lord Võ Quan.

nón lá—literally a straw (conical) hat.

Pham Vien—a herald in the employ of Lord Trưng (fictional).

Phan Minh—keeper of the names, Minh the dog, and the gardener's son (fictional).

Phật Nguyệt—famous general in the Trưng Sisters' army (historical).

Phùng Thị Chính—mother of six, and general in the Trưng Sisters' army (historical).

Quách A—lieutenant in the Trưng Sisters' army.

Răng—the tiger who terrorizes the city of Mê Linh. Literal translation: "Teeth."

Sun Bin (Chinese)—ancient Chinese philosopher.

Tay Vu—city led by Lord Dũ Chí.

Thi Sách—first, a tutor to Trưng Trắc and Trưng Nhị. Later, Trưng Trắc's husband (historical).

Thi Vũ—father of Thi Sách (fictional).

Thuan—Nàng Quế's extraordinary horse.

Tô Định—the governor of Jiaozhi (historical).

Trần Ngai—a guardsman at Cung Điện Mê Linh (fictional).

Trần Thuận—the love interest in the story of Hoang Tam.

Triệu Ẩu—both the name of Phùng Thị Chính's youngest daughter and only surviving child *and* the name of a legendary leader in Vietnamese history.

Trinh Sang—Lord of Hợp Phố (fictional).

Trưng Nhị—younger daughter of Lord Trưng and Lady Man Thiện (historical).

Trưng Trắc—older daughter of Lord Trưng and Lady Man Thiện. Later, named Trưng Vương (historical).

Trưng Vương—"She-King of the Việts" (historical).

Tượng Lâm—the southernmost point of the Hán Empire.

Việt—the people of Lạc Việt.

Võ Danh—eldest son of Phùng Thị Chính (fictional).

Võ Quan—Lord of Nhật Nam (fictional).

Võ Tuyen—Phan Minh's mother, who was mauled to death six years earlier by Răng the Tiger (fictional).

Vũ Thơm—heroine of "The Lament of Vũ Thơm," who dies by suicide after eating "heartbreak grass."

Wan Fu (Chinese)—Hán officer who orders the beheading of Duy the beggar (fictional).

Wu Sheng (Chinese)—an elite Hán soldier (fictional).

Wuwei (Chinese)—a frontier region and colony of China.

Xam—an elephant.

Xấu—Trưng Nhị's pet dog, formerly Ngoan.

Xingping (Chinese)—city in China and home to General Ma Yuan.

yi (Chinese)—a Confucian virtue meaning "the moral disposition to do good."

Yu (Chinese)—a river in China.

Zhangyi (Chinese)—a frontier region and colony of China.

READING GROUP GUIDE

DISCUSSION QUESTIONS

1. Why do you think the Trưng sisters wanted an army of women? What did this symbolize to you specifically?

2. Why do you think Trưng Nhị stepped back and allowed her sister to assume the role of leader of their rebellion?

3. How do you think the story would've been different had Trưng Nhị been successful in her attempt to kill Wan Fu instead of Trưng Trắc stopping her?

4. Discuss the relationship of the nobility to the people of the Lạc Việt region? Do you think the Trưng family truly understood the reality of these people's lives?

5. Do you think Lord Trưng should've heeded his dreams more? What could he have done to change the course of their future?

6. Discuss the ways this novel portrayed historical attempts of erasing a culture. How does it make you consider the

current world and the ways this is repeated throughout history?

7. Do you think the mountain people were correct to want to keep to themselves and wary of opening up to outsiders like Trưng Trắc? Why or why not?

8. Discuss why the different regions were so reluctant to join a second war against the Hán? Do you think that if they had all stood strong together, they would've won again and been able to keep their freedom?

9. Discuss your response to the character of Kha. What additional layers did he bring to the novel in terms of tone and emotion?

10. Describe the ways that Thi Sách and Phan Minh are similar to each other. In what ways are they different? What do they tell the reader about Trưng Trắc and Trưng Nhị by being chosen as their husbands and lovers?

Q & A

1. How did you first hear the story about the Trưng sisters?

My father told me the story of the Trưng sisters when I was a young boy. It stuck with me because it was completely unlike any other revenge story with which I had been familiar. Instead of ending with the death of the guilty party (the governor), the Trưng sisters' revenge galvanized the women against the greater enemy, which was the occupying forces of the Hán. The point wasn't just "an eye for an eye"; it was to use one's anger and passion and ferocity for the good of the people.

2. What did growing up with the story of the Trưng sisters mean to you and the way you viewed the world?

For whatever reason, I have always connected the story of the Trưng sisters to my family's history. I never met my paternal grandmother because she and her one-year-old son (my uncle) were killed during a French air attack when she was twenty-seven years old. By all accounts she was as formidable as Trưng Nhị and as pious as Trưng Trắc; had she lived, I fully believe she could have launched a revolution. One effect of growing up with this story is, I suppose, that I've always been most comfortable under the leadership of women.

3. What does the role of mythology and oral tradition play in Vietnamese culture? What does it mean to you?

I won't presume to speak for Vietnamese culture. I myself was born in Boston and grew up in central New Jersey. But mythology and oral tradition play a major role in my life because they create archetypes that enable one to rise into these roles and inhabit them. Growing up in the 1980s, screen media offered few if any positive portrayals of Asian, Asian American, or, especially, Vietnamese characters. Hearing stories that featured Vietnamese heroes likely saved me from the self-loathing that I might have felt if my only exposure to Vietnamese characters was through depictions of the Vietnam War.

4. You have written other fiction. What made you want to get this story of the Trưng sisters into readers' hands?

It is a story I've always wanted to write but felt prepared to do so only after I'd written a few other books. It's a big-canvas story, requiring a scale that is daunting, almost Shakespearean in scope. I wanted to make sure I could do it justice. To me, the worth of the Trưng sisters' story is self-evident, and I just hope that I succeeded in sharing aspects of the story that were so special to me growing up.

5. As a creative-writing professor, what's a common piece of advice that you give to your students, and did you follow that advice yourself when writing *Bronze Drum*?

I like to tell my students to "follow your curiosity." I certainly followed that advice when writing *Bronze Drum*, which I spent more than a year researching before I typed a single word. Writing it was a process of discovery, which is essential for any writer, because without discovery, how can there be joy?

6. What was your process for researching an ancient true story especially given it's treated practically as myth as so much of the story is passed down through oral tradition?

If you go to the library and look up "Vietnamese History," you will find shelves and shelves full of books on the Vietnam War and very little that goes back further than 1900, and almost nothing from ancient Vietnamese history. At first, I got my information from single chapters and articles from books with titles like *Women of Vietnam*, *Women Warriors in History*, and *Tigers in the Rice*. But then I found some more substantial accounts in books by Keith Taylor and Nam C. Kim. I must have had hundreds of email exchanges with the archaeologist Nam C. Kim, who helped me imagine the physical details of this ancient society. I leaned heavily on his input when it came to constructing their world.

7. What was the process for you in writing historical fiction? How did you find the balance between "truth" and weaving a tight narrative?

As a fiction writer, I feel that my primary allegiance is to telling a good story. If I can incorporate historical fact and can draw from myth, that can strengthen and deepen the narrative. But I didn't set out to teach history with this book, and I didn't always validate contemporary Vietnamese myth making about the Trưng sisters. One of the things I love most about fiction is its honesty—it makes no claims to truth and simply asks you to live in the world of the story for a while.

8. What is your writing process like? Do you do a lot of planning, or do you like to write freely and get it all on the page?

That varies depending on the project. With *Bronze Drum*, the movement of the narrative was straightforward because it was driven by historical events, so it did not require detailed planning. I did have an outline, which I followed very closely, but it was broad. The original draft was more than six hundred pages long, so the most challenging part of the process was cutting out a third of the novel and, in the process, having to determine what was truly dispensable.

9. Do you have a favorite character from *Bronze Drum*? Were some characters easier to write than others?

I don't have a favorite individual character, but I do have favorite relationships in the book. My favorite relationships in the book are between 1) Trưng Nhị and Lady Man Thiện, 2) Trưng Trắc and Lord Trưng, 3) Kha and Thi Sách, and, of course, 4) Trưng Nhị and Trưng Trắc. Character is best revealed through interaction, and to me these dyads were the most illuminating. As a side note, I quite enjoyed writing about Ma Yuan, actually, because I like writing sympathetic villains, and there is so much historical record when it comes to Ma Yuan.

10. Who are the writers that have inspired you and informed your work?

My favorite American writers are Mark Twain, Willa Cather, Herman Melville, James Baldwin, and Edith Wharton. More recently, there is Louise Erdrich, Min Jin Lee, Madeline

Miller, Karen Russell, Zachary Mason, George Saunders, and Colson Whitehead. My favorite international writers are Italo Calvino, Marcel Proust, Chinua Achebe, Naguib Mahfouz, Jin Yong, and Eiji Yoshikawa. Recent short fiction authors I admire include Alexander Weinstein, Nafissa Thompson-Spires, Nana Kwame Adjei-Brenyah, Ted Chiang, and Anjali Sachdeva. Among all of those writers, I would say that the ones who have most directly informed my work are Mark Twain, Louise Erdrich, Italo Calvino, and Eiji Yoshikawa. Readers who are familiar with my other books will notice how different they are from one another. Each book has to be a departure from the others for me to become genuinely excited about it, and I consider each book I write to be a part of a different literary lineage.